The Truth
Lies
Out There

A Family Drama of Suspense, Intrigue and Passion

Sahasranam Kalpathy

ACKNOWLEDGEMENTS

I owe immense gratitude to my family for their unwavering support throughout the process of writing this book. Their encouragement has been invaluable.

I am also deeply thankful to my colleagues in the Author community who generously assisted me and provided constructive feedback on my previous works.

Special recognition goes to Mr. Som Bathla, my mentor on this journey, and the members of the Author-Helping-Author (AHA) community, whose guidance has been instrumental in shaping my writing and publishing endeavors.

I want to express my thanks and appreciation to my daughter Sandya for her technical assistance in preparing the manuscript.

Additionally, I extend my appreciation to 'revandesigns' for crafting the beautiful cover for this book.

COPYRIGHT

Disclaimer

This book is a work of true fiction, drawing upon authentic sources for its facts and statistics. The locations and names mentioned are real, but the characters, their names, and the events depicted are entirely imaginary. The author has no intention of defaming any individual, group, or religion. Any similarities to actual persons are purely coincidental. The opinions and facts presented in the book are solely those of the author and are not meant to offend or disrespect anyone or any religious beliefs.

To my parents

Who inspired the

Creativity in me.

AUTHORS NOTE

Thank you for purchasing and reading my book. This work is a piece of fiction. Names, characters, and certain locations and incidents are either the products of the author's imagination or used fictitiously. Any resemblance to actual persons — living or deceased, business establishments, events, or locales is purely coincidental.

*Given the narrative's focus on a South Indian Tamil Brahmin family, numerous Tamil words, and occasional Malayalam, Hindi or Sanskrit terms are employed. The **Glossary** provided at the end of the book offers the literal meanings of these words which are given in italics in the text.*

The story primarily unfolds in Calicut, a city situated in the Kerala state of India, and its environs. While some mentioned places like the Malabar Botanical Gardens, Mananchira Square, the Town Police Station, the Puthiyapalam Crematorium and Medical Colleges, are real, others are fictionalized.

The names of central government agencies referenced are those of actual governmental entities in India.

Any opinions expressed, whether political or otherwise, are solely those of the author and are not intended to defame or disparage any individual or political party.

And dear readers, please give me a candid review in Amazon after reading this fictional novel of mine. It will be a big boost to me.

Sahasranam Kalpathy

A Humble Request to the Reader

Thank you for buying and reading this book. May I request your indulgence for one more favor.

I hope you enjoyed reading this book and derived benefit from the various topics discussed.

Kindly give your sincere and valuable review of this book in the Amazon site. Your rating and candid review will be a great inspiration and encouragement to me.

I would also request you to check my other two books – *Tell Me a Story, Grandpa* and *Grandpa Tell Me More Stories* which are a compilation of short stories with morals, mainly written with children in mind.

Also, the book of *'In Search of a Bridegroom'* is an interesting Autobiographical Fiction which will be of great interest to the reader.

You can contact me at my email address kvsauthor@gmail.com

https://www.linkedin.com/in/sahasranam-dr-k-v-3231a13a/ (Linked In)

https://medium.com/@ramani2911/membership (Medium.com)

https://www.amazon.com/author/sahasranamkalpathy

(Amazon Author Central)

About the Author

Sahasranam Kalpathy (Dr. K. V. Sahasranam) is the author of eleven books previously on various subjects like Short stories for children, an Autobiographical fiction, a book on *'Understanding the Electrocardiogram'* and two books on *'Health Problems in Old Age'*. His first book on *'Understanding Hinduism series'* is named **"Demystifying Hinduism** and the second one **"The Avadhoota"**. In the book **"Daily Musings"** he has given inspirational messages for daily living derived from the scriptures and Hindu Mythology.

His two books on 'Skillsets for Success' were named **"How to Master Essential Life Skills"** and **"How to Achieve Professional Excellence".** In these books he has described skills needed to be successful in life from the point of view of a Medical Director.

He is a Cardiologist settled in the U.S.

Part I

Prologue

1989

The lifeless body was discovered at dawn on the beach.

The first light of dawn stretched its warm fingers across the horizon, painting the sky from inky black to shades of violet and orange. The waves in the Arabian sea lapped gently against the shore, their rhythmic symphony the only sound that broke the silence of the early morning. The air was thick with the briny scent of the sea, a mixture of salt and decay that clung to everything it touched.

A tired group of fishermen, having spent the entire night fishing in the deep sea, pulled their boats onto the sandy beach. Their faces showed signs of arduous work, marked by lines and weathered by the constant sea winds.

"Elelo Eilasa, hi Elelo Eilasa" they intoned in unison as sweat poured from their brows in the hot, humid weather and their sinews strained to pull the boats to the sandy shore.

The coarse sand crunched beneath their worn-out rubber sandals as they secured their vessels, their movements and their voices synchronized from years of repetition. The wooden boats bore the scars of countless battles with the unpredictable ocean, patched up with mismatched planks and frayed ropes.

As the fishermen unloaded their night's catch, the scent of fresh fish mingled with the sea breeze, creating a pungent aroma that hung in the air. Silver scales glinted in the early light as they spilled from the nets on to the woven bamboo baskets. The fish, still flopping in their last desperate attempts at life, added a discordant note to the otherwise serene scene.

Among the men, a grizzled fisherman named Ramu glanced towards the beach, his senses alert to any unusual sight or sound. He caught a glimpse of something on the shore, a dark form half-buried in the wet sand. Thinking it to be a beached shark, the intrigued, fisherman motioned for his companions to follow him, their curiosity overcoming the weariness that clung to their bodies.

As they approached, the rhythmic crashing of the waves grew louder, drowning out the distant calls of seabirds. The sand beneath their feet shifted, soft and yielding, with each step leaving deep imprints that were quickly erased by the advancing waves. The air, heavy with the scent of salt and decay, carried a hint of something more ominous.

There, lying prone on the sand, was the lifeless body of a youth probably in his early twenties. His clothes were drenched, clinging to his body like a second skin. He wore a red T-shirt and faded blue jeans. The damp strands of his hair plastered against his forehead, and his skin, pale and cold, bore the pallor of death. The waves, uncaring, continued their relentless assault on the shore, washing over the body in a macabre dance of death.

Ramu, his weathered hands trembling, knelt beside the young man. He reached out tentatively, fingers brushing against the cold skin. The touch sent a shiver down his spine, a visceral reminder of the fragility of life. The others gathered around, their faces etched with a mixture of disbelief and concern.

"Who could do such a thing to himself?" muttered Koya, another fisherman with a gnarled beard that matched the twisted nets slung over his shoulder.

"Too young to die", commented an old veteran who had seen many a death at sea.

"Why should the youth of today decide to take their own life for silly reasons!", exclaimed a third fisherman. "So young, so handsome."

Ramu shook his head, unable to tear his eyes away from the lifeless form. "We need to inform the police. Let us rush to the nearest police station." He looked around him but found that the beach was deserted but for them. "Two of you stay here", Ramu ordered, "The rest of us can go to the Town police station which is nearest to us."

The fishermen exchanged uneasy glances, their minds grappling with the reality of the situation. They rose, leaving the body untouched, and hurriedly made their way toward the narrow alley that led to the heart of Calicut city.

The scent of the sea hung in the air, now tainted with the odor of death. The distant screeching of seagulls provided an eerie soundtrack to their journey, their mournful calls echoing the somber mood that enveloped the group.

The sun had fully emerged on the eastern horizon, casting its warm glow on the city waking up to another day. But on the beach, the warmth seemed to elude them, replaced by a cold unease that clung to them like a persistent shadow.

Ramu set off at a trot. As they jogged through the narrow alleys of the city, the aroma of freshly brewed chai wafted through the air, mixing with the lingering scent of fish that clung to the fishermen's clothes. The streets were still mostly deserted, the city not yet fully awake. Shutters of small shops creaked open, revealing glimpses of colorful spices and vegetables arranged in neat rows.

The footsteps of the fishermen echoed against the narrow, macadamed pathways, each step resonating with the weight of the discovery they carried with them. The distant hum of a motorbike grew louder as they approached the police station, its engine cutting through the quiet morning like a sharp knife.

The police station stood stoically, its peeling paint and rusted gates a testament to years of service. The fishermen hesitated for a moment before pushing open the creaky door, the hinges groaning in protest. The air inside was heavy with the scent of old paperwork, a musty odor that clung to the worn-out furniture and faded walls.

A uniformed officer, sleepy eyes framed by dark circles, looked up from his desk as the fishermen entered. "What brings you here so early?" he asked, his voice a weary monotone. "What mischief were you fellows up to?"

Ramu, the leader of the group, stepped forward, his expression grave. "We found something on the beach. Something you need to see – the body of a young man."

The officer became alert immediately, the weight of another day's responsibilities settling on his shoulders. He summoned a constable who brought the jeep around and with the fishermen drove towards the beach grabbing the wireless handset on the way.

As they reached the shore, the sun had climbed higher in the sky, casting a golden hue over the sand. The rhythmic waves now seemed less ominous, the relentless cycle of life and death that the sea held in its grasp. The body, still lying on the shore, appeared even more lifeless in the harsh light.

The officer knelt beside the body of the youth, examining the scene with a practiced eye. The wind carried the salt-laden air, mixing it with the acrid scent of the nearby fish market. The waves, now a constant backdrop, seemed to whisper the secrets of the night as the officer took note of every detail.

"Any idea who he is?" the officer asked, not looking up from his inspection.

Ramu shook his head, his weathered face etched with lines of concern. "No one from our colony, that's for sure. We've never seen him before."

The officer nodded, standing up and dusting the sand off his uniform. He pulled out his wireless handset, calling for backup and a forensic team. The city would wake up to a different kind of morning, a morning that carried the weight of unanswered questions and the lingering scent of tragedy.

As the fishermen waited for the authorities, the beach seemed to hold its breath. The distant cries of seagulls faded into the background, replaced by the hum of approaching sirens.

The cavalry had arrived.

The sun, now a harsh spotlight in the east, cast long shadows of the nearby coconut trees on the sand, highlighting the eerie stillness that had settled over the once serene landscape.

The officer turned to the fishermen, his expression serious. "Thank you for reporting this. We'll take it from here. You may leave now but leave your names and addresses with the constable. We may need to question you later."

Ramu nodded solemnly, his gaze lingering on the lifeless body that had disrupted the tranquility of their morning. "So young... so young and so handsome, poor soul," he muttered as he turned away shaking his head.

The fishermen walked away, leaving behind the scene that would become a haunting memory etched into the sands of Calicut. The waves continued their monotonous dance, washing over the shore, as if trying to cleanse the beach of the darkness that had touched its shores.

Chapter 1

Nestled amidst the lush landscapes of Calicut in Kerala, the traditional *Nalukettu* stood as a testament to the state's rich cultural heritage. Set against a backdrop of vibrant greenery, Anantharama Iyer's house stood with its distinctive architectural style prevalent in Kerala. Literally, *Nalukettu* meant 'four blocks'. The entrance, marked by a magnificent *Padippura*, led into a spacious courtyard, providing a warm welcome to visitors. Built on a vast plot, the *Nalukettu's* layout emphasized symmetry and harmony, reflecting the principles of *Vastu Shastra*. The central courtyard or *Nadumuttam* within the house, open to the sky, served as the heart of the *Nalukettu*, allowing natural light and ventilation to permeate the living spaces. The *Nadumuttam*, often a spacious area at the center of the *Nalukettu*, acted as a communal space for family gatherings and celebrations.

The wooden pillars intricately carved with traditional motifs stood as silent sentinels, supporting the expansive verandas that wrapped around the courtyard. The quintessential *Thulasi Thara* at the center of the *Nadumuttam* symbolizing prosperity — a raised platform adorned with a holy basil plant, added a sacred touch to the courtyard. The elaborate woodwork and the ornate polished brass plates and locks called the *Manichithrathazhu* on doors and windows highlighted the exquisite craftsmanship of Kerala's artisans, with each detail telling a story.

The traditional sloping roofs, made of terracotta tiles, sheltered the *Nalukettu* from the monsoon rains and exuded a timeless charm. Juxtaposed against the verdant landscape, the earthy tones of the *Nalukettu's* walls created a harmonious blend with nature. Inside, rooms furnished with antique furniture and time-honored decor transported inhabitants to a bygone era, embracing simplicity and elegance of a Tamil brahmin household.

Fragrant flower gardens and vegetable plants surrounded the *Nalukettu*, adding a sensory richness to the ambience. Mango and jackfruit trees, in the compound cast a soothing shade upon its surroundings. A small, traditional family temple, situated within the premises, served as a spiritual anchor, fostering a connection with ancestral roots. Within the temple, an imposing one-foot high granite idol of *Bhagawan Ganesha* commanded one's attention. As a living testament to Kerala's architectural legacy, Anantharama Iyer's ancestral house stood not just as a physical structure but as a repository of Tamil brahmin culture, embodying the timeless beauty of the region. The *Kolam* is a customary art drawn with rice flour on the floor of South Indian homes, both in front of the house and inside pooja rooms. It is believed to bring prosperity to the home. In Anantharama Iyer's home, womenfolk always drew beautiful *Kolam* designs in front of the home. This is a customary way to welcome Goddess Lakshmi, who brings wealth, into the home.

A single-storey, two-bedroom outhouse, a modest bungalow, stood just a few feet away from the main building of the Nalukettu. It was a cozy dwelling, complete with its own small garden at the front and surrounded by trees offering shade. Initially, Anantharama Iyer had rented it out to an underprivileged family for a nominal rent. However, as his children grew and started families of their own, he decided to keep the outhouse vacant. It would serve as a guest house for relatives or in-laws of his sons and daughter whenever they visited the Iyer household.

The ancestral home of the Iyer family was more than bricks and mortar; it was a haven for laughter, shared stories, and the echoing resonance of familial bonds. Today, the expansive hall within the *Nalukettu* pulsed with the vibrant energy of a birthday celebration.

The air was saturated with the rich aroma of ghee-laden sweets, and the delicate fragrance of jasmine flower streamers that were strung from the beams. The family, adorned in vibrant hues, moved with purpose as they prepared to celebrate Arjun's 22nd birthday. The young

15

man, having recently completed a B.A course in Economics awaiting exam results, stood at the threshold of a new chapter in his life.

"*Hum Honge Kamyab... Hum Honge Kamyab...*" sang Arjun as he came down the stairs in his jeans and kurta.

"*Tamizh-le paadu-da*" urged his mother Meenakshi as she emerged from the kitchen, presenting her husband Anantharama Iyer with a steel tumbler brimming with hot filter coffee as he sat in his customary spot, the easy chair in a corner of the hall.

"*Naam Peruvomei Vettri... Naam Peruvomei Vettri...*" sang Arjun in Tamil, laughing at his mother's silly request. She could not understand Hindi.

In the midst of the bustling scene, Anandu, the eldest brother and the manager of a finance company, found himself amusing himself with his two spirited, eight-year old twins, Aadi and Akhil.

"Aadi, my little explorer, leave the vase alone. Akhil, you brat, let go of your brother's hair," he chuckled, a playful glint in his eyes as he attempted to maintain order amidst the joyous chaos. The kids were prancing about expecting the birthday cake to be cut soon and licking their lips in anticipation.

Uma, Anandu's wife, clad in a bottle-green saree brocaded with silk jari, moved gracefully through the crowd, her eyes sparkling with an infectious love for her family.

"Arjun, *kanna*, your cake is ready!" she called out, her voice a melodic tune that cut through the cheerful chatter like a harmonious melody. "I have also made your favorite *Paal Paayasam.*"

Nandini, younger to Anandu, the gynecologist sister from Calicut Medical College, made a grand entrance with her six-year old daughter Aathira. "Happy birthday, Arjun *mama!*" Aathira giggled, presenting him with a lovely birthday card that she had crafted herself, using crayons, watercolors, and a collage of beautiful pictures to decorate it.

Nandini winked at Arjun, mischief dancing in her eyes, "May your marks in the examination be as impressive as your birthday celebration."

"Don't worry *akka*," Arjun retorted, "I will get nothing short of a first class – don't be surprised if I come first in my college. Then you must give me the gift that you promised me."

Satya, the fourth sibling, and his recently married wife Janaki came down the stairs entering the hall hand in hand. As newlyweds, their eyes sparkled with the promise of shared dreams and adventures.

"Welcome to the chaos, Janaki. Get ready for a rollercoaster ride," Satya whispered to his wife, his words creating ripples of laughter that echoed through the hall. Janaki, the new bride in the home blushed with shame.

Nandini's younger brother, who is third in the family order, Sreeni, and his wife Mamta, who live in the United States, had already phoned Arjun in the morning to wish him a happy birthday and success in his exams.

At the heart of the family, Anantharama Iyer sat comfortably in his easy chair sipping the filter coffee that his wife Meenakshi had handed him. Wisdom etched into the lines of his aging face, he exuded a serene aura, even as Parkinsonism claimed some of his physical strength and the left half of his body. The undiminished twinkle in his eye spoke volumes of a lifetime filled with love and resilience.

Anantharama Iyer, the patriarch of the family, was a man of illustrious history, etched with the indelible ink of a self-made success story. His journey began in 1935 when he left the shores of India for Burma, lured by the promise of opportunity. Recruited by an English firm for his unmatched intelligence and numerical acumen, Anantharama Iyer embarked on a professional journey that would define the trajectory of his life. Having passed his Matriculation with flying colors, he possessed proficiency in shorthand and typewriting, a highly sought-after qualification by the British rulers of that era. Diligently he dedicated his evenings to study and attended evening classes to acquire qualifications, culminating in his attainment of the esteemed title of Fellow Chartered Accountant (FCA). Within a decade of his arrival in Burma, he established ownership of an esteemed accountancy firm named *'AR Iyer & Co.'*

Burma became the canvas upon which he painted his success. With unwavering dedication and a keen mind, he ascended the professional ladder, carving a niche for himself in the competitive corporate landscape of Burma as a successful chartered accountant. His journey was not merely a tale of professional triumph but a testament to perseverance and the pursuit of excellence.

After gaining independence in 1948, insurgent activity and the winds of political uncertainty swept through Burma. The specter of military dictatorship hung over Burma, with signs of this direction appearing as early as 1959. In view of this, Anantharama Iyer made a pivotal decision in 1961. Anticipating the looming instability in that country, he chose to return to the embrace of his homeland, India. Calicut in the Malabar region of Kerala, with its cultural richness, beckoned him, and there, he laid the foundation for a new chapter of his life.

In Calicut, he manifested his dreams into reality, constructing a grand residence that echoed the architectural splendor of the past – a *Nalukettu*. The dwelling not only served as a testament to his success but also as a haven for family gatherings and celebrations, a place where the echo of laughter would reverberate through the years.

Beyond his professional prowess and the material success that enriched his life, Anantharama Iyer was a man of profound personal traits. His scholarly disposition was evident in the meticulously curated collection of books that lined his study. A connoisseur of knowledge, he found solace in the pages of literature that spanned cultures and eras. The study of Sanskrit and the profound teachings contained within the ancient Hindu scriptures were subjects exceptionally dear to his soul.

However, it was his extraordinary tolerance and philanthropic spirit that defined him in the eyes of those who knew him intimately. Anantharama Iyer was more than a successful professional; he was a benevolent figure who never turned down anyone seeking monetary help. His generosity extended beyond his immediate family, reaching out to numerous relatives and the underprivileged, during his time in Burma. Each act of financial assistance showcased not just his wealth but, more importantly, his compassion and commitment to uplifting those around him and sharing his hard earned wealth.

As the patriarch of the family, Anantharama Iyer's legacy wasn't confined to the pages of corporate success; it extended into the hearts of those he touched with his kindness. His residence became a symbolic center, not just architecturally but emotionally, representing the heart of a man whose journey from Burma to Calicut was marked by resilience, success, and an unwavering commitment to his roots. It was a household rich in ancestral traditions, known to all as Iyer's *Tharavadu* or the ancestral home, despite being built as recently as 1962.

Meenakshi, the steadfast companion of Anantharama Iyer, carried a history as rich as him. Their marriage in 1940, saw a young Meenakshi embarking on a journey to Burma alongside her newlywed husband. At a tender age of fifteen, having received education up to the eighth standard in a government school in the Koduvayur village, Palakkad, she stepped into the realm of matrimony, her commitment to her husband and family becoming the cornerstone of her identity.

In Burma, Meenakshi, with her limited formal education, proved to be a practical and resourceful woman. Devoted to Anantharama Iyer and nurturing a kind and caring environment for her children, she became the steady anchor of their family life. Despite the challenges of adapting to a new culture and environment, Meenakshi's gentle demeanor and practical approach laid the foundation for the family's stability during their stay in Burma.

Upon returning to India and settling in Calicut, Meenakshi experienced the joys and trials of family life. Having her first child relatively late in life, her children were still young and in school when they made the transition from Burma to India. During this time of change, her practical and careful personality made things feel safe and steady in their new home, which was still strange to them.

However, life wasn't without its share of tribulations. Meenakshi, in her mid-forties, began suffering from high blood pressure, asthma, and diabetes. These health challenges became a significant factor in her later years as her three sons and only daughter grew up and married, leaving her grappling with the complications of these diseases. The once vibrant and resilient woman found herself navigating the intricacies of managing her health, a journey fraught with both physical and emotional complexities. Her youngest son, Arjun was born late in her life after they migrated to India and was completing his graduation only now.

In the quiet times of her life, Meenakshi's personality traits became key aspects of her character, shaping who she was. Though a quiet woman, she demonstrated flexibility in her role as a wife and mother. Her practical approach and constant love for her family, even when health problems assailed her, showed how strong she was. She didn't let her troubles stop her from taking care of her loved ones.

Throughout their time in Burma and while raising a family in Calicut Meenakshi's unwavering support and quiet strength enriched the family's history and dynamics. In the larger story of the Iyer family, she represented a quiet yet powerful presence, illustrating the sacrifices and determination required to build a life with her husband, Anantharama Iyer.

Arjun, youngest of the children and the center of attention, stood beside his father, ready to cut the cake. Tall, lanky and handsome, he was the blue-eyed boy of the family. "Come on, Arjun, make a wish!" his sister Nandini teased him, her eyes glinting mischievously like the twinkle lights that adorned the room.

"May the sweetness of this cake be a prelude to the joy in my exam results!" Arjun grinned, his laughter harmonizing with the chorus of the family's claps and cheers as he blew out the candles.

"Before I cut the birthday cake, *akka*, let me seek the blessings from *Amma* and *Appa*." Arjun prostrated before his parents who stood in front of him and blessed him with the words, *"Deerga Ayushman Bhava."*

The hall filled with joy as everyone sang the birthday song together, their voices blending harmoniously in a beautiful celebration. Aathira, for her part, joined the singing in her tinny voice. Anantharama Iyer, though seated, joined in with a voice that was a bit shaky but filled with the warmth of a loving father.

Post-song, the hall echoed with the delightful sound of unwrapping gifts and the crackle of laughter. Anandu handed Arjun a small package, "From your favorite brother, of course." It was a beautiful Titan watch with a golden dial and a golden strap. "This is the latest watch in the Indian market," his brother remarked, "I got it through a client of mine working in the Titan company. There is one more gift for you from Uma."

Uma, ever the organized one, handed Arjun a meticulously wrapped packet. "It's a planner, *kanna*. For all those big dreams you'll be planning after acing those exams."

Arjun thanked her, "Thanks, *Manni*, I'll make sure to fill it with my dreams and achievements." Nandini presented a beautifully wrapped gift, a mysterious smile playing on Nandini's lips. "Open it later, when you're alone," she winked, causing Arjun to raise an eyebrow in curiosity.

Satya and Janaki, the newlyweds, gifted a photo frame capturing a candid moment from their recent wedding showing the newlyweds with Arjun wearing a maroon kurta. "May your life be as colorful and beautiful as this picture," Janaki said with a warm smile.

As the evening progressed, the family congregated in the hall, sharing cherished anecdotes, genuine laughter, and the pure delight of each other's company. Anantharama Iyer observed the scene with a contented smile, his eyes reflecting not only the celebration but also a lifetime of love and sacrifice that had woven the intricate fabric of their familial bond.

"Arjun," he called, beckoning his youngest son. "Come here."

Arjun approached, a mixture of reverence and love reflected in his eyes. Anantharama Iyer patted his cheek, "You make us proud, *kanna*; Chase your dreams, and remember, this family will always be your anchor. My blessings are always with you."

The atmosphere, though initially characterized by joviality, evolved into a moment of profound connection. The family, bound by blood and affection, savored the essence of togetherness. The laughter persisted, filling the *Nalukettu* with a timeless melody that spoke volumes about their shared happiness.

Aathira came up with her small camera which her father had sent from Australia, "*Mama*, stand with the others so that I can get a group photo of all of you together. All of you stand near *Thatha*, so that he doesn't have to get up."

"Say cheese", she shouted as she clicked a couple of snaps as everyone burst into a chorus of laughter at her little comment.

As the night gradually drew to a close, the family dispersed, their hearts full, leaving the hall with the lingering warmth of shared laughter and unconditional love. In the quiet moments that followed, Anantharama Iyer and Meenakshi stood together, watching their children find their way in the world. In the heart of the *Nalukettu*, where tradition and modernity embraced, the Iyer family celebrated not just Arjun's birthday but the unspoken bond that held them together – a fabric of love and the exquisite beauty of a joint family.

Meenakshi's face, however, betrayed a palpable unease, as if the echoes of an unsettling premonition reverberated within her. Anantharama Iyer, her stalwart companion through countless years, was swift to discern the gloom that cast its shadows across her countenance. In a tender inquiry, he probed, "What ails you, Meena? There's a turmoil in your eyes, I can see something is troubling you."

Meenakshi emitted a profound sigh, burdened with the weight of unspoken concerns. "It's nothing," she began, "I was thinking of my recent visit to the astrologer, with Arjun's horoscope. Dark times are predicted for Arjun after his birthday due to the influence of his new onset *Ketu dasa*. I've arranged for rituals, sacred poojas in the temple, with a fervent plea to *Bhagawan Guruvayurappan* to safeguard him through this foreboding juncture."

Unrecognized by Meenakshi, as she sought solace in her actions, a dark future created by destiny loomed ahead. Misfortune and the threat of disaster approached silently, unknown to her compassionate heart. Troubles were brewing, poised to disrupt the lives of the once happy and contented family.

Chapter 2

The early rays of the morning sun peeked through the gathering clouds, casting a gentle glow upon the Iyer household. The soulful melody of the *Venkatesa Suprabhatham*, sung by the renowned musician Sreemathi M. S. Subbulakshmi, drifted through the air, filling the home with a sense of tranquility and hope. The music served as a gentle nudge, urging each member of the household to awaken from their slumber and embrace the new day with vigor and enthusiasm.

As the sweet strains of the sacred hymn wafted through the corridors, it stirred something deep within the hearts of the Iyer family. "What a beautiful way to start the day," remarked Meenakshi, her voice tinged with appreciation.

"Indeed," agreed Anantharama Iyer, a soft smile gracing his lips. "It feels as though the divine itself is blessing our home with its presence," he added, his eyes reflecting a sense of reverence.

In the kitchen, Uma paused in her chores, her hands stilling as she listened to the melodious rendition of the *Suprabhatham*. "Such divine music," she murmured to herself, a sense of peace washing over her. "It fills the heart with joy and uplifts the soul," she reflected, a fond smile playing on her lips.

Meanwhile, in the pooja room, young Arjun adorned with *Vibhuti* and sandal paste, sat cross-legged on the floor, his eyes closed in quiet contemplation. The music seemed to transport him to another realm, where worries and care melted away in the presence of such divine beauty. "I feel so blessed to be able to listen to such music," he whispered to himself, a sense of gratitude swelling within him.

And so, as the *Venkatesa Suprabhatham* continued to weave its enchanting spell, it brought the Iyer family together in a moment of shared reverence and appreciation. For in the midst of life's trials and tribulations, it was moments like these — moments of music, of harmony, and of divine grace that reminded them of the beauty and wonder that surrounded them each day.

Anantharama Iyer, the esteemed patriarch, was dressed in the traditional attire of a pristine *dhoti* paired with a sleeveless banian as he leisurely reclined in his cherished easy chair. With a steel tumbler of meticulously brewed, steaming filter coffee cradled in his hands, the room was filled with the comforting aroma of freshly brewed coffee.

Having engaged in his morning rituals and pooja, Anantharama Iyer's forehead displayed the revered markings of three horizontal lines of *Vibhuti*, and a central mark of sandalwood paste. The sacred symbols added a touch of divinity to his visage, creating an impression of a devout individual basking in the satisfaction of life's fulfilled aspirations.

As the patriarch reflected on his familial blessings, a tranquil feeling of contentment enveloped him. The joy derived from witnessing the prosperity and settled lives of his children was palpable, a testament to a life well-lived. However, a solitary exception lingered in the form of Arjun, the youngest scion of the family.

Gazing out of the window, he murmured to himself, "Arjun's journey is still unfolding. Soon, his endeavors will bear fruit, and my family responsibilities will be complete."

Meenakshi came and stood by his side with a glass of coffee, "Do you want more coffee? Did you say anything?"

His musings were interrupted by her enquiry, and he added with a gentle smile, "Our responsibilities in this *Grihasthasrama* are ever evolving. Arjun's impending success in his examinations will mark a blessed conclusion to this chapter. He has still not let go of his childish nature and pranks."

24

Anantharama Iyer continued to savor his second tumbler of coffee this morning, his gaze fixed on the horizon through the window. The beginning of the day promised more than just sunlight; it signaled the fulfillment of aspirations and the natural cycle of life in the Iyer household.

His spectacles perched on the bridge of his nose, he scanned the newspaper, a contented smile playing on his lips browsing the newspaper for the latest political scandal in the country. The room echoed with the joyous banter of the Iyer siblings – Anandu, Satya, Arjun, and Nandini. Everyone was busy getting ready to leave for their respective places of work. The kids had already left for school.

Arjun was sprawled on the divan reading a magazine, his lanky frame taking up most of the space. Awaiting his examination results, his mind oscillated between anxiety and anticipation. Anandu, the eldest brother, sat beside him, a mischievous glint in his eyes. Satya, engrossed in his transistor radio, tried to tune in to his favorite station, while Nandini, the sister, busied herself helping her sisters in law in setting the table in the dining area for breakfast.

"Hey Arjun, when are your results coming out?" Anandu teased, nudging him with an elbow as he polished his shoes. "Are you not nervous?"

Arjun lowered the magazine and shot him a sideways glance, a playful smirk playing on his lips. "Soon enough, *anna*. I'm not nervous like you were when you were awaiting your results."

Anandu chuckled, remembering the nerve-wracking days of his own youth. "Well, you better pray you've inherited my intelligence."

"But not your looks," Arjun quipped. Anandu smiled. Arjun was proud of his handsome looks. He inherited his fair complexion from his mother, who was notably lighter-skinned compared to his darker-skinned father.

Satya, still fiddling with the radio, chimed in, "Speaking of good looks, Arjun, you could you help me get my transistor radio repaired? It's been acting up lately."

Arjun sighed dramatically, his hand on his heart. "Ah, the burdens of being the helpful brother. Fine, I'll take it to the repair shop for you. No worries."

Nandini, joining the banter, added, "And while you're going, can you drop me off at the hospital? I have to check in on a patient and I have three major surgeries lined up for today."

Arjun mockingly saluted with a bow. "Sure thing, doctor Nandini. Your chariot awaits."

Amidst the laughter, their mother's voice was heard from the kitchen. "Arjun, *kanna*, when you go out, pick up the groceries from the Udaya store and the vegetables from Bharatan's. We're running low on essentials."

Arjun nodded, already mentally noting down the growing list of tasks. "Consider it done, *Amma*."

Anantharama Iyer looked up from his newspaper, a twinkle in his eye. "Arjun, while you're in the city, could you drop by the City Optical on SM street? I need to get my spectacles repaired."

Arjun raised an eyebrow. "Spectacles, *Appa*? Did you accidentally sit on them again?"

Anantharama Iyer chuckled. "No, no, just a loose screw and a broken nose pad. Nothing too complicated," said he laughing.

The banter continued as the family gathered around the dining table for breakfast. Plates clinked, and the aroma of home-cooked food filled the air. The Iyer household was a symphony of voices, laughter, and the occasional clatter of utensils.

"Where's Aathira?" Arjun enquired after his affectionate niece.

"Gone to school already. Devaki amma, the maid took her to the bus shelter to wait for the school bus," Nandini answered placing two *iddlis* on Arjun's plate. "Aadi and Akhil left for school early today."

As they enjoyed their breakfast, Anandu couldn't resist poking fun at Arjun. "Hey, Arjun, since you're in the mood for favors, can you also take my scooter to the repair shop? It's been making some weird noises of late."

Arjun feigned exasperation. "Am I the family mechanic now? Fine, I'll take your noisy scooter for a tune-up. Everything except the horn makes sound in your scooter. Why don't you trash it and get a new one?"

Nandini, who had a special bond with Arjun, leaned in and whispered with a wink, "You're the glue that holds this family together, Arjun. Don't forget it."

He smiled at her, appreciating the sentiment. After all, she had practically been a second mother to him, having cared for him since his birth when she was only sixteen. When he was a toddler, she had helped Meenakshi with tasks like feeding and bathing him. As a child, Arjun also had wished for his sister, Nandini a*kka*, to assist him with everyday activities such as getting him ready for school and helping with his homework. He held a deep affection for her − a sort of motherly affection.

Once breakfast was over, the siblings dispersed to their respective corners of the house busy preparing to leave for work. Arjun, now shouldering a laundry list of tasks, began his mission to fulfill everyone's requests.

First, he gathered Satya's transistor radio, giving it a dramatic examination. "Ah, the patient is in critical condition. I'll do my best, Satya *anna*."

Satya smiled. "Just get it fixed, will you? None of your wisecracks."

Arjun flashed a thumbs-up and headed towards the door. Nandini joined him, ready for the hospital visit.

As they left, Anandu called out, "Don't forget my scooter, Arjun! It's in the portico!"

Arjun waved dismissively. "I am taking it, I'll add it to my superhero to-do list. I am taking it to drop off Nandini *akka* before giving it for repairs." Arjun kick-started Anandu's scooter, inspecting it with a mock-serious expression. "We have a code red, ladies and gentlemen. Anandu *anna's* scooter needs immediate attention."

Anandu chuckled. "Just take it to the repair shop, Arjun. I don't need a running commentary."

As they left home, Nandini turned to Arjun. "You're like a one-man task force. Is there anything you can't do?"

Arjun grinned. "Well, I can't fly. *akka*. Not yet at least. One day I might even do that."

Nandini rode pillion on the scooter with Arjun. As they left, Nandini asked, "Don't you ever get tired of helping everyone, Arjun?"

He shrugged. "Not really. It's who I am, you know? The all-round helpful guy."

They reached the hospital, where he dropped off Nandini and went about finishing his assigned tasks.

The day continued with Arjun juggling various tasks – picking up groceries, dropping by the optical store for his father, and finally, taking Anandu's scooter to the repair shop.

As the day wound down, the family reconvened in the living room. Anantharama Iyer, now with his repaired spectacles, beamed at Arjun. "Thank you, *kanna*, You've saved my eyesight."

Arjun chuckled. "Just doing my duties, *Appa*."

The room echoed with mirth, the joyous atmosphere a testament to the love and intimacy that bound the Iyer family together. As they settled in for the evening, Arjun couldn't help but feel grateful for the chaos and the constant requests. After all, it was these moments that made their family unique, vibrant, cohesive and undeniably, filled with love.

Yet, fate consistently unfolds its own plans for individuals. What a person ardently wishes for doesn't invariably come to pass, and what unfolds may not necessarily be in their best interest. Little did anyone in the family fathom that destiny held a distressing jest in store, ready to unravel a tempest in the midst of a family accustomed to tranquil seas. The impending storm was an unforeseen twist in the narrative of their usually placid existence.

Chapter 3

As the evening sun cast a warm, golden glow through the windows of Anantharama Iyer's cozy home, the aroma of *sambar* and *rasam* wafted from the kitchen, where Uma, the eldest daughter in law, was engrossed in her usual routine of cooking. Janaki, the younger daughter in law was in the hall neatly folding and sorting the laundered clothes of the day. The rhythmic creaking of the *Aattukattil* echoed in the dining area, where Meenakshi, the elderly matriarch sat swaying gently, her eyes closed, lost in a world of memories.

Seated on the floor nearby, Nandini's daughter Aathira, the vivacious six-year-old with pigtails and sparkling eyes, diligently scribbled in her notebook. Nandini, a dedicated gynecologist and an assistant professor in the Medical college at Calicut, sat beside her, guiding her through the labyrinth of homework.

"*Amma*, can you please explain this arithmetic problem again? I don't understand," Aathira looked up with a pout, her tiny fingers gripping the pencil.

Nandini chuckled, her eyes crinkling at the corners. "Alright, let's go through it one more time. You see, if you have nine mangoes and you give five to your friend, how many do you have left?"

"Four," Aathira answered with a triumphant smile, calculating using her fingers,. "But why would I give her five mangoes?" she remarked naughtily.

"Don't crack jokes, *kanna*," Nandini chuckled pinching her nose in a playful manner. "Anyway good job, my little mathematician," Nandini praised, ruffling Aathira's hair. "Now, finish the rest, and we'll have dinner soon."

As mother and daughter immersed themselves in the world of numbers, Meenakshi opened her eyes and observed them with a tender smile. Her gaze then shifted to Nandini, who looked weary yet determined. Meenakshi's heart swelled with pride at the sight of her accomplished daughter.

"Nandu, you're working so hard. Don't strain yourself too much," Meenakshi advised, her maternal concern, soft and caring.

Nandini glanced at her mother, a gentle smile playing on her lips. "I'm fine, *Amma*. Aathira keeps me on my toes, but I love it."

"I was not referring to Aathira, I was referring to your job in the hospital", Meenakshi sighed, the lines on her face revealing the years of wisdom she held. "You take after your *Appa*. Always working hard, never complaining. What with your night duty and all."

Nandini chuckled, a hint of nostalgia in her eyes. "True, *Amma*. But you and *Appa* taught me well. Dedication and hard work are our family's trademarks. I remember the days when we were in Burma, just before the civil unrest. Father, working late in his office, used to come late from office with the curfew on, and how you used to be anxious till he reached home."

Just then, the shrill ringing of the phone in the hall interrupted their conversation. Nandini sprang up from where she was seated to pick up the phone. It was a call she had been waiting anxiously for. Rajaram, her husband was calling from Australia. It would be 10.30 at night for him.

Aathira's eyes lit up, and she abandoned her homework, rushing to her mother. "*Appa! Appa!* Can I talk to *Appa*?"

Nandini handed the phone to Aathira, who spoke animatedly to her father in Australia. Nandini observed the joy in her daughter's eyes and couldn't help but smile. Despite the distance, Rajaram made it a point to call every Saturday, creating a virtual bridge between continents. After a few cajoling words to Aathira, Rajaram asked her to hand over the receiver to Nandini.

The intimate conversation between Nandini and her husband was hushed. Meenakshi embraced Aathira who ran to her, sat on her lap and gently swung on the *Aattukattil* as Nandini continued conversing with her husband continents away.

"I will be applying for a visit visa for you, Nandu", Rajaram said, "You can come here with Aathira and stay for six to nine months during which you can try the entrance tests here for you to qualify to join for a fellowship here."

"But what about Aathira's school?," Nandini interposed.

"Oh, don't worry about it. After all she is only in the first grade. Once you come here permanently, there should be no problem with her schooling…" And the conversation went on. Aathira wanted to talk to her dad once again and Nandini handed over the receiver to her.

Meenakshi caught Nandini's gaze and motioned for her to come closer. Nandini joined her mother near the *Aattukattil*, the creaking now a comforting melody. Her mother suddenly seemed to look haggard and weary.

"*Amma*, how are you feeling?" Nandini inquired, concern etched on her face.

Meenakshi sighed, her eyes reflecting a hint of fatigue. "I've been feeling excessively tired lately, Nandu, and slightly breathless. Maybe it's just old age catching up. Never mind."

Nandini's brows furrowed. "Old age, *Amma*? You're only sixty two. Let me check you."

Meenakshi hesitated but nodded. Nandini brought out her stethoscope from her bag, the familiar scent of antiseptic lingering on it. She listened to her mother's heartbeat, her expression growing serious.

"*Amma*, your heart rate is a bit fast, and I can hear a heart murmur. I need to check your blood pressure," Nandini said, her professional manner taking over.

As Nandini wrapped the cuff of her digital blood pressure apparatus around Meenakshi's arm, Aathira finished her call with Rajaram and returned, sensing the change in the atmosphere.

"What's happening, *Amma*? Is *Ammamma* okay?" Aathira asked, her eyes wide with concern.

Nandini smiled reassuringly at her daughter. "*Ammamma* is fine, *kanna*. I'm just checking her blood pressure and health."

Meenakshi shot a playful glare at Nandini. "I didn't ask for a doctor's appointment, Nandu. I'm fine."

Nandini chuckled. "Humor me, *Amma*. I don't want any surprises."

After a moment, the blood pressure monitor beeped, and Nandini read the results. Her expression grew somber. "*Amma*, your blood pressure is higher than usual. Have you been feeling stressed or anxious lately?"

Meenakshi hesitated before confessing, "Well, there is something. I've been thinking about Arjun all the time. Once his results are out, he needs to get a job and get settled in life. Worry about him keeps me concerned."

Nandini sighed, understanding the weight of her mother's worries. "*Amma*, you need to take care of yourself first. Stress isn't good for your health."

Meenakshi nodded, her eyes filled with gratitude. "Yes, maybe you're right."

"Okay, *Amma*," Nandini assured her.

The evening progressed with a hearty dinner, filled with laughter and anecdotes. Meenakshi's weariness seemed to fade as the family gathered around the dining table, sharing stories and savoring the delicious home-cooked meal.

As the night deepened, Nandini tucked Aathira into bed, kissing her forehead. Meenakshi sat in the living room, lost in her thoughts.

Nandini joined her, a cup of hot Horlicks in her hands for her mother. Janaki and Uma had retired to their rooms following cleaning up the kitchen after dinner, as their husbands had already retired for the day.

"*Amma*, I think you should see Professor Menon at the Medical College tomorrow. We shouldn't delay any health concerns," Nandini suggested gently. "I am worried about your fluctuating blood pressure and your heart murmur."

Meenakshi nodded, her eyes reflecting a mix of gratitude and concern. "You're right, Nandu. I'll go with you tomorrow. But promise me, no fuss. I don't want the whole town knowing about my health."

Nandini chuckled, her eyes sparkling. "No fuss, *Amma*. I'll make sure of it."

The next day Nandini accompanied Meenakshi to the Calicut Medical College in a cab. Professor Menon, a seasoned physician, welcomed them into his office, the shelves filled with medical textbooks and awards.

After a series of questions and a thorough examination, Professor Menon delivered his diagnosis. "Meenakshi *Amma*, your blood pressure is elevated, and there is a murmur in your heart. I would like to run some tests to understand the underlying cause. It could be stress-related, but we need to rule out other possibilities."

Meenakshi nodded, her eyes meeting Nandini's for reassurance. The tests were scheduled, and by evening, the duo left the office with a mix of worry and hope.

Back home, Meenakshi reclined on the *Aattukattil*, staring out of the window with a sullen face. Nandini sat beside her, a comforting presence. Aathira, sensing the subdued atmosphere, tiptoed into the room.

"*Ammamma*, *Appa* said he's sending a surprise for you. He wants you to smile," Aathira announced addressing Meenakshi, a mischievous twinkle in her eyes.

Meenakshi couldn't help but smile at her granddaughter's antics. "A surprise, is it? Well, I better start practicing my smile then."

Nandini juggled between work, taking care of Meenakshi, and assisting Aathira with her homework as evening set in. The phone rang.

Meenakshi answered the phone and it was Rajaram, her son in law from Australia, checking in on her health.

"How is everyone? *Amma*, are you feeling okay?" Rajaram's voice carried a touch of concern.

Meenakshi assured him, "I'm fine, Raju. Just a bit tired. How's everything with you in Australia?"

"All well here, *Amma*. Anyway you take care and don't worry about anything. I am glad that Nandini is there to help you."

Meenakshi exchanged a worried glance with Nandini, who decided to step in. "Rajaram, maybe you could ask around your workplace if there are any openings there. It might help Arjun get a foot in the door." Nandini knew that half the worries *Amma* had were regarding Arjun and his future.

Rajaram sighed. "I've tried, Nandini. But these things take time. It is not easy. I'll keep trying, though. And ask *Amma*, to take care of herself. I don't want her worrying about Arjun. Everything will be fine."

The conversation continued, with updates about life on two different continents. After the call ended, Meenakshi turned to Nandini. "Nandu, do you think Arjun will find a job soon? Can Raju get him a job in Australia? I am worried. That is one my greatest anxieties. His horoscope shows that astrologically bad times are ahead for him."

Nandini sighed, her heart heavy with concern. "I hope so, *Amma*. We can only wait and see. In the meantime, let's focus on getting you well. And stop worrying unnecessarily about Arjun and his horoscope."

Days turned into weeks, and Meenakshi's health improved with medication and rest. The medical tests showed no major concerns. Dr Menon gave a verdict of high blood pressure causing mild cardiac ischemia and trotted out a list of medication to be taken.

The family breathed a collective sigh of relief. Yet, the underlying stress lingered, woven into the very fabric of their daily existence.

One evening, as Meenakshi rested on the *Aattukattil*, Nandini sat beside her, a sense of calm settling over them. Aathira, ever the source of joy, skipped into the room, holding a letter in her hand.

"*Amma*, look what *Appa* sent!" Aathira exclaimed, handing the letter to Nandini. "*Thatha* gave it to me now and told me to show it to you."

Nandini unfolded the letter, her eyes widening in surprise.

"What is it, Nandini?." Meenakshi was curious.

Nandini smiled at her mother, reading the letter. "Rajaram is sending us tickets and a visa to visit him in Australia. A vacation, he says. May be for a couple of months. He wants us to be with him and take a break from everything here. He wants you to come with us to Australia, *Amma*."

Meenakshi looked at her daughter, her eyes moist with gratitude. "Nandu, can we go? It might do us all good. Aathira and you can be with Rajaram. It will be a welcome break for me too. Uma and Janaki can manage here."

Nandini smiled, her heart swelling with love for her family. "Of course, *Amma*. We'll go. A change of scenery might be just what you also need for your heart."

The news of the upcoming trip brought a renewed sense of excitement to the household. Aathira danced around, imagining the adventures awaiting them in Australia. Meenakshi, though initially hesitant, found herself looking forward to the journey, a chance to be with her son in law Rajaram and create cherished memories.

"Kangaroo... Kangaroo..." Aathira hopped about the house shouting with joy. "I will bring a kangaroo with me when I return from Australia!"

Everyone laughed.

In the following days, preparations for the trip unfolded. Meenakshi, Nandini, and Aathira gathered around the dining table, passports and travel documents spread out before them. The house echoed with the chatter of excited packing and the aroma of traditional snacks being prepared to be taken to Australia.

Little did they know that their joy would be abruptly interrupted. The excitement-filled voyage to Australia, brimming with anticipation and aspirations, was thwarted by an unforeseen and abrupt twist of fate.

Man proposes, God disposes.

Chapter 4

The warm rays of the setting sun painted a picturesque scene, illuminating the quaint surroundings with a sense of tranquility and warmth that enveloped the space like a comforting embrace. Inside the cozy home, the atmosphere was filled with a quiet contentment, as the family gathered together in the fading light of the day.

Anantharama Iyer was settled comfortably in his favorite rocking chair, gently rocking back and forth as he remained engrossed in the day's newspaper. He would often read the paper till the last page, not missing any detail. Meenakshi, his wife, bustled around the kitchen, creating a culinary masterpiece for the evening meal. Her two daughters in law helped her. The scent of sautéed onions now gently permeated the air, embracing the entire household with its comforting essence, tantalizing the senses and eliciting salivation from all who were favored by its aroma.

Nandini, sat in the living room, engrossed in a lively conversation with her father discussing about their imminent trip to Australia. Their laughter filled the room, setting a peaceful tone before the events that were to occur soon. Anantharama Iyer looked weary but bright despite his age and his illness. His words came out in a monotone in a low voice caused by his neurological disability. Occasionally he stuttered groping for words or proper expression. Nandini wondered if her father was getting into the beginnings of dementia which is often an accompaniment of Parkinsonism. Unfortunately, her medical knowledge led her to dwell more on the disease's complications than on how she could help her father. Meenakshi was in the kitchen kneading dough to make *Bhaturas* for the night's dinner.

Suddenly, the tranquility shattered. Meenakshi clutched her chest, a gasp escaping her lips, and the clang of utensils hitting the floor echoed throughout the house. Anantharama Iyer looked up from his newspaper, concern etched on his face. Nandini rushed to her mother in the kitchen, panic seizing her.

"*Amma*, what happened? Are you okay?" she asked, her voice trembling with worry.

Meenakshi struggled to speak, her face contorted in pain. She was sweating profusely and her breath came out in gasps. Her lips were bluish. Arjun, hearing the commotion, ran into the kitchen. One look told him that all was not well with *Amma*. He ran to the hall and grabbed the phone, dialing for an ambulance. Panic thickened the air as the urgency of the situation enveloped the household. Anantharama Iyer could not get up from his rocker abruptly owing to his disability.

"*Enna Aachu.....Enna Aachu.....,*" he kept on repeating. No one seemed to answer him in the confusion.

The wailing siren of the ambulance pierced through the quiet neighborhood as Meenakshi was carefully loaded into it, accompanied by Nandini and Arjun. The doors slammed shut as the ambulance sped away.

Back at home, the atmosphere was charged with an unspoken tension. Uma, the elder daughter-in-law, took charge of the situation, her face a mask of responsibility. She briskly moved around the kitchen, instructing Janaki, the younger daughter-in-law, to assist her.

"Janaki, can you please chop those vegetables? We need to finish cooking," Uma said, her tone authoritative. "I am sure Nandini and Arjun will take care of Amma in the hospital. Meanwhile, we should get things going here. The children will be back from school soon and we have to remain calm without causing them any worry. I will call Anandu and tell him to go to the hospital straightaway from his office."

Janaki, however, was in no mood to take orders. Buried hostilities in her mind began gradually surfacing. Months of hidden anger and frustration in her mind surfaced as negative emotions. She rolled her eyes, an audible scoff escaping her lips. "I'm not your servant, Uma *manni*. I know what I need to do and when."

It was an unprecedented moment when Janaki, driven by a simmering resentment, addressed Uma with an air of defiance giving vent to her innermost thoughts. A simmering tension had been building up between them for days, fueled by Janaki's feeling that Uma, as the elder daughter-in-law, was overstepping her bounds and trying to assert her dominance in the family. But Meenakshi's towering presence had kept Janaki's acrimony at bay till now.

Janaki's feelings stemmed from her belief that her mother-in-law favored Uma excessively, granting her more freedom and privileges than Janaki herself received. In Janaki's eyes, Uma seemed to wield an influence that exceeded her own, leaving Janaki feeling overlooked and undervalued.

As Uma had been present in the family for over eight years, Meenakshi, the mother-in-law, naturally relied heavily on Uma and entrusted her with significant responsibilities in the household. Uma was given charge of the storeroom, in the house – a recognition of trust. Being given charge of the storeroom was considered as conferring an extra privilege on the daughter in law. In contrast, Janaki, being the newer addition to the family, had not yet established a strong connection with her mother-in-law that would warrant granting similar responsibilities or privileges.

This discrepancy in treatment fueled a sense of jealousy and envy in Janaki's unseasoned mind. She found herself grappling with the emotions arising from a perceived imbalance in attention and importance. She developed an erroneous paranoid feeling that she was being sidelined in the family by her mother in law. This unfolding dynamics between the recently arrived Janaki and Uma was laden with complex emotions, as each woman felt that she was wronged.

Janaki's primary source of irritation stemmed from being the sole, indulged daughter of her parents, thus rendering her unable to reconcile with the inevitable challenges and discomforts associated with living in a joint family. She found adjustments in a joint family impossible.

Uma's eyes narrowed, her patience waning. "This is not the time for your arrogance, Janaki. Amma is in the hospital, and we need to ensure everything is running smoothly here."

A flicker of annoyance crossed Janaki's face. "Why does everything have to be your way? Just because you're the elder daughter-in-law doesn't mean you can boss everyone around."

As the tension simmered in the kitchen, Satya, Janaki's husband, entered the scene. He had just arrived from the office and was looking for a cup of tea. He raised an eyebrow at the brewing storm.

"What's going on here?" he asked, his voice a wary undertone.

Janaki pointed an accusing finger at Uma. "She thinks she can order me around like I'm her servant. I won't tolerate it."

Uma, unfazed, replied addressing Satya, "I'm just trying to manage things in Amma's absence. Is that too much to ask? By the way, do you know that *Amma* has been hospitalized? I thought that Janaki would have telephoned you..."

"Oh, I forgot." Janaki's rejoinder seemed rather abrupt.

Satya was aghast on hearing of *Amma's* hospitalization. But even before he could enquire about it, the argument between the sisters in law escalated, each word a spark in the already volatile atmosphere. Satya, caught between his wife and sister in law, sighed in frustration.

"Can we not do this now? *Amma* is in the hospital. We should be supporting each other, not quarrelling." He put an end to the cold war temporarily.

Meanwhile, in the hospital, Nandini and Arjun anxiously waited for news about Meenakshi. Dr. Menon emerged from the ICU, his expression grim.

"She had a heart attack. We've stabilized her for now, but she's in a critical condition. The next forty-eight hours are crucial for her," he explained. "Let us wait for a couple of days before we can declare her out of the woods." The doctor left leaving Nandini and Arjun worried.

Nandini's eyes welled up with tears, and Arjun wrapped his arms around her, both grappling with the harsh reality that their world might be on the verge of shattering. Arjun let out a soft, gentle sob.

Back at the Iyer residence, by next morning, Sadasiva Iyer, Janaki's father, had arrived from Trivandrum. He arrived, holding his long umbrella under his arm, wearing a white shirt with sleeves that reached below his elbows and a towel draped over his shoulders. He always carried his umbrella with him wherever he went. He had been informed by Janaki over the phone about her mother in law's heart attack. He sensed the tension in the house as soon as he stepped in. Putting on an artificial face of gloom, he sat beside Anantharama Iyer and in a few words expressed his grief at the misfortune that had befallen them.

"*Mami*, is such a great and nice woman. It is unfortunate that she was felled so early in life with a heart attack. Life will not be the same for her anymore. She will have to take rest and leave the responsibilities to her daughters in law."

Anantharama Iyer kept quiet. He knew fully well the hypocrisy behind Sadasiva Iyer's statements. He merely nodded. After a few banalities, Sadasiva Iyer rose to speak to his daughter, Janaki.

Sadasiva Iyer, a retired, professor of English from a Government college in Trivandrum, was known for his diplomatic attitude and careful choice of words. Rattling off English quotations especially from the bard of Stratford upon Avon was his usual mannerism. He always gave the impression of exuding confidence and trustworthiness. However, beneath his polished exterior, he harbored a singular, self-centered agenda concerning his daughter's future. His desire was not merely for her happiness but a calculated plan to ensure control over her life, especially in her marital relationship with Satya.

Sadasiva Iyer's aspirations for his daughter went beyond the usual parental concerns. He wished for Satya, his son-in-law, to heed his guidance and fulfill every desire of his daughter. It wasn't just about their happiness; it was about asserting dominance over Satya, his son in law, and shaping him to conform to Sadasiva Iyer's expectations. This undercurrent of control and manipulation ran deep in Sadasiva Iyer's intentions.

Having been employed within the government system in the college where promotions and appointments depended on political affiliations and connections, he had become intimately acquainted with the intricate web of manipulations and machinations. This experience not only shaped his professional outlook but also transformed him into a cunning and scheming individual in his personal life. The deceitful techniques he learned while working in a government college didn't stay there; he effortlessly incorporated them into his everyday life.

Everything he did – from how he interacted with people to the choices he made – was shaped by the sneaky tricks he'd learned while working in powerful circles in Trivandrum. He had mastered the art of manipulating and undermining his rivals in his field.

His cunning wasn't just about looking out for himself. He also used it to ensure a bright future for both himself and his daughter. Every action he took was carefully planned to benefit them both, making sure their opportunities kept improving.

The ultimate goal in Sadasiva Iyer's strategic playbook was to separate his daughter and son-in-law from the joint family setup. His vision involved establishing them in a separate residence, a dwelling where his daughter could escape the perceived burdens imposed by in-laws.

"Why should my daughter cook and launder the clothes of her in laws. I married her off to take care of her husband and children only. Not the *excess baggage*' that comes in a joint family," was his thinking. The core of his plan aimed at creating a space where Sadasiva Iyer's influence could reign supreme, free from interference or opposition from the in laws. *'The better part of valor is discretion'*, was his Shakespearean dictum.

The self-centered nature of Sadasiva Iyer had a profound impact on his daughter, who, influenced by her father's ambitions, began nurturing similar dreams of an independent household—a nuclear family, or as referred to in her mother tongue, a *'Thani kudithanam.'*

Sadasiva Iyer's focus on family, driven by selfishness, clearly showed his strong desire to control his daughter and son-in-law's lives to match his own wishes.

"Don't waste your love on somebody who doesn't value it", he remarked quoting from Shakespeare, as with a subtle shake of his head, he approached Janaki in private in her room. "Janu, my dear, don't let anyone undermine you. You have your own identity. Stand firm," he whispered, imparting fatherly advice. "Remember all that I have told you previously. Get Satya to your way of thinking. That is the only way you can be happy in this joint family. Once your mother in law returns from hospital, things around the house will not be the same. Be ready to assert yourself. Don't give in to the manipulations of others."

Janaki, absorbing her father's words, felt a surge of determination. He continued, his voice lowered to a conspiratorial tone, "It's not wrong to dream of a little home of your own in the city. Independence is crucial."

Continuing his slick method, Sadasiva Iyer approached Satya, a twinkle in his eye. "Satya, a man should provide for his family. It's high time you consider having a place of your own, away from the constant bickering in a joint family."

Satya frowned, unsure of how to respond to his father-in-law's not-so-subtle hints. He preferred to keep quiet.

Sadasiva Iyer made a quick visit to the hospital to enquire after Meenakshi's health. Back in the Iyer household, amidst the chaos, Sadasiva Iyer sat in a corner on the sofa sipping a tumbler of strong coffee that his daughter provided, observing the drama unfold. He couldn't help but smile knowingly, realizing that his subtle nudges had set the stage for a family in turmoil. He muttered to himself with a cunning smirk, *'Now let it work. Mischief, thou art afoot. Take thou what course thou wilt!'*

Later, in the privacy of their room, Janaki subtly slipped the idea into Satya's ear. "Don't you think it would be nice to have our own place, away from all this drama?"

Satya, torn between loyalty to his family and the desire for independence, hesitated. "It's not that simple, Janu. We need to think about it carefully. Leave such thoughts for the time being. Let *Amma* come home recovered."

But he did not outright reject Janaki's idea. Janaki felt that she had scored her first goal in her game.

Anandu was in his room looking at some financial statements from his company. Uma, feeling slighted and overlooked, sought solace in Anandu, her husband in the privacy of their room. She painted a vivid picture of Janaki and the tiff they had in the kitchen that day.

"Anandu, don't you see how I am treated? We deserve our own space too," she lamented, planting seeds of doubt in his mind. "Sadasiva *mama* was prompt to drop in as soon as he heard about *Amma*. I am sure he would have sowed the seeds of malice in Janaki's mind. He spent about half an hour talking to her privately behind closed doors before he left. They must be conspiring something."

Anandu, torn between his loyalty to the family and the desire to protect his wife's feelings, felt the weight of the brewing conflict. His mother being in hospital was worrying him. "Why are you unnecessarily worrying about such things?", he tried to lighten the mood. "Everything will be back to normal when *Amma* returns home from hospital."

"Not necessarily," Uma replied, "Janaki is becoming rebellious. Today she was defying me and being rude when I asked her to do some chores in the kitchen. '*I am not your servant*', is what she said to me. Imagine her cheek!"

"Leave it, Uma, let us put an end to this complaining." Anandu resumed his work.

"You always side with your brothers and your parents. You never heed my words or listen to my side of things. I toil in this house from dawn to dusk and no one gives me any respect or recognition. No one, including you, listens to my problems." Uma was openly annoyed. "Your brother, Satya is not like that. He listens fervently to his wife and fulfills all her desires. I am like a working machine to you and your family."

Anandu kept quiet. Silence is the better part of discretion, he decided.

In the living room, Anantharama Iyer sat in his rocker, blissfully unaware of all these undercurrents happening in the family, engrossed in a classic novel. The distant echoes of his family's discord barely registered in his peaceful world. Partial nerve deafness owing to old age thus was a blessing for him.

The night wore on, the Iyer household becoming a battleground for unspoken resentments and brewing conflicts. The sound of dishes clinking in the kitchen and quiet arguments could be heard, making a chaotic noise that matched the growing tension between the sisters-in-law.

As the night deepened, Nandini and Arjun sat by Meenakshi's bedside at the hospital, their hearts heavy with the weight of impending sorrow. The monotonous beeping monitors and sterile hospital scent became the backdrop to their silent prayers. Meenakshi was deep asleep sedated by the doctors. The rhythmic beep on the monitors lulled Nandini and Arjun to sleep sitting in their chairs. They waited for a new dawn, a dawn they hoped would bring good news from the doctors.

The Iyer household, once a haven of peace, now echoed with the unspoken fears and resentments of its inhabitants. Little did they know that the dawn would bring not only a new day but also the unfolding of a fate none of them could escape from.

Chapter 5

On a Thursday evening, the gentle rays of the sun bathed the peaceful street where the Anantharama Iyer residence proudly stood. The two-storey Nalukettu, with vibrant bougainvillea vines in the garden, seemed to glow in the warm light, casting a serene aura over the surroundings. The golden glow of the sun filtered through the windows, casting soft shadows on the walls and creating a cozy ambience that enveloped them like a comforting blanket. Inside the charming home, the atmosphere was filled with a sense of quiet serenity, as the Anantharama Iyer family gathered together to enjoy the tranquil evening.

The air was filled with the aroma of spices as Meenakshi, frail and recently discharged from the hospital, reclined on her bed in her room. On the bedside table beside her were strewn strips of medications and bottles of potions. Nandini's blood pressure apparatus stood in the midst of these, a silent reminder of the serious nature of Meenakshi's illness. The atmosphere in the house held a hushed tone, as if the walls themselves were privy to the secrets and conflicts brewing within the family.

Downstairs in the living room, Anantharama Iyer sat on his favorite easy chair, a sense of weariness etched on his face. He seemed to have aged more during the past few weeks. His sons, Anandu, and Satya, flanked him on either side sitting on stools and wicker Ottomans. The tension in the air was palpable as Anantharama spoke, "Children, gather around. I have something important to discuss. Where is Nandu, I want her also here."

Nandini entered the room with a tray of steaming filter coffee for all of them, its aroma wafting through the air. The two daughters-in-law, Uma and Janaki were engaged in the preparation of the evening meal in the kitchen. Though out of earshot, their keen ears were tuned to pick up the conversation going on in the hall. Once Meenakshi returned home, the tension between the sisters-in-law had slightly diminished. The overt confrontation between the sisters-in-law had diminished considerably after Meenakshi returned from the hospital.

"Nandu, come here and sit with us as I want to tell the three of you some important decisions that I have taken," said Anantharama Iyer. All three of them look at him with eagerness mixed with apprehension.

Anantharama Iyer cleared his throat, "As you all know, Meena is back home, but she is advised complete bed rest for another month. Dr. Menon has further cautioned that she shouldn't be exposed to any upsetting or stressing situations at home." He paused, eyeing each of his children, aware of the potential storm his words might unleash. "I am also getting older and my Parkinsonism is giving me more trouble of late. Also, I seem to forget things from time to time," he continued in his feeble quivering voice.

Anandu, the eldest son, seemingly impatient, raised an eyebrow, "*Appa*, is there something more that you want to say?"

"Patience... patience..." Anantharama Iyer chided, "Be patient and listen."

The tremors of his left hand seemed to worsen as Iyer became more anxious. He nodded, "I've been thinking about our assets, the liquid ones – my pension fund, mutual funds, government bonds and my fixed deposits in various banks. I feel that the time has come to divide them among you."

The room erupted in a collective gasp as the siblings exchanged puzzled looks. Anandu spoke first, "But *Appa*, isn't it too soon for such discussions? *Amma* needs time to recover."

"But why hurry through this when *Amma* is indisposed?" Nandini voiced her concern. "What made you decide on this all of a sudden?"

47

Anantharama Iyer sighed, "I understand, *kanna*, But I'm not getting any younger. Managing everything is becoming challenging. My memory is also playing tricks on me at times and I don't think that I am as sharp as I used to be. Hence, I've decided to share my savings equally among the five of you."

Everyone fell silent as the news hung in the air, and tension simmered beneath the surface. Anandu and Satya exchanged glances, both contemplating the implications. Nandini remained stoic, her mind racing.

"But *Appa*, why are you saying this to the three of us, especially when Arjun is not here?," Nandini expressed her worry.

Anantharama Iyer nodded, "I've thought this through, Nandu, it's essential to plan for the future. This is the right time to take some firm decisions."

Satya voiced his concerns, "Appa, we can't just decide this without discussing it properly and at length. And what about Arjun? He deserves to know as Nandini rightly said. And Sreeni is in the US. Should he too not be informed of this?"

Father fixed his gaze on Satya, "I don't want Arjun to worry about it now. Let him find his footing first. Let him get through the examination and find proper employment. He is too young now to handle all that money. Satya, you will take care of his assets for the time being as a guardian. Once he is employed and married, you can give him independent charge of his funds."

Satya sighed, exchanging a glance with Anandu, who seemed equally uneasy with the situation. The patriarch's decisions were known for being unquestionably final, but this one had stirred a hornet's nest.

"But what will Sreeni say if we decide all this in his absence?" Anandu posed a rider.

Anantharama Iyer, irritation etching his features, locked eyes with Anandu and stated firmly, "I'm the one making the decision here, not any of you. So, Sreeni doesn't get a say in this. I will inform him when he chooses to come to India to meet us. Not till then. He has not bothered to come to see us for the past five years. Why can't he come at least once in two years? After all, both Meena and I are getting old and God knows how long we will be with you. And... Sreeni is mature enough to know that he should visit his parents. What is the use of his coming after we are dead and gone!" Anantharama Iyer was getting emotionally worked up and annoyed. At this, all three of them fell silent.

Anantharama Iyer continued, "I've also made up my mind about your mother's jewelry. I have told her to consider dividing it among the five of you. It's time both of us take some concrete decisions."

Nandini, who had been silent until now, interjected, "*Appa*, *Amma* won't agree to this. She values her jewelry; it's not just about the money. There are some antique pieces in her collection belonging to grandma."

Anantharama sighed, "I know it won't be easy, but it's necessary. We must prepare for what lies ahead. Neither Meena nor I are going to be around for long. My instincts tell me this. Meena can earmark the jewelry for each of you. She need not hand them over right now. At least she can list them out."

"Oh! *Appa*, don't talk like that you and *Amma* will be with us for a long, long time to come," tears glistened at the corner of Nandini's eyes. "You are scaring us."

"Don't be superstitious," he admonished her. "Speaking about death won't bring it upon me or Meena. Don't be excessively sensitive or superstitious about such matters. Learn to accept the truth with equanimity. That's what *Bhagavan Krishna* advises in the *Bhagavad Gita*."

The quiet of the Iyer household was suddenly shattered by the piercing ring of the telephone. On the line was Sreeni, the third son, living in the US. Nandini picked up the receiver and handed it over to her father. "It is Sreeni."

A total change occurred on Anantharama Iyer's face. His demeanor   dissolved into one of paternal concern and affection. Excitement filled the room as Anantharama Iyer answered, "Sreeni! How are you? How are Mamta and Pooja?"

The voice from the other end was filled with enthusiasm, "*Appa*, we're coming to see *Amma* and you. Mamta and Pooja are with me. We are starting tomorrow and will be there on Sunday morning."

The news sent a ripple of excitement through the family. Anandu and Satya exchanged glances, while Nandini rushed to Meenakshi's room to convey the happy news to her. She also passed the message to Uma and Janaki who were busy in the kitchen.

Janaki, unable to mask her envy, scoffing, muttered under her breath, "Must be nice, living in the US, free from all responsibilities. It is enough if you come to see your parents and brothers on vacation once in four or five years. How convenient!"

Uma, catching Janaki's words, shot back, "Responsibilities? Sreeni is coming to see his parents. It's not a vacation for them."

Janaki, impetuously, retorted, "Oh, please! They're probably enjoying their freedom there while we handle everything here. And while they are here mother will pamper them and make us work like slaves to keep them happy and satisfied. They get to be pampered as they are the '*phoren*' son and daughter in law."

Meenakshi, from her room listening to this exchange between her daughters in law, winced at the rising tension and envy between the daughters in law. She whispered to herself, "Not now. Please, not now. Don't start all over again. Oh! *Bhagavan Guruvayurappa*, give these children a sane mind!"

Anantharama Iyer, unaware of the brewing storm between the daughters in law, continued talking to Sreeni excitedly, "We're eagerly waiting for all of you. Take care, *kanna*."

The call ended, and the room fell silent. The anticipation of Sreeni's visit mingled with the unresolved tension regarding the impending division of assets. The calmness in the house hid a mix of feelings that could burst out suddenly.

In Meenakshi's room, she closed her eyes, silently praying for a moment of peace amid the gathering storm. She could not guess what problems would surface once Sreeni and his Telugu wife, Mamta land amidst these controversial times.

She closed her eyes in silent prayer.

Chapter 6

The city lights of New York twinkled outside the window, casting a warm glow on the spacious apartment where Sreeni and Mamta lived. The air was crisp, the faint scent of Mamta's homemade *rasam* lingering in the kitchen. The walls were adorned with artifacts and antiques from Sreeni's collection, each piece telling a story of a distant past.

Sreeni, in his mid-thirties, sat in the living room surrounded by shelves of books and carefully curated artifacts. His face reflected the sharp intellect that had propelled him through his academic and professional pursuits. Mamta, an elegant woman with a grace that belied her strong-willed nature, moved around the kitchen, the clinking of utensils a familiar melody in the kitchen.

"Sreeni, the *rasam* is ready. Come and have your dinner," Mamta called out in her dominating voice, a hint of a Telugu accent in the words.

"Where is Pooja," Sreeni asked as he worked on his computer. Pooja, their five-year old daughter was always bustling around the house with her naughty antics.

"She had her dinner early and has gone to bed," Mamta replied from the kitchen.

Sreeni looked up from his Compaq Deskpro computer which he had purchased only recently, his brow furrowed in concentration. "I'll be there in a minute," he replied, his mind still immersed in the complex equations on the screen. Mamta sighed, understanding the intensity that consumed her husband when he immersed himself into his work.

As Sreeni joined Mamta at the dining table, the aroma of the *Jeera rasam* filled the air, creating a comforting atmosphere. The table was set with delicate silverware, a stark contrast to the rugged artifacts that decorated the apartment. Mamta served a generous portion of rice and *rasam*, a testament to her culinary skills. "I have also made your favorite potato *Podimass*. *Pappadams* are there in the steel container."

"*Appa, Amma* must be missing our cooking in Calicut," Mamta remarked, using the Tamil words for father and mother. Mamta struggled with Tamil proficiency. Despite her attempts to grasp the language, her interactions with Sreeni primarily occurring in English and Hindi hindered her progress in learning Tamil. Consequently, her knowledge of Tamil remained limited to a mere smattering of words. Sreeni nodded absentmindedly, his mind still occupied with the challenges of his research.

"Did you call them today?" Mamta asked, concern evident in her eyes.

"Call who?" Sreeni was distracted.

"Your parents."

Sreeni looked up, his gaze meeting Mamta's. "Ah, I'll call them later. I have a deadline to meet," he said curtly, his tone revealing the distance that lingered between him and his family in India. "Don't forget to call them." Mamta exclaimed.

Mamta realized that despite being married for seven years, the bridge between herself and Sreeni's family was still under construction. She had navigated the delicate path of being a wife to a man who valued his independence above all else. The cultural differences between her Telugu roots and Sreeni's Tamil Brahmin heritage added another layer of complexity to their relationship.

Mamta's deficiency in speaking in Tamil posed a challenge in conversing with her mother-in-law, Meenakshi, who lacked fluency in English. While Mamta could comprehend Tamil to some degree, she faltered in responding or engaging in conversation. This limitation significantly impeded her free communication with her less proficient

Tamil-speaking sisters-in-law, fostering feelings of inadequacy that manifested as envy and, to some extent, antipathy. However, their ability to converse with her in English helped to a certain extent to bridge the gap of understanding.

After dinner, as they settled into the plush sofa, Mamta mustered the courage to broach a sensitive topic. "Sreeni, we've been married for seven years, and I feel like our families are living in two separate worlds. Your family is our family, and yet, you keep them at arm's length. We haven't gone to India for the past five years."

Sreeni sighed, a deep furrow forming on his forehead. "Mamta, I've made a life for myself here. I can't be entangled in the affairs of a joint family back in India. Besides, I visit them occasionally, isn't that enough?"

"But we haven't gone to India for the past *five years*." Mamta repeated with emphasis.

"I am busy, as you can see." Sreeni was always ready with an excuse.

Mamta's eyes softened with understanding, but a flicker of disappointment remained. "It's not about how often you visit, Sreeni. It's about being emotionally present and connected with them. Especially now, since your mother had a heart attack. Your parents are aging, and they need your support. I'm not asking you to abandon your life here, but just to be there for them when they need you."

Sreeni looked away, a trace of guilt clouding his features. He kept hearing his own criticisms of his brothers in his mind, which reminded him bitterly of his own contradictions. He considered himself much above his brothers in education. They were only mere graduates, he felt, while he had a doctorate.

Mamta reached out, her hand gently touching his. "I married you knowing your priorities, but I hoped that love could bridge the gap. I want our home to be filled with the warmth of both our families. Pooja also should get to know her cousins — the children of your brother and sister — and her grandparents."

For a moment, Sreeni softened, the walls he had built around his emotions momentarily crumbling. "Mamta, I don't want to hurt anybody. But I can't change who I am. My focus is on my career, on building a secure future for us, especially our daughter, Pooja."

Mamta nodded, a hint of sadness in her eyes. "I understand, Sreeni. But remember, relationships need tending too. Just like your artifacts, they need care and attention."

The room fell into a contemplative silence, broken only by the distant hum of the city outside with its ongoing traffic and mad rush. The artifacts on the shelves seemed to observe the scene, silent witnesses to the complexities of human relationships.

Mamta continued to strike a delicate balance between the demands of Sreeni's ambitious world and the longing for familial connection. The apartment became a blend of Tamil and Telugu traditions, a tapestry of cultures woven together in an attempt to create a home.

Two days later, one evening, as Sreeni sat engrossed in his research, Mamta entered the room, a package in her hands. "Sreeni, I thought you might like this. It's a traditional Tanjore painting – a piece of your roots in our home."

Sreeni looked up, surprise registering on his face. He carefully unwrapped the package, revealing the intricate details of the Tanjore painting – a vivid portrayal of deities and mythological stories. A surge of nostalgia swept over him, connecting the dots of his past to the present.

"Mamta, this is beautiful," Sreeni said, genuine appreciation in his voice. Mamta smiled, a subtle victory in bringing a piece of his heritage into their modern life. "Where did you get it from?"

"A Tamil lady in California is making these in her spare time. I came across her details from a friend of mine and ordered these paintings from her. It's exquisite, isn't it?" Mamta admired the painting from all angles. "I will put these up in the foyer so that those who enter the house can appreciate it."

Encouraged by the small breakthrough, Mamta decided to take a bolder step. "Sreeni, why don't we plan a trip to India? Spend some time with your family. Pooja also has not seen her grandparents since she was an infant. She wouldn't remember them. You mother is also recovering from a heart attack; we should go to see her."

Sreeni paused, his mind conflicted. The very idea of immersing himself in the intricate web of family dynamics made him uneasy. He cherished the intimacy of his nuclear family and wasn't inclined to extend that joy to his relatives beyond. Yet, Mamta's earnest expression and the flicker of hope in her eyes tugged at the edges of his resolve.

"Maybe," he replied, a non-committal word that hung in the air. Mamta nodded, accepting the inch he had given, knowing that change, especially for someone like Sreeni, was a gradual process.

"It would be nice to visit them now, as *Amma* too would be glad to see all of us after her recent hospitalization." Mamta continued.

The next few days became a delicate balance between Sreeni's world of equations and research and Mamta's attempts to infuse their home with the warmth of familial bonds. The aroma of incense arising from the pooja corner, created a fusion of flavors and traditions in the cozy home of the Sreenis.

A couple of days later, as dusk colored the skyline of New York, Mamta approached Sreeni, "Sreeni, I spoke to your *Appa* today. *Amma* misses you, and *Appa* too is not keeping well. They want to see you."

Sreeni looked up from his desktop computer, a twinge of concern in his eyes. "I have a conference this weekend. Maybe after that," he replied without looking up from his computer, his words carrying a promise that felt like a fragile thread.

Mamta took a deep breath, the weight of responsibility settling on her shoulders. "Sreeni, life is unpredictable. We can't always plan when to be there for our loved ones. Sometimes, we just need to show up."

Sreeni nodded silently.

The words hung in the air, a gentle reminder of the power of presence. Sreeni sighed, a conflict raging within him. Mamta reached out, her hand finding his. "I'm not asking you to change overnight, Sreeni. Just take a step, be there for them. It's a journey we should take together. We can't forget our families back home in India."

Mamta's words lingered in the air, a silent plea for connection. The apartment echoed with the clinking of utensils and the hum of conversations in Hindi and English, creating a symphony of cultural harmony. Sreeni, though still attached to his ambitious career pursuits, found himself softening under the persistent warmth of Mamta's love. Pooja also had acquired a basic understanding of Hindi. For her Tamil was a foreign and incomprehensible language. Hence most of the time, she ended up replying to Sreeni in English even if he tried to speak to her in Tamil.

A week later, one evening, their five year old daughter Pooja was playing in the living room with her newly acquired doll's house while Sreeni and Mamta sat on the balcony, the city lights below them. Sreeni spoke, his voice carrying a vulnerability he seldom revealed. "Mamta, maybe it's time. Let's plan a trip to India. I want them to see the life we've built, and I want to be there for them. Let's mend our relationships." Even then, Sreeni's primary aim was to flaunt his accomplishments to his family in India rather than rebuild their strained relationships. His self-centeredness consistently overshadowed any genuine connection he sought.

Sreeni's relationship with his parents had become strained when he decided to marry Mamta, a Telugu girl. Initially, Anantharama Iyer and Meenakshi objected, but eventually relented due to Sreeni's adamant nature. Although his brothers weren't fully supportive, they stayed quiet since their parents had already, though reluctantly, agreed to the marriage. Since getting married, Sreeni sensed a distance between himself and his parents, a chill in their relationship. He visited them in India only once — a year after marrying Mamta, when their daughter Pooja was born. This disconnect was the main reason Sreeni hesitated to visit his parents in India.

Mamta's eyes sparkled with joy, a silent victory for love over solitude. "Sreeni, that's all I've ever wanted. I want our home to be filled with love and connections. While we are there, I could make a quick visit to Hyderabad to visit my parents and brothers too. I'll start the preparations straightaway and book the tickets."

Two years ago she had made a short visit to Hyderabad to meet her parents along with Pooja during the summer holidays. Sreeni had stayed back. At that time Mamta, however, did not visit Calicut to meet her parents in law.

Listening to their conversation, Pooja who was playing in the living room came to the balcony and climbed on to Sreeni's lap. "Daddy, are we going to India?" Pooja, with her innocent baby talk, asked, her eyes widening with wonder.

"Yes, dear," Mamta replied with a tender smile. "We're going soon to see your *Ammamma*, *Thatha*, and your uncles, aunts and cousins. There are three mischievous kids there, just like you, but a bit older."

"Oh, I want to see them! I'll give them lots of my candies and lollipops that I got for Halloween. Can we also see the Taj Mahal? My school miss, Catherine told me it's beautiful to see."

"No, dear, we can't see the Taj Mahal this time. It's far, far away from where *Ammamma* and *Thatha* live. Maybe we can visit it next time when you're a bit older," Mamta reassured, her words filled with maternal warmth.

Pooja's lips pouted in apparent displeasure, her disappointment evident. She shifted her attention to playing with her doll's house, excited about the travel to India.

As they decided to embark on a journey back to their roots, the artifacts and antiques in the apartment seemed to nod in approval, witnessing the evolution of a man who, despite his independence, had discovered the richness that family and love brought to life. The lights of the city kept twinkling outside the window, spreading a cozy glow over a home now united by love and connection rather than distance.

However, unknown to them, a subtle tempest was quietly taking shape within the confines of their ancestral home. Little did Sreeni and Mamta appreciate that their seemingly ordinary visit would act as the catalyst, awakening dormant embers and igniting a blaze that could potentially alter the destiny of the entire family.

Chapter 7

The Malabar Botanical Gardens embraced Arjun and Divya in a lush symphony of greens. Tall trees towered overhead, their branches interlocking to form a verdant canopy that filtered the sunlight into shining golden beams. A gentle breeze carried the fragrance of blooming flowers, and the distant hum of nature and the chirping of birds enveloped the two figures as they strolled through the winding pathways hand in hand.

Arjun's hand found Divya's, their fingers intertwining effortlessly. The touch spoke volumes, a silent affirmation of the connection that had blossomed between them since their college days. They walked along the cobblestone path, surrounded by a carpet of colorful flowers that had fallen on the path from the trees overhead. An occasional fluttering butterfly overhead seemed to lead them through the garden. The cooing of a cuckoo heightened the mood. Divya's almond-shaped brown eyes shimmered with a mixture of joy and contentment.

Despite originating from a background rooted in tradition, Divya possessed an extraordinary knack for adapting to diverse situations and surroundings. This remarkable ability enabled her to gracefully navigate the intricate challenges posed by the conventional values upheld by her family, which consisted of her widowed mother and two elder brothers.

This was another factor that drew Arjun to her. Her caring nature and strong empathy were central to who she was. She consistently put others' needs and feelings before her own, making her a reliable and empathetic friend.

In her traditional family setting, Divya struggled with a deep-seated fear of letting down both her close relatives and the wider community. She accepted that there was a chasm of difference between the cultures of her traditional Malayalee Nair family and that of Arjun. Arjun's family was steeped in the Tamil brahmin orthodoxy that stuck to their cultural roots. This fear, at times, became a hindrance, preventing her from pursuing her authentic desires and aspirations. This contributed to her internal conflicts, making certain decisions a formidable challenge for her.

After the loss of her father during her formative years, Divya found solace in the affection bestowed upon her by her two brothers. However, as of late, their attention had been absorbed by their respective business endeavors, leaving Divya longing for the warmth of love and affection. It was in this void that Arjun emerged, generously drenching her with the love and care she craved. For Divya, the absence of paternal love found its surrogate in her affection towards Arjun.

Despite facing internal struggles, Divya's love for Arjun remained strong and sincere. Arjun's charisma and kindness played a pivotal role in dismantling societal norms, allowing their mutual affection to flourish. In Arjun, Divya found a kindred spirit who not only understood her aspirations but actively encouraged her to liberate herself from the constraints of tradition. Their love served as a wellspring of strength for Divya, emboldening her to confront and challenge the expectations thrust upon her.

Divya was jolted out of her reveries by Arjun nudging her.

"Hey!... daydreaming, eh?"

She suddenly composed herself and smiled.

"Divya, do you remember the first time we met at the Fine Arts society meeting in college?" Arjun asked, a smile playing on his lips. Both of them had been active members of the society.

Divya chuckled, her laughter like a melody that resonated with the natural harmony around them. "Of course, Arjun. You were belting out that soulful melody, and I was captivated. I never thought an economics student could sing a passionate song like that."

Arjun grinned, a glint of pride in his eyes. "And you, with your graceful dance moves, stole my heart right there."

As they continued their leisurely walk immersed in their sweet memories, they found a secluded spot under the shade of a sprawling banyan tree. Large, gnarled roots provided a natural seat, and they settled down, facing each other.

"I miss those college days," Divya admitted, her gaze lingering on the distant horizon. "The Fine Arts society, our impromptu performances, and the thrill of waiting for exam results — all that is behind us and those glorious days are over."

Arjun nodded, his expression nostalgic. "It feels like a lifetime ago. But those moments shaped us, brought us together."

The sun dipped lower in the sky, casting a warm glow over the botanical gardens. Arjun reached for Divya's hand again, his thumb gently caressing the back of hers.

"I've been thinking a lot about our future," Arjun confessed, his eyes searching hers for understanding.

Divya looked up, her gaze softened, a silent invitation for him to continue.

"I want to find a job, make a stable life for us, I am done with studying." Arjun said, his tone filled with determination. "But more than anything, I want you by my side. Divya, I can't imagine my life without you."

Divya's heart swelled with emotion, her eyes reflecting the depth of her feelings. "Arjun, I've been thinking too. I want to pursue my MA degree, explore the world of literature. But I want you to be a part of my journey. I can't imagine facing the unknown without you."

Their hands tightened around each other, a silent promise exchanged between souls deeply entwined.

"You study, I'll work," Arjun chuckled. Both burst out laughing.

"Do you remember the first time we came to this garden?" Arjun asked, breaking the tender moment with a mischievous glint in his eyes.

Divya raised an eyebrow, her curiosity piqued. "Of course, I do. It was during the college field trip. We sneaked away from the group and explored this magical place."

Arjun chuckled, his gaze intense. "I brought you here because I wanted to show you something special. Come on, let us go to that spot again together."

He led Divya to a secluded corner, where a small clearing overlooked a pond covered in water lilies. The setting sun painted the sky with hues of orange and pink, casting a reflection on the still water.

"Divya, this is where I first realized I was in love with you," Arjun admitted, his voice carrying the weight of unspoken emotions. "The spot where our friendship blossomed into love."

Divya's eyes widened mischievously, her heart fluttering with a mix of surprise and joy. "Really?"

Arjun nodded, his eyes never leaving hers. "This place, this moment — it became etched in my heart. I knew then that you were the one I wanted to share my life with."

Divya felt a lump in her throat, overwhelmed by the sincerity in Arjun's words. "Arjun, I love you too. More than words can express. "But..." she hesitated, a slight pause hanging in the air.

Arjun, curious, raised his eyebrows. "But what is it?"

Divya took a deep breath, her words tinged with uncertainty. "You haven't informed your parents about us, and I haven't shared our relationship with my brothers or mother. I believe my elder brothers would support my dreams, but still, there's a lingering fear in my heart."

Arjun, with a reassuring smile, urged, "Come on, Divya, let's not dwell on that now. We'll handle it when the time comes. I understand that caste may pose a minor challenge, though religion doesn't. I'm confident my parents won't and can't object to us being together."

Divya's eyes betrayed her doubt as she questioned, "Why do you think so?"

Arjun, eager to ease her worries, shared a family anecdote. "My elder brother, Sreeni, married a Telugu lady, and they are happily settled in the US. Despite initial reservations, my parents accepted their union out of emotional compulsion. So, marrying you shouldn't be a problem for me. Besides, my Telugu sister-in-law struggles to converse with my mother due to her lack of knowledge of Tamil. With you, communication won't be an issue as mother is well versed in Malayalam. I'm sure my mother will adore you, and once she approves, our future is secured."

Divya, frowning slightly, responded, "Let's hope for the best." Her words held a mix of anticipation and concern, lingering in the evening air.

"I believe you should tell your brothers and mother about us. I will also bring this up with my parents, particularly my mother, when the right moment arises." Arjun voiced his opinion.

Divya nodded her agreement.

They stood there, wrapped in the quiet beauty of the botanical gardens, their hearts speaking a language only they understood.

As darkness began to embrace the garden, Arjun and Divya found a bench overlooking the city lights twinkling in the distance. The Arabian sea glittered like a vast expanse of stardust on the horizon.

Arjun sighed, his fingers tracing invisible patterns on Divya's hand. "Divya, I know our families are different, our paths filled with uncertainties. But I want to face all of this with you."

Divya leaned her head on Arjun's shoulder, a sense of comfort enveloping them. "Arjun, love is a journey, and I'm ready to embark on it with you. No matter what challenges come our way, we'll face them together."

They sat there, wrapped in the quietude of the emerging night, their hearts beating in sync with the rhythm of their shared dreams.

Days turned into weeks, and their meetings in the Malabar Botanical Gardens became a ritual. Each visit was a celebration of their love, a sanctuary where words were exchanged in whispers, and the language of their hearts spoke louder than any external noise.

"I embroidered this handkerchief especially for you," Divya said with a warm smile, presenting Arjun with a beautiful white silk handkerchief adorned with the initials '*A & D*' delicately stitched in two corners.

Arjun held the handkerchief gently, admiring the intricate embroidery. "It's exquisite," he remarked, a hint of playfulness in his tone. "It's so lovely that I might hesitate to use it to wipe my dirt-covered face."

Divya chuckled, her eyes twinkling with amusement. "Oh, don't worry about that," she said, her voice light. "It's meant to be used. Consider it a reminder of our friendship."

"Friendship or love?" Arjun grinned and winked at her, touched by Divya's thoughtful gesture. "Thank you, Divya. I'll treasure it always."

The warmth between them filled the surroundings as they shared a moment of genuine connection, their laughter ringing out harmoniously.

Later, as they sat together, Divya shared the story behind the handkerchief. "I spent hours working on it," she explained, her expression earnest. "Each stitch was done with you in mind."

Arjun listened attentively, moved by her dedication. "It's truly special," he replied, his voice sincere. "You have a talent for this."

Their laughter echoed once more, a reflection of their deep friendship and shared joy.

One evening, as they sat on their favorite bench, the air thick with the fragrance of blooming jasmine, Arjun broke the silence. "Divya, what if I start something of my own? A business, a venture that reflects my dreams and aspirations."

Divya looked at him, her eyes reflecting a mix of surprise and awe. "Arjun, do you think you can do it? I mean, breaking away from the conventional paths our families expect us to tread."

"Conventional...? What do you mean?" Rahul looked at her in in astonishment.

"I mean going for a 9-5 salaried job in a bank or any other institution."

Arjun smiled, his gaze unwavering. "Divya, I believe in myself. We can create our own path, build something that's uniquely ours. And I want to do it with you. With your support and you beside me, I will be able to achieve success in life. A conventional job, as you say, will not make us rich. But a business can, especially if I hit it off."

"Don't think of riches, Arjun," Divya chided him. "It is more important to be happy than be rich."

As the full moon ascended in the night sky, casting a silver glow over the botanical gardens, Arjun and Divya made a silent pact to embark on a new journey together.

They sat there, hand in hand, gazing at the city lights far away. The same city that had witnessed the blossoming of their love now stood as a testament to their shared dreams.

As they stood up to leave the botanical gardens, Arjun pulled Divya into a warm embrace. "This is just the beginning, Divya. Our journey together is bound to be extraordinary. God help us."

Leaving the garden, their hearts intertwined, they were ready to face whatever lay ahead. The Malabar Botanical Gardens had quietly witnessed the sweet love story of Arjun and Divya — a love that had overcome obstacles and flourished, destined to thrive as they embarked on their journey together.

As the bard said, '*Our wills and fates do so contrary run*' so did fate have distinctive designs for both these passionate lovers. With its complex designs, fate had another path in store for these romantic lovers. The universe with its own set of scripts, however, had a different narrative penned for Arjun and Divya.

Chapter 8

The air inside the Anantharama Iyer household hung thick with unspoken tension. The orthodox Tamil Iyer home was spruced up with intricate *kolams* at the entrance. The aroma of delicious cooking lingered in the air, but it was overshadowed by the simmering resentment between the two key players in this domestic drama — Uma and Janaki.

Uma, the eldest daughter-in-law, clad in a maroon cotton saree moved about the kitchen with a determined air, her eyes narrowed as she inspected the ingredients for the day's meals. Janaki, no less formidable, sat in the dining room, chopping vegetables. The monotonous clinking of utensils, the whistle of the pressure cooker and the occasional sizzle of mustard seeds hitting hot oil filled the background as the sisters-in-law prepared for another round of verbal sparring. Ever since Meenakshi became ill, she avoided being active in the kitchen. As a result, the two sisters-in-law often clashed over small issues.

"Janaki, can't you at least get the salt right?" Uma's voice tasting the *sambar*, laced with annoyance, cut through the kitchen's hum.

Janaki clenched her jaw, her eyes narrowing at the unrelenting criticism. "*Manni*," retorted Janaki, as she addressed her elder sister in law, "I too have been managing a kitchen for years in my home. I know how much salt to put in a dish."

Uma, her slender frame tensed with suppressed anger, continued sautéing the onions, ignoring Janaki's comment. She scoffed, "Well, it seems like you forgot today. Maybe you should let someone else handle it for a change. Meanwhile, it's already past ten, and *Appa* is waiting for his medicine."

Janaki felt the seething resentment bubbling inside her, but she bit back her retort. The tension had spread beyond the kitchen into every corner of the house. She resented being the 'newcomer' constantly scrutinized and compared to Uma. She felt ostracized and unheard, constantly battling the feeling of being treated as the lesser daughter-in-law. This resentment manifested in snide remarks, passive-aggressive behavior, and a constant need to point out Uma's perceived shortcomings. Even the gods in the puja room seemed to be observing the brewing storm with apprehension.

Uma was also upset at Janaki's behaviour. She complained to Meenakshi who was in her room, her breathing eased now due to the nebulizer which Uma had provided. "*Amma*, I woke up late because Aadi wouldn't stop coughing all night. I managed to get them both ready for school, and that's about all I could do. Now Aadi has come back from school with a high fever. I am waiting for Nandini to come from the hospital to ask her to examine Aadi and prescribe some medicine for him."

"Excuses, excuses," Janaki scoffed. "I don't neglect Satya's or anyone's needs with all this extra work thrust upon me."

Uma's eyes welled up with tears of frustration. "This isn't a competition, Janaki. We both have our share of responsibilities."

"Responsibilities!" Janaki's voice rose a notch. "You get all the praise and attention from everyone just because you're the elder daughter in law. Meanwhile, I'm stuck doing all the thankless jobs."

In the living room, Anandu, Uma's husband, sat with a furrowed brow, listening to the verbal duel, sensing the mounting tension in the kitchen. He glanced at his son, Akhil, who, though aware of the brewing storm, seemed more engrossed in his homework than the domestic turmoil.

As Uma continued to toil in the kitchen, she couldn't help but feel the weight of expectations pressing down on her. She wanted to be a good wife, a dutiful daughter-in-law, and a caring mother to her two twin sons, Akhil and Aadi. However, the constant scrutiny and criticism from her younger sister in law Janaki was making it increasingly difficult for her to keep up with the demands.

Meanwhile, Janaki, as was her wont, took her complaints to her husband, Satya, who sat in the living room trying to concentrate on the newspaper sipping a cup of steaming coffee. "Satya, I can't take this anymore. *Manni* is always finding fault with me, and your mother always takes her side."

Satya sighed, folding the newspaper. "Janaki, we've been through this before. Just try to adjust. It's our family, after all. You should not flare up at every tiny bit of criticism or comment."

Janaki's eyes flashed with frustration. "Adjust? Who me? I feel like I'm singled out here. I can't breathe in this atmosphere. I feel stifled by the atmosphere in this house. And... you want *me* to adjust!" She flared.

Satya, seemingly caught between the loyalty to his wife and his family, patted Janaki's hand trying to pacify her. "I'll talk to Uma, alright? We'll find a solution. Now get back to what you were doing."

While Satya promised Janaki a solution, Uma sought solace in a conversation with Anandu. "Anandu, I can't handle all this anymore. The pressure is too much. I want to move away from here, live separately with you and the kids. Janaki always finds a reason to pick a quarrel with me. She is reluctant to take on the chores around the house and is finding an excuse always to avoid them. Let Janaki remain here with your parents... we should leave. I can't put up with her anymore."

Anandu looked at his wife, concern etched on his face. "Uma, be patient. After all, every household has its minor problems and an occasional tiff. Don't magnify such small matters."

"You always side with your brother and his wife. I am the one left out here in this house. I have to slog from morning to night looking after all of you and no one has even a bit of gratitude." Uma went on grumbling.

"Uma, I am going out to the grocers to get some provisions that you had asked for. Do you want anything?" Anandu asked as he put on his shirt, trying the escape from the present situation.

Later that evening, as Anandu returned home with the grocery, he found Uma sitting on the porch steps, her face streaked with tears. "Uma, what happened?" Anandu asked, his voice laced with concern as he sat on the steps beside her.

Uma hesitated, tears threatening to spill over once more. "It's Janaki," she finally choked out. "I can't take it anymore, Anandu. The constant snide remarks, the feeling of being judged, the unfair comparisons... it's tearing me apart."

Anandu sitting on the verandah beside her said in an undertone "Uma, I have a chance of getting transferred from Calicut. Once that happens, we can move away and start fresh. But don't tell this to anyone else as yet – even mother. I'll tell them when it is finalized."

Uma's eyes softened with relief. "Promise?"

Anandu smiled and nodded, squeezing her hand. "Promise. Just a little more time, and everything will fall into place. Keep up your spirits till then and be patient."

While Uma found a glimmer of hope, Janaki persisted in her efforts to have Satya intervene in the escalating conflict. "Satya, you need to do something about this. I can't put up with them any longer. Everyone expects me to do the mean and dirty jobs around the house."

Satya, feeling the weight of his wife's dissatisfaction, sighed. "I know, Janaki. I'll talk to them, all right? Just give me some time. Be patient. We'll find a solution to it."

Meanwhile, Janaki, in the midst of her escape, called her father, Sadasiva Iyer, in Trivandrum. "*Appa*, I can't continue like this. I need to leave this house. I can't put up with Uma and all the problems here."

But time seemed to be a luxury the household couldn't afford. One evening, Janaki decided to break free from the suffocating atmosphere. She came down from her room dressed in a vibrant saree, complete with makeup and lipstick, announcing her plans to go to the movies with Satya. "Let me get off this horrible place for some time and be free of the irritations here" she announced to no one in particular.

Akhil, now down with fever, lay on the couch, his face flushed with illness. Meenakshi was having one of her asthma attacks, and Uma was attending to her adjusting the nebulizer to make her comfortable. Anantharama Iyer, in his cozy easy chair, was dozing oblivious to the drama that was being enacted in the hall. Yet, Janaki, unmindful of the chaos at home, was determined to escape for a few hours of respite along with her husband, Satya.

"And, by the way, Satya and I plan to dine out after the movie. No one need to wait for us." Janaki announced as she walked out of the house towards the porch, where Satya was waiting with his scooter.

Uma, witnessing Janaki's blatant disregard for the family's pressing issues, couldn't hold back her frustration. "Janaki, Akhil is sick, and *Amma* is having an attack of asthma. How can you leave at a time like this?"

Janaki waved her off, her eyes filled with defiance. "I need a break, *Manni*. I can't slog like a donkey in this house all the time."

Meenakshi, struggling for breath, managed to utter, "Janaki, have some sense. Your duty is at home, not in theaters. At least help Uma look after Akhil who is ill now."

Ignoring the plea, Janaki stormed out, leaving chaos in her wake. Uma, fuming, approached her ailing mother-in-law. "*Amma*, I can't bear this anymore. Something needs to change. Janaki is becoming too arrogant and haughty. All because Satya is dancing to her tune."

Sadasiva Iyer, concerned for his daughter, decided to visit Anantharama Iyer's home in Calicut. He reached Calicut early morning by the Trivandrum express and hired an auto to take him to the home of Anantharama Iyer. As he entered, he could feel the palpable tension hanging in the air. The household, once a haven of familial warmth, now resembled a battleground.

Sadasiva Iyer, as was his habit of fishing in troubled waters, took Janaki aside, speaking in a soothing tone. "Janaki, my dear, these things happen in every family. We'll find a solution soon. Don't worry. Keep up your humor and be patient."

Janaki, tears streaming down her face, clung to her father for comfort. "*Appa*, I can't bear it anymore. I feel like an outsider in my own home."

Sadasiva Iyer patted her back, his eyes filled with concern. "I'll talk to them, find a solution. Don't lose hope. I will return by the evening train today and will be back here next month. I will talk to Anantharama Iyer about your problem." His words partially soothed Janaki's ruffled temper.

As father and daughter tried to navigate the troubled waters within the household, the rift between Uma and Janaki continued to widen. Each passing day brought new tensions, untold frustrations, and a mounting sense of helplessness.

Amidst the family turmoil, Anandu struggled with the burden of responsibility, torn between his wife's appeals and Janaki's distress. With tensions rising, the once-tight-knit family faced imminent and irreversible change.

Chapter 9

Nestled within the outskirts of Calicut, the *Kurukankaattil* residence exuded an air of grandiosity that once represented wealth. The exterior of the mansion mirrored the family's bygone prosperity, currently obscured by an imminent descent into decadence and hardship. The walls, once coated with pristine paint, now displayed peeling layers, and the once-prominent woodwork, now unvarnished and flaking, silently bore witness to the family's fall from opulence.

Stepping inside, the atmosphere was laden with the rich scent of aged wood, permeating the air with a sense of history and nostalgia. The spacious hall contained antique furniture, each piece echoing a past era. These relics told stories of the grand moments the ancestral *Kurukankaattil* home had experienced, displaying its former magnificence.

Yet, the grandeur had faded, leaving the hall in a state of sad disrepair. The delicate curtains on the large bay windows hinted at neglect, yearning for a much needed wash. Amidst this silent decline, a majestic bison head, hunted by their great-grandfather, commanded attention on the eastern wall, serving as the lone reminder of their esteemed lineage.

The mansion, once a symbol of wealthier days, was now caught in a state of decay. The chipping paint and worn wood silently told the tale of a family that had once prospered but now struggled against time and circumstance. As its grandeur diminished, the *Kurukankaattil* household served as a solemn reminder of the unstoppable march of time.

In a quiet corner of the room, Kuttykrishnan Nair, the venerable patriarch of the family, lay motionless on a luxurious fourposter bed. He was bald with a wisp of silvery white hair adorning his occiput. He was clad in a white dhoti and was bare chested with a shawl thrown across his shoulders. His once-sharp gaze had given way to vacant eyes, and the left side of his body remained paralyzed, the consequence of a debilitating stroke that had sapped his vigor. Stress and years spent toiling, grappling with business tensions and contending with high blood pressure had exacted a toll on his once robust health. He felt comfort in a half-asleep state, exhausted by both tiredness and the strong medications in his body.

Since KK Nair fell ill, his business suffered greatly. His competitors seized the opportunity of his absence and managed to snatch many of his clients, causing chaos in his business. Expenses rose while profits fell, leaving the business as weakened as KK Nair himself. Consequently, the once prosperous days of the KK Nair household faded away.

By his bedside stood his sons, Sukumaran and Divakaran, who fancied themselves as the 'KK brothers.' Their movements exuded a calculated efficiency, their eyes revealing an underlying agenda beneath their apparently caring facade.

Kuttykrishnan Nair, the architect of a thriving business empire, had commenced his entrepreneurial journey at the age of thirty with a lone lorry transporting agricultural goods and groceries from North India to Kerala under the banner of 'KK Transport.' As his business flourished, within a matter of five years his fleet expanded to sixteen lorries, and branches sprouted in different towns across the Malabar region. A quarter-century of dedication transformed the KK Transport as industry's unrivaled luminary in North Kerala.

Hailing from the illustrious *Kurukankaattil tharavadu*, a prominent *Nair* lineage in Kerala, Kuttykrishnan Nair was his father's sole heir. His half-sister, Narayani also referred to as Nani Amma, a widow at a tender age, resided in a separate house with her only son, Mohandas. Despite adversities, Kuttykrishnan Nair steadfastly supported her financially, ensuring her son's education up to college.

Upholding a commitment to integrity, he avoided unethical business practices, earning respect even from his rivals. Although he briefly flirted with politics, disillusionment led him to abandon it.

He had firmly expressed his belief that his sons too should steer clear of the complex world of politics and its practitioners. Despite this, in order to sustain the prosperity and triumph of his business endeavors, he consistently extended generous support to various political parties, regardless of their underlying principles and precepts. This decision was not born out of a lack of principles on his part but rather arose from his practical outlook on life. This astute and pragmatic individual possessed a deep understanding of where the advantages resided and identified those individuals within the political sphere who could offer assistance in his business affairs. When dealing with political connections, he tackled it wisely, knowing that success often depends on forming strategic partnerships and wisely using the resources for one's benefit. This stood him in good stead in his business. His complex character showed a man who, though hesitant to involve his family in politics, understood its crucial role in the intricate web of power and influence.

He strongly believed that if his sons got involved in politics, it would put their family business at risk. He feared that without honesty and ethics, the business he had built with earnest effort would suffer. He imagined a situation where the good values of his business would be destroyed by the dishonesty and unethical behavior often found in politics and politicians.

His wife, Kathyayini Amma, embodied simplicity amid opulence. Content in her roles as wife and mother to her sons Sukumaran and Divakaran, she always adhered to the traditional attire of a cotton *mundu* and *vesti*, a reflection of Malayali women's modesty.

Following Kuttykrishnan Nair's incapacitation, the responsibility of managing the business fell upon his sons, Sukumaran and Divakaran. Initially aided by their aging accountant Swaminathan, an aged widower, and their father's stalwart confidant, the brothers gradually took charge of the sagging business. Swaminathan, whom they referred to as 'Swami' was a godly person, an embodiment of honesty and principles. Thus he was best suited to Kuttykrishnan Nair's business and liking. Nair also treated him with respect more as an equal rather than as an employee.

But as the sons took over the business, their intention was to make a quick buck and often Swami seemed to stand in their way as his honest and virtuous advice often fell on deaf years. Hence a time came when they decided to part ways with the seasoned accountant after they mastered the intricacies of their familial enterprise.

"Suku *Etta*, it seems this business is reaching its limits. We must seek more avenues," Divakaran softly murmured, his eyes fixated on the ledger laid out in front of him, as both the brothers sat in the office of the KK Transport. Being the younger of the two siblings, he harbored an earnest desire to propel the business forward, to witness its growth and expansion. Dissatisfaction loomed within him as he scrutinized the financial records. His philosophy centered on a pursuit of higher profits, increased wealth, and greater influence. The shrinking profits unnerved him.

Sukumaran, the elder brother, shared his sibling's sentiments. "Diva, you're right. We must discover some easier ways to improve the business and accumulate wealth. The legacy our father has left behind is slowly dimming, and we cannot stand by idly as it crumbles. Father's charisma is no longer working in this business ever since he is laid up. The competition is tough. It's imperative that we seek alternative methods to fortify the business, ensuring its prosperity continues to flourish." But Sukumaran was the cautious type, not willing to take risks for the sake of improving the business.

As the brothers contemplated the path ahead, a blend of determination and concern crossed their faces. The business was more than just a means of livelihood; it was a testament to their family's history and the values they held dear. They felt it was important to explore other ways to improve the business or diversify, with a shared dedication to protecting their father's legacy from being weakened.

Their glances locked, silently contemplating schemes in their minds, as Mohandas, their cousin, sauntered into the room. He had arrived on his motorbike and had parked it in front of their office. Despite being roughly the same age, Mohandas stood apart in character from his cousins. His manner showed him to be a shrewd, small-time politician, with greying hair meticulously arranged to conceal the passage of years. He was clad in a white dhoti and a *Khadar* shirt — characteristic of politicians.

Engaged in a prominent political party within the region, Mohandas held sway over his minions, yet his aspirations for a noteworthy role in the administration of a *Panchayat* or the city council remained unfulfilled. Ambitious and hungry for political ascent, he recognized the indispensable role money played in realizing his dreams. In this pursuit, he was willing to follow any crooked path, embracing mean strategies without hesitation. He knew where the money lay.

Presently, his sights were set on a cunning plan: to embed himself as a partner in the KK brothers' business. This covert collaboration was intended to be the initial step in his intricate plot to insinuate himself into the fabric of their enterprise. The ultimate goal was to exploit the business as a stepping stone, helping him toward the achievement of his political and financial ambitions.

Entering the room, Mohandas skillfully concealed his ulterior motives beneath a façade of geniality. As he exchanged pleasantries with his cousins, his mind whirred with Machiavellian calculations. "What a fine establishment your father has built," he remarked, his words dripping with apparent admiration. "Now it's your responsibility to elevate it to greater success."

The brothers, unaware of the deceitful web being woven around them, reciprocated with genuine warmth. "How is our aunt Nani *Amma*?" asked Divakaran enquiring about Mohandas's mother who was ill with rheumatoid arthritis and undergoing Ayurvedic treatment. "How is her joint pains now?"

"Better," commented Mohandas nonchalantly. "She feels better after the new treatment from the Ayurvedic *Vaidyar*. In fact, she was mentioning today that she wanted to see her brother — your father."

"Sure, tell me when she is free, I'll send my driver around with the car to fetch her to our house." Sukumaran was only too willing to oblige.

"By the way," remarked Mohandas as if casually, "I have some savings with me which I want to invest appropriately. I thought of asking you first. I thought that investing it in your business would be the best thing, as the money is safe in your hands. Moreover, since you're my family member, I trust you more than giving it to a total stranger. Don't you agree?" Mohandas looked at Sukumaran expectantly.

"Well, let me think it over," Sukumaran, being the cautious type, did not show his eagerness immediately, though any new capital investment was welcome in their business at this juncture. He decided to talk to his father about it before committing himself to Mohandas. He was not unaware of the devious nature of the wily politician.

"Sure," Mohandas was quick to feel the pulse of the situation. "Think it over, both of you and tell me within a couple of days. I have to think of other avenues, if not, to invest the amount."

The stage was set for a secret manipulation, with Mohandas orchestrating the moves. Using subtle hints and clever conversation, he planted seeds of greed and desire in the minds of his cousins while hiding his true motives behind the friendly demeanor. "Partnership has its mutual benefits, both in business and politics," he mused, casting a sly glance toward the brothers.

The seemingly ordinary room turned into an arena where alliances were forged not from family allegiance, but from ambition and deception. Mohandas, with his clever strategies, aimed to balance family connections and self-interest, intricately insinuating himself and his plans into the unsuspecting KK brothers' business.

Despite the reservations of the patriarch, Kuttykrishnan Nair, who harbored a deep-seated distrust towards his nephew Mohandas due to his political affiliations and perceived loose character, Sukumaran and Divakaran opted for a path less conventional. In defiance of their father's objections, they chose to accept Mohandas as a limited partner in their business venture.

The infusion of Mohandas's capital of ten *lakh* rupees, became not just a financial transaction but a symbolic gesture of trust and shared enterprise. The brothers elevated him to their 'core group' — a select circle comprising the three of them authorized to make critical business decisions.

Their meetings, once confined to the sterile ambience of the transport office, was now shifted to the secluded outhouse nestled within the vast expanse of Kuttykrishnan Nair's ancestral abode. This ancestral house, sprawling majestically over five acres of land, bore witness to the ebb and flow of generations. The secluded outhouse, once a rest house for esteemed guests and business colleagues, evolved into a dynamic setting where the brothers and Mohandas convened to discuss the future of their shared enterprise. The presence of alcoholic beverages and delicious food, though seemingly insignificant, symbolized the shared bonds of friendship and openness. With their father indisposed, the brothers seized the opportunity to repurpose the space in the outhouse for not only serious business discussions but also as a haven for informal gatherings and moments of respite.

In the outhouse, Mohandas turned to the KK brothers, a sly grin spreading across his face as he poured whisky for the three of them, "Suku, Diva, we need to think beyond the fertilizer business. There are better ways to make quick money, you know."

Sukumaran raised an eyebrow, intrigued. "What do you have in mind, Dasa?"

"Smuggling, my dear cousins. Smuggling is the key for a quick buck," Mohandas replied with a glint in his eyes.

The brothers exchanged a cautious look before Sukumaran spoke, "Smuggling what, Mohan? Isn't that dangerous business? And smuggling gold from the Gulf is not easy."

"Who said about gold?" Mohandas snickered, "Fertilizers from Punjab, my friend. The same business as of now." Mohandas suggested winking, a sly smile playing on his lips. "We can make a fortune, and no one will suspect a thing. Trust me, I have connections."

"But fertilizer is what we are already transporting from Gujarat." Divakaran raised an eyebrow.

Mohandas chuckled, "Don't be naïve. Along with sacks of fertilizer, we will bring something else into Kerala from Punjab. No one will know. We'll extend our fertilizer business to Punjab for this."

"What...?" began Sukumaran. He was always the timid type, not ready to take risks and cautious about the business.

"Leave it to me, the less you know the better," interjected Mohandas. "Let us do justice to this tasty chicken-65 appetizer lying in front of us for now. Once we have accepted it in principle, I will work out the details and get back to you."

They drank to the success of their new venture.

The room resonated with whispered conversations, and the decision was made. The KK brothers, enticed by the allure of easy money, agreed to Mohandas's proposition. The fertilizer business became a façade for their illicit activities, a mask that concealed the treacherous dealings beneath.

Mohandas refrained from disclosing his smuggling plans at that moment. He reasoned that he would reveal them once he had laid the groundwork for the deal. His cunning mind brimmed with schemes he intended to execute through the KK brothers. He still held some secrets up his sleeve.

Chapter 10

Excitement was high that morning. The sun had climbed high, casting warm hues over the ancestral home where the Iyer family gathered. Meenakshi, the matriarch, was bustling around the kitchen, preparing a feast to celebrate the arrival of her son, Sreeni, along with his wife, Mamta, and their five-year-old daughter, Pooja. Meenakshi, despite her recent hospitalization, energetically set the table with aromatic dishes, aided by Nandini and her two daughters in law.

Sreeni with his family had arrived by the morning Mangalore Mail train after reaching Madras from New York by air. Everyone was thrilled to welcome them. Meenakshi and Anantharama Iyer were especially delighted to see them after five years. They couldn't believe how much Pooja had grown! She instantly captured everyone's hearts with her cute looks and baby-talk. Sreeni had changed too, with his hairline receding and signs of baldness appearing. His slight paunch indicated his prosperity. Mamta remained as modern and reserved as ever.

Uma had set out the traditional brass lamps and lit incense sticks in the pooja room from where wafted the sweet scent of sandalwood incense. The lamps were lit in front of the deities their soft glow flickering in anticipation. Janaki had arranged marigold garlands around the pooja room, infusing the space with a burst of color. Nandini played with her daughter, Aathira and her niece Pooja, in the corner of the living room, the laughter of the little ones adding a joyful note to the ambience.

The atmosphere was filled with joy and expectation. Soon after their arrival, Sreeni and Mamta had gone upstairs to freshen up after the tiresome journey and weary jetlag. Pooja, their daughter had stayed back below to play with Aathira. The family awaited them in the dining room. Meenakshi, donned in a colorful silk saree, stood by the doorway, her eyes lighting up as she saw Sreeni and Mamta come down the stairs, their arms around each other. Pooja clung to her father's hand, her eyes wide with curiosity. Everything in India was a curiosity for her.

"*Amma*, how have you been?" Sreeni greeted, touching his mother's feet in a traditional gesture of respect.

"*Ennada, nalla than irukken*, Sreeni. How was the journey?" Meenakshi replied, hugging her son.

The warmth of the reunion was palpable. Mamta, with her cosmopolitan demeanor, surveyed the surroundings with a hint of disdain. Her eyes, accustomed to opulence, flickered over the traditional decor, and a subtle sneer played at the corner of her lips. But she managed to control her emotions from getting the better of her.

Uma approached with a smile, "*Va*, Mamta. Welcome home!"

"Thank you," Mamta replied, her tone polite yet distant. "How are you, *manni*?" She exchanged pleasantries with Uma in English, language serving as a subtle barrier between them.

As they settled in, Arjun, Meenakshi's youngest son, rushed in with a triumphant grin. "*Amma*, *Appa*, Exam results are out. I've scored a first class in the examination! And surprisingly, I am the topper in my college!"

Cheers erupted, joy doubling in the household. Meenakshi hugged Arjun, a proud smile on her face. "*Kanna*, I knew you would make it."

The news created a celebratory atmosphere, temporarily bridging the divides within the family.

In the midst of the jubilation, Pooja, the youngest member, became the center of attention. The little girl, doll-like, with her baby talk in English, clad in a bottle-green silk *paavadai* and a matching yellow blouse, charmed everyone. However, her inability to converse in Tamil left her grandparents, especially Meenakshi, with a sense of longing.

"Nandini, why are you not moving to the US with us?" Sreeni asked, genuinely curious. "You can pursue your post graduate studies there. Medical education is far advanced in the US compared to India."

"As Rajaram is in Australia, Aathira and I plan to join him there," Nandini replied, her eyes reflecting a mix of hope and uncertainty. "I plan to do a Fellowship in Gynecologic Oncology. It is an upcoming specialty."

Sreeni turned to Arjun, "Arjun, what about your future plans? What next after your BA? Further studies, or employment? Education in India is not as good as in the US. I was lucky to escape from here early in my career." He never passed up a chance of praising the US and undermining India's educational system. It was his nature.

A sudden silence engulfed the room on hearing Sreeni's comment. Sreeni was noted for bragging.

"I'm thinking of starting a business venture. Nothing finalized yet, just exploring some ideas with friends," Arjun responded.

"Be careful, Arjun. Choose your partners in business wisely, and don't rush into investing money," Sreeni cautioned, a hint of wisdom in his words. "Business is a two-edged weapon. It can cut both ways. In America, the youngsters venture on their own early in life. The MBA course is attractive for the younger generation now. They leave their homes soon after college to pursue their higher studies elsewhere. They don't stick to their parent's homes as in India."

"And also, they don't look after their parents when they get old, isn't it so?" Satya's remark was tad caustic.

Sreeni fell silent, his ego hurt.

Meanwhile, Mamta retreated to the living room, finding it challenging to connect with Meenakshi. She preferred conversing with her sisters-in-law in English, distancing herself from the cultural nuances that seemed alien to her Telugu roots. Crossing her legs, she sat in front of her father-in-law, Anantharama Iyer who lay in his easy chair, engaging him in a conversation that the old man struggled to

81

comprehend. Her American accent was a bit strange to him and he had to frequently interrupt her while she spoke.

Everyone sat for lunch. *Keerai molakoottal* and *Vendakkai pacchadi* were on the day's menu — favorite of Sreeni, mother commented. "Sreeni, Uma remembered that these were your favored dishes. And she has made your favorite *Palada Pradaman* also. Come on, do justice to the dishes."

"Okay, Amma, I will take the *Paayasam* after lunch as a desert. Give it to me in a cup after my lunch, *manni*," he said addressing Uma.

After lunch Uma and Janaki retreated to the kitchen to clear the dishes, while the Anandu, Sreeni, Satya and Nandini sat around Anantharama Iyer who was in the easy chair fanning himself with his palm leaf fan. Meenakshi sat on the sofa beside her husband. Mamta took Pooja upstairs to their room for an afternoon nap. The discussion veered around dividing the assets. Anandu, broached the subject as all of them were present in the hall. Arjun had left after lunch saying that he had to meet some of his friends to share the news of his success with them.

"Sreeni," began Anantharama Iyer, "The other day I was telling these people that I would like to divide my cash and deposits among you. It is time that you take the burden of looking after the funds off my back. Each one of you can take care of your assets which I will allot for you. Arjun's share will be temporarily managed by Satya till he is employed, settled and mature enough to manage it himself."

"But why the hurry to do it, Appa," interjected Sreeni.

"We have already gone through this once," said Anantharama Iyer exasperated, "I am getting old and weak. Meena is also recovering from a repaired heart." he said smiling. "It is time you guys learnt to manage things on your own and relieve us of the burden."

"So, when do you want to do all this?" Sreeni anxiously asked.

"I have asked my auditor to come to see me this weekend. I will discuss the formalities with him. I have also asked our lawyer Subramania Iyer to come one of these days for me to draw up my will regarding this ancestral house."

"Okay then," commented Sreeni, "I can take the auditor's advice on how to repatriate the funds to the US. I have to get RBI sanction and what not."

"Why don't you leave the money in my bank in an NRO account?" posed Satya.

"Oh, no," Sreeni cut in, "I don't trust my money in banks in India."

Satya began to protest, then kept quiet.

"What are you planning to do with the house?" Satya asked turning to his father.

"That, I will decide in consultation with my wife and my lawyer. For the time being, none of you need to worry about that." Iyer was firm.

"Since the compound is quite large, almost an acre, shall I construct a small house for myself in the southeast corner of the plot which is now vacant? My bank will give me a housing loan at a very nominal interest and repayment in EMI's over a fifteen year period." Satya, hesitatingly made his request.

Meenakshi who was listening to the conversation, rather put out, immediately objected, "No, no... not now. That will create problems if you alone construct a house in this compound. Forget it. This house is quite large and all of you can stay here in it. Don't talk of constructing any separate house in this compound as long as *Appa* and I are alive."

"Yes, true," Sreeni cut in, "No one need think of constructing a house in this compound. This is for all of us together. Moreover, I don't plan to come and stay here. So no one else also need construct a house in this premises."

Anantharama Iyer added, "Listen to me. Before I transfer my assets to you, there are some pieces of advice I wish to impart. It's imperative that you heed them attentively, as they arise from my firsthand experiences and challenges. Meena and I have diligently worked over the years to construct this tale of success and raise all of you admirably. I wish to inform you of certain values and principles that will serve you well in your future endeavors and pave the path to your success."

"If you have problems, resort to an open and honest communication between yourselves. Don't let misunderstandings fester. You are mature adults. Learn to respect each other's differences instead of blaming each other and trying to change one another. I have noticed some disagreements and small arguments starting to arise within this family. Put yourself in the other's shoes and try to understand where the other person is coming from before jumping to conclusions and making judgements. Learn to forgive and forget minor issues. Remember that you are all now part of the same family. Strive for harmony and cooperation rather than discord and rivalry. Recognize and appreciate each other's contributions to the family. Also, it is ideal not to borrow or lend money because borrowing can strain relationships and lending can make people less careful with their resources."

"Whether it's managing the household or caring for children, every role is valuable. Learn to respect each other's personal space and privacy. Try to understand each other's perspectives and feelings. Empathy can go a long way in defusing tensions and fostering unity. When conflicts arise, communicate calmly and respectfully. Instead of playing the blame game, work together to find solutions to your problems. Focus on resolving issues rather than assigning fault. If you're unable to resolve conflicts on your own, don't hesitate to seek advice or support from other family members."

"See that your spouses also follow these rules. When they are older, teach these principles to your children also. These are some of the principles that have helped me carve out success in my professional and personal life."

All of them nodded. No one spoke as the weight of their father's words sank in.

Mamta coming down the stairs was gesturing Sreeni about something. Sreeni nodded. A silent message seemed to be conveyed to him.

Sreeni got up from his seat and sat beside mother, "*Amma*, Mamta has a small request."

Meenakshi looked up. "*Enna?*"

"She would like to see the jewelry collection which you have — yours and grandma's. The others would have seen it previously. Mamta has not had a chance to see them. Can you arrange for it?"

Meenakshi looked up at Nandini. Nandini nodded imperceptibly.

"Sure, *kanna,* Nandini and I will go to the bank tomorrow and bring all the jewelry home. Once all of you have seen them, we should return it to the bank locker as it is not safe to keep it here. I can also make an inventory of the jewelry with Nandini's help and decide how to divide it among the five of you."

The next day, Meenakshi and Nandini left for the bank, returning with the boxes of jewelry. The central hall became a stage for the display of ornaments, the teapoy in front shined with the glimmering treasures. Meenakshi sat on the sofa as Nandini opened the small jewelry boxes one after another and placed the items one by one on a large table cloth that was spread on the teapoy.

Mamta's gaze fixated on Meenakshi's pearl necklace with the blood red ruby pendant and matching ear drops. Janaki, on the other hand, couldn't take her eyes off the blue sapphire necklace with a peacock-shaped pendant ringed with tiny green emeralds set in a beautiful pattern as if the peacock was dancing. A large blue sapphire was set in the center of the pendant. It was an exquisite piece of art. Subtle envy hung in the air as Mamta and Janaki made childish requests, vying for Meenakshi's favor.

"*Amma,* that pearl-ruby necklace is for me," said Mamta smilingly. "Give it to me please, I can pass it on to Pooja as your legacy."

"Yes, Mamta, wouldn't this pearl necklace look stunning on you?" Sreeni endorsed her, pointing to Meenakshi's cherished possession.

"*Amma,* why don't you give Mamta the pearl necklace? It would suit her sophisticated style," Sreeni suggested, his words laced with persuasive intent. "It will enhance her reputation within her circle of friends."

Janaki smirked on hearing this. But she kept silent.

Sreeni joined his wife in making comments, showing interest in some of the bangles and rings also. The atmosphere became charged with envious glances and covetous desires.

"And the blue sapphire necklace for me," chipped in Janaki. "It is so beautiful. It will look nice on me with my navy-blue reception silk saree." Janaki added, "*Amma*, this sapphire necklace is truly exquisite. It would suit me perfectly." She could not take her eyes off it.

"And the Star Sapphire ring for me." Sreeni smilingly, but firmly put in his request.

Mother just looked at each of them silently and smiled.

"And who gets your diamond necklace, Amma," Sreeni was curious. He wanted to stake his claim on that too.

Meenakshi did not answer him.

Uma and Nandini kept silent. They knew fully well that *Amma* would take the decisions herself and decide who should get which ornament. "Nandini," Meenakshi accosted her daughter, "You make a list of all of these ornaments to the last sovereign and give it to me. I will decide on the division later." Nandini nodded.

Mother, sensing the growing tension, decided to defuse the situation. "I will make a list of the jewelry and decide on the division in the coming days. We'll keep them in the safe in my room for the time being."

Nandini watched passively, her eyes betraying a mix of amusement and resignation. The sisters-in-law competed for attention, their requests becoming increasingly persistent. As Meenakshi spoke, Mamta's eyes lingered on the coveted pearl necklace, her mind already envisioning the elegance it would add to her persona.

The scene portrayed envy, greed, and covetousness, with the jewelry symbolizing desire and status. Inside the Iyer household, amid the jubilation, emotions simmered beneath the surface, as each character pursued their own ambitions and desires.

Chapter 11

Arjun was returning home from college after alighting from the bus, clutching a file containing his mark list. He was deep in thought about his future and it was in this contemplative state that he unexpectedly ran into   Divakaran, a senior from his college days. Divakaran had parked his car — a 1978 model Mercedes Benz, a car too large for the narrow streets of Calicut, on the side of the road leading to his home and was smoking a cigarette. As Arjun passed him, he called out to him.

"Hey Arjun!" Divakaran greeted him, a sly glint in his eyes.

A warm smile spread across Arjun's face as he reciprocated Divakaran's greeting. "Oh, hey Divakaran! It's been quite a while. How have you been?" He remembered with nostalgia his college days, as Divakaran, senior to Arjun by two years, and they had once shared camaraderie in the college union activities. Back then, Arjun had served as the union secretary, leaving an indelible mark on those who he came across.

In those years in college, Arjun had emerged as a prominent figure, excelling not only in academics but also in sports. His popularity soared, making him the cynosure of both the teaching staff and the girls on the campus. His easy-going nature and pleasant demeanor endeared him to everyone he encountered. Arjun's innocence and his eagerness to lend a helping hand became his greatest assets, drawing people toward

87

him like a magnet. Even his rivals during college union election times couldn't help but admire him, acknowledging the genuine charm that he radiated.

As they exchanged pleasantries, memories of the past weaved through their conversation. Divakaran, reminiscing about the college union activities, couldn't help but express his appreciation for Arjun's charismatic presence. "You know, Arjun, those union days were something else. You were a natural leader, and everyone admired you, even your rivals."

Arjun, modestly acknowledging the compliment, replied, "Those were good times, Divakaran. We had some great moments together."

The genuine bond they shared during their college days was apparent in the way Arjun spoke. Divakaran continued, "You made a lasting impression, my friend. Your easy-going nature and willingness to help stood out. No wonder everyone was drawn to you."

Arjun, reflecting on those times, smiled nostalgically. "It's the people I met, like you, who made those years special."

The conversation unfolded like a stroll down memory lane, with dialogues punctuating their shared experiences. Divakaran, couldn't help but add, "Arjun, I've always admired your sincerity and charm. You've got something special about you."

Arjun, appreciating the genuine friendship they had, responded, "Thanks, Divakaran. It means a lot coming from you." The warmth of their conversation painted a vivid picture of the friendship they once shared.

But unknown to Arjun, Divakaran had undergone a transformation, veering away from the ideal friend Arjun once knew during their college days. The changes in Divakaran revealed a shift in perspective, where the businessman within him consistently calculated profits and benefits whenever engaging even with his friends. As years had passed since their college camaraderie, Divakaran's priorities had changed. He had become more self-centered. Arjun, unaware of the change in Divakaran, still believed that Divakaran was the same old friend he had while in college.

Arjun told Divakaran about his success in the B.A. examinations. Divakaran, always quick to get to the point, wasted no time. "So, what are your plans for the future? Any grand schemes?"

Arjun hesitated for a moment, then replied, "Well, I'm actually exploring self-employment opportunities. You know, trying to find my way. I like to enter business rather than take up a salaried job."

A mischievous smile crept across Divakaran's face. "Self-employment, huh? Business? Interesting. You don't have any experience in that, have you? Starting a business from scratch is not an easy task, Arjun, don't you think?"

"Yes, I know," Arjun agreed, "I know the difficulties and the teething troubles that I would face if I started new."

"What business do you have in mind?"

"Oh, I haven't thought about any particular business yet. Must give some thought to it. I was discussing with some of my friends."

"How about joining our business? I'm on the lookout for someone with potential, and you fit the bill." said Divakaran with a twinkle in his eye. "My brother and I are looking after my father's established business. So you will not be having any trouble if you join us."

Divakaran was well-informed about Arjun's family background, including his wealthy father who had returned from Burma. Connecting the dots, he realized Arjun could potentially finance their growing business. With his cunning nature, Divakaran was already plotting how to rope in Arjun in his schemes.

Arjun, taken aback, scratched his head. "Join your business? But Diva, I don't have any money to invest... yet."

Divakaran's eyes twinkled with a hint of cunning. "Money can be arranged, my friend. If you're interested, we can work something out." He knew quite well that Arjun's father was rich and his brothers were well employed. Arjun could prove to be a milch cow for him and his business if he played the cards right.

Arjun, the innocence radiating from his face, replied, "I'll think it over. My father might divide his assets soon, and I might have some money coming to me then." Arjun, in his naivety inadvertently disclosed his family affairs to Divakaran including his father's decision to divide his assets.

Divakaran's mind, fueled by greed, began to scheme. "Money, eh? This could be interesting. Well, that is a good thought. You can invest your share of your father's money in our company when you get it. Meanwhile, you could come to our company and begin learning the basic things about the business from us." Divakaran shot a sideways glance at Arjun. He was sure that Arjun was hooked on to the idea.

"Okay, Diva, let me think it over. I will be back with a reply soon. Give me your phone number. I'll get back to you."

Divakaran scribbled his phone number on to a pad taken from the dashboard of the car, tore off the page handing it over to Arjun. "I'll wait for your call."

Later, Divakaran shared the encounter with his confidants, Mohandas and Sukumaran. Mohandas, always drawn to the scent of wealth, eagerly voiced his interest. "Money talks, my friend. Trust me. We should take him in."

But Sukumaran, always the cautious type, hesitated. "Including an outsider in our business? Is it worth the risk?"

Divakaran reassured him, "Arjun is naive, intelligent, and gullible. We can easily lure him in. He's young, impetuous, but manageable. Let's give him a chance. We can always ease him out if we find him unfit."

Sukumaran had his reservations. "Should we take advantage of a naïve boy like him. He does not know the nuances of business. Furthermore, you say that he is a straightforward and honest guy. Will he prove to be an advantage for our business or will he be counterproductive?"

"Sure, why not," Divakaran interjected, "We can get him to invest his father's money with us as we are planning new ventures as per our cousin's advice." Divakaran smiled at Mohandas.

Sukumaran finally agreed with Divakaran and they decided to give Arjun a chance.

The atmosphere in the Iyer household was charged with anticipation as Sreeni and Mamta prepared to leave on their journey back to the United States. They were busy packing the various savories and sweets that Meenakshi had ordered her two daughters in law, Uma and Janaki to prepare for them to take to the US. Mamta, throughout her stay, confined herself to the solitude of her room upstairs, venturing downstairs solely for the purpose of sharing meals. In the bustling kitchen, Uma and Janaki tirelessly toiled under the watchful eye of Meenakshi, their mother in-law, who managed the culinary affairs of the household from the confines of a couch in the dining room.

Meenakshi, concerned about the workload, gently suggested that Mamta lend a hand in the kitchen. However, Sreeni, ever protective of his wife, swiftly intervened, stating, "*Amma*, she's not accustomed to our traditional cooking methods and gadgets. Besides, she's here on vacation; let her rest." This defense, however well-intentioned, stirred discontent among the sisters-in-law, Uma and Janaki leaving them seething with resentment.

Uma and Janaki, unable to express their grievances openly, harbored their displeasure within. Their discontent surfaced in the evenings when Anandu and Satya, their respective husbands, returned home. Their dissatisfaction was palpably, affecting the family harmony.

The next day afternoon, with Anandu and Satya away at work, Nandini away in her hospital, and the children at school, Meenakshi found a moment of repose on the couch in the corner of the dining room. Uma and Janaki, having completed their culinary tasks, had retreated to their individual rooms upstairs.

Observing Meenakshi alone, Sreeni approached her discreetly, a request lingering in his eyes. "*Amma*, I was thinking about the silver tea set father received as a gift while he was leaving Burma. It's lying idle in the Godrej Almirah. I could use it in the US, creating a lasting impression when I entertain my office colleagues and Mamta's friends. What do you think? Can I take it with me? None of you are using it here."

Meenakshi hesitated, mindful of the need to consult others. "But how can I give it to you without asking the others? I'll talk to Nandini about it."

"Why, *Amma*? Do I not have a say in this house? Why do you have to ask Nandini everything?" Sreeni responded, a touch of exasperation in his voice. "I have a share in the silverware too. Let me take the tea set, and others can have the glasses, plates, or the *Vilakku*. Additionally, I'd like father's silver engraved plate also; it'll complete the beautiful set."

Reluctantly, Meenakshi agreed, unaware of the hidden motives behind her son's request. "Alright, take your father's silver engraved plate also. I'll get it for you. I'll inform the others later."

"Okay, I'll pack them in my suitcase now itself."

With a glint of covetousness in his eyes, Sreeni continued, "And about those ebony elephants and the carved antique side table in the living room? They would appear marvelous in our new residence in the US and would elevate the house's decor. I'll arrange for them to be shipped through my agent within a month. Keep them safe for me, and don't promise them to anyone else."

Meenakshi, nodding at her son's shrewdness, could sense a shift in dynamics within the family, yet she merely nodded, choosing to address the matter later.

In the midst of the bustling household, Anantharama Iyer, engrossed in his own world, remained blissfully ignorant of the unfolding events in the dining room. Relaxing in his rocking chair, he was poring through the day's newspaper. Little did he fathom the artful desires and astute maneuvering of his son, Sreeni. The air was thick with untold emotions. Anantharama Iyer was oblivious of this silent drama unfolding in his home.

As two more days elapsed, the momentous day arrived when Sreeni, Mamta, and their daughter Pooja bid farewell to their familiar surroundings, embarking on a journey to the United States. Sreeni was careful to pack the silver tea set and the engraved silver plate in his suitcase without anyone else knowing about it. He was sure that in course of time *Amma* would forget all about it and wouldn't tell others.

In the emotional farewell scene, Sreeni looked back at his childhood home, promising a return after two years. His words, laden with a mixture of hope and nostalgia, echoed in the ears of those left behind. Certainly, he wouldn't be aware of the changes that would happen in his family in two years.

Amidst the farewells, Anantharama Iyer bid his son and his family adieu with a heartfelt paternal blessing. He didn't realize the complex mix of feelings and wants that had become woven into the family dynamics. The leaving wasn't just about physical distance; it also created an emotional gap, hidden beneath the surface of farewells and promises. Sreeni, Mamta, and Pooja departed from a home where continuing emotions from their leaving lingered beneath the surface.

Meanwhile, Arjun confided in his brothers Anandu and Satya about the KK brothers' promise to assist with his business venture, but Satya, ever cautious, warned him, "Don't rush into anything without thoroughly investigating them. Businessmen can't always be trusted; be careful."

"Get the opinion of a few other friends of yours who may know the KK brothers better, and only then venture into a partnership with them. You never know whom to trust these days." Anandu offered his advice.

A few days later, Divakaran approached Arjun with a proposition. "Arjun, we're having a small get-together at our outhouse this Saturday evening. Why don't you join us? We can discuss business and celebrate your potential partnership."

Intrigued, Arjun agreed. He left home in the evening on Saturday, informing his mother that he would be late that night and would be having dinner with his friends. Satya and Janaki had gone to Trivandrum to attend the wedding of Janaki's cousin. They planned to stay for a few days at Janaki's house before returning. Anandu, Uma and the children had gone to a movie that evening.

Arjun had decided to attend the meeting so as to get to know Sukumaran and Mohandas whom he had not met for a long time. He remembered them from his college days as his seniors and hence decided to renew the acquaintance.

Sukumaran, the elder of the KK brothers had grown up in the traditional family environment, where honesty and integrity were highly valued. He learned the importance of hard work and diligence from a young age, instilled with the belief that success should be achieved through legitimate means. Despite having a business-oriented mindset, Sukumaran's approach differed significantly from that of his younger brother. While his brother was more daring and willing to take risks, Sukumaran preferred a more cautious and ethical approach to business dealings. He believed in building long-term relationships based on trust and mutual respect rather than short-term gains at the expense of others. As a result, he often served as the voice of reason within the KK brothers group, advocating for ethical practices and steering the company away from potential legal or moral pitfalls.

Divakaran on the other hand, had grown up with a rebellious streak, often challenging authority and pushing boundaries. Unlike his elder brother Sukumaran, who valued tradition and ethics, Divakaran was more interested in living life on the edge. From a young age, he was drawn to the allure of fast money and was willing to take risks to achieve financial success. He admired his cousin Mohandas, who shared his disregard for the law and often looked to him for guidance in business matters. Divakaran's was not afraid to bend or break the rules to achieve his goals. Despite his flaws, Divakaran's boldness and charisma made him a formidable force within KK Brothers, often driving the company's riskier ventures and pushing boundaries in pursuit of profit.

From an early age their cousin, Mohandas had been groomed to navigate the murky waters of politics, where he saw an opportunity to amass wealth and influence. His father had been involved in the same political party he was currently serving. During a political protest, his father had tragically lost his life to a stray bullet fired by the police.

Mohandas grew around a background of deceit and corruption, where dishonesty was not only tolerated but encouraged. Unlike the KK brothers, who may have had some ethical reservations, Mohandas embraced the world of illegal activities and backdoor deals without hesitation. He saw the brothers as useful pawns in his game of power and used his influence to lure them into a web of illegal activities. Mohandas's selfish ambition knew no bounds, and he would stop at nothing to achieve his goals, even if it meant destroying the lives of others in the process. He epitomized the dark side of politics, where greed and corruption reign supreme, and morality was nothing more than a hindrance to be overcome. He also had perfected the art of manipulating people to achieve his desired ends.

Arjun found himself in the outhouse of the opulent *Kurukankaattil* mansion. The outhouse was separate from the main ancestral house and was secluded surrounded by a thick foliage of trees and bushes. This provided some privacy and possibly secrecy to the outhouse. There was a dim light on the porch of the outhouse. A couple of wicker chairs stood on the porch with a matching tea table. Arjun entered the house with trepidation. He was not sure of what he would encounter.

"Ah! So you are here, Arjun." Divakaran met him on the porch having seen him approaching. C'mon I'll introduce you to Suku. I think you know him already from the college days. Mohandas will be arriving soon." He put a friendly arm around Arjun's shoulder and ushered him into the hall where Sukumaran was seated with a glass filled with whisky on the coffee table in front of him.

Divakaran introduced him to his brother. Sukumaran struck him as a more mature and down-to-earth type on individual. Mohandas had not yet arrived. They invited him to take a seat. The preliminaries over, Sukumaran spoke to him.

"Arjun, my friend, you need to loosen up a bit," Sukumaran said, offering him a chilled beer. "Start with a beer; you can upgrade to the hot stuff later. We'll begin our discussions once Mohandas gets here."

Arjun hesitated, glancing around the room filled with an air of sophistication. "I don't drink."

"Come on, it'll only taste like soda." Divakaran chuckled, patting him on the back. "Come on, it's a celebration. You're going to be part of something big. This is not a *usual* meeting for us."

The unmistakable blare of a car horn resonated outside, at which Divakaran stepped onto the porch to receive Mohandas, who had just arrived in his recently acquired Maruti car. The vehicle, a captivating shade of shiny post-office red, gleamed under the evening sunlight, catching Divakaran's eye as he greeted his cousin.

As Mohandas gracefully exited the car, Divakaran couldn't help but jest, "So, you've officially joined the ranks of Maruti owners? When did you manage to snag this beauty?"

With a grin, Mohandas replied, "Oh, I got it second-hand from one of our party leaders. He had only used it for a year and a half before upgrading to a second-hand Mercedes. It was a real bargain for me."

Divakaran, eyeing the rear windshield graced with a color picture of Gandhiji's bust and the phrase '*Satyameva Jayate*' written in Malayalam, couldn't resist a playful jab. "The Gandhiji picture suits you politically, but '*Satyameva Jayate*'? Does that align with your penchant for deceit and untruthfulness? Who are you trying to fool?" Divakaran remarked roaring with laughter.

Mohandas, looking a bit sheepish, chuckled, "I'm in the game of politics, my friend. Some theatrics and pretense are necessary for the public, you know. One needs to survive in the field of politics."

Their banter continued, the camaraderie evident in their easy exchanges. Divakaran, leaning against the car, prodded further, "Politics, my dear friend, has turned you into a real actor! But seriously, how's life treating you, Mohandas?"

As they strolled towards the house, Mohandas's tone turned more reflective, "It's a rollercoaster, Divakaran. The constant balancing act between principles and the demands of politics can be quite the challenge. Sometimes, a symbolic gesture, like Gandhiji on the windshield, is the compromise we make. '*Satyam*', of course not, but '*Jayate*', that is victory and success, I need it in politics." Mohandas said chuckling.

Divakaran, ever the thoughtful friend, nodded understandingly, "I get it. It's not always black and white in the political arena. But don't lose yourself in the act, my friend. Authenticity is a rare commodity in your world of politics."

The evening unfolded with shared laughter, reminiscing about old times and new adventures. The beer and whisky flowed freely, and soon the clinking of glasses filled the room. Without his knowledge, Arjun had already downed three mugs of beer. Amidst laughter and camaraderie, the KK brothers subtly introduced Arjun to the world of smoking, handing him a cigarette. Arjun did not know at that time that it was laced with a dash of cannabis.

Divakaran grinned as Arjun took a drag, coughing as the effects slowly seeping into his consciousness. "Feels good, doesn't it?"

Neither of them spoke about their business or Arjun's joining them in this preliminary encounter. The bait was ready, they would gradually tighten the noose around his neck.

Arjun, his inhibitions, gradually fading, catalyzed by the alcohol and the pot nodded with a dazed smile. Little did he know that this seemingly innocent camaraderie was a prelude to a perilous journey which was the beginning of his decadence. With every puff he took, the Tetrahydrocannabinol [THC] that coursed through his veins accessing the frontal and temporal lobes of his brain triggered his already genetically predisposed brain to slide into the deep chasm of schizophrenia. He did not know it at that time that he was prone to this dreaded psychological disorder, which would be unmasked like a specter and consume him and alter his future.

Cannabis and alcohol would prove to be his downfall – his nemesis. Little were the Machiavellian trio aware that they were unleashing a Frankenstein monster by introducing Arjun to the world of alcohol and cannabis. The days ahead would take him into a downward spiral, a quagmire from which he would find redemption difficult, if not impossible.

As the inhaled smoke coursed through his veins, Arjun felt more and more relaxed. He reached home in a daze. His mother opened the door to him. In her sleepy mood, she did not notice the change in Arjun's behavior. Arjun did not speak to her as he went upstairs to his room and fell on to his bed deeply unconscious.

As the days passed, Arjun was required to report to the office of the KK Brothers in downtown Calicut and familiarize himself with the intricacies of the business. He received instruction on monitoring fertilizer shipments from Gujarat and Punjab. He learned how to oversee the transportation of fertilizer bags by trucks and manage inventory in the warehouse. Assigned tasks were straightforward and did not entail financial management. Additionally, he received training on salary disbursement and assisting with the employees' daily duty schedules. They did not request him for any investment at this stage. He was being groomed for the business, he felt.

At the same time, the KK brothers gradually escalated Arjun's indulgence. The meetings in the outhouse to discuss the details of the business became more frequent and Arjun was drawn into the vortex of deception. Beer evolved into whiskey, and smoking became a routine habit, each cigarette carrying a hidden dose of cannabis. The once-reluctant Arjun was now hooked, a puppet in the hands of his deceitful mentors. More and more evenings were spent in the outhouse, each one sinking Arjun deeper and deeper into the murky depths of addiction.

One evening, in the dimly lit study, the brothers broached a new topic with Arjun. "Arjun, we've been thinking. You're like family to us now, and we want you to be a part of our flourishing business," Sukumaran declared.

Arjun, blissfully unaware of the illicit activities surrounding him, perked up. "Business? What do you have in mind?"

Divakaran leaned in, his voice a conspiratorial whisper. "We're expanding our fertilizer business, and we need capital. Five lakhs from you, and you'll be a partner."

Arjun's eyes widened, a mixture of excitement and apprehension coursing through him. "Five lakhs? That's a lot of money."

"But think of the returns, Arjun. You'll be swimming in wealth," Mohandas added, a cunning glint in his eyes. Sukumaran, however, kept silent. He was not in favor of the other two taking undue advantage of the innocent boy. He felt a soft corner towards the unsuspecting youth in front of him. But he was powerless by himself and had to give in to the machinations of the other two. He had to agree to their decisions without dissenting.

The room echoed with the clinking of glasses as they toasted to Arjun's potential partnership. Unknown to him, the brothers had a sinister plan in motion and Arjun was a puppet in their chain.

Chapter 12

Days, weeks, months rolled by.

The air in the Iyer household was thick with tension and gloom. The former lively and happy atmosphere had now turned into a deep sadness, filling every corner of this old family home. Anantharama Iyer, the patriarch, further weakened by Parkinsonism and dementia, sat in his easy chair, his once robust frame now a mere silhouette of its former self. Progressive memory loss clung to him like a shadow, often distorting the names of his sons as he addressed them wrongly. His eyes, once lively, now mirrored confusion and disorientation. Despite experiencing memory loss, he occasionally had moments of clarity when he spoke more coherently and recalled old memories. During these rare lucid intervals, his dementia appeared to improve significantly, allowing him to converse clearly with others without any apparent neurological issues.

In the labyrinth of fading memories, Meenakshi, the devoted wife, stood as the sole beacon of recognition for Anantharama Iyer. In the midst of his cognitive decline, she became the anchor, a source of solace in the turbulent sea of confusion that engulfed him. When he reached out during his lucid moments, it was her hand he sought, the warmth of her touch offering a fleeting connection to the past. "Meena, come and sit beside me," he would call her, "And talk to me." They would lose themselves in memories of their past, the days in Burma and the halcyon days of their youth. He had vivid memories of his past; it was the recent events and names that eluded him. He found it difficult to focus his mind on anything. His memory lapses were becoming more frequent.

In those tender moments, Anantharama Iyer, lost in the maze of his own mind, would delicately clasp Meenakshi's hand. The lines on his forehead, etched with the weight of forgotten memories, seemed to momentarily ease as he gazed into the eyes of the woman who had been his lifelong companion. It was as if, in that brief connection, a flicker of recognition danced in the depths of his gaze. Softly, almost in a hushed whisper, he would murmur endearments to Meenakshi. The words, though seemingly disjointed and nonsensical, carried the weight of a love that transcended the boundaries of time and memory. Meena, as he would address her, with a tender smile, would listen to the gentle cadence of his voice, understanding that the coherence of his words mattered less than the sentiment behind them.

Their interactions resembled a graceful dance of emotions, a serene conversation where words merely conveyed the profound feelings they exchanged. Meenakshi, assuming the role of a steadfast anchor, replied to his whispers with comforting gentleness. "I'm here, *Kettela*," she would softly say, her voice carrying a mixture of empathy and sorrow for the man she had shared a lifetime with.

As Anantharama Iyer continued to deal with the challenges of progressive dementia, Meenakshi took on the role of a caring guide. She would softly help him navigate through moments of confusion and memory lapses, offering support to bring him back to the present. This was a sensitive task, a blend of emotions where Meenakshi, despite her own concerns, stayed strong for her husband in need.

As they held hands, their silent communication showed the human heart's strength to withstand forgetfulness and still find solace in the touch of a loved one. Meenakshi, the matriarch, sat by her ailing husband, often engaging in one-sided conversations. Her words, like whispers to the wind, at times seemed to barely register with Anantharama Iyer. His declining health worried and burdened her greatly, leaving her exhausted and overwhelmed. Often she forgot to take care of her own deteriorating health. As his condition worsened, the household descended into despair.

One gloomy day, Meenakshi, struggling with her own health, found herself increasingly breathless and Nandini rushed her to the hospital where she was admitted for severe congestive heart failure. Dr. Menon's diagnosis was a cruel reality that left her confined to the sterile hospital bed for a week. Nandini, the devoted daughter, stood by her mother's side, managing the household in addition. Unlike previously, Arjun was not available to share the task of looking after his mother. He was in a world of his own.

Arjun further complicated the already tense family dynamics by his behavior. His erratic behavior and increasing addiction only fueled the flames of annoyance and resentment within the family. Satya and Anandu, the elder brothers, attempted to counsel him, admonish him and urge him to seek rehabilitation. However, Arjun's rage at times knew no bounds. He would listen to no one but himself. Gradually he was sinking into a hellhole of disaster. No amount of advice and counseling helped him. He knew that his father had already divided his assets among his children and now he wanted to get at his share of the funds. Satya was the temporary custodian of this, as had been ordained by his father. Arjun's paranoia had become so severe that he viewed everyone at home as an enemy.

"Give me my share, and I'll handle it," he shouted at Satya, his eyes reflecting a mix of anger and desperation. "I know, all of you are plotting against me. You want to swindle me of my rightful share," he would shout as his paranoia became more and more evident day by day.

Satya, trying to maintain composure, replied, "Arjun, this is not the solution. You need help. We can't stand by and watch you destroy yourself."

Arjun's aggression escalated, flinging vessels and words alike at home. Uma and Janaki, the sisters-in-law, wisely kept their distance, avoiding the storm that brewed within the walls of their home.

Meenakshi, torn between her ailing husband and troubled son, felt helpless. The once harmonious family now echoed with the unsettling sounds of anger and despair. The once serene household now reverberated with Arjun's tantrums.

One morning, as the sun shrouded by clouds struggled to cast its feeble light on the household, Arjun, appearing haggard and agitated, approached Satya. "I need money, Satya *Anna*. I can't live like this."

Satya sighed, his empathy overshadowed by the frustration of the situation. "Arjun, we've been through this. You need to seek help for your addiction. I can't keep giving you money."

Arjun's eyes flashed with resentment, his voice dripping with desperation. "You and Anandu have everything. Just give me what's rightfully mine! I know you all are plotting against me! *Appa* has already allotted my share." He stormed out of the house.

During these tough times, unexpected problems added more stress to the family members who were already struggling. Out of the blue, the next surprise emerged from Anandu, the eldest son, catching everyone off guard. The tense atmosphere reached its peak when Anandu, the eldest son, dropped a bombshell that shattered the fragile peace of the household.

Chapter 13

As the day bid its farewell, the sun gracefully dipped below the horizon, allowing long shadows to stretch and embrace the Iyer household. Anandu, wearied by a day's toil at the office, entered the living room where his family had congregated. Uma, his devoted wife, was occupying the wicker chair by the window, diligently sewing a button onto Aadi's shirt. In the adjacent dining room, Janaki engaged herself in the household chores. The corner table served as her impromptu ironing station, where she meticulously pressed shirts and pants for Satya, preparing for the demands of the next day. Aadi and Akhil, Uma's sons, sat cross-legged on the floor, immersed in their daily homework. Nandini was in the dining room sitting at the table reading a book while helping Aathria do her homework.

Meanwhile, Anantharama Iyer, the patriarch of the household, found solace in his rocking chair, fanning himself with a sense of regular monotony. At times, he would drift into brief periods of sleep. Meenakshi sat in the corner chair hooked on to the nebulizer and took deep breaths as the equipment whirred and spiraled its contents into her lungs.

"Amma," said Anandu, addressing Meenakshi who looked up from her chair removing the face mask of the nebulizer. "I have some news." Uma, sensing something important was to be announced, looked up from her sewing, her eyes searching Anandu's face for any sign of what was to come.

Anantharama Iyer, the elderly figurehead, lowered his handheld fan, his eyes narrowing in concern. "What is it, Anandu? What are you going to say?" He was going through one of his lucid intervals when he could grasp what was being said and responded equally well logically.

Anandu, continued, "I've been transferred to Poona and I have to join within a fortnight. I will be taking Uma and the children with me."

Silence descended upon the room, as if time itself had paused to absorb the impact of his words. Uma's hands momentarily stilled over the shirt. The room, once filled with the ordinary sounds of familial activities, suddenly became quiet. The children looked up from their homework with a look of surprise writ on their faces. Janaki glanced up from ironing clothes, her expression a blend of surprise and shock.

Anantharama Iyer, his brows furrowed, struggled to grasp the sudden turn of events. "Poona? Why? And what about the family? You can't just uproot everyone like this." Despite his dementia, he could understand the gravity of the situation.

Anandu, in careful tones, explained, "It's a promotion transfer, *Appa*. If I let go of this opportunity, I'll miss a promotion for the next five years."

Iyer's eyes pleaded with a silent desperation, "But the family, Anandu. You can't take Uma and the children away. They'll find it difficult if you uproot them from here."

Uma, caught between loyalty to her husband and duty to her in-laws, looked down, a conflicted expression clouding her features. She kept quiet, unable to decide or comment. Her mind had jumped with joy at the news, but she could not voice her delight.

Anandu, though empathetic, remained steadfast, "This is an opportunity for all of us, *Appa*. A new beginning. Uma needs a respite from the daily struggles here, and I need to seize this chance for our family's future. Shouldn't we carve out a life for ourselves too?"

The profound weight of his words hung in the room, enveloping every family member like a dense, melancholic veil. The calm feeling in the air changed as they sensed something different about to happen, which could disturb their peaceful lives.

Seated on her sofa, Meenakshi found herself assaulted by a myriad emotions surging within her. A complex host of sentiments unfolded within her, revealing the internal struggle between her deep affection for Anandu, her commitment to family, and her unwavering devotion to her husband.

As Meenakshi grappled with these conflicting emotions, she sensed a profound realization settling over her – the dawning realization that her hold over the family had dwindled. Decisions, once a collaborative effort, were now orchestrated by her sons and daughters-in-law, leaving her as a passive observer. Decisions were now thrust upon her by her children. She seemed to be losing hold on her family. It was a juncture in her life where the roles had reversed, and the time had arrived for her to listen, not speak — a universal truth, she mused, that befalls everyone as old age takes hold, gradually usurping both body and soul. The children govern the parents when they grow old.

She grasped the significance of 'Vanaprastha': in old age, after fulfilling familial duties, one should relinquish control of the family and retire to the forest. This practice was followed by the *Grihasthasramas* and kings in ancient days. Today, it equated to releasing control of the family and withdrawing from active involvement in its affairs, leaving them to the children. The children would grow independent and care for themselves. Elderly parents would devote their time to God and prayers, serving merely in an advisory role in the family, without involvement in decision-making or daily management.

Unfortunately, Meenakshi couldn't help but release a sigh of profound despair. The room, once a sanctuary of familial harmony, now echoed with the muted strains of change. She could not do anything about it. She had to accept it. It was fate. It was destiny. Change was bound to happen. She was helpless.

Amidst this silent turmoil, the unspoken words echoed louder than ever. Anandu, sensing Meenakshi's internal conflict, approached her gently. "*Amma*," he began softly, "I understand this is difficult. But we are family, and our decisions are not meant to diminish your voice but to ensure the well-being of everyone. Uma and I have to chart our own course in life just as you and *Appa* did when you moved to Burma. Don't you realize that? You must let us go. Poona is not in a faraway country, I can be here within a day whenever you want me."

Meenakshi, looking into Anandu's understanding eyes, felt a mixture of gratitude and heartache. She placed a gentle hand on his head and ruffling his hair, she nodded. The conversation kept going, as the family tried to understand each other better. The room, full of feelings and understanding, became a place where families connected and life unfolded. "Yes, Anandu, *kanna*, you should go and carve out a life for yourself and your family. You have our blessings." She wiped the tears that had formed in the corner of her eyes.

Uma, feeling torn, glanced between her husband and her in-laws. She sensed the tension building, and her heart sank. Anandu remained firm in his decision, ignoring his father's plea.

Nandini, who remained quiet so far, looked up from a book she was reading and came into the hall. "How can you do this, Anandu. Mother is ill, father is ill, and now you want to leave us. Who will take care of them?"

"You are the doctor, Nandini. Take care of them. Get their medicines. You're capable," Anandu retorted, his eyes not wavering. His self-centeredness was showing up. "I have been shouldering the burden all these years. Why not others also take a share of the burden?"

Satya, their brother spoke up. "And who will pay for their medications, Anandu? We alone can't afford it. You're the one leaving, but you should also share in the expenses in their treatment."

Nandini's eyes widened with disbelief. "Satya, we are a family. We share burdens. We can't let our parents suffer due to our differences of opinion."

But Satya, with his calculating eyes pitched in with his argument, dismissing Nandini's plea. "I alone can't share the medical expenses. Nandini, you are the doctor. You should look after them. You have access to medications from the hospital and your salary can cover it."

Nandini, earning a paltry sum of Rs 2800 (approx. $170) from the Kerala Government, shook her head. "I don't have enough to spend on the whole household. We need to share the expenses. All of you must cooperate."

Satya, the ever-envious brother, interjected with a caustic smirk. "Get money from your husband in Australia. He's an NRI, and he can afford to support you."

Walking in from the dining room where she was surreptitiously listening to the arguments, Janaki, the scheming sister-in-law with self-seeking intentions, added venomously, "Why not, Nandini *akka*? Your husband is living a luxurious life alone abroad, and you're struggling here. Ask him to pay."

Nandini, feeling affronted, stood her ground. "I won't beg for money. We are a family, and we should support each other. I cannot ask Rajaram for money to treat *my* parents. It wouldn't be right. And by the way, Janaki, you have no right interfering in our family affairs!"

Janaki, sulking moved away from the room.

Meenakshi, the silent observer, couldn't hold back her tears. "Why are you crying, *Ammamma*?" Aathira, the innocent granddaughter, asked. "Nothing my dear *kanna*," Meenakshi managed to hide her true feelings behind a feeble excuse hugging her granddaughter affectionately. She couldn't digest the fact that her children were fighting over the expenses for the treatment of her husband and herself. Self-pity overcame her and poured out as hot tears.

Amidst the chaos, Arjun stumbled into the room, his eyes bloodshot and glazed. "What's happening here?" he slurred, his speech garbled.

"Arjun, you're drunk again," Nandini sighed, her patience waning.

"No, no! I'm not drunk. I am hearing voices, voices in my ear, saying my brothers are plotting against me. My life is at stake," Arjun rambled on, his paranoia overcoming him. With his addiction to alcohol and small doses of cannabis which his business associates were feeding him, he was spiraling down into an abyss of schizophrenic paranoia.

Anandu scoffed, "Arjun, stop with your delusions. We have more important matters to discuss."

The tension escalated as each character fought for their own interests with raised voices. Nandini felt the weight of the family's expectations and her limited financial resources. Arjun, lost in his addiction, saw threats in every shadow. Anandu, torn between career and family, stood firm in his decision. The once peaceful home turned into a place of conflict and selfishness, resonating with the noise of different desires clashing. Arjun stood swaying in front of Nandini and his brothers and spoke in a loud voice.

"Regarding the money for treating *Appa* and *Amma*, if that's all your concern," Arjun spoke, his words clear despite his drunken state, "You can take the money *Appa* gave me. It's *his* hard-earned money. I'm willing to contribute my whole share for their treatment if you brothers are too selfish and stingy to pitch in."

His statement left everyone momentarily stunned, the room falling into a heavy silence. Arjun's culture of selflessness shone even in his drunken state. Nandini, in frustration, expressed these words to all present. "This serves as a lesson to every parent who gives away their wealth and possessions to their children upon retirement without reserving anything for themselves to sustain them in old age. No parent should repeat the grievous mistake our father made. They should retain their earnings to ensure they can cover expenses for their treatment and upkeep in old age. It's a lesson for all of us."

Nandini rose and hugged Arjun. "Arjun, *kanna*," she said gently, "That was a courageous and generous offer. I'm truly proud of you. But the issue isn't about who foots the bill; it's about all of us sharing the responsibility."

"If that's the case," Arjun countered, "Why not ask Sreeni *Anna* as well? He should chip in too. He is enjoying life in the USA."

Nandini felt tears welling up. "Arjun, you're the epitome of a devoted son, willing to sacrifice your own money for them. Now, please go to your room and rest." She gently guided him to the stairs urging him to go upstairs to his room. Arjun moved up the stairs.

"Anandu, please reconsider," Iyer pleaded one last time, desperation in his eyes. But Anandu, unyielding in his pursuit, turned away. "Sorry *Appa*, I've made my decision. It's final."

After the room fell silent, the family didn't realize a terrible truth: something bad was about to happen. It was like a dark storm gathering in the horizon, ready to bring unexpected tragedy and suffering.

Chapter 14

Mananchira Square, bathed in the warm hues of the evening sun, witnessed the meeting of two souls entangled in a web of emotions. Arjun and Divya, once inseparable, now found themselves at the heart of a storm that threatened to separate them. The sprawling lawn, dotted with people enjoying the serene atmosphere and the cool breeze that wafted from the Arabian sea, couples enjoying a tête-à-tête, and children prancing about with colorful balloons, became the scene for a confrontation that would redefine their relationship.

As Arjun and Divya found a quiet spot on the lawn, the air was thick with unspoken tension. Divya, her eyes reflecting concern, broke the silence, "Arjun, I heard about your new... habit. Is it true?"

Arjun, slouched and slightly slurring, looked away momentarily before meeting her gaze. "What's it to you, Divya? It's my life, and I can do what I want."

Divya sighed, her frustration evident. "Arjun, you've changed. This isn't the person I fell in love with. Why are you doing this to yourself?"

Arjun, leaning back, countered with a defiant tone, "I'm not doing anything to myself. I know what I am doing. I'm planning joining a business with my friends. We'll be successful, you'll see."

Divya with raised eyebrows, probed further. "Who are these friends? Why haven't you told me about them before?"

A smile played on Arjun's lips. "The *Kurukankaattil* brothers, Divya — KK brothers. We're starting something big. I am planning to go into partnership with them. I am already learning the ropes of their business."

Divya's eyes widened, a tinge of worry crept in. "The KK Brothers? Arjun, be careful. I have heard my brothers comment about them. My brothers mentioned that they might not be as trustworthy as their father was."

Arjun's face suddenly contorted with anger. "Why do you have to suspect my friends? Are your brothers the epitome of honesty?"

Divya, her voice firm, replied, "Arjun, your business is my business if we plan to continue like this. I won't stand by and watch you ruin your life and your health."

"Why are you interfering in my business, Divya? I can handle it," Arjun retorted, his agitation rising. "Everyone seems to be plotting against me!" he burst out, his paranoia cropping up.

"Because your business is also my future, Arjun. I can't be with someone who's spiraling down a destructive path," Divya's eyes glistened with unshed tears. Divya realized that Arjun had undergone a sea change in his behaviour and attitude. He seemed like someone possessed.

The tension escalated, and Arjun's frustration erupted. "Why can't you trust me? I don't need your interference in my business matters. I'll handle my life the way I want." His voice was becoming loud.

Divya, hurt and desperate, whispered, "Quieten down... Arjun, there are other people around us. I love you. But I can't watch you destroy yourself like this. You need to change, if not how can we have a future together."

Arjun, momentarily softened by her words, reached for her hand. "Divya, I promise I'll change. I'll give all this up and be the person you fell in love with."

Divya, her emotions a tumultuous storm, struggled to keep her composure. "You promise, Arjun?"

"Sure, I promise," Arjun affirmed, his eyes locking with hers, squeezing her hand in assurance.

The weight of that promise lingered in the air, an unspoken pact that would determine the course of their relationship. Little did Divya know that fate was preparing a cruel twist, threatening to shatter the foundation of their love.

Days passed, and the promises made in the golden glow of the Mananchira Square began to fade like footprints in the sand, washed away by the waves of enticement. Arjun, ensnared in the grip of addiction and lured by the promise of a dubious partnership by the scheming KK brothers, found himself unable to keep his word. The rift between him and Divya thereby widened, fueled by resentment.

Days passed by. One evening, in the quiet confines of Divya's home, Arjun sat alone with Divya on the divan in their elegant living room. Her brothers were away at their office and her mother had gone to the temple to attend the *Sapthaham* that was going on. Divya, her eyes searching Arjun's face for a glimmer of the man she once knew, asked, "Have you really changed, Arjun?"

Arjun, avoiding her gaze, hesitated before muttering, "It's not that simple, Divya."

Tears welled up in Divya's eyes. "You promised me, Arjun. You promised you'd change."

"I know, but things are complicated. The business, the pressure..." Arjun trailed off, unable to meet her eyes.

Divya, her voice tinged with desperation, pleaded, "Arjun, don't let this destroy us. I can't bear to lose you."

Arjun, a mixture of guilt and defiance in his eyes, suddenly snapped, "You think I want this? You think I'm doing this on purpose?" His anger was increasing.

Divya, undeterred, retorted, "No, Arjun, but you're letting it happen. You're letting it consume you. You are destroying yourself."

Arjun, anger simmering beneath the surface, stood up abruptly. "You don't understand. This is my life, my choices."

"And what about us, Arjun? What about the promises you made? What about our future?" Divya's voice trembled.

Arjun, a bitter laugh escaping his lips, shot back, "Promises? They're just words, Divya. Don't act like they mean anything. I made the promise only to appease you... then."

Divya was stunned.

The room echoed with the silence of shattered dreams and unfulfilled promises. Divya, eyes brimming with tears and her heart breaking, whispered, "I can't do this anymore, Arjun. If you choose this path, we can't be together. My brothers and my mother already know about us. They'll never accept a relationship with you if you keep acting like this."

Arjun, his eyes reflecting an admixture of emotions, watched as Divya stood up and walked away into her room banging the door shut, leaving behind the echoes of their love. The weight of his choices hung heavy in the air, a bitter reminder of what could have been. Arjun walked out of the house, crestfallen.

In the aftermath of that fateful evening, the once vibrant love between Arjun and Divya withered away. Arjun was caught up in depression, anger, and addiction, becoming a shell of his former self. Fate had caused a split between them, hinting at even more trouble ahead.

That night Arjun drank more than he should have.

Chapter 15

As the dawn broke, painting the sky with soft pinks and golds, the morning sun rose, casting a warm glow across the land. Just as its rays stretched down, a blanket of fluffy clouds floated by, like wisps of cotton on a gentle breeze. Rather than dimming its light, these clouds only made the sun's beauty more captivating, adding a dreamy touch to the scene. Then, as if answering the sun's call, the clouds released tiny droplets of rain, each one sparkling like a precious gem in the light, creating a shimmering curtain over the landscape. The rain brought life to the earth, with the ground eagerly soaking up the moisture, releasing the sweet scent of wet grass into the air. In that moment, it felt as if nature held its breath, waiting for something wondrous. And as the rain continued to fall, each drop became a small miracle, transforming the world into a canvas of beauty, a testament to the timeless dance of sun and rain.

The home of Anantharama Iyer stood grand and imposing, surrounded by the lush greenery of Calicut. The aroma of incense lingered in the air as the morning sun cast its golden glow on the sprawling courtyard. The *Vilakku* had been lit in the pooja room in front of the altar in which stood the large bronze idol of *Bhagawan Ganesha* flanked on either side by equally exquisite idols of Sri Krishna gracefully playing the flute and that of *Devi Mahalakshmi* astride the lotus. Tiny silver idols of *Bhagawan Dharma-Sastha*, *Bhagawan Venkitachalapathy*, *Devi Saraswathy*, and *Bhagawan Subramanya* stood on either side of these large idols. In the front of the altar stood a five-wicked large silver *Vilakku* adorned with vermillion and a bunch of jasmine flowers atop it. The aroma of sandalwood incense permeated the air giving the whole area a divine ambience.

Janaki moved about the house with a purpose, her mind buzzing with discontent and suppressed indignation. The ancestral home, once a haven of peace, now seemed burdened with complex emotions. With a sense of determination, Janaki approached the shelf in the corner and lifted the receiver of the phone off the cradle and dialed her father, Sadasiva Iyer in Trivandrum.

"*Appa*," Janaki's voice held a note of frustration as she looked furtively around to ascertain that she was alone in the hall. Anantharama Iyer was not seen in his ever present perch – the easy chair, and Meenakshi was in her room lying down after having her breakfast.

"I can't take this anymore, *Appa*. The house is drowning in chaos. You must understand the predicament I'm in. Do something about this, *Appa*. You don't seem to understand my difficulties." Janaki was in a state of hysterical anxiety.

Sadasiva Iyer, on the other end of the line, listened intently. "What happened, Janaki? Tell me everything."

The next morning, as the Trivandrum express chugged into the station, Sadasiva Iyer with his distinctive umbrella and a tote bag made of yellow cotton cloth, disembarked. He made his way to Iyer's ancestral home, where Janaki, clad in a simple green cotton saree, awaited him with a mixture of relief and anticipation.

"*Appa*," Janaki greeted, touching her father's feet in a gesture of respect.

"*Deerga Sumangali bhava*," intoned Sadasiva Iyer as he patted her head affectionately. "Tell me, Janaki, what troubles you?"

"*Appa*, I will get you a strong decoction coffee first." Janaki offered, "We will discuss matters after that."

Sadasiva Iyer perfunctorily paid his respects to Anantharama Iyer who was reclining in his easy chair and to Meenakshi, before accompanying his daughter to the courtyard in front of the house. He needed privacy for their huddle. The scent of jasmine permeated the air as Janaki began, "*Appa*, I can't bear the tension in this house anymore. Anandu *anna's* transfer, Arjun's addiction, both the parents ill, it's all too much for me! The whole burden on the household is on me. Nandini *akka* is busy with her hospital practice and is rarely available in the kitchen." She poured out what was in her heart amidst tears and sobs. "Now, *Amma* being indisposed, everything is on my head!"

Sadasiva Iyer, the one to quote Shakespeare in times of crisis, nodded knowingly. "Family life is like that –'*All the world's a stage*', my dear. But tell me, what do you want me to do?"

"I want to live separately, *Appa*. With Satya," Janaki confessed, her eyes revealing a longing for a life of luxury and tranquility. "I want to move out of here, somehow."

Sadasiva Iyer, thoughtful, responded, "Luxuries come at a price, Janaki. What troubles you specifically?"

Janaki sighed, her voice laden with frustration. "I have already told you. Arjun comes home almost every day, stoned and drunk, creating trouble. Anandu *anna's* family has left for Poona, and all the heavy responsibilities of the house have fallen on my shoulders. I can't handle this excess workload. *Amma* being sick, the burden of cooking for the whole family is now on my shoulders."

Sadasiva Iyer raised an eyebrow. "Excess workload, you say?"

"Yes, *Appa*. It's suffocating. I need peace of mind," Janaki implored, her eyes seeking understanding. "I hardly get any time for myself."

Her father, scanning the courtyard, observed, "I see. Let me talk to your mother in law about this."

Approaching Meenakshi who was swinging gently on the *Aattukattil* in the dining room, Sadasiva Iyer gently broached the subject. "Meenakshi *mami*, my Janaki is finding it difficult to manage everything. Perhaps, it's time for Satya to move to a smaller home where things will be easy to manage."

"*Mama*," anger and disgust were obvious in Meenakshi's voice despite her illness, "Who will take care of the two aging souls in this house if they also move away? What are you implying? Do you want to break up this family? What has Janaki been telling you?" Her angry eyes searched for Janaki who tactfully avoided her and moved into the confines of the kitchen.

"No, no... mami, Janaki has not been telling me anything," Sadasiva Iyer, his cunning mind at work, quickly composed himself, "What if I send a servant from Trivandrum? An elderly man who can manage the house, cook for you and take care of you both. He will be an additional help around the house."

Meenakshi, her face etched with disapproval, replied, "We don't like food cooked by outsiders. My husband won't like it either."

"No, no, *Mami*, he is a brahmin – a sixty year old widower from Vadakkanchery. He is well known to me and will be willing to come here to be with you. His only son has moved with his family to New Delhi and this man is alone in Trivandrum. He is a homely person. He will only be too glad to come here if I request him What do you say?"

Meenakshi, hesitant yet desperate, reluctantly agreed. She knew she had no choice in the matter. The kitchen was now under the control of Janaki. "But I need someone trustworthy, *Mama*. And let me have a word with Nandini too."

"Sure, he is reliable and will take care of you and Iyer. Also he is a very good cook able to make all our customary dishes. He will be an asset to this household. You will definitely like him"

Meenakshi nodded half reluctantly.

"Don't worry, I will send him at the earliest, before *Pongal* itself if possible." Sadasiva Iyer assured her, glancing over at Janaki, who had now discretely moved into the dining room by his side. She eagerly endorsed the idea vigorously nodding her head.

"Appu — for that is his name, can cook, help around the house, and ensure the safety you desire," Sadasiva Iyer added, his eyes portraying his cunning nature. "He can also take care of Iyer and his needs."

Meenakshi, still reluctant, nodded. "If you say so, *mama*. Okay, let him come. Meanwhile Satya and Janaki will stay here itself. They need not shift anywhere. Janaki will feel relieved if she gets an additional hand to help her in the kitchen. That is enough for the time being." Meenakshi felt that her children were planning to leave one by one like rodents deserting a sinking ship.

The plan set in motion, Janaki looked at her father with a glint of triumph and gratitude. "Send him as soon as possible, *Appa*. I feel unsafe in this house with an alcoholic roaming around." She muttered to her father under her breath. For the time being, at least, problems were settled, she felt.

Meenakshi, however, overhearing the conversation, fell into further despair, her once harmonious home coming apart at the seams. As evening approached, Sadasiva Iyer bid his daughter and Meenakshi goodbye, promising to send the trusted servant Appu, soon.

As he left the house, he promised Janaki, "I'll talk to Satya later over the phone. For the time being take it easy, we will think of a *Thani kudithanam* later."

In the quiet of their bedroom that night, Janaki approached Satya, her eyes shimmering with a secret. "Satya, *Appa* visited today."

Satya, curious, sat up. "Why? What happened? Why didn't he stay?"

Janaki shrewdly avoided telling him that she had called him the day before and told him about the problems here — Arjun's addiction, Anandu's transfer, the ailing oldies and the chaos in this house. "Appa came in the morning and returned by the evening express to

Trivandrum. He just wanted to see *Amma* and *Appa*, to enquire after their health." She had no hesitation in lying about it.

"But what brought him here all of a sudden? It cannot be his concern for *Amma* and *Appa* alone." Satya was persistent. He could see through her clever ruse.

Janaki knew that she could not keep up the pretense anymore.

"I can't manage it all alone here, Satya," Janaki admitted, her voice tinged with urgency. "I told you many times but you do not do anything to solve my problems. Matters seem to go from bad to worse day by day What am I to do?"

"So,...? You called your father?" Satya looked up his face reddening.

"I called *Appa* yesterday and told him to come here and talk to your mother." She went on to narrate the incidents of the day and her father's decision to send Appu, an elderly widower for help around the house. She concluded saying that she could not manage alone with two ailing oldies and a drunkard in the house.

Satya, irked, responded, "So, what do you want *me* to do?"

"I want us to live separately. Appa will send a servant to take care of everything here," Janaki revealed, watching Satya's reaction carefully.

Satya, his temper rising, snapped, "Live separately? Have you lost your mind, Janaki? And calling my parents 'oldies' and my brother a 'drunkard' – that's disrespectful!"

"Don't snap at me, Satya. It's the truth," Janaki retorted, her frustration bubbling to the surface. "I can't live like this. Either take me away from here or do something about it."

"As your father is sending this elderly guy... whatever is his name, let him come. Let things be as of now. We are not leaving..." Satya, miffed, climbed into bed without another word, turned away from her and went to sleep, leaving Janaki alone with the weight of her desires.

As the night deepened, Anantharama Iyer's home remained quiet, concealing secrets and plots that could alter its destiny. The scent of jasmine filled the cool night air and wafted in through the open windows, its sweet fragrance masking Janaki's selfish ambitions and the risks to family unity. The stage was set for manipulation; only time would reveal Janaki's intentions and their consequences.

Chapter 16

It was the first day of the vibrant *Pongal* festival, heralding the *Uttarayanam* season. The sun, on its journey from south to north, cast its benevolent rays upon the house. Tradition dictated that this time was auspicious, a period when divine grace flowed abundantly. Hindus believed that *Bhagawan Vishnu*, after his yogic slumber, awakes during *Uttarayanam*. In the *Mahabharata*, Bhishma, the grand sire who had been felled by Arjuna's arrows, breathed his last and attained *Moksha* during this season. The *Makara Sankranti* day which usually fell on January 14ᵗʰ or 15ᵗʰ, marked the beginning of *Uttarayanam* was celebrated by Tamils as *Pongal*.

The morning sun peeped from amidst the clouds and bathed the *Nalukettu* in a warm glow, signaling the start of a new day. A gentle chill hung in the air, as though the unseen hands of time were reaching out to the aged walls. Birds chirped on the mango tree in the courtyard, their melody welcoming the dawn of a new chapter. January was a relatively cold month. A mild fog hung over the city.

True to tradition, Meenakshi, Nandini, Uma and Janaki awoke early, performed the traditional bath and clad themselves in rustling silk sarees. Anandu from Poona, along with Uma and her two sons, Aadi and Akhil, had joined the household for the festival. The silver *Vilakku* with five wicks flickered in the pooja room, and after a brief ritual, they prepared the '*Pongal*' — a dish made of rice boiled in milk with sugar, offered as *Nivedyam* to the gods. The air was filled with the odor of the festive delicacy. The aroma of powdered cardamom, sprinkled over the Pongal, filled the air in the household, delighting everyone's olfactory senses. The incense from the pooja room assailed the senses and the whole house was bathed in a divine ambience. A sumptuous lunch awaited. Nandini, having taken leave from the hospital, shared the joy as it was a holiday for her daughter Aathira. Satya, too, had secured a day off from his office. It was a memorable get together after a long time.

The morning unfolded in a joyous revelry. Children burst crackers and lit sparklers in the courtyard, their laughter echoing through the house. It seemed as though happiness and joy had returned to the *Nalukettu*, filling the home with the echoes of laughter and vibrant energy. Even Arjun, who had seemed lost the night before, having bathed and sporting the traditional Vibhuti and sandalwood paste on his forehead, joined the children in their playful festivities bursting crackers and lighting sparklers.

Amidst the festivities, Anantharama Iyer, supported by his walking stick, made his way to the verandah. His raucous laughter and toothless grin enlivened the atmosphere. For that moment, it seemed as though the celebrations had given him a new lease on life and made him child-like. Aathira, Akhil, and Aadi reveled in the fireworks, their laughter and enthusiasm adding to the overall jubilation. It was a day filled with shared joy and familial bonds.

The day after Pongal, Anandu and his family who had come on a week's leave left for Coimbatore to visit Uma's parents. Appu mama, the elderly cook and helper sent by Janaki's father, had arrived before Pongal, easing the tension and pressure of the bustling household. Everyone was back to their routine monotonous duties. Nandini resumed her hospital duty the following day as she did not have enough leave to her credit.

As the festivities waned, the house sank back into its previous gloomy nature. On Jan 18th — four days after *Pongal*, on a lovely sunny morning, Anantharama Iyer woke up incredibly early and took a bath.

Meenakshi, surprised at his unusual behavior, teased him, "*Enna Aachu*? Why did you get up so early and bathe?"

"I wanted to read the *Vishnu Sahasranama Stotram,*" he replied with a toothy smile, surprising her. Meenakshi handed him the book with large print, along with his reading glasses, and switched on the overhead lamp.

"*Adisayama Irukku*" she exclaimed laughing.

Reclining in his easy chair, Anantharama Iyer began chanting the slokas in a mumbling tone. After about half an hour, as he completed the recitation, he called out to Meenakshi in a feeble voice, "Meena, can you get me a glass of strong hot coffee? I want you to make it specially for me with your own hands. Add a little extra decoction and extra sugar."

"What happened?" Meenakshi teased smiling at him, "You are behaving like a newlywed bridegroom today!"

Grinning, she brought a flask of steaming hot coffee for him. She sat beside him, pouring the coffee little by little into a steel tumbler, blowing it to cool it down so that he could slowly savor it. She couldn't help but smile at his eagerness to slurp down the warm brew. She sat beside him blithely appreciating him. From time to time, he looked at her face and smiled as if he was seeing her for the first time. Anantharama Iyer handed back the tumbler to her and lay back on the easy chair, closing his eyes and fanning himself rhythmically with his dilapidated handmade palm leaf fan. "Coffee, *nanna irukku,*" he remarked. He gleefully cackled with his customary laughter as he closed his eyes continuing to fan himself.

Within a few minutes, the fan silently slipped from his hand, his hand dropped to his side, and his head rolled to one side. With a deep sigh, he breathed his last. The atmosphere in the room changed instantly, as if time itself paused for a moment.

Meenakshi, realizing something was wrong, exclaimed, "*Enna*?!" Her voice carried a mix of shock and disbelief. She gently shook him, "*Enna, Ezhunthirungo!*" Tears welled up in her eyes as the melancholic truth sank in. "*Ayyo, Ayyo,* Nandini, Satya, Janaki....!" she wailed and sank on to the floor.

In the adjacent room, Janaki heard the commotion and rushed in. "*Amma*, what happened?" she asked, concern etched on her face.

"He's not responding, Janaki. Help me!" Meenakshi's voice trembled.

Janaki checked his pulse and his breath, her face turning pale. "*Amma*, he's gone." She shook her head and burst out in sobs.

Meenakshi clung to Anantharama Iyer's lifeless form, tears streaming down her face. Janaki, and Appu mama stood in shocked silence. Satya was contacted in his office and Nandini rushed home from the hospital. Anandu and family who were in Coimbatore left immediately by road to reach Calicut. Neighbours and relatives began trickling in.

A deep, solemn quiet settled over the house, replacing the earlier sounds of laughter and joy. The warmth seemed to dissipate, leaving behind a heavy sense of loss. Amidst the grieving silence, Arjun, who had been wandering in the background, stood still, absorbing the weight of the moment. He seemed paralyzed with shock.

Appu mama, the elderly help sent by Sadasiva Iyer from Trivandrum, who had seen generations come and go, quickly took charge. "Let's give Anantharama *anna* the farewell he deserves. We'll make the arrangements." He rose to the occasion like an elderly uncle in the family. His avuncular nature had endeared him to all.

The family, enveloped in sorrow, began the process of bidding farewell to Anantharama Iyer, the patriarch of the household. Dialogues were exchanged in hushed tones, words of comfort were shared, and amidst the grief, a sense of togetherness prevailed. Friends, neighbors and relatives began trickling in to offer their condolences.

As the day unfolded into the evening, rituals were performed, prayers were offered, and the house echoed with the chants of the priests in the mourning family. The once-celebratory mood had transformed into a somber atmosphere, a stark contrast to the revelry of just a few days ago. Sreeni phoned from the US expressing his inability to come immediately. Hence the family began the proceedings for the funeral. As the three sons were already there, the funeral was planned for the same evening as is done in Hindu households.

In the dim light of the oil lamps lit around the stately figure of the patriarch, the family gathered for one last look at Anantharama Iyer's peaceful face as he lay in state on the bare floor with his head facing south as the Hindu tradition demanded. The weight of the loss settled on each member, and the reality of the empty easy chair in the living room sank in. The body had been washed and adorned with *Vibhuti* and sandalwood paste. A *Panchagaccham* dhoti with golden braid at the edges was draped around his waist and an *Angavastram* was placed across his shoulders. He looked divine as he lay in state.

The sun was transiently shrouded by a cloud as if it was in mourning over the passing of a great soul. Wreaths and garlands were strewn in the courtyard as the four pallbearers lifted the bamboo bier on their shoulders and made their journey towards the crematorium at Puthiyapalam amidst the sobs of the womenfolk of the household. The children, Akhil, Aadi and Aathira looked on uncomprehendingly at the tragedy happening in the family.

As Anantharama Iyer began his final journey, a chapter closed in the corridors of the ancestral house, leaving behind a legacy of joy, laughter, and the echo of his raucous laughter that once enlivened the atmosphere. The mourning household embraced each other, finding solace in their shared grief, as the echoes of a vibrant life slowly faded into the quiet of the night.

Meenakshi sat alone on the dining room couch, overwhelmed by sorrow. She felt as if a part of her had been taken away, like losing a limb. After sharing over five decades with her husband, it felt as if the light had gone out of her life, leaving her in darkness. "*Ellaam Pocchu!* When will it be my turn?" she whispered to herself as she cried herself to sleep.

Chapter 17

The Iyer household was limping back to normalcy after the storm caused by the death of the patriarch, Anantharama Iyer: but one member refused to sail with the wind – Arjun, the youngest son, felt wronged, as if the very walls of his home conspired against him.

It was a tranquil Sunday morning, the air thick with warmth as the fragrance of freshly brewed filter coffee wafted through the air, saturating the living room with its rich aroma. Satya, a contemplative figure, paced the room with a steaming tumbler of coffee, occasionally sipping its warmth.

After her morning bath, Janaki lit the lamp in the pooja room, carefully adorning it with a garland of jasmine flowers she had plucked from the garden and strung meticulously. A new addition adorned the wall, nestled beside the myriad deities from the Hindu pantheon – a portrait of the late Anantharama Iyer, now festooned with a sweet-smelling jasmine garland. It stood as a sentimental tribute to the patriarch, a towering presence that once held the family together. The lingering scent of incense, lit on the altar in the pooja room, diffused its subtle fragrance, enveloping the entire house.

Nandini had gone to Madras as Rajaram's mother was unwell. His father had passed away five years ago. Aathira was having her school holidays, so Nandini saw this as a good opportunity for a well-deserved break. She took a three-week leave from her position at the medical college to care for her ailing mother in law at Madras.

Arjun was lounging on a well-worn sofa, his thoughts heavy and brooding occasionally mumbling to himself illegibly. Satya, the elder brother, paced with a watchful eye, a silent observer of the emotional undercurrents. The silence pregnant with tension hung heavily between the brothers. Dialogues, though unspoken, lingered in the air, charged with unspoken empathy.

Satya, glancing at Arjun, gently inquired, ""What's troubling you, Arjun?" He seemed a bit subdued this morning.

Arjun, eyes clouded with unspoken turmoil, replied, "It's just… everything feels problematic, *anna*."

The morning unfolded, the familial rituals serving as a gloomy backdrop to the unspoken tension. Janaki, from the kitchen with a grace that only heightened the solemnity, addressed Satya, "Is everything okay with Arjun? He seemed distant. He refused to have his morning cup of coffee."

Satya, a furrow forming on his forehead, responded, "He's going through a rough patch. It's been tough on him. Father's demise seems to have shaken him."

The jasmine garland swayed gently in the pooja room, almost mirroring the delicate balance of emotions in the household. A silence hung in the air, broken only by the occasional sip of coffee by Satya.

As the sun continued its ascent, the living room became a canvas of shadows and sunlight, a reflection of the emotional contrasts within the family. Arjun's brooding figure on the sofa seemed to absorb both the warmth and the shadows.

The door creaked open as Meenakshi, the matriarch of the family entered from her bed room, the bright vermillion bindi on her forehead had now been replaced by a streak of *Vibhuti* — the mark of a Hindu widow. Her eyes, keenly observant, scanned the room before settling on Arjun. "What's going on, Satya? Why does Arjun seem so lost, that too so early in the morning. What happened?"

Satya, struggling to find the right words, replied, "It's complicated, *Amma*. He's grappling with something, and it's affecting all of us. He is refusing to be open with me."

The intricate family relationships were evident in the hushed conversations and meaningful looks. Each person bore hidden worries, bound together in a silent battle.

On that Sunday, the family went through their usual routines, like lighting lamps, making coffee, and having their breakfast like automatons. Everyone could feel the emotions in the air, even though no one talked about them. The family was dealing with some difficult emotional feelings.

Satya finally spoke, his voice clipped. "By the way, Arjun, you can't keep using my scooter without asking. It's not right."

Arjun scoffed, resentment seeping into his tone. "What's the big deal, Anna? It's just a scooter. Why can't I use it?"

Satya's brows furrowed. "It's not about the scooter. It's about respect, about basic courtesy. You can't just take my things without asking me."

Arjun leaned back, a sly smile playing on his lips. "Respect, huh? You want respect, Anna? Why don't you respect my freedom? I'm not a child anymore."

Satya sighed, the weight of responsibility etched on his face. "Arjun, *Appa* authorized me to manage the funds in your name. I have to ensure they're used wisely and not squandered away. I know that is the reason for your anger towards me."

Arjun's eyes flashed with anger. "I don't need your management, *Anna*. I want the right to withdraw my money when I need it. I'm not some charity case. After all, it is my share of the money which *Appa* left me."

Satya shook his head. "It's easy to earn money, Arjun, but exceedingly difficult to manage it and keep it safe. You know, that's what *Appa* used to say always. It is his hard earned money, after all."

The words hung in the air, a silent battlefield between brothers. Meanwhile, the matriarch, Meenakshi, observed from a distance, her eyes reflecting a mixture of sadness and helplessness. She was torn between the affection for her two sons but knew that both of them were right in certain aspects. She remained a silent spectator to the dialogue.

The tension wasn't confined to the brothers. Arjun's relationship with Janaki, Satya's wife, was equally strained. Small sparks between them frequently ignited into squabbles, like flint against steel.

One evening, as Janaki served dinner, Arjun, arriving at an odd hour, couldn't help but create a storm.

"Why can't you come home at normal times, Arjun? Must I always be available to open the door for you? You know that *Amma* cannot always get up to answer the door." Janaki's voice was sharp, irritation dripping from her words. After all she was elder to him in age and hierarchy.

Arjun smirked sarcastically, pushing her buttons. "Oh, poor Janaki *manni*, the guardian of the night. What a burden it must be, to open a simple door."

Satya, who had come down from his room upstairs, intervened, attempting to ease the tension. "Arjun, be respectful. Janaki is managing the house all alone."

Janaki's eyes flared with anger. "I'm not your servant, Arjun. If you can't respect the people in this house, maybe you should leave."

"How can you ask me to leave, *Manni*," Arjun retorted, a cunning smile playing on his lips. "This house belongs to me as much as it does to Satya *anna*."

Janaki left the room offended.

A few days later, a seemingly innocuous dinner escalated into a full-blown confrontation. Janaki, while serving food to Arjun, made a comment as to her inability to work in this house because of the attitude of some people. Arjun became the unwitting target of her pent-up frustration. Arjun, in a fit of frenzy, threw his plate on to the floor. It crashed to the ground, food scattering like broken promises. He stomped out of the room in a huff.

Janaki stormed out, tears streaming down her face. "I won't serve him again. Let him starve to death, for all I care!"

Satya, torn between loyalty to his brother and his wife, tried to console Janaki. "He's going through a rough patch, Janu. Give him some time."

Mother Meenakshi, wailing in the background and choking with emotion clutched her chest. "My heart, it hurts. Oh, God! I am not able to bear all this tension," she said lying in bed.

It was then that Satya decided something needed to change. He spoke to Arjun, urging him to see reason, to mend his ways. He suggested seeing a psychiatrist, as a desperate attempt to salvage what was left of the family.

"Come on, Arjun. Let's go see Dr. Mohsin. He is a well-known psychiatrist. Maybe he can help you," Satya implored. "I will take you to him. I'll fix an appointment tomorrow itself."

Arjun resisted at first, but Satya's persistence and mother's entreaties prevailed. Arjun agreed to accompany Satya for the appointment.

The psychiatrist's office became a confessional, unraveling the tangled threads of the Iyer family's history. Dr. Mohsin, a perceptive man and a seasoned psychiatrist, with an air of calm, listened intently as Arjun's history unfolded. The family background, the habits, the resentments, the love affair with Divya, the business dealings with the KK brothers, the strange whisperings in his ear that he heard warning him of others plotting against him, and his introduction and habituation to alcohol and pot — they spilled like a long-buried secrets from Arjun's bosom.

After thorough questioning and physical examination, Dr. Mohsin diagnosed Arjun with schizophrenia, aggravated by alcohol and cannabis use. The prescription became a lifeline, a beacon of hope in the darkness.

"Don't worry," the doctor assured him, "You can be all right. But there are two important things you must promise me. Firstly, you must take my medicines properly at the right times. Secondly, you must say goodbye to alcohol and ganja forever. They can worsen your mental problems and disturb your mental balance."

Arjun silently nodded.

"A mere nod isn't enough. I need a definite and absolute commitment from you that you won't touch alcohol or ganja again. Only then can I guarantee an improvement in your clinical condition." The doctor was persistent.

"I'll quit them, doctor," Arjun replied.

Satya thanked Dr. Mohsin and both of them returned home.

Back home, Meenakshi addressed Arjun sternly in the privacy of her bedroom as Arjun sat at the foot of her bed. "I want you to become normal, get a good job, and then get married. Can you promise me that, Arjun? You should be normal like your brothers and be successful in your line of work. Don't waste away your life in such useless pursuits."

"Arjun, in today's world you have to be extremely careful when you deal with people especially if you want to be in the field of business. I would like to share some advice tailored to the challenges you might face, even though I have not been very experienced in these matters. But two things that should guide you are our culture and common sense."

"First and foremost, always stay true to your values and beliefs. Don't go against our cultural beliefs and morals. Be careful to surround yourself with friends who uplift and support you — they're your tribe. Choose your friends very carefully. Remember, effective communication is the key to success in life; hence learn to be careful in what you say. Listen actively to others and think well before you react. Learn to manage your emotions wisely. Don't allow your emotions to cloud your judgment or lead you astray.. Don't get into unnecessary conflicts; Always try to seek peaceful resolutions for problems."

"Financial prudence is crucial. When it comes to money be responsible. Save and invest wisely, steer clear of debt, and cultivate good financial habits from the get-go. That is how your father was able to be successful while in Burma. He used to say these things always. Try to be like him and follow his footsteps."

"These are the most essential qualities for confidently and gracefully navigating the complexities of your life. Arjun *kanna*, heed these words with care and diligence; they serve as a compass guiding you

131

through life's myriad challenges. These are pieces of advice which Appa gave your brothers and sister. You were not there then."

Arjun listened to her intently and then with a bit of hesitation, brought up a new topic. "There's something I need to tell you *Amma*... about a girl I really like. And, well, she likes me too." He took his time, explaining to her all about Divya, her family, and the long-term connection they shared.

Meenakshi listened attentively, a mix of surprise , curiosity and shock in her eyes. "Divya, you say. Tell me more, Arjun. How did you two meet?"

Arjun, a hint of a smile playing on his lips, unfolded the story. "We met at college, *Amma*. She was my classmate. She's from a good family, and we've known each other for a while now. I thought you should know. She is a Malayalee — a *Nair*."

Meenakshi was torn between her affection for her son and the problems which such an alliance could cause.

Meenakshi, nodding thoughtfully, asked, "What are your plans, Arjun? Do you see a future with Divya?"

Arjun, his eyes reflecting determination, replied, "I do, Amma. She's a wonderful person, and we understand each other well. I want to build a life with her. You will also like her."

'But she is not our caste." Meenakshi, subtly hinted. "What will your brothers and our relatives say?"

"But she is a Hindu, *Amma*," retorted Arjun, "None of you objected to it when Sreeni *anna* came up with the proposal to marry Mamta *manni*. So, how can you all stand in my way?"

Meenakshi was at a loss to reply. She kept silent for a minute. Then, Meenakshi, her worries giving way to understanding, offered a gentle smile. "Well, Arjun, if you're happy and she's a good person, I trust your judgment. But remember, relationships come with responsibilities. Unless you mend your ways, marriage with Divya is out of the question."

Arjun, appreciating his mother's support, assured, "I know, *Amma*. I want to make things work, for both of us. I will change, definitely."

Their conversation continued, each word weaving an array of emotions. The hesitant revelation by Arjun transformed into a heartfelt dialogue between the two, deepening the connection between a mother and son.

The proposition regarding Divya stirred conversations between Satya, Janaki, and Meenakshi. They initially objected to the relationship, but eventually, they acquiesced, but with a condition—Arjun needed to change. He needs to stop behaving recklessly and give up his addictive habits. There was to be no compromise on that.

"First, change yourself, Arjun. For the next three months, stay away from drugs and alcohol. Take Dr. Mohsin's medications regularly. Be at home," Meenakshi instructed.

For a brief period, it seemed like Arjun was turning a new leaf. The medications cast a temporary spell, bringing a semblance of normalcy to the Iyer household and to Arjun's behaviour.

But this was short-lived.

Meanwhile, Nandini returned from Madras with Aathira to rejoin her post in the medical college. Though initially shocked to hear about Divya, she agreed with Meenakshi that if it would change Arjun for the better, it was an acceptable proposal.

Old habits die hard. A few days later, the magnetic pull of his past led Arjun back to the KK brothers. They invited him for a meeting, a clandestine gathering in their outhouse on a Saturday evening.

"I'm on medication. No alcohol or drugs," Arjun insisted.

The KK brothers exchanged sly glances. "Sure, Arjun. No alcohol, no drugs. We respect that."

In the dimly lit outhouse, Arjun was handed a glass of what seemed like fruit juice. Without his knowledge, it was laced with vodka. After two glasses, the room started to sway, the world becoming blurry.

"They won't know. Just one cigarette, Arjun. It's not laced with anything — it's a simple cigarette," one of the KK brothers whispered.

The ganja hit Arjun like a freight train. The psychiatric medications and the vodka intertwined, a lethal disco that left him disoriented and confused.

He stumbled home at 11 pm, a disheveled figure. Mother Meenakshi opened the door, shock etched on her face. "What happened to you, Arjun?"

"I'm sorry, *Amma*," he said and staggered to his room, leaving the unanswered question hanging in the air. His addiction, once tamed, roared back with a vengeance. He had slithered down to square one in this treacherous game of snakes 'n' ladders.

Despite Satya and Nandini's sincere attempts to communicate with him, Arjun's mind remained a fortress, impervious to external influence. Dr. Mohsin's prescribed treatment, unfortunately, proved ineffective, unable to work its expected magic. In a distressing turn of events, Arjun, already grappling with his mental health, exacerbated the situation by combining his medications with alcohol and cannabis. This lethal concoction heightened his schizophrenic symptoms to a distressing peak.

As time progressed, the Iyer household transformed into an emotional battlefield, where the warmth of affection gradually gave way to the chill of anger and mutual resentment. Attempts at persuasion morphed into a frustrating struggle. The once-strong bonds within the family now seemed irreparably fractured. Arjun, caught in the chaos of his inner struggles, felt himself sinking deeper into his personal challenges.

Satya, ever concerned for his brother, earnestly pleaded with Arjun, "You need to understand, Arjun, the path you're on is destructive. The medications are meant to help you, not work against you."

Nandini, her eyes reflecting empathy, added, "Arjun, we're here for you. You don't have to face this alone. Let us help you."

Despite their genuine efforts, Arjun's response was a hardened resolve. "You don't get it. None of you do. This is my battle, and I'll fight it my way. You are all against me!" he shouted ; his paranoia overshadowing his sanity.

Days passed in a never-ending cycle of emotional upheaval, as every effort to connect with Arjun was met with opposition. The laughter and warmth that once filled the home now felt like distant echoes. Amidst this chaos, Arjun's journey into his own struggles persisted without pause.

The matriarch, Meenakshi, approached Arjun with a mixture of concern and sadness. "*Kanna*, we want to help you. There's a way to find peace, but you need to let us in."

Arjun, seemingly distant, responded with a bitter edge, "I don't need anyone's help *Amma*. I can handle my own life."

The air in the household grew heavy with unspoken words and unresolved tensions. Satya, sharing a concerned glance with Nandini and his mother, spoke softly, "Arjun, we're not your enemies. Let us be your allies in this battle." Despite heartfelt pleas, the emotional divide grew wider. Kind gestures were met with Arjun's icy anger, and all efforts to reach out were blocked by the walls of isolation he had built around himself. The family members, once close-knit, now found themselves on opposite sides of a painful conflict, with Arjun in the midst, fighting not only his mental health but also the isolation he had embraced.

In this sad situation, Meenakshi watched helplessly as the family bonds weakened. Everyone struggled with their own feelings of powerlessness in dealing with Arjun's inner struggles. It seemed as though a profound void was expanding, consuming not only Arjun but also eroding the unity that had once bound the family together.

Meanwhile, Meenakshi's health was deteriorating and her nocturnal breathlessness was giving her trouble incessantly. She had to be hospitalized frequently for nebulization, intravenous medication and oxygen therapy. However, the family was not prepared for another shock, catching everyone off guard, especially Meenakshi. It came in the form of a phone call from Rajaram, Nandini's husband in Australia.

Chapter 18

Nandini's heart weighed heavily as she walked through the gloomy corridors of the hospital. The acrid smell of disinfectant and the low hum and beep of medical equipment formed a dissonant symphony, a constant reminder of her mother's progressively deteriorating health. Meenakshi lay in the sterile white hospital bed, a frail figure surrounded by machines and tubes, her once vibrant eyes now puffy and dimmed by the weight of illness. The bleep of a cardiac monitor added a background rhythm to the silence that prevailed.

"Nandu, my child, come closer," Meenakshi beckoned weakly, her voice barely audible above the soft beeping of the monitors. Nandini approached, her eyes brimming with concern and weariness.

"*Amma*, how are you feeling?" Nandini inquired, her voice tinged with a genuine concern. "Would you like me to prepare a glass of soothing Horlicks for you?"

Meenakshi wearily shook her head, letting out a heavy sigh, her eyes searching Nandini's face for the reassurance that seemed elusive. "I am tired, Nandu. The recurrent chest pain is simply unbearable. But what choice do we have? Such is the price we pay for a lifetime filled with both joys and sorrows. I don't know why God is tormenting me like this. I don't think that I have long to live."

With a tender touch, Nandini tried to comfort her mother. "*Amma*, don't worry. We can go to Madras, to a multispecialty hospital there, and have you undergo further investigations. If necessary, we can explore surgery or angioplasty options available. Please don't worry; you'll be all right."

Meenakshi vehemently shook her head, her resolve unwavering. "No, Nandu, I don't desire any investigations or interventions. I've already conveyed this to all of you. Don't insist. I am old, and I've nearly fulfilled all my duties towards my children. My only concern is Arjun. He hasn't returned to his usual normal self. I fear leaving this world without ensuring my duty towards him is complete. That's my sole regret." Tears streamed down her cheeks, mirroring the depth of her concern.

"Don't fret, *Amma*. Satya and I will look after him. I am confident he will regain his senses and return to a normal life. You can trust us, *Amma*," Nandini reassured, her words carrying a soothing tone.

"I fear I might die before witnessing that brighter day," Meenakshi remarked tearfully, her heart laid bare with the weight of her emotions.

Nandini nodded in understanding, swallowing the lump in her throat. The emotional toll of witnessing her mother's vulnerability was almost overwhelming. Gently, she cradled Meenakshi's frail hand in her own, offering the solace of her touch. "*Amma*, you've been the anchor of our lives. We'll overcome these problems together,"

The room felt filled with unspoken emotions, creating an atmosphere that demanded empathy and understanding. Nandini, torn between her roles as a caring daughter, a responsible doctor and a practical analytical person, endeavored to strike a delicate balance in her words and actions.

"*Amma*, let me make you comfortable," Nandini suggested, adjusting the pillows behind her mother. "I know it's not easy, but we're in this together."

Meenakshi managed a weak smile, gratitude reflecting in her eyes. "Nandu, my child, your care means the world to me. I've always known you'd be the strength we need."

As the day unfolded, the conversations between Nandini and Meenakshi turned towards shared memories and unspoken fears. Every word was heavy with meaning, and every action tried to make the pain in the room better.

"Nandu," Meenakshi's voice trembled as she broke the silence, "Promise me one thing."

Nandini leaned in, her eyes meeting her mother's with unwavering attention. "Anything, *Amma*. You know I'll do whatever it takes."

Meenakshi took a deep breath, her gaze unwavering. "Look after your siblings, Nandu. They need your strength now more than ever. I trust you to be their pillar of support, especially Arjun. Anandu has left to pursue his own interests. Sreeni is completely disconnected from the family, having established his own life in America and showing little concern for what occurs here. Satya desires to remain connected to the family, but Janaki and her personal pursuits obstruct him. He finds himself torn between two responsibilities. Both he and Janaki prioritize their own self-centered interests. Moreover, it pains me to observe that he pays greater heed to the counsel of his father in law than he does to us."

Nandini was surprised at how Meenakshi had so correctly assessed each one's nature. She nodded solemnly, the weight of her mother's trust settling upon her shoulders. "I promise, *Amma*. I'll be there for them, just as you've been for me. Don't worry."

As the night wore on, the hospital room became a sanctuary for shared reflections and unspoken love. In the subtle exchanges of words and glances, Nandini found solace in the connection that bound them. The journey ahead was uncertain, but in that moment, surrounded by the echoes of a lifetime, they found strength in each other's company.

Satya sat in the corner of the room, his eyes reflecting a mix of exhaustion and frustration. His strained relationship with Nandini and his refusal to contribute to the treatment of his mother had only intensified with Meenakshi's frequent hospitalizations. He could not bear sharing the hospital expenses. The burden of medical expenses weighed heavily on Nandini, and Satya remained adamant in his disregard to contribute to the medical expenses.

"My salary is just adequate to cater to Janaki's and my expenses. I am helping with running the household also, you must know," was Satya's excuse.

"Satya, please," Nandini implored, her eyes pleading with him." I cannot bear all the expenses alone. We need to share this responsibility. It's our mother's health at stake. All of you think that being a doctor, I have enough money for everything. People hardly realize that a government doctor in this country is underpaid and overworked."

Satya scoffed, his irritation evident in his curt response. "You are the doctor, Nandini. It's your job to take care of her. And remember, our parents have contributed more to your education than they have to mine. I have my own expenses, my own dreams. I cannot keep pouring money into this endless pit of hospital bills."

Nandini's frustration bubbled beneath the surface, but she chose to remain composed. The atmosphere suddenly felt suffocating, fueled by resentment and helplessness.

Just as Nandini grappled with the mounting challenges, a sudden turn of events altered the course of her life. A phone call from Australia brought unexpected hope amidst the prevailing darkness. It was a message from her husband, Rajaram — one of hope and despair at the same time. It was with mixed feelings that Nandini reacted to the message.

"Hello, Nandini. It's me. I have some good news," Rajaram's voice crackled through the phone, breaking the oppressive silence.

Nandini listened eagerly as Rajaram revealed the unexpected news. He shared the glad news that he had sent a visa, for both her and

Aathira to visit Australia. A prospect had emerged offering a golden opportunity to write the test of the Australian Medical Council (AMC) and embark on a fresh career move in a distant land. This opportunity, a cherished dream of hers, had materialized, presenting a chance to fulfill aspirations she had long held.

Nandini had nurtured dreams of furthering her studies in Australia, particularly specializing in Gynecologic Oncology – a burgeoning field in her medical field. The prospect of overseas training had been a fervent desire, and now, as the news sunk in, conflicting emotions brewed within her. She faced a difficult decision: should she prioritize caring for her sick mother or pursue her dream of joining a Fellowship in Australia? She grappled with the dichotomy between the hope and joy of realizing her dreams and the heart-wrenching reality of leaving behind her ailing mother and her wayward brother, Arjun.

"Rajaram, are you serious?" Nandini's eyes widened with a mix of disbelief and excitement.

Rajaram continued, "It's a golden opportunity, Nandini. You can pursue your dreams, and Aathira can start her school anew in a different environment."

As the significance of the moment unfolded, Nandini felt a surge of conflicting emotions. Her dream of studying abroad, especially in a field she was enthusiastic about – Gynecologic Oncology, seemed like the stars aligning. However, the weight of responsibilities at home, with her mother's fragile health and Arjun's unpredictable behavior, threatened to eclipse the joyous prospect.

"This is incredible, Nandini! Just imagine the opportunities awaiting you," Rajaram exclaimed, trying to infuse optimism into the moment.

Nandini, however, still remained torn, her thoughts drifting to her mother. "But *Amma*... What about her? And Arjun... he's not stable. How can I leave them alone?"

Rajaram's expression shifted, understanding the gravity of Nandini's concerns. "Nandini, I know it's not easy. But this is a chance of a lifetime. You've sacrificed enough. It's time to think about yourself and your future – our future, our daughter's future. Last time itself you missed the chance when I sent you the tickets because *Amma* fell ill and was hospitalized with a heart attack. Satya and Janaki are there.

Moreover, Appu *mama* is there to help them. They should be able to manage in your absence."

As the reality of the situation settled in, Nandini found herself at crossroads. On one hand, the allure of fulfilling her dreams and advancing her career beckoned from across the seas. On the other, the obligations and emotional ties tethering her to her ailing mother and the challenges at home rooted her firmly in the present.

"Think about it, Nandini. Australia could open doors you've only dreamed of," Rajaram added, his words hanging in the air, emphasizing the potential that lay ahead.

Nandini nodded slowly, her mind a whirlwind of conflicting thoughts. She found herself standing on the precipice of a life-altering decision, one that promised personal growth but demanded a painful sacrifice.

"*Amma* must understand, Nandu. It's a chance that might not come again so easily," Rajaram urged, his voice tinged with a mix of urgency and reassurance. "Talk to her and convince her," Rajaram said. "I'm sending the visa by express post. Make arrangements, Nandini. Apply for leave from the medical college, get a TC for Aathira. We can sort everything out once you're here," Rajaram's urgency echoed in his words. "This is your best chance, Nandini. Don't pass it up."

As the weight of the decision settled upon her, Nandini felt an unspoken dilemma. The opportunity to carve a new path beckoned, but the emotional ties binding her to her family tugged at her heartstrings. In the ensuing days, she found herself engaged in heartfelt conversations with her mother, handling the delicate balance between personal aspirations and familial responsibilities. Nandini thought that her mother would be dismayed on hearing the news. But she was in for a surprise.

"*Amma*, I know I've always been by your side, but this chance... it's something I've waited for," Nandini confessed, her voice filled with a blend of hope and guilt. "But at the same time, I don't know how I can leave you in this present state."

Meenakshi, though frail, understood the significance of the situation. She placed her hand on Nandini's head, "Nandu, my child, life offers such chances rarely. Don't let this slip away. I'll be fine. Take this opportunity for yourself. Go to Australia and create a life alongside Rajaram for yourself and Aathira. My blessings are always with you. Last time when we planned a trip there, I fell ill and upset all your plans. Don't miss this golden chance." She understood that it was time to let go her daughter.

The room became a refuge for emotions as Nandini found herself torn between embarking on a new journey and holding onto her familiar life. She yearned to pursue her dreams yet longed for the comfort of home and the duties she held dear. As Nandini pondered this unexpected crossroads, the weight of her family responsibilities bore down heavily upon her. With ailing mother, troubled brother, and resentful sister-in-law, her fractured family teetered on the brink of collapse.

The Iyer household had become a battleground of conflicting emotions. Satya's frustration mingled with Janaki's growing resentment, and Arjun's unruly behaviour clashed with Nandini's internal turmoil. Satya felt deeply upset upon hearing the news. He realized that he would now be responsible for taking care of his mother and managing the household. Additionally, he dreaded Janaki's response to this news.

Days passed, and as Nandini prepared for her impending journey, Meenakshi called her to her bedside. The air in the room felt heavy with the weight of unspoken farewells.

"Nandini, my child, sit with me," Meenakshi whispered, her eyes searching Nandini's face. "I know I may not have much time left. I need you to do something for me."

Nandini hesitated, her heart heavy with the realization of her mother's impending farewell. "*Amma*, don't say that. You'll be fine," Nandini nodded, holding back tears. "Anything, *Amma*. I will do whatever you ask."

Meenakshi requested Nandini to retrieve the jewelry box she had recently brought from the bank and placed in the safe. She had not yet found time to return it to the bank.

"These are for my five children," she said, "Get me five small boxes and label them with their names. I will put the jewelry for each of them in the respective boxes. I will also leave a sealed envelope with you containing the list of the ornaments for each one of you. Open it only when the time comes. I want you to keep the five boxes back in the bank locker tomorrow itself. You will be the one to operate it. You need not inform the others about this for the time being."

Meenakshi smiled weakly. "Life is uncertain, Nandini. Promise me you'll do this for me."

Nandini nodded solemnly and hugged her mother, her throat tight with unshed tears. "I promise, Amma. I'll take care of everything."

The day of departure arrived, casting a somber shadow over the household. Satya, Janaki, and Arjun moved about with a palpable tension, the absence of Nandini already being felt like an unspoken void in the family.

As Nandini hugged her mother goodbye, Meenakshi whispered, "Take care, my child. And remember, your home will always be here."

Nandini took a moment to bid farewell to Satya and Janaki. Conversations with Anandu and Uma had transpired over the phone the previous day, and she had relayed her decision to Sreeni a week ago during their conversation. Now, as she confronted Arjun, a wave of emotions washed over her, and tears welled in her eyes.

"Arjun, please, return to the person you used to be. Listen to *Amma* and Satya – I have no more words left for you," Nandini implored her younger brother tousling his hair affectionately, her voice tinged with a mixture of concern and frustration.

Arjun, overwhelmed by the weight of the moment, broke into tears. "*Akka*, you're the only one in this house who understands me. And now, you're also leaving. I feel like an orphan here." His sobs echoed through the room, his vulnerability laid bare like that of a child seeking comfort.

Nandini, despite her own emotional turmoil, embraced Arjun, offering solace as tears streaked down her cheeks. At that emotional

143

moment, their family bond provided solace as they shared their sorrow. Little Aathira, caught in the crossfire of emotions, stood silently, torn between the excitement of joining her father in Australia and the heartache of bidding farewell to her dear *Ammamma* and others. The ancestral household, a witness to shared joys and sorrows, now bore witness to a farewell steeped in intense emotions.

"Goodbye *Mama*," she tugged at Arjun's shirt as he passionately hugged her. "Be good *Kutty*," he smiled amidst tears. "I don't know when I will see you again."

"Good bye *mama* and *mami*," she smiled waving to Satya and Janaki, who hugged her affectionately.

The air in the house vibrated with the heaviness of unspoken sentiments. The upcoming departure created a deeply emotional atmosphere, evoking a range of feelings within the old family home.

"Arjun, my brother, take care of the house and *Amma*. I trust you to be the anchor in my absence," Nandini said, her words carrying a weight of responsibility.

Arjun, wiping away his tears, nodded solemnly. "I'll try, *akka*. But it will never be the same without you."

During the goodbyes and heartfelt hugs, the house resounded with a mix of happy and sad feelings as things changed. Every part of the house was filled with memories of joy and stories shared, now marked with the sadness of leaving.

As Nandini stepped out into a new chapter in her life, the legacy of her family's struggles clung to her like a familiar companion. The journey ahead promised new beginnings, yet the echoes of the past lingered in the recesses of her heart. With a heavy heart, Nandini left her home behind, carrying the weight of her family's troubles in her heart. Australia beckoned her, offering a chance for a new beginning, but the echoes of her family's struggles persisted in her heart.

Chapter 19

In the softly lit hall of Kuttykrishnan Nair's outhouse, the scent of aged wood and hushed conversations filled the air. Dim twilight peeked through the dusty curtains, casting a subdued light on old wooden furniture that had been witness to countless secrets. The room felt secretive, its walls embellished with traditional South Indian tapestries, hiding the ominous intentions that dwelled within.

A large, ornate wooden table stood at the center, on which were spread out maps of India, and the states of Kerala and Punjab, highlighting the intricacies of the smuggling route. Multiple colored marker pins marked certain spots on the maps, indicating towns and villages in the route between the two states. The aged parqueted wooden floor creaked beneath the weight of the conspirators, their hushed discussions masked by the ambient sounds of the imminent night.

In the absence of electrical power owing to the power cut which was regular in Kerala, dimly flickering candles cast elongated shadows on the ancient walls, masking the trio – Sukumaran, Divakaran and Mohandas, in a mood of deception. The atmosphere of the room mirrored their deceitful expressions as they plotted the details of their secret scheme.

In one corner, a vintage globe gathered dust, symbolizing the vast expanse of their illegal trade. The room's temperature fluctuated, mirroring the heated discussions that unfolded within its confines, the discussion taking them further into the realm of illicit gains.

The subtle aroma of tobacco filled the room, merging with the underlying scent of anticipation. A worn-out Persian rug hugged the floor, bearing silent testimony to the countless intrigues that had transpired upon its intricate patterns. The room's windows, draped in moth-eaten curtains, allowed minimal light to seep through, shrouding the conspirators in an atmosphere of mystery.

In one corner of the room, an antique wooden chest stood open, revealing bundles of currency – the initial capital for their nefarious venture. The room, a stage for their plotting, harbored within its weathered walls the plans for a budding criminal enterprise. In the sparsely lit room adorned with vintage wooden furniture and the distinct aroma of whisky which perfused the air, Sukumaran poured himself a drink from the side table, his eyes reflecting the amber liquid. Divakaran reclined on a cushioned chair, his eyes narrowing with curiosity. Across the table, Mohandas, the mastermind behind their ambitious plan, leaned forward, a glint of cunning in his eyes, explaining his plans.

The room filled with the sound of glasses clinking as Sukumaran raised his drink, saying, "Here's to a successful venture, bros! May we have much wealth in our pockets."

Divakaran chuckled and responded, "My friend. True wealth lies in the favorable outcome of this endeavor. If successful, it will yield unexpected results."

Mohandas, the orchestrator of their clandestine plot, smiled with satisfaction, "Indeed! Imagine the riches flowing in like a river, and no one suspecting a thing. We'll be kings in our own right within a short while."

Meanwhile, Elias, their loyal servant, moved silently, placing a tray of crispy snacks before them. The trio fell silent till Elias left the room. The clinking glasses paused momentarily for the servant to withdraw before Mohandas continued, "Now, listen carefully. We'll be bringing in the ganja from Punjab, concealed in the guise of fertilizer. The trucks will be our carriers, each bearing the key to our fortunes."

Mohandas added, "In a recent development, a new substance has emerged on the market, bearing the nickname 'Ecstasy'. This particular compound, true to its name, purportedly instills a profound sense of euphoria in those who partake, even in minuscule doses. However, the cost of obtaining this sensation is exorbitant, rendering it a luxury beyond the reach of many. Although it's expensive, we're drawn to it because it offers the chance to make a lot of money. It's tempting because we could potentially earn huge profits. It can be sold to the high-worth individuals who can easily be hooked on to it. This drug will also be added to our consignment of cannabis."

"But how do we conceal it in our trucks?" Sukumaran was curious.

Mohandas continued, "Each truckload is carrying about two hundred large bags of fertilizer at present. Secretly nestled within two of these bags, we'll cleverly conceal twenty small packets of cannabis and Ecstasy in each bag. These will be placed inside the polypropylene bags bearing the name of the fertilizer manufacturing company. The bags will bear labels proclaiming their contents as fertilizer, a camouflage to deter any suspicion."

"Underneath the bulk of the fertilizer bags, our hidden packets will remain undetected. This strategic concealment ensures that our clandestine operation remains unseen, allowing us to slip through the eyes of scrutiny without a hint of suspicion. What's more, the overpowering pungent smell emitted by the fertilizer serves as our shield, expertly masking any trace of the distinct cannabis aroma. Even the keen senses of a police sniffer dog, trained to detect illicit substances, will be confounded by the potent odor of the fertilizer. This guarantees that our shipments remain secure during transit, evading any unwanted attention from law enforcement."

"But how do we recognize these two bags if they look like the other bags of fertilizer?" Divakaran interposed a question.

"No problem," Mohandas was ready with the answer. "These two bags will have secret markings on the outside which will be known only to us. This will help us to identify the bags easily from the rest of the lot."

"Each truckload, carefully laden with this deceptive cargo, becomes capable of transporting two bags with our hidden stuff. It's a meticulous plan that not only ensures our products reach their destination but also safeguards our operation from prying eyes."

"But what happens when these packets reach Calicut?" Sukumaran inquired.

"Don't fret. They won't make it to Calicut," Mohandas assured him, a smile playing on his lips. "'They'll be intercepted along the way before the trucks arrive at Calicut and removed."

"Where? How will you intercept them?" Divakaran's curiosity was piqued.

"I'll keep that information to myself. The less you know, the safer it is for both of you," Mohandas replied enigmatically. "Initially we'll bring two such bags in each truckload of fertilizer. Later on we can increase the number of bags to three or four depending on the demand and availability of the stuff."

"As part of our scheme, I've already secured a network of distributors poised to handle the sale of our concealed cargo. We will have nothing to do with them. They will not know who their suppliers are. All this will be handled through two middlemen who are loyal and sworn to secrecy. This strategic move thus ensures that our involvement remains confined to the shadows, sparing us the risk associated with street-level transactions. Hence, each link in the chain will not be aware who the others are. This assures anonymity for us."

"Our venture, thus remains shrouded in secrecy. It's a business strategy that hinges on discretion, allowing us to navigate the treacherous waters of illicit trade with finesse and precision undetected by the prying eyes of the authorities." Mohandas concluded with a flourish emptying his glass.

Divakaran smirked, "Cannabis with the scent of fertilizer! Genius, Mohandas! Even a police dog won't catch wind of our little secret. You are a criminal genius, Dasa!"

Sukumaran, ever the skeptic, raised an eyebrow, "And how do we get the initial capital for this grand scheme? You mentioned fifteen lakhs, but we can only manage ten at present. Where will the rest come from?"

Mohandas leaned back, swirling his second drink, "Ah, my brothers, that's where our friend Arjun comes in. His father has passed away, leaving behind a fortune. We can convince him to invest five lakhs as a silent partner. The rest of the amount we have here in this chest," he said pointing to the chest in the corner.

"But remember," he continued, "Arjun should never discover the true nature of our business. That should remain a secret strictly among the three of us."

Sukumaran interjected, "Arjun? But why would he invest in such a risky venture?"

"He's dependent on us now, isn't he?" Mohandas replied with a sly grin. "We have him in our grip. By the way, do you know that he's in a relationship with Sadanandan's sister, Divya, which I came to understand recently."

Divakaran's eyes widened in surprise, "Sadanandan's sister? That's quite the connection. We must handle this delicately, Mohandas. Sadanandan is well known to us too."

"Sadanandan holds a special place in my heart; not just as a friend but also as a fellow member of our shared political journey. We've stood shoulder to shoulder, moving through the rough terrains of both friendship and politics. Politics may be our common ground, but it's the trust we share that makes our friendship enduring." Mohandas commented. "He was the one who told me about Arjun and Divya. His revelation about his sister's relationship with Arjun came as a surprise to me!"

"Let us plan to invite Arjun for a meeting and a celebration here. We'll make him an offer he can't refuse. Just be cautious, my friends. We need him, but we can't let him become a liability," Mohandas declared. "We'll tell him the bare minimum to tempt him to invest in our venture; nothing about the Punjab connection or the packets in our truck loads. We'll talk to him about the fertilizer business only."

The room buzzed with excitement as they discussed the details of their nefarious plan. As the night deepened, Elias served them dinner, and blended seamlessly into the background.

A few days later, the atmosphere in the outhouse living room was filled with anticipation. The brothers, dressed up in traditional dhotis, awaited Arjun's arrival. Mohandas, the puppet master, sat on the sofa, a confident smile playing on his lips. "Suku, you must broach the

149

subject to Arjun as he trusts you most. He considers you like his elder brother."

The door creaked open, revealing Arjun's nervous countenance. "Hi, friends! What is this grand celebration about?"

Sukumaran stood up, embracing Arjun warmly, "Our dear friend, we have a proposal for you. Something that could change your fortunes." Sukumaran, unlike Mohandas, had a real fondness for Arjun because he remembered him from their college days as a sincere and innocent person.

Arjun's eyes flickered with curiosity, "What is it?"

As they settled around the table, Sukumaran laid out the plan. He spoke with conviction, "Arjun, my boy, we're on the brink of a lucrative business opportunity – a venture that promises wealth beyond your imagination."

"We are planning to expand our fertilizer business and propose to extend our reach to Punjab in addition to Gujarat. This will almost double our profits... But there is a small catch," he paused significantly.

"What is it?" Arjun's interest was aroused.

Sukumaran added, "We need an initial investment of fifteen lakhs. This is an opportunity for you to pitch in. Among the three of us, we have managed to raise ten lakhs. You'll be a silent partner and when the profits start rolling in, you'll be counting money as we count our blessings. Your share will be five lakhs."

Arjun hesitated, glancing at the faces around the table. Mohandas leaned in, "Think of it, Arjun. A golden opportunity to secure your future. And besides, we're family now."

"But what is this new business, Suku *Etta*?" Arjun questioned, a hint of suspicion in his eyes.

Mohandas smiled reassuringly, "It's the same fertilizer business, my friend. We're expanding our ventures and extending it to Punjab also. You know how profitable that can be. Later on we plan to extend it to the North-east also."

Arjun pondered, "I need time to think about this. It's a significant amount. I have to ask my brother, Satya."

Mohandas carefully filled a glass with a soothing drink for Arjun, his eyes reflecting false empathy. "Take as much time as you need, Arjun. We have complete faith in you. However, it's crucial to realize that you can't always rely on your brother Satya's financial guidance. At some point, you must start making decisions on your own. After all, it's your father's hard-earned money that Satya is currently overseeing for you, isn't that right?" Mohandas shared these words, accompanied by a subtle glance in Arjun's direction with the corner of his eye, conveying both concern and a hint of cunning.

Arjun, feeling the weight of responsibility, took a sip of the drink and let out a deep sigh. "I know, Das *Etta*, it's just that managing this wealth feels overwhelming at times. Father entrusted it to me, and I want to honor that trust, but it's not as easy as it seems."

Sukumaran leaned back, his expression understanding. "I know Arjun. Managing substantial wealth comes with its challenges and responsibilities. However, remember that everyone, including Satya, started somewhere. It's about finding your footing and gaining confidence in your decisions. You must begin taking your own decisions."

Arjun stared into his glass, contemplating Sukumaran's words. "I guess you're right. I need to step up and take control. But what if I make the wrong choices? What if I let my father down?"

Sukumaran placed a reassuring hand on Arjun's shoulder. "Mistakes are part of the journey, Arjun. Your father believed in your ability to learn and grow. You have a support system here, and we'll guide you through it. Don't worry. We are there always for you. We'll help you manage your money."

Encouraged, Arjun nodded. "You're right, Suku *Etta*. I need to trust myself more and learn from the experiences, both good and bad. I'll talk to Satya *Anna*."

Sukumaran smiled warmly. "That's the spirit, Arjun. We're here for you every step of the way. And remember, your father's legacy lives on through you. Make decisions that reflect his values and your own. You cannot go wrong."

As the conversation unfolded, the air in the room became charged with a sense of shared responsibility and understanding, fostering an atmosphere where Arjun felt supported in his journey toward financial independence. Little did Arjun suspect that he was being driven towards a catastrophe by this trio who had nothing but their own interests at heart.

As the night progressed, laughter and friendship filled the room. The brothers cleverly hid their real motives, ensnaring Arjun with their convincing charm. Unaware, he found himself on his fourth glass of whisky.

A few days later, a storm brewed within the Iyer household. Anandu had come from Poona on a weekend to attend the marriage of his friend's brother in Calicut. He had come alone. That evening, Arjun confronted the brothers, as they sat in the hall, a mixture of anger and betrayal in his eyes, "All of you are tricking me. Father has left me enough funds, but neither of you are allowing me to access that. You are probably embezzling those funds."

"Arjun, why are you speaking like this," Anandu remarked trying to pacify him. "If you need money ask me or Satya. Satya is only helping you by taking care of the funds for you."

"Arjun, don't unnecessarily blame me. I do not want your money. I am doing what *Appa* asked me to do – to look after your funds till you become responsible enough to handle them on your own." Satya burst in anger.

"Why do you think that I am not old enough or responsible enough to handle my own money? I need money to invest in a business."

"Is it the one with those *Kurukankaattil* brothers?" Satya asked.

"Yes, I want five lakhs as initial investment. They are expanding their business and have promised to include me as a partner. I want to join them."

"Do you think that this is a good idea?" Satya asked skeptically. "Those guys do not have a good reputation, I hear."

"Why do you think so? I am not a fool to squander away *Appa's* money. It is a promising investment and will fetch good returns, I am sure. Don't unnecessarily stand in my way." Arjun became belligerent.

Satya in a resigned manner replied, "Okay, come to the bank tomorrow morning with me. I will transfer the entire amount to you and hand over all your funds to you completely. If you squander or lose them, it is none of my concern." So saying he stormed out of the room in a huff.

The next day Satya gave Arjun the control of all his funds. Arjun in turn handed over a cheque for five lakh rupees to Divakaran.

Days turned into weeks, and their plan unfolded seamlessly. The trucks laden with cannabis and Ecstasy disguised as fertilizer rumbled through the night, crossing borders undetected. The brothers reveled in their cunning success, toasting to each triumph.

However, beneath the surface, tension simmered. Sukumaran, ever the worrier, voiced his concerns to Divakaran one evening, "What if Arjun discovers the truth? We've entangled ourselves with him, and now he holds a piece of our secret."

Divakaran, confident as ever, dismissed his fears, "He won't find out. We've played our cards well. And besides, he's too deeply invested in us and his relationship with Divya to jeopardize everything."

Occasionally, they would give Arjun a wad of cash, claiming it was his share of the profits, ensuring he spent it on alcohol and drugs, gradually making him reliant on them. With each passing day, they tightened their grip on him.

In the cozy room where secrets were exchanged and sinister plots hatched, the trio spoke freely, confident in their assumption that the depths of their conspiracies were concealed from prying eyes.

Meanwhile, Elias, their aging servant, apparently absorbed in his duties of serving them food, cleverly blended into the background. The trio, blissfully ignorant, remained oblivious to the discreet presence of their servant Elias, who surreptitiously lingered on the periphery, intermittently overhearing fragments of their conversations. Little did they realize that their seemingly dim-witted servant, in his own unassuming way, was gradually getting the hang of their deceitful schemes and eavesdropping on their conversations. Without their knowing, Elias, was realizing the subtleties and details of their treachery, a revelation that would eventually lead to their downfall.

One evening, as the brothers gathered to discuss the escalating profits, Sadanandan, Divya's brother paid them an unexpected visit. Mohandas greeted him with a forced smile, "What brings you here, my friend?"

Sadanandan's eyes narrowed as he came straight to the point, "Arjun — he's been acting strangely lately. Did you do something to him? I know that he has been hanging with you people recently."

Divakaran feigned innocence, "No, we didn't do anything to him. Why... why would we harm our own kin? He's part of our business family now."

Sukumaran added, "Maybe he's just stressed after his father's death. We'll talk to him, make sure everything is fine. Why do you ask this?"

"No, he was a good student at college and he is in a relationship with my sister Divya. Both Prabhakaran and I had no objections to this as he belongs to a good brahmin family here in Calicut. But of late, his behaviour seems strange and Divya also expressed hesitation to meet him. That is what piqued my curiosity. I thought I will check with you."

"I will talk to him," Sukumaran assured him, "I will tell him to meet Divya and speak to her."

Sadanandan remained skeptical, "See that you do. Divya is worried, and I won't tolerate any harm befalling my sister."

He was becoming agitated.

"Divya is our beloved sister, and since our father's passing, we have cared for her with immense affection and tenderness. We are deeply committed to ensuring her future remains bright and untarnished. If anyone dares to harm her, including Arjun, Prabhakaran and I will take decisive action to remove them from her life — permanently, if necessary. It is crucial that Arjun understands this unequivocally. If he continues down a troubling path, he must be warned to stay away from our sister. You had better warn him about this." Sadanandan did not mince words.

The weight of the conversation hung in the air, emphasizing the deep-rooted concern and protectiveness the brothers felt for their sister, Divya.

As he left, the brothers exchanged uneasy glances. Divakaran muttered, "This Arjun could turn out to be a thorn in our side. We have to be careful with him."

As dissatisfaction grew, a sense of impending disaster fell upon the Iyer household. The family was oblivious to the looming threat that could break apart the already fragile fraternal bonds. Another catastrophe was approaching, set to worsen the tension caused by Arjun's behavior.

Chapter 20

Lost in the haze of alcohol and pot, Arjun roamed aimlessly, a soul adrift in a sea of despair. The only source of comfort he had was his sister, Nandini. However, she had also left to pursue her own future. He now felt deserted and isolated, like an orphan surrounded by relatives — lonely in a crowd. He felt completely alone, convinced that nobody in the world could truly grasp the profound turmoil he was experiencing inside. In the state of this distorted reality and paranoia, he believed his brothers harbored a conspiracy against him, leaving him with an acute sense of betrayal. His worsening symptoms of schizophrenia led him to believe that everyone was plotting against him. The illness was slowly tightening its hold on him. The shores of his life seemed deserted, and a profound sense of desolation engulfed him. It seemed as though there was no refuge, no one to turn to in his turbulent existence.

His father, in an attempt to provide a semblance of stability, had granted him his share, allowing Arjun financial autonomy. However, the freedom only intensified his struggle, for in his clouded state of mind, rational decision-making was impossible. Logic and sensibility eluded him, leaving him unclear as to what to do.

His once-affectionate mother, who had been a source of guidance, now languished in indifference due to her illness. Arjun longed for the affection he once received from her, but her distracted attitude due to her illness, left him feeling lonely in his monotonous life.

In the midst of this emotional abyss, his only flicker of hope was Divya, his beloved. For nearly four years, she had been his unwavering comfort, understanding his aspirations and needs. However, a shift in Arjun's attitude and behaviour had created a rift in their relationship. Divya's once-frequent calls and letters dwindled, leaving Arjun haunted by the fear that her interest in him was waning.

Determined to salvage what little remained of their connection, Arjun, fueled by a newfound resolve, rose to his feet. He decided to meet Divya in hopes of revitalizing their fading relationship and reigniting her love. Arjun decided to meet her in her home during the day time when her brothers would be in their respective workplaces.

When Arjun reached Divya's home, she was alone sitting on the sofa in her living room reading a magazine. Her brothers had headed out for work, and her mother had gone to the temple for a *Satsang*, creating an ideal moment for Arjun to approach her with his plea.

"Divya," Arjun hesitated as he entered, his eyes searching for a connection. "Can we talk?"

Divya, already sensing that something was amiss, nodded and gestured for him to sit down and continue.

Their surroundings seemed to echo the tension that hung in the air as Divya and Arjun faced each other. Their relationship, once filled with the warmth of mutual love, now harbored an underlying gloom, setting the stage for a conversation charged with emotion.

"I... I know things haven't been good lately," Arjun began, fumbling over his words. "But I need you to understand, Divya. I've been struggling, and I don't know whom to turn to."

Divya, though hesitant, encouraged him to speak, "Arjun, I've noticed the changes in you. You have never kept the promises to me. It's been hard for me too. What's going on? Why are you still like this?"

Reluctant to dive into the heart of the matter, Arjun felt the weight of strain in their relationship. He jumped up restlessly and paced nervously, choosing his words carefully.

"I've... I've lost my way, Divya," Arjun admitted, his eyes avoiding direct contact. "The drugs, the alcohol – it's like I'm drowning, and I can't find a way back."

Divya, listening intently, couldn't help but feel the surge of annoyance and pity building within her. "Arjun, we had plans, dreams. What happened to all those promises you made?"

"I know, Divya. I've let you down," Arjun confessed, a sense of remorse evident in his voice. "But I need you to believe that I can change. I just need your support."

The plea lingered in the room, creating an uneasy silence. Divya, grappling with conflicting emotions, finally spoke, "Arjun, our relationship was my solace, but now it's turning into a nightmare. I can't be part of this destructive path you're on. You are destroying yourself and you have no one but yourself to blame. You have a nice family, an affectionate mother, understanding brothers and a loving sister. Still you are not putting in an effort to change. I cannot live with that!" She was in tears.

As Arjun absorbed the weight of Divya's words, the realization hit him – the consequences of his actions, the promises he had shattered.

"I didn't want it to come to this, Arjun," Divya sighed and continued, her eyes revealing the emotional toll. "But I can't keep waiting for a change that might never come. We need to end this for both our sakes."

The moment's vulnerability made their once-promising relationship gloomy. Divya sadly understood she had to end things, while Arjun struggled with their falling apart.

"Divya," he whispered, desperate and defeated, "I don't want to lose you."

"I don't want to lose you either, Arjun," Divya replied, her voice breaking. "But we both need to find a way back to who we used to be, separately. Don't come to see me or try to meet me again. Things are over between us. Your promises to me that you'd stop drinking are like words written on water."

Arjun, consumed by the effects of his substance abuse, acted out of character and forcefully grabbed her hand. His nails bit into her delicate skin. Divya, feeling a mix of frustration and hurt, couldn't contain her emotions.

"Arjun, what are you doing?" Divya exclaimed, her voice a blend of shock and dismay, as she tried to free herself from his grip. "You are hurting me!"

But Arjun, lost in his altered state, was oblivious to her distress. The tension in the air thickened as Divya, overwhelmed by the hurtful situation, found herself compelled to respond. In a moment of emotional intensity, she slapped him... hard.

The sound reverberated in the room, reflecting the emotional discord that had poisoned their relationship. Divya, her hand trembling slightly from the force, looked at Arjun with a mixture of sorrow and disappointment.

"I can't do this anymore, Arjun, get lost!" she uttered tears streaming from her face and her words burdened with a heavy heart. The slap showed how something once hopeful had fallen apart. A bond seemed to have snapped. She turned and walked out of the living room into her bed room banging the door shut, leaving Arjun to brood over his misfortune.

Hanging his head in dejection, he walked out of the house. "Damn it..." he cursed himself.

Arjun, eager to join the business, approached Divakaran and gave him a second check for five lakh rupees. He had already given them five lakhs as the first instalment of his share in the business. When Arjun asked for a written agreement to confirm their partnership, Divakaran slyly replied that they didn't need one, insisting their friendship and trust should be enough.

"Why bother with an agreement, Arjun?" he smoothly replied. "We're good friends, and friends trust each other. Your ten lakh rupees is safe with us."

Divakaran promised Arjun a large share of the profits once the business succeeded, keeping Arjun unaware of the specific details.

With each passing day, Arjun's mental and physical health declined, showing increasing signs of schizophrenia. His unpredictable behavior caused frequent arguments with Janaki and Satya. His temper tantrums were intolerable. He often stayed away from home at night, finding solace in the KK brothers' outhouse. Arjun's uncontrolled drug and alcohol use worsened, dragging him deeper into despair.

The once-promising relationship between Divya and Arjun had unraveled into a tragic tale of substance abuse, broken promises, and emotional turmoil, leaving both parties ensnared in the consequences of their choices.

Regrettably, the residents of the Iyer household were unprepared for the impending cataclysm that would strike them in the coming days — a shocking disaster that would bring waves of despair and chaos to their already fragile family.

Chapter 21

On a fateful morning, the quiet abode of the Iyer family became the stage for a heart-wrenching scene. Meenakshi was found collapsed on the bedroom floor, discovered by Janaki as she descended from her room upstairs early morning, heading to the kitchen to brew coffee for both herself and mother. The gravity of the situation was obvious – mother had fallen, possibly during the night when she ventured to use the toilet. She was bleeding from a jagged injury on her forehead, possibly injured by the impact against the doorpost during the fall. Blood had caked on the floor beside her head. Janaki immediately shouted to Satya who hurried from upstairs. Hearing the commotion, Appu mama, their cook also was promptly by their side to help. They lifted the unconscious Meenakshi on to her bed. Janaki immediately applied a piece of gauze to the injury on her forehead to staunch the bleeding.

The household was engulfed in shock, a palpable tension hanging in the air as Meenakshi remained unconscious. The urgency of the situation demanded immediate hospitalization, and an ambulance was immediately summoned. Satya, contacted Dr. Menon, who told him to rush her to the hospital. He assured Satya of an immediate visit to the hospital to see her in the ICU. Panic rippled through everyone, anxiety and fear etched on their faces.

"Dr. Menon said he would come soon. We need to get her to the hospital immediately," Satya urged, his voice reflecting both concern and anguish. The urgency in his words propelled Janaki into action. She rallied together to assist in transporting mother to the waiting ambulance, their worried expressions mirrored in the flashing lights of the emergency vehicle.

In this challenging time, Satya emerged as a steady pillar of support. He, along with Janaki accompanied Meenakshi to the hospital, while Appu mama remained at home to hold the fort. In the hospital, the grim diagnosis unfolded – an acute myocardial infarction and cardiogenic shock. Her blood pressure was extremely low. The weight of the revelation hung in the air as Satya grappled with the severity of mother's condition.

Amidst the unfolding crisis, Arjun's absence cast a shadow of concern. His room stood empty, an unsettling reminder of the unknown. Satya realized that he might not have returned home the night before. Hence, Satya and Janaki were left to manage the crisis without any help from Arjun.

As they waited in the hospital, Satya shared his apprehensions with Janaki. "I don't understand where Arjun could be at a time like this. His absence is adding to the worry," he confided, his worry evident in his furrowed brow.

Dr. Menon arrived, his presence bringing a momentary sense of relief. Yet, the seriousness of the situation remained, hanging like a heavy cloud over the anxious family. The hospital corridors witnessed a flurry of emotions – fear, hope, and an underlying sense of helplessness.

Satya and Janaki sat in the waiting room outside the ICU with anxiety writ on their faces. Satya huddled with Janaki, exchanged concerned glances, "We need to stay strong for Mother," Satya encouraged, attempting to bolster the spirits of Janaki who seemed to be a complete wreck.

"Where could Arjun be at a time like this? We can't reach him. He could be of help if he were here," Satya moaned. Anandu was contacted over the phone informing him of mother's critical state. Satya voiced his concerns, the uncertainty fueling the tension in the room. Anandu promised to come by the next available flight to Coimbatore and thence by road.

The hospital's sterile walls witnessed the ebb and flow of emotions as they oscillated between hope and fear. In the midst of it all, Satya remained steadfast, concern etched on his face. "We just have to wait for the doctor's word. Let's hope for the best," he reassured Janaki who sat with a sullen face, his words attempting to infuse a sense of optimism.

As they clung to each other for support, the weight of uncertainty pressed heavily on their shoulders. Little did they know that this distressing morning marked the beginning of a tumultuous journey, testing the strength of the family and its resilience in the face of adversity.

Contrary to their optimistic hopes, Meenakshi breathed her last in the afternoon. She never regained consciousness. The news devastated Dr. Menon, his words filled with sorrow as he shared the grim reality with Satya and Janaki.

"We tried our utmost, Satya, but her blood pressure never stabilized. The infarction was extensive, with the main coronary artery on the left side and its branches, completely blocked. She had been lying unconscious for perhaps a few hours, and during that time, we lost crucial moments. I am sincerely sorry. She was a wonderful woman. My condolences for your loss," Dr. Menon expressed, his voice heavy with regret. Gently patting Satya on the shoulder, he left the intensive care unit, leaving the bereaved family to grapple with the burden of their grief.

Satya and Janaki, still in shock, stood by the lifeless form of their beloved mother, a figure that had weathered numerous adversities throughout a lifetime. The sterile silence of the room enveloped them as they confronted the harsh reality of her death.

"How much she must have endured, both mentally and physically," Satya mourned, his voice a mixture of anguish and reflection. He tenderly held his mother's lifeless hands, memories flooding his mind of the struggles she had faced and the resilience she had exhibited.

Amidst the sorrow-filled atmosphere, Janaki sought solace in an embrace with the lifeless body of her mother-in-law. Silently sobbing,

163

she expressed her grief, the weight of loss echoing through the hushed corridors of the hospital. Regrets are often voiced after it's too late.

In this poignant moment, Satya and Janaki shared memories of his beloved mother. "She was the heart of our family, the one who held us together through thick and thin," Satya reminisced, his eyes reflecting a mix of gratitude and sorrow.

Janaki, wiping away her tears, added, "She was not just a mother in law to me; she was a pillar of strength for all of us. Her kindness and strength were unparalleled." The exchange of heartfelt sentiments served as a cathartic release, an acknowledgment of the profound impact Meenakshi had on their lives.

Regrets, often arriving too late, are a testament to one's emotions. It is a common occurrence for people to forget expressing their love and affection while someone is alive, only to grieve deeply at their passing. They overlook the importance of showing appreciation and kindness to those around them while they're still here. Instead, they find themselves offering condolences and expressing remorse at funerals, realizing the missed opportunities too late.

In moments of reflection, they remember the times they could have said 'I love you', offered a simple gesture of kindness or a touch of affection. The weight of these missed chances settles heavily upon them as they grapple with the permanence of loss. In the end, they come to understand that it's not the grand gestures or extravagant displays of sentiment that matter most, but the simple acts of love and kindness that make life meaningful. *They forget that it is important to give bouquets to the living than wreaths to the dead.*

As they stood by her lifeless form, the hospital's environment seemed to amplify the emptiness left in Meenakshi's absence. A nurse, entering the room with a solemn expression, offered words of comfort. "I am terribly sorry for your loss. If there's anything you need, please don't hesitate to ask," she said, her empathy bridging the gap between medical protocol and human emotion. She proceeded carefully to prepare the lifeless body for transport to their home.

Grieving, Satya and Janaki nodded appreciatively, grateful for the compassion extended during this trying time. As they came to terms with Meenakshi's death, the two of them had to face the practicalities of bidding her farewell for the last time.

As they prepared to leave the hospital, Satya's voice trembled with a mixture of grief and acceptance. "We have to inform our relatives and make arrangements for the funeral. I shall call Sreeni and Nandini from the ISD booth outside by the time the nurse finishes her formalities. It's time to say our last goodbyes to *Amma*," he said amidst sobs, his words carrying the weight of responsibility.

Returning home, they faced the challenging task of informing relatives and friends about the tragic turn of events. The air was thick with grief as loved ones and neighbours began trickling in to offer condolences and share memories of the departed soul.

While arranging the funeral, Satya and Janaki managed the fine line between grieving and coordinating the last rites. The household was engulfed in a pervasive sense of despair. Anandu and Uma had already departed from Pune to ensure they reached home in time. Their children were left with a friend of theirs. Sreeni, though expressing his inability to come immediately, promised to be present for the obsequies. Nandini promised to join them later after the funeral.

Anandu and Uma had arrived at midnight. Next morning, the cremation unfolded at the solemn Puthiyapalam crematorium, with Arjun arriving in time, silently participating in the funeral rituals, his demeanor akin to a dazed, grieving soul. The compassionate family priest guided the funeral ceremonies. The obsequies, a detailed thirteen-day affair, cast a gloomy pall over the entire household. Friends and relatives provided solace, with Sadasiva Iyer making a timely appearance for the funeral and staying back to offer support. "*When sorrows come, they come not single spies. But in battalions!*," he commented quoting the bard, "I never thought that Meenakshi *Amma* would leave us so soon. She was a brave woman, a stalwart who held the family together like reinforced concrete." He continued, "*So wise, so young, they say, do never live long.*"

In the days that followed, the house became a haven for shared stories and comforting embraces. Friends and family offered words of solace, attempting to fill the void left by Meenakshi's absence. The collective grief became a testament to the impact she had on those around her.

By the time, the fifth day had dawned, bringing with it a sense of gradual healing, Sreeni and Nandini had arrived on a short visit of two weeks from the US and Australia, respectively. As the heartaches began to abate on the sixth day, a subtle shift unfolded, casting an emotional shadow over the grieving family. It was during this delicate juncture that Sadasiva Iyer, taking on the mantle of the elder in the house, felt compelled to address a matter close to his heart with Anandu and Sreeni.

Worried about Janaki's well-being in the aftermath of Meenakshi's demise, Sadasiva Iyer delicately broached the subject. His concern for Janaki's peace of mind and security led him to propose that Satya and Janaki shift from the family home. He emphasized the erratic behavior displayed by Arjun. Hence, following Meenakshi's demise, he underscored the need for a change. His concern for his daughter seemed genuine. As the family gathered, grappling with the weight of the recent loss, Sadasiva Iyer, a voice of reason, shared his thoughts.

"It's essential for Janaki's peace of mind that we consider a separate living arrangement for her and Satya. Arjun's recent behavior has been unpredictable, and we must prioritize her safety, especially since none of you are here now," he suggested, his words laced with concern and subtlety, taking a dig at Nandini and Anandu.

The recommendation, conveyed with empathy, was crystal clear – a suggestion for Satya and Janaki to shift to a separate rented house nearby. In this arrangement, Arjun would assume responsibility for the family home, with certain rooms locked down. Sadasiva Iyer, recognizing the need for guidance, took on the role of an elder, gently steering the family towards a path he said was considered the best for their collective well-being. But in fact, he was aiming for the welfare of his daughter and son in law only.

Anandu, listening intently, responded, "It's a tough decision, I agree, but we must prioritize Janaki's well-being. We need to consider what's best for her at this point." The conversation happened as everyone worked together to understand the challenges faced by a grieving family. Anandu could not offer a better suggestion. Neither could Satya. Nandini kept silent as she had no solution to offer.

Sreeni weighed in, "I understand the concern, Satya and Janaki leaving the house might be a momentous change for them. Let's consider all perspectives before making a decision. Let's not jump to make a decision immediately." His measured response added a layer of thoughtful consideration to the ongoing conversation.

Sadasiva Iyer, with a deep sense of responsibility, continued to guide the family. "*What's done cannot be undone*, and as the saying goes, *What's past is prologue*. It's time to forge a path forward that ensures the well-being of each family member," he remarked, drawing from his scholarly reservoir of wisdom. "I think my suggestion is the best at the present time — unless there is a better suggestion." He looked at each one of them by turn.

No one had a better solution.

The family's conversation developed into a detailed discussion, with each member sharing their thoughts and worries. Though change seemed overwhelming, they all worked together to create a supportive atmosphere during this sensitive period. Eventually, they agreed that Sadasiva Iyer's solution was the most suitable. The decision was accepted in principle.

Arjun was nowhere to be found while these matters were discussed.

Upon the conclusion of the funeral ceremonies on the thirteenth day, the siblings convened to discuss the future. Arjun displayed indifference, while Satya expressed his intention to live separately nearby, unwilling to share a space with Arjun. He would start looking for a suitable accommodation soon. Arjun could stay in the ancestral house. The fate of the family home hung in the balance, with the decision to sell deferred. As the financial matters surfaced, it was revealed that Arjun had assumed control of his funds, a fact Satya distanced himself from. Sreeni and Nandini attempted to advise Arjun to mend his ways, but it seemed to fall on deaf ears. Sreeni had already transferred all his funds to the US.

After the last of the obsequies were over, Sreeni and Nandini planned to leave the following week. Anandu and Uma had to leave within two days as they had entrusted the care of their twin boys to a close family friend in Poona.

The family gathered in the hall two days after the conclusion of the ceremonies after all the other relatives including Sadasiva Iyer had left. Arjun sat in one corner of the sofa aloof from the group, brooding.

167

As conversations moved towards mother's jewelry, Sreeni broached the subject and inquired about the details. Nandini, anticipating this, had been to the bank the previous day and brought the jewelry boxes home from the locker along with mother's list dividing them for each of her sons and daughter. Nandini, armed with the list, presented the five boxes on the teapoy in the living room.

She detailed mother's division of the jewels among her children. Joy crept into Sreeni's heart as he learned that the coveted pearl necklace with the red ruby pendant was bequeathed to him. Satya, however, received a simple pearl necklace with an emerald pendant, not the one Janaki had yearned for. He was miffed at this but kept silent brooding to himself. Janaki's face wilted on hearing this. She had her heart set on the blue sapphire necklace featuring a peacock-shaped pendant.

Arjun, in his list, acquired bangles, rings, and a couple of simple gold chains. The blue sapphire necklace with the peacock pendant with the large, beautiful sapphire in the center which was coveted by Janaki, was bequeathed to Arjun to the great consternation of Satya and Janaki. Anandu, on the other hand, was gifted an emerald necklace with a beautiful pearl pendant. Uma smiled at this putting on a stoic expression.

Nandini, the only daughter, inherited mother's diamond necklace, leaving Sreeni feeling slighted. He had hoped *Amma* would leave the diamond necklace to him as Mamta was from a rich aristocratic family. Everyone received other jewelry which included bangles, rings and chains. The decision to take the jewels abroad to the US by Sreeni created a ripple of emotions, with Nandini feeling peeved. Anandu, mindful of his share, collected the boxes, intending to transport them to Poona. Nandini decided to keep the jewelry in the locker which had been shared with her mother.

The room, which had once silently observed both joy and sorrow, now reverberated with unspoken emotions, blending grief and memories together.

In the aftermath of the mournful events, Satya, driven by a sense of responsibility, shared his plans regarding the precious jewels left behind by mother. "I've decided to open a separate locker in my bank to secure the jewelry. It seems the safest course of action,"

The conversation then shifted towards Arjun, who had been silent during the recent discussions. His indifference was attributed to his deep affection for his mother being the last child and mother's pet. He had not yet got over her loss, they reckoned.

Satya, ever the compassionate brother, extended an olive branch. "Arjun, I understand these are tough times. If you're comfortable, I can open a locker for you too in my bank. It's crucial to keep these valuables safe until you're settled in life and perhaps married," he offered, his words a delicate blend of empathy and concern.

Arjun, meeting Satya's gaze, nodded nonchalantly, "Thank you, Satya *anna*. I appreciate your offer. We can have a locker in our combined names."

Days rolled by. Satya was on the lookout for a suitable rented house or apartment nearby. One day Arjun returned home late appearing disoriented and dazed. Janaki, diligently placing the food on the dining table, retreated to the living room, engrossed in a television program. In solitude, Arjun consumed his meal with a palpable silence lingering in the air. Eventually, he joined Janaki in the living room, breaking the uneasy stillness with a query, "Why do you treat me like an outcast? I have an equal right in this family."

A cloud of discomfort settled between them as Janaki, visibly perturbed, responded, asserting her identity, "I'm not your servant or cook, Arjun. Appu mama, our cook, has taken leave, leaving me to manage everything." The simmering tension soon escalated into a war of words, when Arjun, in a fit of anger, impulsively hurled a piece of delicate pottery lying on the shelf onto the floor.

The atmosphere became charged with emotion as Janaki, her patience exhausted, lashed out, "Why don't you just leave? *Yama* should have taken you instead of Amma. You should have been the one to die instead of poor *Amma*," her words echoed with the pain of loss and resentment. "Only your death will release us from this misery." With that, she stormed upstairs, leaving Arjun standing alone in the aftermath of their heated exchange, dejected and forlorn.

Haunted by fear, Janaki refused to stay alone in the expansive house when Satya was absent. The specter of Arjun's unpredictable behavior fueled her apprehensions, leading her to resent him even more.

In a moment of frustration, she had shouted, "Why don't you just die?" But later she regretted those words.

Faced with this tumultuous situation, Janaki, in a desperate attempt to find solace, implored Satya, "As my *Appa* advised, we must relocate from this place as soon as possible. The atmosphere here is stifling, and I cannot bear the weight of these emotions any longer." The plea, filled with both fear and despair, highlighted how fragile their family ties were, revealing the deep vulnerabilities hidden beneath the surface.

The next week they moved to a rented house nearby.

Arjun discovered himself in a large but lonely house which echoed with the footsteps of departed family members and memories of a lively past. He felt lonely. Solitude enveloped him like an unexpected maelstrom, casting shadows upon his soul.

The sounds of his siblings' laughter and the bond with his sister Nandini, along with the unconditional love of his mother, lingered in the empty rooms, now filled only with the haunting silence of their absence. Arjun felt deserted, confronted by the harsh reality of loneliness. His past haunted him, and the void left by his loved ones' absence felt overwhelming, weighing heavily on his fate. He felt both depressed and angry.

"I am to blame for all of this," he thought with a heavy heart. "My reckless behavior and lack of direction have caused these terrible events within our family." As he reflected on his actions, Arjun felt a deep sense of remorse. He realized how his choices had impacted those he loved most. "If only I had been more responsible," he murmured to himself, "Perhaps things would have turned out differently."

As he rambled through his memories, scenes from the past few months unfolded in his mind like a tragic movie. Regret and remorse plagued his thoughts constantly, dragging him into despair. Alone and confused, Arjun stood at life's crossroads, facing the looming question of "What next?" like a giant question mark. Tears streaked his cheeks. With determination etched on his face, he made decisive choices within his heart. As he rose to his feet, wiping away the tears cascading down his cheeks, a sense of resolve filled his being.

He stood there, grappling with the weight of the decision before him. His brows furrowed in deep concentration as he wrestled with conflicting thoughts. The momentousness of the situation was evident in the lines etched on his face, reflecting the turmoil within. Arjun took a step forward, ready to confront the challenges that lay ahead. He felt lonely and depressed. Life felt meaningless – not worth living.

Chapter 22

One serene evening, under the comforting shade of an old banyan tree in their coconut grove, Sukumaran, Divakaran, and Mohandas gathered to discuss the unfolding events in Arjun's household. Mohandas, his eyes gleaming with a newfound piece of information, eagerly revealed, "I've heard that Arjun has recently inherited both wealth and a trove of precious jewelry after his mother passed away."

Intrigued by this unexpected revelation, Divakaran leaned forward, his eyes twinkling with envy and inquired, "How did you come across such valuable information?"

A playful smile danced on Mohandas's lips as he shared, "Devaki amma, the maidservant who tends to both our homes and occasionally to theirs part-time, overheard the hushed conversations of the brothers while she was tidying up their dining room. You know, these maidservants, they are the conduits of information into which we can discreetly tap. I gave her twenty rupees when she gave me this bit of juicy info. I overheard her telling my mother about this." Mohandas declared triumphantly.

The setting sun cast a warm glow on the trio as Divakaran continued, "Now, my friends, we have a unique opportunity in front of us. We must devise a plan to gently nudge Arjun into considering our ventures more seriously. Perhaps, he could even contemplate sharing a portion of his splendid jewelry collection with us. What are your thoughts on this?"

Sukumaran, contemplative, joined the conversation, "It's true; we need to approach this delicately without arousing his suspicion. After all, we are bound by a longstanding camaraderie with Arjun, and we wouldn't want to strain that friendship by rushing into anything. After all, the jewelry is his legacy from his parents. He is an innocent soul not competent enough to handle all this unexpectedly inherited fortune."

Divakaran, known for his strategic thinking within the group, proposed, "Why don't we try to appeal to his self-interest? If we can show him that our plans align with what he wants, he might be willing to help us all succeed together. It's not about taking his money but using it for the good of all."

As the full moon began to rise in the eastern sky, casting a gentle glow on their faces, the three friends continued to discuss their plans. They decided they would ask Arjun to show them the jewelry inherited from his mother – just to have a look, they would say. The trio all agreed to this plan with a greedy gleam in their eyes.

Initially, Arjun expressed hesitation when asked about the jewelry. "It's securely stored in Satya *Anna's* bank in my locker. I can only access it when he's away. Otherwise, he would know that I opened the locker and he'd ask me why I did so. He has explicitly mentioned that the jewelry is earmarked by our mother for my future wife once I'm married and settled," Arjun admitted innocently.

Engagingly, he continued to share more details, "Once a month, Satya *anna* and his wife head to Trivandrum to visit her parents. That's my chance. I'll fetch the jewels, show them to you, and return them the same day. Hence, no suspicion should arise."

True to his commitment, one fine morning, Arjun arrived at their office, clutching the jewelry box. Satya was away in Trivandrum, and so Arjun could bring the jewelry to the office. Mohandas was there too. The air was filled with a palpable sense of excitement as opals, sapphires and emeralds caught the light and glittered with heavenly brilliance, and the brothers marveled at Arjun's splendid collection.

Sukumaran, his eyes drawn to the blue sapphire necklace featuring a peacock pendant with a sizable blue sapphire at its center, expressed his admiration. The exquisite design was eye-catching. With Arjun's permission, he snapped a photograph with his Canon camera, sharing his intent to make a replica as a gift for his wife.

Having shown the jewelry to them, with a conscientious regard for safety, Arjun promptly returned the jewels to the bank that very afternoon, explaining, "I need to return them to the locker today itself, as my brother is due to arrive tomorrow."

Sukumaran, appreciating the trust shared, offered his assurance, "If you ever decide to part with any piece, do inform me first. I would be genuinely interested in making a purchase."

"You are not seen now a days in our outhouse for the get-togethers," remarked Mohandas smirking. "Why don't you come for a drink and a puff with us this evening?"

"I have made up my mind to give up both alcohol and ganja," Arjun remarked. "I want to take life more seriously. I have made a promise to myself to do that." Arjun's determination seemed genuine.

The trio exchanged amazed glances. They realized it was crucial for their benefit for Arjun to stay addicted to alcohol and drugs. That was the only way they could carry out their deceitful plans successfully and have a hold on him.

Mohandas's eyes had sparkled with treachery as he had observed the exquisite collection of jewels and ornaments. Even though a bachelor, Mohandas was captivated by Arjun's collection of jewelry, imagining owning some of it for his future bride, whoever she might be. It would be worthwhile possessing some of these pieces, his mind told him.

In the thriving world of smuggling, Mohandas carefully supervised his co-conspirators, ensuring secrecy surrounded their activities. "The less you know the details, the smoother our operation runs. Profits are practically guaranteed. Our ingenious maneuverings allowed us so far to successfully transport five shipments of fertilizer from Punjab, camouflaging our special packets of ganja and Ecstasy within, resulting in a net profit of sixty *lakhs* from that alone. At this rate, we're on the path to becoming millionaires within a year, truly."

Within the secret circle, conspiracies brewed without Arjun's knowledge. He still thought he was part of a legal fertilizer business. Mohandas gently suggested a visit with the others to reconnoiter the ancestral property of Arjun's family. He delicately hinted at the potential opportunity for them to stake their claim to buy the property at a cheaper price. Mohandas and his companions felt a surge of anticipation as they discussed the possibility of acquiring the property that held such sentimental value to Arjun.

"We can ask Arjun if his brothers are willing to sell the *Nalukettu* to us. We can give them an offer for it. In these distressed times, they may opt to sell it off at a cheaper price, one cannot be certain. Especially since their family is now scattered." Mohandas was scheming in his mind. His mind was filled with delusions of grandeur.

Divakaran contributed to the plan, suggesting, "With Arjun's parents gone, he has inherited a sizable portion of his father's wealth. We should use this chance to convince him to invest more in our business."

The deceitful plans kept progressing, veiled under the guise of camaraderie and friendship. Within the tight-knit KK brothers' group, every interaction was carefully planned to exploit opportunities for financial gain and trap Arjun deeper in their web of lies. There was an unspoken tension in the air, revealing hidden motives as the trio plotted methodically to strip Arjun of his wealth.

Chapter 23

As the initial rays of the morning sun embraced the tranquil Calicut beach, a gradual awakening of activity began to unfold. The dawn painted the horizon with a delicate blend of hope and despair, casting a gloomy atmosphere over the scene. The prone lifeless form of Arjun, clothed in a red Tee shirt and blue jeans, lay on the sandy shore. The tender, foamy waves gently caressed his motionless body.

In the sad scene, a group of fishermen who had been out fishing at night came across this heart-rending sight. Among them, Ramu, a seasoned fisherman with a weathered face, was the first to notice Arjun's lifeless figure. He hurriedly approached, squatting beside the inert body, reaching out to touch it gently in a futile attempt to look for signs of life. The coldness of the skin drowned any little hope of life. Ramu, with a heavy heart, called out to his comrades, who quickly gathered around him.

One young fisherman, his face etched with concern, suggested, "Shouldn't we rush him to the hospital?" Ramu, the voice of practical experience, responded, "What's the use? He must have been gone for hours. We need to inform the police." His words carried the weight of acceptance, acknowledging the grim reality they faced.

Promptly, the police were summoned, stepping onto the scene to take charge of the unfolding tragedy. Following preliminary inquiries, they released the distressed fisherfolk, recording their addresses for further questioning, if needed. The usual routine exchange between the officers and the fishermen ended as the police prepared their inquest into the circumstances surrounding Arjun's death.

Called to the solemn duty at hand, the police, under the guidance of Inspector Vinod, had arrived early at the scene to investigate the mysterious circumstances surrounding the death. With a pair of latex gloves taken from the pocket of his uniform, Inspector Vinod approached the lifeless form, delicately turning the prone corpse. In the face of death, Arjun's visage exhibited an eerie calmness, a few stray pieces of seaweed clung to his nose and mouth. There was some foam around his mouth and on his face, indicating that he had drowned.

A deep gash was present on the forehead, the only sign of external injury in the body. The autopsy would, however, reveal more, if any. Absent were the telltale ligature marks on his neck which would have suggested strangulation or foul play. The cause of death remained uncertain, waiting to be revealed after a thorough autopsy. At first glance, it seemed a likely case of drowning, yet the doubt lingered. Accident or suicide? The distinction eluded the inspector. A heavy sigh escaped the lips of Inspector Vinod, a tangible expression of the burdensome task ahead of him.

In the waterlogged pockets of Arjun's jeans, inspector Vinod discovered a piece of sodden paper – a counterfoil of a pay-in slip from a nationalized bank, accompanied by a few drenched rupee notes and coins. Illegible words, a signature, and an amount of Rs. Five thousand entered on the counterfoil hinted at a potential lead to the identity of the deceased. Furthermore, a wet handkerchief, meticulously hand-embroidered with the initials '*A & D*,' was recovered from another pocket. Footwear was absent on the lifeless body.

Determined to unlock the mysteries surrounding the death, Vinod dispatched a constable to the bank with the crucial piece of evidence. The unfolding investigation sought not only the cause of death but also the background of Arjun's life leading up to this tragic juncture.

The bank confirmed that the initials on the paper belonged to Arjun, adding another layer of pathos to the unfolding tragedy. Satya who was the cashier in the bank where Arjun had deposited the five thousand rupees two days ago was quick to recognize the scribble which was Arjun's initials. He rushed to the scene on the beach along with the police and to his horror found that it was the body of Arjun, his dear younger brother lying lifeless in the wet sand. A sob broke from his throat.

Two of Satya's colleagues, having learned of the tragedy, arrived from the office to offer their support. The police diligently initiated their investigation, conducting a thorough inquest. Subsequently, the lifeless body was carefully loaded onto an ambulance and transported to the Calicut Medical College for an autopsy. Satya, accompanied by his colleagues, followed the police convoy, anxiously awaiting the completion of the autopsy.

Fortuitously, being the morning hours, all forensic surgeons were present at the medical college. Hence, without any delay, the autopsy was completed. Satya and his colleagues, fraught with anticipation, stood by, waiting. A group of Arjun's friends had gathered at the medical college forensic department, seeking a final glimpse of their departed companion. By noon, the body, now wrapped in a simple white cloth, was handed over to Satya. Together, they embarked on the solemn journey back to their ancestral home. In the quiet atmosphere, conversations reverberated as Arjun's friends reminisced about fond memories and stories, trying to come to terms with the sudden loss.

Externally, the lifeless form displayed a deep linear gash on the left side of the forehead. During the autopsy, minuscule fragments of decayed wood shavings were discovered within the wound, indicating they had been driven in by a forceful impact from either a wooden stick or stump before death. These fragments were meticulously gathered and preserved for subsequent analysis at the forensic laboratory. At autopsy, the primary cause of death was determined as seawater drowning. The comprehensive autopsy report, though, would only be available after a few days. Further insights from the chemical examiner's report needed additional time and would be available weeks later.

The entire episode cast a heavy shadow over the grieving household, enveloping them in a gloomy atmosphere. Interviews with Arjun's friends and Satya emerged as vital components of the ongoing police inquiry, gradually revealing fragments of a promising life that had been abruptly snuffed out. Satya, grappling with his own grief engaged in heartfelt dialogues with the police investigators. The unfolding events painted a vivid picture of sorrow, empathy, and the inexplicable nature of life's uncertainties.

In the midst of overwhelming sorrow, Anandu, arriving from Poona with Uma, joined the grieving family, embracing their shared anguish. With tear-filled eyes, he questioned the circumstances, expressing his deep emotion.

"How did this happen? Why did he do it?" The unexpected tragedy had shattered his perception of the departed, as he remarked, "I thought Arjun was a tough guy, not one to take his own life in this manner." His grief flowed uncontrollably, mirroring the profound impact of the loss.

As the cremation ceremony unfolded, an immense crowd gathered, comprising friends, college mates, and well-wishers, far surpassing the attendees at even his father, Anantharama Iyer's funeral. Arjun had been highly popular. Throughout his college days and beyond, he had cultivated a large circle of friends through his sincerity and honesty. His openness and willingness to assist others had earned him numerous friends. Unfortunately, addiction turned out to be his only weakness.

Satya, arranging for the funeral, sought solace in the unwavering support extended by friends and family. In the midst of the mournful proceedings, Anandu and Satya engaged in conversations with fellow mourners, sharing memories of their dear departed brother.

The air was thick with sorrow, punctuated by moving dialogues that echoed the sentiments of those grappling with the inexplicable tragedy. Anandu, in a heartfelt exchange with a close friend, reminisced about the shared experiences and moments that defined their intimacy with the departed. "I never saw this coming. It's hard to understand why he chose this path," he expressed, struggling to come to terms with the unexpected turn of events. "He was strong-willed, even though he had his idiosyncrasies."

The aged helper, Appu mama, a silent but steadfast presence, stood by Satya's side, offering support and assistance as needed. The ceremonies were like a painting of feelings, with conversations in the air that were full of sadness and understanding. Anandu, surrounded by a circle of mourners, continued to express his disbelief and sorrow. "He was the last person I expected this from," he shared, his voice laden with a mix of sadness and confusion.

Friends and family gathered in small groups, exchanging stories and memories of the departed, attempting to find solace in the shared recollections. Uma and Janaki were seated in the dining room of their ancestral home, where Arjun's lifeless body was placed. They expressed their sorrow through silent tears for their young brother-in-law's passing. At times, their uncontrollable sobbing filled the halls of the ancestral residence, where Arjun's lifeless figure lay adorned with flowers and wreaths from those who cherished his memory.

The crematorium, a solemn witness to the departure of their parents in bygone days, now stood poised to receive the mortal remains of their dearly beloved son. As the sun went down gracefully, coloring the sky with beautiful shades, it marked the sad end of another young man's life. At the peaceful Puthiyapalam crematorium, where memories of past goodbyes remained, the burning pyre became a backdrop for deep talks. People talked solemnly about how unexpected tragedies affect those left behind.

At the funeral, the KK brothers stood together with their cousin, Mohandas, showing a powerful display of unity as a touching tribute to their strong friendship with Arjun.

At home after the funeral, Anandu, Satya, Uma and Janaki, their countenances obscured by the weight of grief, occupied chairs in close proximity, wrestling with the profound sense of loss that enveloped them. Anandu and Uma, having undertaken the journey from Poona, silently provided unwavering support.

Over the telephone, Nandini succumbed to tears upon receiving the heart-wrenching news of Arjun's suicide, lamenting, "He wrote to me only a week ago. How could he do such a horrible deed to himself!" she sobbed over the phone.

Sreeni, while expressing condolences and inquiring about the tragic circumstances, maintained a composed attitude in the face of this shocking revelation.

In the quiet hallways of their old family home, they talked, each word filled with the sadness of what had happened. Satya and Anandu engaged in heart-to-heart dialogues, attempting to find comfort in shared memories. Uma and Janaki, amidst the somber atmosphere, offered silent gestures of support, their presence a testament to the love and affection they had for their young brother in law.

As the day unfolded, the weight of grief hung heavily, and conversations served as a release for those grappling with the inexplicable loss.

After carefully completing their investigation, the police finally determined that Arjun's death was a result of drowning, deemed to be a suicide due to an overdose of cannabis and alcohol. They closed the case without further inquiry.

Part II

Interlude

1990

It was Sunday. The early morning sun cast a golden hue over the sleepy city of Calicut as Colonel Chandrakanth, clad in his half trousers and a worn-out T-shirt, embarked on his usual morning stroll with his faithful companion, a labrador retriever named Buddy. As they made their way through the quiet streets, Colonel Chandrakanth inhaled the pleasant cool December air as he thought of the plans for the day.

Buddy, in a long leash, trotted beside him, his keen senses alert to every sound and scent that wafted through the neighborhood. The air was heavy with the aroma of freshly bloomed flowers mingled with the faint smell of damp earth. It had drizzled the night before.

His leisurely stroll led him behind the boys' high school which was close to his residence. Passing by the school, Colonel Chandrakanth noticed the half-constructed building looming in the distance behind the school premises. During his morning stroll, it was a glaringly unpleasant sight along his route. The half-built house was intended for a businessman from the Gulf. However, due to financial constraints, the construction had been halted six months ago, leaving it vacant and incomplete, surrounded by thick, overgrown shrubbery. The unfinished structure had become a gathering spot for antisocial elements and petty criminals. Empty bottles and stubs of beedis and cigarettes strewn about hinted at frequent visits by alcoholics and gamblers. Rumors circulated about drug deals taking place in the vicinity. It was a stark reminder of the decay that had seeped into the heart of their community. But the responsible authorities seemed to turn a blind eye to all this.

Buddy's ears perked up, sensing something amiss. With a low growl, he tugged at his leash, urging Colonel Chandrakanth to follow at a quickened pace. Intrigued, the retired army officer allowed himself to be led towards the derelict building.

The dog entered the house and began barking at something in the hall. Curious, the colonel followed and was stunned by what he saw. In the dim morning light, he discovered three teenage boys in school uniforms slumped against the wall, seemingly unconscious.

He knelt beside the boys, his hands trembling as he reached out to check for signs of life. But deep down, he knew it was futile. The stench of alcohol and cigarette smoke hung heavy in the air, a grim reminder of the darkness that lurked within their midst. A swift examination, drawing on his army training, revealed that the boys were dead. Beside them lay a few cigarette stubs and a small packet resembling ganja and some white powder. Nearby, an empty bottle of rum rested against the wall. One look at the scene, the colonel could guess what would have taken place.

"Dear God," the colonel muttered to himself, his voice barely audible over the deafening silence that engulfed the room. "I... I think they're gone," he said to himself, his voice choked with emotion.

Buddy whimpered softly, his tail tucked between his legs as if sensing the gravity of the situation.

With a heavy heart, Colonel Chandrakanth made his way out of the building, careful not to disturb any evidence that could aid the police in unraveling the mystery behind the boys' unnatural demise.

Once outside, he wasted no time in alerting the authorities, his mind reeling with the grim reality of what he had just witnessed.

The headlines screamed across the newspapers the following day, announcing the tragic fate of three high school students discovered in an abandoned building, their lives claimed by drug overdose. The article examined the details uncovered by the police, shedding light on the alarming rise of drug-related incidents among teenage school children in Kerala. With a heavy heart, the reporter lamented the growing number of young lives lost to the scourge of illicit substances.

In heartfelt words, the article expressed frustration with the failure of the authorities to apprehend those responsible for supplying drugs and cannabis to vulnerable children. "How many more innocent lives must be lost before action is taken?" the reporter questioned, echoing the sentiments of a community plagued by grief and outrage.

As the news spread throughout the town, murmurs of sorrow and disbelief filled the air. Parents clutched their children closer, fearing for their safety in a world fraught with danger. "It's a tragedy," one concerned citizen remarked, shaking his head in dismay. "Something must be done to protect our children from such senseless loss."

The heartbreaking reality of the situation weighed heavily on the minds of all who read the article. Tears were shed for the young lives cut short, their potential snuffed out before it could fully bloom. "We cannot let their deaths be in vain," vowed another member of the community, determination shining in their eyes. "We must come together to demand justice for these innocent souls."

With each passing moment, the urgency of the situation became clearer. The need for action grew more pressing, driving individuals from all walks of life to stand united in the fight against drug abuse and its devastating consequences. "We owe it to them," declared a local activist, their voice ringing with resolve. "We owe it to all the children whose futures hang in the balance."

And so, amidst the sorrow and grief, a glimmer of hope emerged.. The government, at last, was catalyzed into action by the protesters from all quarters of state.

Chapter 24

Six months had passed after Arjun's death, marking the slow ticking away of time. Nandini, finally returned to Calicut, her hometown. Her early arrival had been hindered by the pressing demands of her exams in Australia, preventing her immediate return when Arjun met his untimely end. The shocking revelation that Arjun's death was deemed a suicide by the authorities had left Nandini emotionally devastated.

Almost an entire year had slipped away since Nandini had bid farewell to her homeland. The past experiences had made her take a crucial decision — to spend the next six months in India. Within this period, she aimed to find out the truth about Arjun's death, rejoin the medical college, seek a five-year leave for advanced studies, and later return to Australia to join the fellowship in Gynecologic Oncology.

The ancestral home, once vibrant with the sounds of life and joy, now stood engulfed in a mournful silence. The echoes of laughter that thronged the corridors were replaced by a melancholic solitude. The jolting events of the past had left the grand mansion devoid of inhabitants. In the shadow of the imposing structure, Nandini chose to stay in the modest outhouse which stood within the compound of the sprawling ancestral estate. It was a single-storied, two bedroom, modest bungalow that stood a few feet adjacent to the main building.

Satya, Janaki, and the elderly helper, Appu *mama*, who had been an integral part of the household during the last days of their parents, had chosen to relocate much earlier due to differences of opinion with Arjun. They had moved to a rented house a few blocks away, leaving the once lively mansion desolate. Only memories remained in the large empty *Nalukettu*.

Nandini found herself surrounded by solitude in this vast estate. Driven by curiosity to know more details, and a need for closure regarding Arjun's death, Nandini set out to meet Satya and Janaki. She hoped to find a reason for Arjun's perplexing behavior in the days leading up to his tragic end. She felt a fervent desire for answers, and she approached the situation feeling both nervous and determined.

Entering into conversations with Satya and Janaki, Nandini delicately probed regarding the details surrounding Arjun's death. She sought to understand the changes in his life, piecing together the fragments of his existence that seemed to elude her mind. Her emotions were a blend of sorrow, confusion, and an unspoken yearning for closure regarding his death. She wanted to know more about his death — whether it was really a suicide or an accident. Her mind still refused to accept the fact that Arjun would voluntarily take his own life.

In the living room of Satya's rented house, Nandini sat on a worn-out sofa, her eyes searching for answers in the faces of Satya and Janaki. The air hung heavy with unspoken tension as she broached the topic that had been haunting her thoughts for months.

Nandini, leaning forward eagerly said, "I needed to talk to both of you about Arjun. I can't shake the feeling that there's more to his death than what the police report says. Arjun was not a person to take his own life. I want to know what happened."

Satya exchanged a hesitant glance with Janaki before responding, his eyes clouded with a mix of sorrow and uncertainty.

"Nandini, it's been tough for all of us. Losing Arjun was unexpected, and the police concluded it was suicide." Satya seemed to be on the defensive as if the blame for not taking care of Arjun would fall on him. His facial expression belied the fact.

Nandini was persistent, "When I received Arjun's letter a week before his death, he sounded optimistic. He claimed to be turning his life around, cutting back on alcohol and steering clear of ganja. But the autopsy report paints a different picture – drowning while under the influence of alcohol and cannabis. I need to understand what really happened. It seems incongruous."

Janaki, who had been fidgeting nervously, finally spoke up, her gaze avoiding Nandini's penetrating eyes. "Arjun had his struggles, Nandini *Akka*. Sometimes things are more complicated than they seem."

Nandini remarked, "Sometimes the most complex problems have the simplest of solutions. Janaki, you're not telling me everything. There's a sense that something's being held back. Did Arjun confide in you about something troubling him?"

Satya sighed, his eyes flickering with hesitation, and he exchanged a knowing look with Janaki. Both of them appeared to be nervous discussing Arjun's death.

Satya: "Look, Nandini, Arjun had his demons, but he didn't share everything with us. We're as puzzled as you are."

Nandini leaned forward, her voice firm, "I need to know the truth. If there's even a hint that Arjun's death wasn't what it seemed, I have to find out the truth. I came to India in search of the truth about Arjun's unnatural death."

Janaki shifted uncomfortably, glancing at Satya before finally meeting Nandini's gaze.

"Nandini *akka*, we cared for Arjun deeply, but some things are best left in the past. Opening old wounds won't change anything. It won't bring Arjun back."

Nandini her face set grim with determination responded, "I still can't ignore this, Janaki. I owe it to Arjun to uncover the truth. Tell me everything you know, no matter how insignificant it may seem."

Satya, sensing Nandini's resolve, sighed and began sharing fragmented details of Arjun's last days. Nandini's eyes bored into Janaki, searching for any hint of an unspoken truth. Janaki's responses remained guarded, her gaze darting around the room as if trying to evade the weight of Nandini's inquiry.

As they talked, the room felt heavy with hidden secrets, making Nandini feel uneasy. The truth was hard to find, and the more she asked, the more she felt there might be hidden feelings and stories about Arjun's sudden death.

"When was the last time you saw Arjun?" she inquired.

Satya replied, "I saw him a week before he passed away. He came to collect his locker key from me, which I had been keeping for him. We haven't seen him since then."

"The truth lies somewhere out there," she thought. She was bent on finding it at all costs.

With a determined resolve, Nandini decided to go to the Town police station, hoping to find answers about Arjun's mysterious demise. Her quest for the truth led her to the familiar surroundings of the police station. But she was disappointed upon learning that Inspector Vinod, the officer who had conducted Arjun's inquest, had been transferred out of Calicut.

As she stood there, grappling with uncertainty, an unexpected face caught her eye — Ranjit Menon! her previous college mate, now wearing the badge of the new Assistant Commissioner of Police (ACP). A spark of recognition lit up Ranjit's eyes as he glanced in her direction.

Nandini was surprised to see him there. "Ranjit, is that really you? I can't believe you're here!"

Ranjit, equally surprised responded, "Nandini! What a surprise! It's been ages. How have you been? And, by the way what brings you here, of all places?" Their spontaneous reunion sparked a wave of nostalgia.

"Where have you been all these years?" Nandini went on happy to see a familiar face at the police station.

"I was posted in Delhi, but now I have been asked to take up charge in this police station." ACP Ranjit replied smiling.

"Oh, is that so," Nandini responded smiling. "From a large metro like Delhi to this small city in Kerala? Surprising."

"Oh, strange are the ways of the government bureaucracy," replied ACP Ranjit and left it at that. He seemed reluctant to talk about his transfer to Calicut. Nandini did not press him for details.

The rumor circulating was that ACP Ranjit had been transferred from Delhi to Calicut as a form of punishment. The specifics were a mystery to most, but chatter in the police station suggested that Ranjit had been demoted to work at the Town Police Station in Calicut due to some misdemeanor during his time in Delhi. Despite the rumors swirling around him, Ranjit chose not to address or verify these claims. He simply ignored them allowing them to circulate freely.

"I came seeking answers about my brother Arjun's death, but I find that Inspector Vinod who had investigated the case has been transferred. Can you, by any chance, help me?" Nandini voiced her concern.

"C'mon, let's sit in my office," he invited her into the comfort of his office.

Ranjit's expression shifted, his brows furrowing with concern as Nandini poured out the details and her concerns about Arjun's demise. She detailed his addictions and shared that in his last letter, received a week before his death, he had expressed giving up alcohol and drugs, aiming for a normal life. She handed over Arjun's last letter to the inspector, emphasizing his newfound commitment to self-restraint, and expressed her suspicions regarding the autopsy report.

"I feel there's more to Arjun's death than what's on paper. I don't think he drowned while under the influence of alcohol and drugs, if what he said in the letter is true. He had stopped alcohol and drugs according to this letter. There are some inconsistencies that I am not able to understand. Can you help me find the truth? Can you reopen the case, inspector?"

ACP Ranjit, initially hesitant, read the letter and listened attentively to Nandini's details, his eyes reflecting a mixture of empathy and determination.

"Nandini, I can't promise immediate answers, but I'll look into it. The fact that his death is reported as drug related really intrigues me. We shared college days, and I owe you that much. I'll go through the case file and get back to you. Meanwhile leave me a phone number where you can be reached."

Nandini scribbled the phone number of the outhouse where she stayed on a paper and handed it out to him.

As the weight of their shared history settled between them, over a cup of tea, they began to reminisce about the college experiences that bound them together. Ranjit, the stellar athlete, and Nandini, the brilliant student, found solace in the sweet reminiscences of their shared past. They remembered their platonic relationship when they enjoyed a close friendship with each other during their college days. Nandini continued her conversation with Ranjit, peeling back the layers of their present lives. They talked about her current profession as a gynecologist and discussed how Ranjit, after his M.A. degree, found his calling in the IPS cadre of the government. His time as an NCC cadet in college proved beneficial to him.

She told him about her husband Rajaram who was in Australia and her daughter, Aathira. Inspector Ranjit in turn said that he was married and had a son aged ten. Memories of the past collided with the present, creating a complex interplay of emotions that engulfed both ACP Ranjit Menon and Nandini. As inspector Ranjit learnt about Arjun, the weight of nostalgia mingled with his determination to seek justice for him.

"From the details you have given me, Arjun is also like a brother to me, Nandini; yes, he reminds me of my younger brother Rajiv," he murmured, his voice tinged with emotion. "I won't rest until we find the truth. I will reopen the case. I will pull up the case file."

"Thank you, Ranjit. It means a lot to me." Nandini watched him with a mixture of gratitude and apprehension, her heart heavy with the burden of uncertainty. She had never expected to find solace in the company of a police officer, yet here she was, clinging to the flicker of hope ignited by Ranjit's unwavering resolve. "Thank you," she whispered again, her voice barely above a whisper. "For believing in me."

Ranjit offered her a reassuring smile, his eyes reflecting a depth of understanding that spoke volumes. "We're in this together," he assured her, his tone firm yet compassionate. "I'll do everything in my power to bring justice to Arjun and closure to his loved ones."

In the heart of that police station, a connection forged in college days sparked a newfound determination by ACP Ranjit Menon to seek justice for Arjun, and Nandini couldn't help but feel a glimmer of hope reignited by the unexpected ally she found in him.

Chapter 25

Nandini decided to meet Divya after reading Arjun's four-page letter to her, for the nth time. Just a week before he passed away, Arjun had written to her in detail about changing his ways, quitting alcohol and drugs. In addition, he had shared the story of his relationship with Divya, mentioning that they had dreamt of their plans for the future. Also, *Amma*, before her demise had given a green signal to their relationship if he promised to mend his ways. Arjun also explained how Divya had turned him away during their last meeting because he was high on ganja. He asked Nandini to help him make amends with Divya and intervene to patch up their misunderstandings when she returned from Australia. The letter also gave information about Divya's life, her two brothers, her widowed mother, and where they lived.

Picking up her handbag after having a hurried breakfast, she took an autorickshaw to Divya's house.

Nandini hesitated at the doorstep, nerves pulsating with anticipation. Divya was alone at home. Engrossed in a book, she glanced up with a guarded expression.

Awkwardly, Nandini addressed her, "Divya, right?... I'm Nandini, Arjun's sister... We need to talk. I hope this is a convenient time for you."

Divya looked up, her eyes betraying a flicker of discomfort and rather abruptly asked, "Arjun's sister?... er... What do you want?"

Nandini discerned a mild uneasiness and perhaps belligerence in her features. Nandini, stood uncertainly and took a deep breath, trying to gauge Divya's reaction. "I just returned from Australia. Arjun had written to me about you in his last letter. He had wanted me to help him mend things between you two."

Divya's gaze narrowed, a defensive edge creeping into her voice which seemed distant, "I don't know what he wrote to you, but those are past now. What is the use of talking about that. He is gone..." her voice trailed away. She did not even ask Nandini to take a seat.

"May I sit down?" Nandini persisted, her tone growing more urgent.

Divya gestured toward a chair.

Nandini leaned forward, "What happened between you two, Divya? When did you last see him?"

"Why does it matter now? He's dead. Why open past wounds?" Divya looked down at her feet as she answered refusing to meet Nandini's gaze.

Nandini's eyes narrowed, suspicion clouding her expression. "He mentioned something about meeting you here in your home. What happened here?"

Divya averted her eyes, fidgeting uncomfortably, avoiding eye contact remarked, "He met me here a few days before he died. We had an argument. That's all."

Nandini pressed on, a mixture of frustration and desperation in her voice. She wanted to know what transpired between them on that day, but Divya seemed reluctant to speak to her about it, confining herself to monosyllabic responses or brief replies. "He mentioned that you told him not to meet you ever again. Is it true?" Nandini persisted.

Divya nodded indifferently. She refused to meet Nandini's eyes. "I did not want anything more to do with him. He had promised me more than once that he would change his ways and give up alcohol and drugs, but always he went back on his promises. He seemed to go from bad to worse. There seemed to be no going back for him. I could not tolerate

194

that. I had had enough. How could I bear to live with such a person? My future would be ruined!" Her voice assumed a tinge of hysteria.

"What did you do, Divya, after you met him that day?" Tell me. "Did you meet him after that day?"

Divya teary-eyed, shook her head. "No, I didn't meet him after that day. I... I had a few letters that he had written to me over the years. That day after meeting him, in a fit of frustration, I burnt all of them. I didn't want any reminder of the pain. He... he... hurt me, Nandini." Divya's body was racked with sobs.

Nandini had an intuition that Divya was not revealing everything but couldn't seem to get anything more out of her.

"Is that all you can tell me about your last meeting? Did you meet him after that – any time before his death?"

Divya shook her head and whispered, "No." She hesitated for a moment and continued, "I... I received a letter from him just before he died. I never bothered to open it."

"Nandini was immediately alert, "Do you have it with you now?"

"Yes, I put it in my table drawer and forgot all about it. Let me check." Divya went inside and returned with an unopened envelope and handed it to Nandini.

"You can keep it. I did not even open the envelope. I do not want to read it nor know what is written inside." Then hesitating she looked up at Nandini, "I'm engaged now to another person, trying to move on. Please don't dig up the past. I don't want my past to mar my future."

Nandini, sensing Divya's reluctance, decided to leave. "Okay, Divya, I understand your concern. I'll leave now. But is it okay if I come back to speak to you sometime later. If you happen to remember anything... anything at all that will help clear my doubts about Arjun, please give me a ring." She placed the unopened envelope in her handbag and handed over a slip of paper with her name and phone number scribbled on it. Divya carelessly glanced at it and placed it in the folds of the book she was reading.

As Nandini rose to leave, she remarked, "I'll come back later. May be we can discuss a few more things when you are more relaxed and in a mood to talk to me." Nandini had a feeling that Divya was not opening up to her. Something seemed to gnaw at her mind, but she was covering it up with a shroud of silence.

"Don't come back, Nandini. I'm trying to forget him. Don't remind me of Arjun by coming back." Divya called after her when Nandini descended the steps from her house.

From Divya's house, Nandini went straight to the medical college and completed the formalities, submitting her joining papers. The clerk advised her to await further instructions by post. She returned home, the weight of recent events heavy on her shoulders.

Placing her handbag with Arjun's unopened letter on her dresser, Nandini went to take a shower. As she emerged from the shower, the shrill ringing of the phone interrupted her thoughts. It was her husband Rajaram from Australia inquiring about her joining the medical college. She explained that she was awaiting posting orders from the medical college. Continuing the discussion with him, she had a light dinner, conversed with her daughter, Aathira, and attended to the routine of the evening.

As she was preparing for bed, suddenly she remembered Arjun's letter given by Divya. She had forgotten all about it in her conversation with Rajaram. With a sense of anxiety, Nandini opened it, expecting perhaps a message of reconciliation. However, as her eyes moved across the pages, surprise, shock, and remorse gripped her. The room seemed to spin, and she collapsed onto the bed, her head reeling from the unexpected emotional turmoil.

The letter had very troubling news, suggesting things that seemed unbelievable. Nandini was completely shocked by what she read, feeling frozen and unable to think clearly because of Arjun's unexpected revelations. Strong feelings filled the room as she tried to imbibe the shocking news, not sure what to do next.

Chapter 26

The next morning, she hurried to Inspector Ranjit's office after contacting him over the phone. She was in a state of near hysteria. Nandini clutched Arjun's letter tightly in her hands as she entered the office of the inspector.

Inspector Ranjit, always looking stylish like a Bollywood actor, glanced up from his desk with a smile as Nandini walked in. His hair was neatly groomed, showing touches of grey at the temples, and his face exuded a sense of assurance. He motioned her to take a seat, and she hesitantly lowered herself onto the cold, hard chair.

"Good morning, Nandini, what brings you here so early in the morning?" Ranjit inquired, peering at her troubled expression, with a mix of curiosity and concern. "You look disturbed."

"I found something that might shed light on Arjun's death," Nandini replied, her voice trembling as she handed over the letter to him.

"Ranjit, you must read this letter. Arjun had written it to Divya a few days before his death. I got it from her yesterday." So saying, she described the previous day's incident when she had been to meet Divya.

Ranjit leaned forward, intrigued. "Show me the letter. Doing a bit of sleuthing on your own, eh?" he teased her as he removed the three-page letter from the envelope.

As he unfolded the letter and began reading, the atmosphere in the room shifted. The weight of Arjun's confessions hung heavily in the air.

"Ten lakhs? Business dealings?" Ranjit muttered to himself, as he read the letter, his eyebrows furrowed. "This is much more than a simple case of a son's guilt."

Ranjit continued reading Arjun's letter, each sentence tightening the knot in his stomach. "*A showdown was needed,*" he quoted Arjun's words, his voice quivering with anger and pity. "Maybe Arjun was angry with them and confronted them with his suspicions that they were deceiving him," the inspector commented as he read the letter.

Arjun had hinted in the letter that he had advanced ten lakh rupees to the KK brothers in two instalments as they had promised to include him in their business, but they had not given him any agreement or drawn up a partnership deed. He had blindly trusted their word. As per the contents of the letter, they had given him a small share of the profits from time to time, but now that he had given up his old errant habits, he wanted to take interest in the business and straighten his life. That was the gist of it.

This lack of transparency had left a lingering doubt in Arjun's mind that the KK brothers were up to some mischief or indulging in some illegal methods in their business dealings. They had been evading questions from him about the business. He had felt that they were not being straightforward in their dealings with him. He had hinted as much in the letter but was not privy to the real nature of their business. He had mentioned in the letter that he would confront them one of these days with that. A showdown was inevitable, he had felt. But before anything could be done, the cruel hands of fate had plucked him from this world.

Ranjit's gaze met Nandini's eyes, searching for answers. "Did you know about all this? And he wrote all of this to Divya, of all persons and not in his letter to you." Ranjit commented, looking up from reading the letter.

"No, Inspector. Arjun never spoke to me about his business dealings, nor did he write to me about them." she replied, her eyes welling up. "Furthermore, for almost a year I had been in Australia, and hence did not know about the goings on here... unfortunately."

As he continued reading, the second half of the letter really shocked Ranjit. Another matter Arjun had wanted to get off his chest in this long winded letter, was regarding his mother's death. On the night before his mother's death, he had come home drunk and high on cannabis. Mother had opened the door for him. After having served him dinner, she had moved to the bed room and called out to him. When Arjun reached the room, she had scolded him for his wayward behavior and his late night arrivals which was upsetting everyone in the house. One thing had led to another and a war of words ensued. And in a fit of rage, impulsively he had pushed his mother.

> ".......... I truly didn't mean to hurt her, but in my wicked state of mind, I did something I deeply regretted. I've never been able to forgive myself for this awful act. I don't even deserve forgiveness from God. No son should ever harm his mother like I did. I never imagined it would lead to her death. It was never my intention. Rage, ganja, and alcohol clouded my judgment. I wasn't aware of what I was doing... "

She had fallen hitting her head against the doorpost. Arjun had stormed out of the house without looking back and spent the night in the outhouse of the KK brothers' residence. The next morning, he had woken up late and returned home only to learn of his mother's hospitalization and subsequent death. Extreme guilt engulfed him. Was her death due to his pushing her and her fall hitting her head against the doorpost — he did not know. The thought shattered his already devastated soul. He would carry the burden of this guilt to his grave. This was a secret he could share only with Divya and could not tell his brothers or Nandini.

Ever since that day, Arjun had decided to give up both cannabis and alcohol, deciding to take control of his life. He would seek the help of Dr. Mohsin to get relieved of his addiction. In this three-page long letter he had entreated Divya to forgive him and forget the past. They could be together again and he was willing to improve his ways and go steady with her and make amends. The letter ended with his profuse apology to Divya asking her to give him one more — last chance.

Divya had never read that letter.

"Since you said that your mother's death was due to a severe heart attack, it is unlikely that her fall and head injury were the cause of death. The intense stress of arguing with Arjun could, however, have caused the heart attack." Inspector Ranjit endeavored to soothe Nandini's ruffled emotions. "I am sorry, Nandini but I think since both are dead, it is best to put it behind you and move on."

Nandini nodded dejectedly.

"It's quite possible that Arjun's overwhelming sense of guilt was the reason behind his decision to end his own life," the inspector mused, returning the letter to Nandini with a solemn expression. "Considering this, it could shed light on the mystery surrounding your brother's demise. He could have been severely depressed after that event."

Nandini left the police station taking leave of Inspector Ranjit ruminating on the thought, her heart heavy with anguish.

Back at the police station, ACP Ranjit, the seasoned detective, thought to himself, "There was more to be done apart from solving the puzzle behind Arjun's death." The letter that Nandini had shown him might point to suicide as the cause, but he wanted to be sure before closing the file. He decided he had work to do before closing the file.

ACP Ranjit decided it was time to confront the *Kurukankaattil* brothers or the KK brothers, as they chose to call themselves and ask them about their dealings with Arjun and his investment with them. He called them in together for questioning before closing Arjun's file.

The air became thick with tension as Sukumaran and Divakaran entered Inspector Ranjit's room in the police station with trepidation writ on their faces.

"Sit down," Ranjit commanded, in a stern voice, his gaze piercing through the façade of the brothers. Initially, he chose to question both of them together. The inspector opted to start by questioning them about Arjun, with his case file open in front of him. Following his initial inquiries about Arjun and his business dealings with them, he proceeded to ask them about Arjun's final days.

"When did you see Arjun last before his death?" Ranjit came straight to the point.

"We don't know where Arjun was before his death. Hadn't seen him for days," Divakaran answered his voice shaking.

Sukumaran interjected, "We saw him about a week or so before his death. After that he never came to our office.

Ranjit's next question shattered their confident demeanor: "Did he visit your office only, or did he also come to your home to meet you?"

"Occasionally... rarely, we used to meet him in our outhouse, when we had a get together... on some evenings."

"And was it there that you fed him alcohol and drugs?" Ranjit persisted.

Both the brothers feigned innocence. "Drugs? Oh no, Inspector, we never use drugs, occasionally we have a drink or two in the evenings, which is all. Arjun seldom joined us. We don't know how he got into drugs."

"Well, how much money had Arjun invested in your business?" The brothers looked at each other before answering, "Five lakhs," said Divakaran.

"Are you sure?" Ranjit's eyes bored into his. "May be ten lakhs... Yes... he invested ten lakhs."

"Was he a partner in your business?"

"No, he was not a registered partner as per record; he sort of invested the money with us so that we could pay him a share from the profits." The brothers had begun to sweat now, trying to wriggle their way out. They wrung their hands in anxiety. Divakaran grabbed at the glass of water that was offered by a constable and wiped his forehead with his handkerchief.

"Did you give him any receipt, a signed agreement or promissory note when you accepted this amount?"

Both sat silent.

Ranjit leaned back, studying their reactions. "Business dealings... ten lakhs, without any record or agreement! Care to explain that?"

....

"What is the nature of your business?" Ranjit's stared intently at both of them.

"We bring fertilizer from North India, mainly Punjab and Gujarat and distribute it here — all over Malabar... wholesale."

"How do you bring the fertilizer?"

"We have our own trucks — the KK Transport company."

"How many trucks do you own?" Ranjit persisted.

"Our fleet has a strength of fifty five trucks plying between North and South India." Sukumaran answered.

"Our business is transparent, Inspector," Divakaran interjected.

The brothers' faces betrayed a sense of unease. "We have nothing to hide, Inspector. We are honest businessmen. Arjun was free to do as he pleased with the money his father left him. Being friends, he opted to invest it with us... of his own accord; we never compelled him." Divakaran replied, a forced smile playing on his lips.

"Okay, both of you may leave for now," Ranjit rose from his seat and put on his beret, "But be available for questioning whenever you are summoned."

"Okay, sir, thank you sir," both answered in unison.

As they were going out, Ranjit called out to them, "By the way who is Mohandas?"

"He is our cousin, my aunt's son. He is a politician and a small-time leader in a political party. He is also a partner in our fertilizer business."

"I want to meet him also. Tell him to be available tomorrow."

After the brothers had left the police station, the inspector summoned their chief head constable Raghavan an elderly, sincere constable who had put in long years of service in the department. He was an individual honest to the core, a devout Hindu, always sporting a sandalwood mark on his forehead as a sign of devotion to *Bhagavan Guruvayurappan*. He had been a resident of Calicut since he joined the force. Head constable Raghavan, who was set to retire in a year, had been a trusted confidant of ACP Ranjit ever since the inspector assumed charge in Calicut.

"Ah, Raghavan sir," Ranjit accosted him, giving him the respect he deserved, "I have an assignment for you. Get me all the information you can about a certain Mohandas, a petty politician who is a partner in the business with the KK brothers who just left. I want you to be discreet while making enquiries as I don't want him to get even a whiff of doubt that we are gathering details about him. Also, get me details about the KK brothers and their business. I want to know whether they are legitimate or are cutting any corners."

"Yes, sir," said Head constable Raghavan, "I know him – Mohandas is a small time politician who has curried favors with the leadership of his party in Delhi and is now rumored to be trying to contest for the post of an MLA in the next state assembly elections. It is rumored that he has been able to raise quite a hefty sum of money as funds for his party here, so much so the leadership is happy to give him a ticket for the next election."

"Is he a reliable and honest chap?" Ranjit's skepticism was obvious in his question.

The head constable smiled sardonically, "Honest? No, sir he is as honest and trustworthy as a viper. There is a rumor that he has many underhand dealings including blackmail by which he amasses his fortune."

"Okay, get me all the particulars about him."

"Sure sir," replied Raghavan saluting the inspector.

"And, by the way, be careful." Ranjit nodded to the constable who took his leave. "And let's proceed cautiously with investigating him since he has political connections, which could have consequences either way."

Nandini was reclining on the rocking chair which her father used to sit gently rocking to and fro as he read the day's newspaper. She had taken some items of furniture from the ancestral home when she shifted to the outhouse. She sat reading a medical journal gently rocking as she absorbed the contents. Devaki Amma, a weathered maid who was a part time help, approached Nandini with a sense of hesitancy. "*Amma*, I need to tell you something."

The maid used to work in the *Kurukankaattil* house and also at the house of Mohandas as a part-time help. She came thrice a week to clean the outhouse where Nandini stayed.

Nandini raised her eyebrows silently.

"I have to tell you something," the elderly servant whispered as if in a conspiratorial tone.

Nandini raised her eyebrows, "What is it?"

"I wanted to tell you about the dirty games that the brothers at the *Kurukankaattil* house played on your dead brother. Your brother was a gem of a person. Occasionally he used to tip me discretely ten or twenty rupees." She chuckled exposing her betel stained teeth.

Nandini listened intently as Devaki Amma spilled the beans about Arjun's drunken escapades, in the outhouse of the KK brothers, the pranks, and the twisted games the brothers played on him.

"They made him dance while drunk and do unimaginable things," Devaki Amma whispered, her eyes filled with pity. Nandini's eyes widened with horror as the maid went on with more particulars. The news about the dirty tricks those brothers had played on her innocent brother pierced Nandini's ears like red hot lead.

"How did you know all this?" Nandini was skeptical as to whether the maid was telling the truth. "Were you working there in the outhouse?"

"Well..." hesitated Devaki Amma, "Elias, their man servant told me. He is often there in the outhouse when the brothers entertain Arjun. Their cousin Mohandas is also there. Elias and I are close... well... he told me." Devaki amma said blushing. "He is the one who told me what pranks they played with your brother, Arjun."

"Why do you go to their house?"

"I work part time in their house and also at their aunt – Narayani Amma's house. Their son Mohandas is close friends with the brothers in the main house."

But that was not all.

On another occasion, Devaki amma, had inadvertently overheard a conversation between the elder brother Sukumaran and his wife. It was a conversation centered around the precious jewels that Arjun had inherited from his late mother. Sukumaran had shared his memories of having seen Arjun's jewelry collection. He had shown his wife a photograph capturing the elegance of an exquisite necklace with a beautiful peacock shaped pendant with a large blue gemstone in the center ringed by shiny green gemstones.

Sukumaran's wife was fascinated by the snapshot of the exquisite necklace.

"Could you not ask Arjun if he would sell us the necklace. It is so stunning. It will look nice on me!"

"I don't think he would sell it now, but I have told him already. I will try to get the necklace for you. If he is not prepared to sell it, we will think of something else." Sukumaran had winked with a cunning smile.

Sukumaran had told his wife, "Arjun cherishes these jewels; they are more than mere ornaments for him. They carry the essence of his mother's love, a connection to his roots. I don't think he will voluntarily part with it."

Sukumaran's wife, a silent participant in this emotional exchange, had nodded in agreement. "Yes, these jewels are not just material possessions; they are a living testament to the bonds that tie him to his past memories. No wonder Arjun wants to hold onto this legacy with pride."

As the couple exited the room, the photograph was left lying on the bedroom table. Devaki amma, the snoopy maid, had entered the room to carry out her daily chores of sweeping the room. In the midst of dusting and sweeping, she couldn't help but pause, to take a peek at the photograph of the necklace. She was fascinated by the design of the necklace, of course, fully well knowing that this was something beyond her reach. But she could not but admire the exquisite piece of jewelry.

Nandini, now armed with this new gossip disclosed by Devaki amma, relayed it to Ranjit, who added it to his growing list of suspicions surrounding the *Kurukankaattil* brothers. He assigned two plain clothes men to shadow the brothers and report directly to him. The inspector sensed that Arjun's case was growing increasingly intricate — perhaps more than a simple case of suicide. Perhaps the ramifications of the case were greater than he initially thought.

Nandini felt sad and frustrated. She sensed betrayal around her. The dark mood matched the shadows at the Iyer house.

Chapter 27

When Nandini mentioned Devaki Amma's gossip to Inspector Ranjit, his response had been, "Find out what's in Arjun's locker. You said that you had the list of the jewelry your mother bequeathed to him. You might be in for a surprise. You never know whether Arjun sold any of the pieces of his jewelry."

Ranjit's words echoed in her ears as the weight of suspicion and intrigue swept over her. Determined, she decided to pursue Ranjit's request, starting with a call to her younger brother, Satya.

Nandini dialed Satya's number and waited for him to answer.

"Hello?" Satya's voice crackled through the phone.

"Satya, it's Nandini. We need to talk about Arjun's bank locker. Can you come to the outhouse?" Her voice betrayed a mix of urgency and anxiety.

"Why? What happened?" Satya seemed anxious and surprised. His voice was cautious.

"We will discuss it in person." Nandini was noncommittal.

Within the hour, Satya arrived at Nandini's outhouse. He seemed anxious. Nandini wasted no time and cut to the chase.

She explained to him that the police had reopened Arjun's case on her request.

"Why? What is the need for that?. It has already been closed by them as a case of plain and simple suicide." Satya seemed perplexed. "Why do you insist on dredging up past events?"

"In light of some new findings, the police wanted to know if there was any foul play associated with Arjun's death. The police — Inspector Ranjit in particular, wants Arjun's locker opened and inventoried." Intentionally, she did not mention about the gossip that she had heard from Devaki amma and her discussion with Ranjit regarding the jewelry.

"We need a power of attorney to open Arjun's locker. The bank won't allow it otherwise," Satya's eyes narrowed as he mentioned the legal complexities.

"Did you get the POA from Anandu and Sreeni?" Nandini persisted.

"Anandu said he'd come in person. to sort this out together. Sreeni has already given me a POA from the US." Satya asserted, "Since you are here, you can easily give me a POA. We can get it done tomorrow itself."

"But why? Since I am here, I can come with you to the bank directly. There is no need for my POA." Nandini was quick to answer.

Satya seemed reluctant at the suggestion and hesitated but eventually nodded. "Why should you bother to come with me to the bank. The bank manager and I together can inventory the jewels in Arjun's locker."

"No, I shall come in person to the bank," Nandini insisted. "I want to be present when the locker is opened and inventoried."

"Is it enough if we do it a week or two later?" Satya asked.

"Why?… why should we delay it. Let us do it tomorrow or the day after itself. ACP Ranjit has asked me to report to him soon about this."

Satya seemed to hesitate peeved at Nandini's insistence, "Alright, but let's get it over with quickly. We can do it tomorrow itself. I will inform Anandu to come by tonight's flight. He can fly to Coimbatore and come from there by train. I am leaving for Bombay the day after along with Janaki."

Nandini raised her eyebrows, "Bombay? What gives?"

"Janaki's cousin — uncle's son, is getting married on Sunday. He is working in a multinational company in Singapore. The bride is from Bombay. Hence the marriage is in Bombay. As you know our marriages are a two-day affair. Janaki wants to be present on both days — Saturday and Sunday. So we are leaving by the Friday morning flight to Bombay. That's why I am in a hurry to get this behind me soon."

"Sure, tomorrow is perfectly okay for me," Nandini was ready.

The paperwork had been a tedious process, complicated by the bureaucratic red tape that had delayed obtaining the legal heirship certificate. As Sreeni, in the U.S., had already provided his power of attorney, leaving Anandu and Nandini as the remaining persons to grant access. Satya had got all the papers ready.

Anandu arrived by noon and Nandini, accompanied by him, reached the bank after lunch.

The air inside the bank was charged with anticipation as the siblings handed over the necessary documents to the manager. After the essential preliminaries, the manager, a stoic figure in a formal suit, led them to the vault.

As the locker door creaked open, revealing the secrets locked within, Nandini felt an uneasy shiver run down her spine. The trio, with the manager as their witness, removed the jewel box from the locker.

As the jewelry box was opened, memories gleamed like precious gems. Nandini's eyes gleamed with unshed tears as the memory of her dear mother and Arjun assailed her mind. But when her gaze landed on the empty space in the box where the blue sapphire necklace should be, she was aghast! Her heart sank. All other pieces of jewelry were present intact.

"Where is *Amma's* blue sapphire necklace, Satya?" she demanded, her eyes drilling into his.

Satya's indifferent and rather indignant shrug only fueled her frustration. "How do I know? Arjun might have sold it or pawned it. You should ask him," he retorted callously raising his eyes upwards towards the heavens.

Nandini felt peeved and humiliated at this insult. Anandu kept quiet, frowning deep in thought.

Nandini's disbelief transformed into determination. "I'll talk to Inspector Ranjit about this. This is not right. Something is fishy. We should get to the bottom of this."

The inventory completed, the bank manager sealed the locker, leaving the siblings to grapple with the sudden suspense that surrounded the disappearance of the necklace from the collection. "I cannot hand the contents over to any of you till this disappearance, which you claim, is sorted out. Since the police are involved, I am sealing the locker for the time being and shall hold the inventory list with me. You can have a copy, he said turning to Nandini." The manager was insistent.

Outside the bank, Nandini made the call to Inspector Ranjit from a nearby STD booth, narrating the events with a mix of frustration and surprise. Ranjit, perceptive as ever, promised to dig deeper.

In his office, Ranjit contemplated Devaki amma's rumors about the necklace and Nandini's account of the events at the bank. He sensed a web of deception and was determined to seek answers. He resolved to interrogate Sukumaran regarding Arjun's necklace.

Sukumaran was summoned to the police station and he faced Ranjit's probing gaze. "Sukumaran, what do you know about a blue sapphire necklace that belonged to Arjun's mother?" Ranjit asked coming straight to the point, his tone firm.

Sukumaran shifted uncomfortably. "I... I don't know anything about it. Why would I?"

Ranjit leaned forward, his eyes piercing through the façade. "I heard that you were interested in the necklace. You even had a photograph taken of the piece. Are you hiding something?"

Sukumaran's eyes darted nervously. "I... I don't know anything about the necklace. It is true that I liked it and wanted it for my wife. I took a snapshot of the necklace with Arjun's permission intending to make a similar replica. I offered to buy it from Arjun. But he refused to sell it to me when I asked him. Why do you ask me about it?"

Ranjit's voice softened, adopting a softer tone. "Sukumaran, don't hide anything from me. If there's something you're not telling me, now is the time. Do you have that necklace with you?"

"God promise, I don't know anything about the necklace."

"You may go now. But don't play any tricks with me." Ranjit cautioned him sternly.

Chapter 28

Chief Constable Raghavan ruminated on the meticulously gathered intelligence on the elusive KK brothers. He sufficiently understood the gravity of the information he had unearthed. A single flickering tube light cast wavering light on the papers spread across Raghavan's desk as he prepared to report his findings to Inspector Ranjit. He arranged the papers into a file to be handed over to ACP Ranjit. The old, dilapidated ceiling fan lazily swung around as it wobbled from side to side creaking due to its aged unoiled joints.

The tale began with the honorable figure, Kuttykrishnan Nair, their father — an honest and straightforward businessman whose reputation for honesty and ethics in his business was admired even by his rivals. Stricken with a stroke, Nair had relinquished the reins of the family business to his two sons, Sukumaran and Divakaran. What emerged from the grapevine painted a disconcerting picture — the brothers, unlike their upright father, harbored aspirations for quick riches, and whispers hinted at the dubious means they employed to achieve their ends. Black money and non-disclosure of profits and income had brought them into the scrutiny by the authorities and they were under investigation by the income tax and sales tax departments. But so far no criminal offences had been charged against them.

Raghavan realized the importance of the information that he had gathered — the rumors about the siblings. Though unconfirmed, the rumors were disturbing. It seemed the siblings were balancing between legal and illegal activities. Despite the cloud of suspicion that hung over them, the KK brothers had managed to evade any formal accusations or legal ramifications so far.

Chief constable Raghavan reported his findings to Inspector Ranjit, "I have collected some details on the KK brothers, sir" he said as he was offered a seat. The aged constable suffered from osteoarthritis of his knees and Ranjit being well aware of this fact, never allowed him to stand in front of him for long.

The constable sat on the edge of the chair, "They bring fertilizer from North India," he continued, his voice a low murmur, as he laid the file containing the details on the inspector's table. "Acting as distributors in the Malabar region, they've carved a niche for themselves, holding a monopoly on the trade. It was the father who built the business to the present level. The brothers are managing the business as their father is now laid up."

"As individuals," Raghavan continued, his gaze fixed on the papers before him, "Both brothers are said to be greedy and dishonest, a stark departure from the integrity their father once upheld. Of late, they have expanded their business and are getting their fertilizer from Punjab also." Their story unfolded like a novel, with characters lurking in shadows and their real motives obscured by layers of deception.

"As you had advised, I've taken the liberty of ordering two constables to tail their every move," Raghavan finally revealed, his expression a mix of determination and concern. "It's time to unravel the mystery that surrounds the KK brothers. I'll report back to you, sir, once I've gathered more concrete facts. They seem to be an unreliable lot. Meanwhile constables Sooraj and Kartik are shadowing Mohandas, their cousin."

The sun hung low in the sky, casting long shadows that stretched across the dusty roads of Mahe. Mohandas skillfully maneuvered his red Maruti 800 hatchback through the narrow lanes, an unspoken secret guiding him. Two police constables, hidden beneath the disguise of *lungis* and turbans dressed as laborers, trailed behind on their motorbikes, the distant hum of their engines adding to the hushed atmosphere.

Parking his car in a nondescript auto garage on the outskirts of Mahe, Mohandas handed over its keys to the owner, a short dark individual with disheveled hair and a thick mustache and an unkempt beard. They seemed oblivious to the covert surveillance. The constables, Sooraj and Kartik exchanged glances, their silent communication weaving a web of unspoken questions. They had been ordered by ACP Ranjit and head constable Raghavan to shadow Mohandas and report on his movements only; not to interfere with whatever he was up to or take any preemptive action. They watched in anticipation as Mohandas mounted a motorbike which the owner of the garage lent him, setting off in the direction of Thalasseri, the constables lingering in the shadows behind at a discrete distance.

The sun descended further, casting the sky in a symphony of orange and pink hues as Mohandas rode along the coast in Mahe. Suddenly, he took an unexpected turn to the right down a secluded side lane. The narrow path led him to an old godown on the outskirts, a dilapidated warehouse bearing witness to clandestine activities. The constables disguised as laborers, approached cautiously, their motorbikes hidden in the bushes a few yards away from the main building, the crunch of gravel beneath their sandals muffled by the ambient sounds from the shrubbery.

Beside the godown, a small wooden shed annexed to the main structure stood with its gloomy interior. The constables entered the unlocked shed quietly, enveloped in shadows of the thick brush around. The shed was dark. Peering through a small aperture in the wall, they could see the interior of the large warehouse lit by a single incandescent bulb hanging from the high ceiling. The air inside the shed was filled with the musty aroma of sawdust mingled with the putrid odor of a dead rodent among the piles of wooden planks. The constables strained their senses to observe the unfolding scene.

Two large KK Transport trucks, ominous silhouettes against the dimming sky, lumbered into view,. The constables held their breath as the trucks, like silent behemoths, were driven into the godown through the large doors at its side.

Within the confined space of the shed, the constables witnessed the tense scene as the truck doors creaked open, revealing stacks polypropylene bags marked as fertilizer. The atmosphere was filled with suspense as many of the bags were unloaded from each of the trucks and out of these, two bags were identified and isolated from each of the trucks. Mohandas, holding a flashlight helped identify these four bags which were removed. These four were no different in size or color from the others and bore the same label of the seemingly legitimate fertilizer company. The rest of the bags were then reloaded into the trucks. Mohandas supervised the whole charade giving instructions to the truck drivers and their helpers as they unloaded the bags and reloaded them. The constables strained to decipher the hidden motives behind this enigmatic exchange. The driver and helper got into the cabins of the respective trucks and the trucks rumbled out of view bound towards Calicut.

As the sun bid its final farewell, casting long shadows that merged with the darkness surrounding the godown, the constables remained rooted to their posts in the dark shed. The night whispered secrets, and the air became resonant with the loud chirping of cicadas and the sounds of fauna of the wild. The constables, bound by duty, continued their secret observation of the drama that unfolded within the dilapidated walls of the godown. Suspense hung in the air as Sooraj and Kartik squinted through the peephole by turns, trying to make sense of the clandestine proceedings.

The constables waited in the dark shed with an unsettling anticipation. Mohandas, the puppet master in this hush-hush theatre, sat smoking on a worn wicker chair, the tendrils of cigarette smoke swirling around him like a web of secrets. The constables, their identities hidden in shadows, remained vigilant, eyes fixed on the dilapidated structure that housed the unfolding mystery. The suspense was deafening. The constables wondered whom Mohandas was waiting for.

The fading light showed Mohandas sitting in the shadows, partly hidden as he smoked his cigarette quietly. There was a feeling of something bad about to happen, a strong tension that grew with each passing moment. The police constables, hidden from view, felt the weight of the secret about to come out.

The constables glanced at their wrist watches. The phosphorescent dial of their watches showed the time to be nearing eight. The covert meeting, held in the shadows of dusk, was about to take an unexpected turn. The sound of motorcycles and a car was heard at a distance. Soon two motorcycles and an aging black Ambassador car arrived. There were two riders in each bike and two in the car. The constables, now just watching the drama unfold, struggled to hear fragments of conversation coming from the warehouse. But it was inaudible.

Mohandas, the mysterious organizer of this nighttime meeting, responded with a nod and a cryptic smile at the new arrivals. The constables, their eyes widened in realization, immediately grasped the gravity of the situation. The air was charged with unspoken tension, as the suspense was revealed. The four sacks recovered from the trucks were now ripped open and the small brick-sized packages concealed within the four sacks left behind were taken out. In the dim light, the parcels were revealed, hidden within the sacks. The six of them were very quick in sorting out the contents of the two bags.

The constables exchanged glances, a silent communication reflecting the importance of their discovery. They could not count the number of packages, but by a rough estimate they could guess the number to be no less than fifty. Colloquial dialogues, soft murmurs of conversation carried by the night wind, fluttered through the air, though the constables could not decipher what was being said. The air was thick with suspense and surprise. The six newcomers, now integral players in this shadowy drama, collected the mysterious packages. During this covert operation, constable Sooraj did not forget to note down the registration number of the vehicles in his pocket notebook.

"Hey, what's in these bags?" constable Kartik whispered to Sooraj, the words laden with both intrigue and trepidation.

"Shh! Keep quiet and watch, it's probably drugs or ganja or both." came the hushed reply, the two constables sharing a moment of understanding amidst the secrecy. "I have noted down the registration numbers of those two motorbikes and the car. We can easily trace their ownership."

Soon the parcels exchanged hands. The reality of what was happening sent shivers down the spines of the constables who witnessed the mysterious exchange. It was apparent that the parcels would contain contraband.

The mysterious exchange concluded as the packets seamlessly disappeared into hidden compartments within the waiting vehicles — an unspoken agreement etched into the secret meeting. The night was a silent witness to the illicit transactions. A duffel bag, obviously a payoff, passed between the newly arrived characters and Mohandas, the orchestrator of this enigmatic rendezvous.

With a deliberate motion, Mohandas unzipped the duffel bag, revealing its contents — bundles of cash. A sense of triumph and a smile played across his features. The constables stood there, their eyes glued to the scene that was played before them.

The car and the motorcycles roared off into the dark night.

As Mohandas mounted his motorbike and departed towards Mahe to retrieve his car from the workshop, his tail lights fading into the distance, the constables lingered in the shadows, silent witnesses to the covert operations they had just witnessed. The cold night air caressed their faces as the constables ensuring that the coast was clear, mounted their motorcycles for their return journey home. The seriousness of their recent discovery showed on their faces, as their expressions reflected the whirlwind of thoughts going on in their minds.

"What do we do now?" one constable finally broke the silence as their bike roared towards Calicut, his voice carrying the uncertainty that mirrored the shadows around them.

The other constable, gaze fixed on the distant horizon where Mohandas had disappeared, contemplated the question for a moment before responding, "We'll report this to ACP Ranjit who deputed us to this task. This is a sensational discovery. It's time to expose the treachery lurking beneath the surface."

The constables, assigned to uncover secrets in Thalasseri's dusty streets, set forth with determination to reveal the truth. As they embarked on their return journey to Calicut on their motorcycles, the scene was set for the unfolding of mysteries.

They were unaware that the registration numbers on all three vehicles were fake, as they had false number plates that couldn't be traced back to the actual owners.

Chapter 29

Nandini sat in the cozy living room of the outhouse holding a cup of coffee, the aroma of freshly brewed filter coffee wafting through the air. The aroma of the filter coffee filled Nandini's senses, transporting her back to cherished memories of her mother. Her mother's brew held a magic that was beyond compare, a blend of warmth and comfort that embraced her soul. With each sip, not only did it tantalize her taste buds, but it also caressed her olfactory senses with its soothing aroma, wrapping her in a blanket of nostalgia. As she savored the familiar scent, Nandini found herself drifting into a reverie, her mind awash with images of her mother's gentle smile and the sound of her laughter echoing through the kitchen.

"Oh, how I miss her," Nandini whispered softly to herself, her voice barely audible over the gentle hum of the coffee machine.

Lost in her thoughts, she reached out to trace the delicate pattern on the porcelain cup, her fingers lingering over the familiar curves and ridges. Each touch brought a flood of emotions, a bittersweet mixture of longing and love that threatened to overwhelm her.

"It's amazing how a simple cup of coffee can hold so much meaning," she murmured, her words tinged with a hint of sadness. "You were right, *Amma*," she whispered, a tear glistening in the corner of her eye. "There truly is nothing quite like your coffee."

The day's letters lay scattered on the table, but one, in particular, seized her attention. The Association of Gynecologists of Kerala had extended an invitation to a state conference in Trivandrum on the upcoming weekend. A wave of excitement surged within Nandini as she envisioned to escape from the routine in Calicut and the prospect of rekindling old friendships. A weekend break would do her some good. She could get her mind away from matters at home.

Taking an immediate decision, she dialed a number, connecting her to Dr. Soumya, a dear friend and fellow gynecologist at the Trivandrum Medical College. The phone rang, and on the other end, a familiar voice exclaimed, "What a surprise, Nandini! I thought you were still in Australia. Have you come back?"

Grinning, Nandini responded, "No, not permanently. I'm back for a brief period, having rejoined the medical college here. I intend to apply for long leave and return to Australia."

After the preliminary generalities, "Oh, by the way, what can I do for you?" Soumya inquired, genuine curiosity marking her words.

"I wish to attend the gynecology conference next week. Just called to know if you'll be there and if you'd be able to put me up for a couple of days."

"Absolutely, why not! I'll be delighted to accommodate you. It's just Shekhar and me here. Our son is in the hostel. We can have a fantastic time and catch up with old times," Soumya responded warmly. Shekhar, Soumya's husband, held the distinguished position of Professor of Forensic Medicine at the Trivandrum Medical College.

As Nandini continued savoring her coffee, the excitement bubbled within her, envisioning the imminent reunion with Soumya and the prospect of spending delightful moments in Trivandrum. She wanted to revisit some of the scenic spots in the city and also wanted to pay a visit to the famous *Padmanabha Swami* temple there. The thought of the upcoming conference made her happy and excited. It made her feel warm and enthusiastic, as if time and distance didn't matter anymore.

In the days that followed, the two friends exchanged phone calls, detailing plans for the weekend. The prospect of rekindling their camaraderie brought a sense of joy to both Nandini and Soumya, turning a routine conference into a cherished opportunity to celebrate the enduring bond of their friendship. She called her travel agent and requested him to book a berth to Trivandrum by the express train on Friday night.

The conference yielded a vibrant mixture of academic highlights that thrilled Soumya. Reconnecting with friends and mentors provided an additional a layer of joy to the event. Friends and mentors alike filled the corridors with animated discussions, creating an atmosphere of fellowship that transcended the boundaries of time. The air buzzed with curiosity about Soumya's decision to specialize in Gynecologic Oncology. Animated discussions and exchange of ideas permeated the hallways, creating an atmosphere of intellectual exchange.

In the evening, despite a plethora of banquet festivities beckoning, Soumya and Nandini opted for a quiet evening at home. The two friends, nestled in the cozy embrace of Soumya's living room, decided to forgo the grand banquet arranged at a Kovalam beach resort. A simple dinner was cooked by Soumya and as the evening unfolded, Dr. Shekhar, Soumya's husband who joined them for dinner, eagerly got into discussions about her future plans. Post-dinner, he retreated to his room for some quiet work, leaving the two friends to their own devices.

As night descended upon Trivandrum, casting long shadows on the narrow lanes lit by the dim tube lights, Soumya reached for her cherished photo album. The room bathed in the soft glow of memories, Nandini and Soumya embarked on a journey through photographs capturing moments of joy and nostalgia. Soumya, with infectious enthusiasm, recounted the tales behind each snapshot, weaving a narrative that transported them back in time to their college days. The room reverberated with laughter and merriment as they reminisced about their days as students in medical college and the days of benign ragging. They hardly realized that it was late at night as they shared nostalgic memories.

In the midst of their banter about old times and recent escapades, Nandini shared the tragedies that had befallen her family. Soumya, ever the empathetic friend, extended her support, saying, "If there's anything I can do to ease your burden, don't hesitate to ask."

A few unmounted photos spilled onto Nandini's lap as she flipped through the pages of the album. Soumya invited her to peruse these recent snaps from her niece's wedding in Bombay. The reception photographs showcased costumes of vibrant colors and joyous faces, but Nandini's gaze froze on a particular image – Satya and Janaki, smiling, stood on the dais beside the newlyweds. Janaki looked glamorous with rouge and lipstick wearing a blue silk saree. Nandini felt shocked when she saw Janaki wearing the blue, sapphire necklace that was missing from Arjun's locker. For a moment she felt as if time stood still. She stared at the photo.

The room, once filled with laughter, suddenly hung in suspended disbelief. Soumya, oblivious to the revelation, continued to narrate the wedding tales, unaware of the storm brewing within Nandini's heart.

A palpable silence lingered in the air as Nandini stared at the photograph, the shock etched on her face. Soumya, her friend, immediately noticed the change in Nandini's demeanor.

Concern etched on her brow, Soumya gently inquired, "What's the matter?"

Nandini, still reeling from the revelation on seeing the blue sapphire necklace around Janaki's neck, took a moment to compose herself before responding, "Nothing... this photo shows my brother Satya and his wife. Satya's wife is related to the bridegroom. He is her cousin. They too attended the wedding at Bombay."

Nandini pointed out Satya and Janaki to Soumya. "Can I have a copy of this reception photo?" Composing herself Nandini continued, "I want to get a similar *lacha* like the one the bride is wearing, stitched for Aathira." She managed to stammer, hiding her sudden embarrassment and concealing the true intention behind the request for a copy of the photo.

The room, once filled with the lightness of shared memories, now brimmed with unspoken questions in Nandini's mind. Soumya, sensing that there was more beneath the surface, chose not to press Nandini further.

In the train, Nandini, on her journey back to Calicut, clutched the photograph tightly in her hand glancing at it frequently, with the burden of thoughts racing through her mind. How did Janaki come to possess the necklace? Nandini racked her brains but could not come up with a logical answer. The rhythmic hum of the engine served as a backdrop to the tumult within. As she reached Calicut, the photograph seemed to contain more than just images; it held the key to unraveling a mystery that had shaken the fabric of her family.

"How did Janaki come to wear that necklace? What were Satya and Janaki hiding?" The thought nagged Nandini's brain as she reached home the next morning.

With a determined spirit, Nandini sought out Inspector Ranjit, her confidant in the enquiry. She handed over the photo to him, emphasizing the need for discretion. "Find out about Janaki and Satya's Bombay visit and the necklace without revealing my involvement," she requested, her eyes reflecting a mix of concern and a burning desire for answers. "Please don't tell them that I gave you the photo. I don't want to ask them about it again. I wonder if it has any connection to Arjun's death."

Inspector Ranjit, always the astute investigator, nodded in understanding. The investigation took a nuanced turn, with Ranjit skillfully promising to keep matters secret and private. "I will ask them without bringing your name into it. It will not show up in my records either." He placed the photo in his table drawer instead of putting in Arjun's case file.

Meanwhile, in the narrow lanes of Coimbatore, the red Maruti car driven by Mohandas weaved through the traffic. Constables Sooraj and Kartik whom Inspector Ranjit had instructed to shadow him, were not far behind. They wore regular clothes like the common folk of Tamil Nadu, with white dhotis and sacred ash on their foreheads and could easily pass off as locals.

Mohandas parked his car in the underground parking space of a mall. From the rear seat of the car he removed a duffel bag and began walking towards a maze of lanes that were opposite the mall. He reached a quiet area and sat down on a bench on a roadside restaurant – a *Dhaba* and ordered a cup of tea. He placed the duffel bag by his side on the bench on which he sat.

Mohandas leisurely sipped his tea, showing no signs of urgency. Before long, a mysterious middle-aged man, dressed in a long kurta, pajamas stopping at his bare ankles, and a white crocheted skullcap known as a taqiyah, joined him on the bench. The stranger had arrived on an old Lambretta scooter. From a distance, Kartik observed, quickly jotting down details of the scooter and its registration number. His instincts hinted at a secret exchange taking place. Meanwhile, Sooraj snapped photos of the stranger and Mohandas with his camera's zoom lens.

After finishing his cup of tea and exchanging a few words with Mohandas in hushed tones, the stranger casually picked up the duffel bag from the bench. Walking over to the scooter, he placed the bag on it and rode off without a backward glance. Kartik found himself torn about whom to pursue. In a matter of seconds, the stranger vanished into the crowd on his scooter. Kartik didn't have time to rush to his own bike and give chase. Instead, he kept watch on Mohandas, who calmly got up, settled his bill for the tea, and left the same way he had come.

What is the meaning of this clandestine meet they wondered.

"Was this another payoff? Was it a payoff for extortion? Was someone blackmailing Mohandas? What is the identity of the man who picked up the duffel bag. Constable Kartik and Sooraj felt that these were beyond their ken and they decided to return to Calicut and report this to Inspector Ranjit.

Chapter 30

Nandini was surprised by the unexpected visit of Mrs. Maya, the perpetual gossip monger next door. Nandini felt suspicious of her as this gossipmonger's visit portended something more ominous. Mrs. Maya pretending to be friendly and warm would have come with some fresh gossip, Nandini was sure.. This was an unusual visit, Nandini reckoned. Nevertheless, she invited her inside.

"How nice to see you, Nandini after such a long time. We missed you while you were away in Australia," Mrs. Maya said, sipping the cup of tea that Nandini placed before her. "After the series of tragedies that wrecked your home, I was totally shocked and grieved. It is good that you took a respite from these sorrowful circumstances going to Australia."

Nandini, maintaining a non-committal attitude, replied, "Yes, I was thoroughly devastated by the events here. I was not here when *Amma* passed away. I came later after her funeral for a short visit."

"Yes, and Arjun too," Mrs. Maya persisted, her eyes searching for any signs of hidden emotions in Nandini's face. "What a handsome man he was. To be snatched by the cruel jaws of death in the prime of youth! God is indeed cruel." She paused looking at Nandini slyly, awaiting a response from her.

Nandini chose to remain silent.

"And by the way," she continued, adopting an air of casualness, "I just ran into him... Arjun, I mean, the evening before his body was found." Mrs. Maya paused, carefully observing Nandini's face for any reaction, hoping to extract some juicy gossip about Arjun's death, before continuing.

At first, Nandini's mind failed to register the significance of Mrs. Maya's statement. Suddenly, a realization dawned upon her – there might be more to this encounter than met the eye. If Maya had seen Arjun the evening before his body was discovered, the question remained, where and when.

"Where did you see him that evening?" Nandini asked trying to be casual but her curiosity piqued.

"Oh, that?" Mrs. Maya feigned nonchalance waving her hand in a gesture of dismissal. "You see, my cousin Reeta stays next to your brother Satya's house. Reeta also knows Janaki very well. I had gone to visit Reeta that evening. As the two houses are adjacent to each other sharing the same wall like those in an *Agrahaaram*, I could hear agitated conversations from Satya's house, but I could not gather what was being said or who it was."

Nandini leaned forward, her eagerness evident. "And... then, what happened?"

Mrs. Maya's eyes sparkled with a mischievous glint. "Both of us saw your brother, Arjun in his red T-shirt, storm out of the house in a rage. He kicked a pot of flowering plant as he left the house, apparently venting his anger on the pot. Janaki, your brother's wife, was standing in the doorway as he left, as pale as a ghost." The revelation lingered in the air as Mrs. Maya reveled in the thrill of passing on a secret.

Nandini regarded her with a searching gaze. It was obvious that she had come with the sole purpose of conveying this piece of gossip. Also, Maya was attempting to pry into Arjun's death to gather a more juicy scandal from Nandini which she could share in her next kitty party.

Nandini realized that this piece of information was crucial and needed to be shared with Inspector Ranjit at the earliest opportunity. However, she remained silent, her expression impassive, not offering any information to Maya as Maya chattered on about her visit to Reeta's house.

Nandini casually remarked, "Oh, yes, Janaki had told me about it." She did not want Maya to think that this news was a jolt to her and hence acted disinterested.

Nandini's nonchalance punctured Maya's ego like a deflated balloon. "Oh, then it's alright, I thought you might not know it." She rose to bid goodbye to Nandini.

Nandini's mind raced with a mix of suspicion and curiosity, thinking of the implications of Arjun's angry departure from Satya's house on the evening before he was found dead. The atmosphere was full of gossip and mystery as Nandini tried to figure out what to do next about her brother's death. She became confused the more she thought of the facts – the visit of Arjun to Satya's house the evening of his death, the absent sapphire necklace from Arjun's locker and the necklace being worn by Janaki in the reception at Bombay. She could not make head or tail of what could have happened. Something was not right, her intuition told her.

The Sunday morning sun cast a warm glow over Calicut. Nandini found herself impatient to wait until Monday to share the crucial information with Inspector Ranjit. She dialed his number, her voice calm but filled with urgency.

"Ranjit, it's Nandini. I am sorry to disturb you on a Sunday morning, I have something important to tell you. Can we meet?"

Ranjit, sensing the gravity in her tone, responded promptly, "Of course, Nandini. Today's Sunday, I'm free. My wife has gone to her home with our son and I was contemplating going out to lunch. Shall we meet for lunch?"

"Sure… Where… and when?" Nandini hesitated.

"The Blue Lotus restaurant in the heart of the city. One o'clock. Can you make it? I hope you know the place."

"Absolutely. I'll be there."

As the clock struck one, Nandini walked into the restaurant. The air was filled with the refreshing aroma of various dishes being served and the gentle hum of conversations. The dimly lit restaurant was almost full. Ranjit, already seated at a corner table, stood up as he saw her approach.

"Nandini, thank you for coming. Please, have a seat."

She smiled warmly, taking a seat across from him. Nandini wore a lotus-pink saree that complemented her grace, and her minimalistic appearance without any makeup accentuated her natural beauty. The fragrance of her Nina Ricci perfume lingered, creating an atmosphere of subtle elegance.

Ranjit, clad casually in a grey colored T-shirt and jeans, greeted her with a polite nod. He appeared different, unlike his appearance in police uniform. "How have you been, Nandini?"

"Surviving, Ranjit. It's been tough," she replied, a hint of sadness in her eyes. "Work at the medical college has also been quite stressful."

They ordered tandoori butter *naans* and a dish of Malay kofta, the menu reflecting the diversity of the city. As they waited for their meal, Nandini described the events of the previous day and the visit of Mrs. Maya.

"Ranjit, I met a Mrs. Maya yesterday. She is my neighbor. She had some interesting gossip to share," Nandini began, her voice hushed.

Ranjit leaned forward, his brows furrowed in anticipation. "Gossip? What is it?"

Nandini recounted the details of her conversation with Maya, her words creating an atmosphere of suspense. "She said she had heard a quarrel between Arjun and Janaki at Satya's house the evening before he was found dead. Arjun had left in a rage. I thought you should know." Nandini went on to describe what Maya had told her.

Ranjit's eyes narrowed, his mind processing the information. "Arjun at Satya's house?... That too on the evening of his death?... A quarrel with Janaki? This is unexpected. What could they be arguing about? Did your brother or Janaki tell you anything about this before?"

Nandini shook her head.

"I don't know, Ranjit. It's strange," Nandini replied, her voice tinged with concern. "And the matter of the necklace..."

Their lunch arrived, the tantalizing aroma of the dishes filling the air. The conversation paused briefly as they savored the flavors of the Malay kofta and the warmth of the tandoori *naans* in silence.

Ranjit, deep in thought, finally spoke. "Nandini, this is crucial information. We need to look into this. Janaki and Arjun quarreling at Satya's house raises more questions than answers. Why did Arjun go there? What were they quarreling about? I'll enquire deeper into this. Thank you for letting me know. I will call them in for questioning."

"And..." implored Nandini, "Please don't bring my name into it. Let it remain anonymous who gave you this information."

"Sure," Arjun nodded.

"One more point," Nandini added, "I have already given you the picture of Janaki wearing the necklace at the wedding reception in Bombay — the one missing from Arjun's locker. You may need it when you meet with Satya and Janaki. I don't know if the Arjun's quarrel with Janaki and the missing necklace are related."

"Sure, I will find out about this too when I question them."

As they continued their lunch, a quiet tension hung in the air. The restaurant became a space where secrets were unveiled, and the subtle exchange of conversation between Ranjit and Nandini hinted at the shared quest for truth.

The scene unfolded with the clinking of cutlery and the soft murmurs of other diners, the formal setting of the Blue Lotus restaurant becoming a backdrop for a conversation that could change the course of the investigation.

Determined to unravel the mystery around Arjun's demise, the next afternoon Inspector Ranjit called Satya and Janaki to the Town police station. The atmosphere within the precinct was filled with tension, a sense of trepidation enveloping the room as the couple entered. Ranjit wasted no time, opting for a direct approach without mincing words.

Addressing both of them, Ranjit began, "Satya, Janaki, some troubling information has come to my attention. A witness claims to have seen Arjun leaving your house in a fit of anger the evening before he died. What do you have to say?" His gaze shifted between the couple, scrutinizing their expressions for any signs of deception.

Satya and Janaki exchanged uneasy glances, their faces betraying the weight of hidden secrets. Satya, typically quick-witted, attempted to dismiss the accusation. "Inspector, this is baseless gossip. I have no idea what your witness is talking about."

Ranjit's steely gaze remained unwavering, he turned his attention to Janaki. "I suggest you start talking. The truth always finds its way to the surface." His eyes bored into Janaki's. She looked scared and her face suddenly became very pale. Ranjit knew immediately that she was concealing something.

Satya, seemingly puzzled, defended himself, "I wasn't at home that evening; I came late due to a heavy workload at the bank. Arjun never came to our house that day."

Inspector Ranjit looked Janaki in the eye and raised his eyebrows.

Unable to withstand his steely gaze, Janaki broke down in tears. "Okay, okay... Arjun did come to our home that evening. I never told Satya. I was alone at home. He... he accused Satya of having taken the sapphire necklace from the locker without his knowledge. He was furious."

"And then?" Ranjit inquired, sensing the gravity of the situation.

"He went on a tirade, claiming that everyone was conspiring against him, wanting his possessions and the money left by father," Janaki continued, her voice shaky.

"And then...?" Ranjit prompted, probing deeper into the unfolding narrative.

"I tried to pacify him, but he wouldn't listen," Janaki confessed, wiping away her tears.

"Was he under the influence of alcohol or drugs?" Ranjit probed, seeking to understand Arjun's state of mind.

"No, he was completely sober. I don't think that he was drunk or on drugs, either. I am certain because his arguments were clear and speech rational. No... he hadn't consumed anything that day, I'm sure of that." Janaki asserted with certainty.

Satya, stunned by this new development stared at his wife.

"Did you take the necklace from his locker?" Ranjit turned to Satya. "You are in the same bank where his locker is."

"I... er..." Satya fumbled for words.

Ranjit, removed the photograph provided by Nandini from the table drawer and handed it to the couple. His eyes shifted between Janaki and Satya's bewildered expression. "What's the story behind the necklace in this photograph?"

The photograph was a shock to both of them. They couldn't understand how the inspector was in possession of this photograph. Janaki, her tears still fresh, stammered, "Arjun accused Satya of stealing it. But we did not steal it, I swear!"

A heavy silence engulfed the room, the weight of the revelation settling in. Ranjit turned his attention to Satya, his voice firm. "Your turn, Satya. What's the truth? How did the necklace come to be in your possession? Come on... out with it!"

Realizing the seriousness of the situation and the fact that he was cornered, Satya confessed, "The locker was jointly in our names – Arjun and myself. He was holding the key but later one day, Arjun gave me the key to the locker for safekeeping. I borrowed the necklace a few days before Arjun's death, planning to return it after crafting a replica for Janaki. I couldn't afford the original. I wanted to make a similar one with artificial gemstones."

Inspector Ranjit's eyes widened in surprise. "So, you *borrowed* it without informing Arjun?" – Ranjit stressing on the word '*borrowed*'.

"Yes, temporarily." Satya remarked crestfallen. I intended to return it to the locker as soon as I could get a replica made. But in the confusion when Arjun died, I forgot all about it. Later, I couldn't open the locker as the bank had sealed it, and hence I could not return the necklace to the locker." Satya explained, guilt and regret evident in his eyes.

"And so his key to the locker remained with you?" Ranjit persisted.

"No, a couple of days before his death, he came to the bank and took back the key from me saying that he would keep it with him. I do not know when he opened the locker, as I was on leave for two days before that evening. I learned from the police that he went to the bank on the day he died to deposit some cash into his account. It seems he must have opened his locker then and discovered that the necklace was missing."

"And you wore the necklace to the wedding of your cousin at Bombay recently?" Ranjit turned to Janaki.

Janaki, her eyes downcast, nodded silently. Tears welled up in her eyes.

"When did Arjun leave your home that evening?" Ranjit asked turning to Janaki.

"Around four o'clock," was her reply. He was there for only about fifteen minutes.

"All this could have been avoided if you had told about this to Nandini and your brother Anandu on the day the locker was opened in the presence of the bank manager. All this heartburn could have been avoided." Ranjit chided them.

Tension hung heavy as the couple grappled with conflicting emotions of responsibility and guilt. The investigation into Arjun's death had just begun, leaving Ranjit and the couple entangled in the mystery of his sudden passing. Ranjit wondered what other secrets were waiting to be discovered.

It seemed everyone had something to conceal.

Chapter 31

Inspector Ranjit was just settling into his routine as the morning sun lazily crept through the blinds of his office at the Town Police Station, casting a warm glow on the worn-out furniture. He looked up as Nandini entered, her eyes filled with a mix of desperation and determination. The air hung heavy with the unsaid as she approached his desk. Now that the matter of the necklace was settled, what brought her here, he wondered.

"Inspector Ranjit," Nandini began, her voice laced with urgency, "I need to see the autopsy report of Arjun."

"Why this sudden request?" Ranjit smiled as he pulled out Arjun's file from the shelf and acknowledged her request. Without uttering a word, he handed her a copy of the document that held the key to unlocking the mysteries surrounding Arjun's untimely demise. As Nandini meticulously scanned the pages, her gaze fixed on the coroner's verdict.

"The death occurred between seven and eight in the evening," Ranjit stated, breaking the oppressive silence as he revealed the unsettling details. "Alcohol, cannabis, and an abnormal presence of Alprazolam."

Nandini's brows furrowed as she absorbed the information. "Alprazolam? That's a sedative for insomnia," she exclaimed, her mind racing with possibilities.

Ranjit, ever the observant detective, raised an eyebrow. "Was Arjun taking any sedatives? I was told he was on medication."

The weight of uncertainty burdened Nandini's response, "Not that I know of. He was on medications for his psychiatric symptoms, but he seems to have stopped those drugs. I have seen his prescription, but Alprazolam was not on it."

A thoughtful expression crossed Ranjit's face. "If so, how did this new substance – Alprazolam, get into his system? This adds a new light to the puzzle," he muttered, his mind already unraveling the threads of a fresh angle in the case.

Looking at the report in his hand, he remarked, "We'll have to look into this aspect more closely. From the autopsy report, I understand that the blood level of Alprazolam was remarkably high compared to the normal therapeutic level. If he did not take it himself, then... perhaps it was given to him by someone."

"The report also mentions about an injury on his forehead and particles of wood in it," Nandini added, looking at the autopsy report. "Does it indicate he was struck with a wooden object by someone?"

"We can't determine that," Ranjit replied, equally uncertain. "It's possible, or he might have hit his head on a wooden surface during the fall – a piece of old furniture or some such thing. We need further investigation."

The room, filled with the scent of old paperwork and the faint hum of fluorescent lights, became a hub of speculation and suspicion. Nandini, driven by the desire for justice, couldn't shake off the feeling that there was more to Arjun's death than met the eye. More facts were coming to light each day.

"Can I have a copy of this autopsy report. My friend's husband is the Professor of Forensic Medicine in Trivandrum Medical college; I wish to get his opinion too."

Ranjit immediately ordered a xerox copy of the autopsy report made and handed it to her.

As the dialogue unfolded, Ranjit decided to probe deeper. "Nandini, I need your help. We need to trace Arjun's recent activities, anyone he might have been in contact with, anything out of the ordinary."

"The truth lies somewhere out there." Nandini commented, her eyes reflecting a mix of determination and worry, "I'll do whatever it takes to find the truth, Inspector. But I think you should start with Divya, again."

"Divya?" Ranjit frowned, "Why do you think I should interrogate her again? The police have already done it previously. It is in the case file."

Nandini looked him in the eye, "The last time I met her she gave me that unopened letter from Arjun, which I showed you, but I strongly felt while talking to her that she was holding something back. Female intuition, you may call it. And she said she never wanted to see me again."

Ranjit leaned back in his creaky chair, his gaze fixed on Nandini. "Okay then. This case is getting murkier by the minute. We need to be one step ahead of whoever orchestrated this. I'll start with Divya."

Nandini, sensing the importance of the situation, replied, "I'll keep my ears to the ground, Inspector. If there's anything... anything that I find out, I'll let you know."

As the lingering mystery of the medication – Alprazolam in Arjun's autopsy report continued to perplex Inspector Ranjit, his determination to unveil the truth intensified. Fueled by the nagging feeling and supplemented by Nandini's revelation that there might be more to Divya's involvement than met the eye, he decided to visit Divya's home, and planned to question her in the presence of her two protective brothers, Sadanandan and Prabhakaran.

Nandini sent her friend Dr. Soumya the copy of the autopsy report. She asked for her husband, Dr. Shekhar's forensic opinion on it. She was concerned about the large amount of Alprazolam in Arjun's body and wanted to understand its importance compared to the presence of alcohol and cannabis.

The air in Divya's living room brimmed with silent tension as inspector Ranjit, carrying the burden of unresolved questions, confronted Divya and her two brothers – Sadanandan and Prabhakaran.

After exchanging pleasantries that disguised the true nature of his visit, Ranjit went straight into the heart of the matter. "Let's talk about Arjun," he said, his eyes piercing through the façade of normalcy that Divya showed. "I need to know when you last met him."

Divya, shifting nervously on the sofa, hesitated before responding, "It was days ago, at my house... I mean... many days before his death. I've already informed the police about this."

Ranjit, sensing evasion in her reply, decided to press further. "It won't hurt to repeat what you've already told the police," he remarked, his tone revealing a hint of skepticism.

Her brother seated nearby, interjected with a touch of bluntness. "She has answered this already."

But Ranjit was not one to be deterred. He continued to scrutinize Divya, looking at her for any subtle signs of deception on her face. The air thickened with suspicion as the protective brothers, sensing their sister's discomfort, stepped in.

Without taking his eyes off Divya, inspector Ranjit remarked, "You may have to repeat your statements many times if needed, till we find out the truth behind Arjun's death."

"But it has already been closed as suicide by the police," her brother Prabhakaran cut in.

"Yes, it was, but now it has been re-opened and I'm looking into it," Ranjit's voice held a finality. "And I will not rest until I get to the bottom of it. I know that your sister is holding something back."

"Please, don't trouble her any further," they pleaded, their voices laced with concern. "She's engaged to be married shortly, and we don't want any scandals surfacing at this crucial time."

Ranjit, annoyed at their attempt to shield Divya, retorted, "Okay... I'll be going now, but if I have any more doubts or if I need to question her further, I will summon her to the police station next time. And I will not be this considerate, either. If she's concealing anything, I will dig to the depths to ferret out the truth. Mind you, the next time it will surely be at the station."

Ranjit's departure left behind a lingering tension in Divya's household, as the siblings exchanged uncertain glances, wondering just how deep the inspector would dig in his quest for the elusive truth.

Inspector Ranjit was determined to uncover the mystery behind Arjun's death. He knew there was more to it than what was obvious. He suspected that some of the key persons were hiding information.

ACP Ranjit decided to extend his interrogation beyond the usual witnesses and interrogate more persons connected with the case. He had a nagging feeling that the case had been closed rather hastily initially without adequately interviewing many of the people involved.

Firstly, He summoned Devaki Amma, the maidservant in Mohandas's home to the station to enquire about the facts she had shared with Nandini. She had nothing more to offer than what Nandini had already told him. So he dismissed her without further interrogation.

Next Ranjit summoned Elias, the helper and manservant of the sleazy KK brothers to the police station. Inspector Ranjit noticed the man's shifty eyes, indicating he was untrustworthy. He was seated in the interrogation room in the police station. The windowless interrogation room lit by a dim, dusty sixty watt bulb hanging from the ceiling became the stage for a tense confrontation with the elderly man servant of the KK brothers. The room was hot and sultry, as the police wanted it — for the suspect to stew in the hot, humid environment in order to break him. The ceiling fan had been switched off — on purpose.

Elias, nervous with beads of sweat forming on his forehead, initially denied any knowledge of the events surrounding Arjun's death. The dimly lit room witnessed the ebb and flow of emotions as head constable Raghavan Nair and Ranjit took turns questioning Elias, determined to unravel the elusive truth. They tried to use the good-cop-bad-cop charade to make him open up. Their efforts ultimately paid off. Hours passed, and Elias's resolve crumbled under the relentless pressure tactics exerted by the police.

It was in the midst of this high-stakes interrogation that Elias finally cracked, confessing to Arjun's unexpected visit to the outhouse on that fateful evening. The air in the room changed, charged with the weight of yet another piece of newfound information.

"Does he frequently come to the outhouse?" the inspector asked.

"Yes, he comes there whenever the brothers and Mohandas have a party. It's almost every weekend and sometimes on weekdays too. The parties often go late into the night, and Arjun ends up sleeping in the outhouse instead of going home. Many times, he has stayed overnight in the outhouse."

"Arjun came to the outhouse of the brothers at about five-thirty in the evening," Elias began, his voice trembling. "I kept quiet earlier, not telling the police anything about this as I feared being implicated in the poor boy's death."

Ranjit, intrigued by the revelation, leaned forward. "What are you implying? Do you think someone caused his death? Perhaps, your bosses?"

Elias, fear etched across his face, hastily clarified, "Oh no, sir! I didn't say anyone killed him. He probably committed suicide. But he was perfectly alive when he left the outhouse that evening."

Ranjit, sensing there was more to the story, urged Elias to provide a detailed account of the events. "Come on, tell me what happened that evening," Ranjit demanded, pulling up a chair in front of Elias and switching the fan on. "If you come clean and have nothing to hide, then you have nothing to worry." His probing eyes sought the truth from the manservant. Night was descending outside the police station, and the surrounding traffic noise had diminished.

As Elias told what happened that evening at the outhouse, Ranjit listened carefully. Elias sounded nervous, and the room made his voice sound even louder. Ranjit tried to understand everything, like putting together a puzzle. Every new detail helped Ranjit understand the story better. He was amazed by what he was hearing as Elias began recounting the reason for Arjun's visit that evening.

Chapter 32

Ranjit listened silently as Elias started narrating the events of that fateful evening.

Elias made some shocking revelations about the awful things happening in the KK brothers' place. It felt like the secrets were thick in the air, and even the shadows showed how deep the betrayal went. He listened with horror and amazement as Elias described in detail the events that transpired in their outhouse that fateful evening and some of the evenings before. Elias recounted bits of conversation he had overheard regarding their illicit transactions and their smuggling operations. That fateful evening had been a culmination of these unfortunate events.

Around five-thirty in the evening, Arjun, unsuspecting and trusting, had entered the outhouse on that fateful day. Elias had allowed him in without any inkling of the storm that would soon break out. Arjun flopped on a wicker chair in the verandah outside the hall as soon as Elias let him in. He seemed drowsy and distracted, yet not under the influence of intoxicants or drugs, as Elias keenly observed. There was no smell of alcohol. Arjun sat there, in the dim light of the verandah pondering over something that seemed to be gnawing at his mind. He seemed to be letting off steam.

Arjun could, however, overhear the muted conversation that was taking place between Divakaran and Mohandas in the adjacent hall.

He listened intently to their conversation. His face seemed to contort with indignation as he listened. As the two conspirators – Divakaran and Mohandas – spoke of fertilizer and a consignment of ganja and Ecstasy from Punjab, Arjun's world shattered. Mohandas, with a boastful air, was detailing the successful transport of nearly ninety packets of the illicit substances in the last few truckloads. Arjun, the unsuspecting victim of their deceit, listened in stunned silence. The truth which they had been hitherto concealing from him unfolded before him like a malevolent force, and the realization that they had been deceiving him all this while struck him with the force of a freight train. They were smuggling cannabis and drugs into the state under the guise of fertilizer. All this without his knowledge. They had been misleading and defrauding him all these months. He had given them his inheritance, under the impression that they were doing legitimate business; and all the while they were doing illegal smuggling! He felt devastated.

In a fury, he stormed into the hall where the duo were meeting and shouted, "Ganja and drugs? You... you never mentioned this to me before! All this while you were cheating me! You had told me about your business of transporting fertilizer only. I never dreamt that you would be a group of drug smugglers! If I had known this, I would never have joined your business or given you my money."

Momentarily taken aback, Divakaran quickly collected himself and sneered, reveling in Arjun's realization and relishing the control they had exerted over him. "It's the real deal, my friend. And you, with your investment, are now knee-deep in it. You are as involved as we are. So don't fret. We have paid you your share and you have greedily accepted it so far."

The room seemed to constrict around Arjun as the treacherous nature of the KK brothers became painfully apparent. Fear gripped him, and panic set in, as he realized the gravity of his situation.

"I can't be part of this! I never signed up for smuggling drugs and ganja!" Arjun was dancing with rage.

Mohandas, gloating in Arjun's discomfiture, let out a mocking cackle that resonated through the room. "You're in too deep now, Arjun. Either you're with us, or you're against us. And trust me, the consequences of betrayal are severe.

In the oppressive silence that followed, Divakaran exchanged a nervous glance with Mohandas and tried to pacify Arjun.

"Arjun, calm down. We can explain." Divakaran interrupted, trying to calm him down.

But consumed by rage, Arjun refused to listen.

Arjun shouted in panic, "I trusted you! I invested in your venture, and this is what you do? I won't let you ruin my life!"

Divakaran stood up, attempting to control the situation. "Arjun, we can work this out. We're family." Divakaran approached Arjun and placed a caring hand on his shoulder trying to mollify him. Arjun shook him off.

The room descended into an uneasy silence. Divakaran exchanged knowing glances with Mohandas, their deceitful plot unfolding with ruthless precision. Hypocrisy and treachery were hanging in the air as they quickly thought of a plan of action to douse the situation.

A cunning plan had already formed in Mohandas's mind. He, with a sly smile, proposed a way to appease Arjun's concerns. Smiling, he approached Arjun, "Okay, Arjun, if you are so particular, we can do one thing. We can easily sort it out."

Arjun raised his eyebrows, his skepticism evident. "How?"

"What do you propose? Will you stop the illegal trade?" Arjun, innocently asked him.

Mohandas with a sly smile answered, "Sure, why not, Arjun? Since you don't like what we are doing, we are ready to give it up for a friend like you. From now on we will give up smuggling the contraband. Anything for a sincere friend like you. We can go a step further and if you wish return the money that you have invested with us."

Arjun, unaware of the hollowness in their promises, naively believed in their sincerity. "Are you sure that you'd stop this business?... And return my money?"

"Sure, why not, Arjun, after all you are our bosom friend. Won't we do at least this for you?" Divakaran stood up with a crafty smirk. "Come on Arjun, don't be peevish, be happy, all will be well. We will put an end to this clandestine business. You can continue with us still if you trust us. Tomorrow itself we will return your investment to you."

"Arjun, let us celebrate this new decision with a drink." Mohandas was standing up already, pouring whisky into three glasses. Divakaran poured a strong drink for Arjun. Initially, Arjun hesitated saying that he had stopped drinking alcohol after *Amma's* death. But they insisted that this was a special occasion for all of them and pried him into taking one drink − just one only. Only this time, they said. Before long, one drink turned into two, and then more, as Arjun unwittingly became a victim in their deceitful scheme.

They then pressured him into smoking a cigarette, which unknown to him, they might have spiked with cannabis − Elias explained. Completely unaware of their deceit, Arjun naively continued to believe they were his loyal friends. He remained oblivious to the extent of their trickery.

"Why don't you have a smoke? It is just an ordinary cigarette. Nothing more." Mohandas enticed him.

"Oh, no, I have stopped smoking." Arjun protested.

"No, no, this is only a plain cigarette." Mohandas lighting a cigarette for Arjun, handed it over to him. He lit up a cigarette for himself.

Arjun, already under the influence of drinks, failed to recognize the subtle hints of duplicity in the air. He failed to recognize the ganja that was rolled into his smoke.

When they saw that Arjun was sufficiently high, Divakaran seized the moment to take a dig at Arjun.

Sneering, Divakaran remarked, "Arjun, do you know that your fiancée Divya is being betrothed to someone else?"

Arjun suddenly became furious, "She told me just now; I am coming from her house only, but I don't believe it. She will marry only me, and I will not allow anyone else to come between us."

Mohandas laughed aloud, sharing a knowing wink with Divakaran.

"And... to whom do you think she is being engaged? Your Divya is being engaged to Mohandas here," said Divakaran with a sneer. "Didn't she tell you that?"

The revelation fueled Arjun's anger. He flung the glass of whisky at the wall and stormed out, dazed and drunk, leaving the room in a fit of fury.

"He is posing a threat to us," Divakaran remarked after Arjun's departure. "We should do something about it since he knows about our secret. When his head clears, he may still try to get back at us. That may prove harmful to our operations."

Mohandas pondered their options.

Divakaran suggested, "We should remove him from the business and return the amount he invested."

Mohandas, with a cunning smile, shattered that possibility. "Not possible, we have already used it up for our new enterprise in Punjab. There is no question of returning any money to him. Luckily, Sukumaran is not here now. If he were here, he would have returned his money straightaway." Mohandas roared with laughter.

"Let us see how we can get him off our neck," remarked Divakaran.

As the duo schemed in the dimly lit room, Elias the silent observer, was serving them onion fritters and finger chips. The cunning duo, their brains befuddled by alcohol, did not know that their faithful servant had been silently observing and listening to every bit of conversation going on in the room.

Ranjit sat across from Elias, absorbing every word of the chilling narrative unraveling before him. Elias, with a heavy heart, detailed the web of treachery woven by the KK brothers and Mohandas, laying bare the sinister underbelly of their deceitful operations. Ranjit listened with a mixture of disbelief and indignation, his mind racing to comprehend the gravity of the situation.

"So, are you saying Sukumaran was not there, eh?"

"No," replied Elias, "Sukumaran sir was not there. He had gone to Mannarkad to tackle some problem in their transport office there. He returned home only late at night. Had he been there, he would not have allowed Mohandas and Divakaran to get Arjun drunk and drugged. He is a more cautious and understanding person. He likes Arjun like an elder brother.

Elias concluded with a sigh, "Arjun, poor soul, fell prey to the machinations of this nefarious gang. The KK brothers and Mohandas, with their cunning plots, lured him into a trap. When in his drunken state, he understood the deception of the threesome and the fact that his fiancé Divya was being engaged to Mohandas, he must have lost his mind and committed suicide that evening."

Ranjit, leaning forward, furrowed his brows in concern. "How could they betray someone so ruthlessly? Arjun trusted them."

Elias nodded in agreement, a profound sadness clouding his eyes.

"What time did Arjun leave the outhouse?"

"It was around six-thirty or six-forty five, I cannot say exactly. The sun had not yet set and dusk had not set in." Elias was doubtful. "It's a cruel world, Inspector Sir," replied Elias shaking his head sadly, "Sometimes, trust becomes the weapon of choice for those who thrive on treachery. And innocent lives are sacrificed on its altar."

"And when did Mohandas leave?" Ranjit's question was pointed.

"He left five or ten minutes after the boy Arjun left." Elias concluded.

Ranjit sighed and muttered to himself, "Yes, I will get them, the bastards."

Inspector Ranjit, usually a calm and collected individual, felt the stirring of a dormant rage that sought justice for young Arjun and all those who had unknowingly crossed paths with the deceitful trio.

The revelations about the KK brothers and Mohandas had unveiled a murky world, and Ranjit understood that navigating through this treacherous terrain required cunning and a meticulously planned strategy. But still the truth eluded him.

The following days found Ranjit meticulously gathering information from multiple sources and weaving an intricate web of evidence to bring to light the clandestine operations of the KK brothers and Mohandas. His actions remained discreet, as a silent force working behind the scenes.

Chapter 33

In the secret world of covert operations in his career, Ranjit had skillfully dealt with lies and betrayal. Now, ACP Ranjit decided it was time to disclose his true identity to the Commissioner of Police in Calicut. He scheduled a meeting and met him in his office.

Ranjit had faced the devastating loss of his younger brother, Rajiv, to drugs when Rajiv was barely fifteen years old and still in school. Alongside two other boys, Rajiv was discovered lifeless in a half-built mansion owned by a non-resident Indian. Their tragic fate was stumbled upon by a retired Army Colonel during his usual morning stroll. The news struck Ranjit and his widowed mother with a heavy blow, leaving them grappling with grief and disbelief.

Ranjit's heartache transformed into a solemn vow, made amidst tears and anguish. He pledged to pursue justice relentlessly, determined to hold accountable those responsible for supplying drugs to vulnerable school children. The drug racket's vile operations, which had shaken the very core of public morality, fueled Ranjit's resolve to take action.

Determined to seek justice, Ranjit made a solemn vow to do everything in his power to hold accountable those responsible for supplying drugs to schoolchildren and dismantle the drug network that had horrified the public conscience. Driven by a fierce determination to honor his brother's memory, Ranjit made a life-altering decision. Despite the option to choose a more comfortable assignment, he volunteered to work in the modest city of Calicut. It was from here that he envisioned launching a covert operation, a clandestine mission aimed at unraveling the intricate web of conspiracy woven by the drug ring which had spread its deadly tentacles in the northern part of the state of Kerala.

As Ranjit embarked on his quest for justice, his mother's trembling voice echoed in his mind, urging him to stay strong and fight for what was right. "Do it for Rajiv," she had pleaded, her eyes filled with tears of sorrow and hope. "No other mother should endure the same fate as mine, losing her son to drugs."

In Calicut, Ranjit found himself immersed in a world teeming with hidden dangers and elusive truths. Yet, amidst the shadows of deceit, he discovered a glimmer of resilience and solidarity among the community. Conversations with locals unveiled tales of despair and resilience, each narrative fueling Ranjit's determination to unearth the truth.

Quietly and with determination, he immersed himself into the task of gathering information about the drug gangs plaguing the area and their harmful influence on the youth. With each piece of data he collected, he felt a sense of urgency and responsibility weighing on his shoulders. As he meticulously compiled the data he had gathered, his mind raced with thoughts of the lives that were being ruined by the drug trade. He couldn't help but feel a deep empathy for the young people caught up in this vicious cycle, their futures hanging in the balance.

With each passing moment, his determination grew stronger, fueled by a desire to put an end to the drug mafia's grip on the northern parts of Kerala. He knew that the task ahead would not be easy, but he was prepared to do whatever it took to make his community safer for everyone. And as he prepared for the massive operation that lay ahead, he couldn't help but feel a glimmer of hope stirring within him. He knew that with the support of his team and the determination of those fighting alongside him, they could make a difference and bring an end to the scourge of drugs once and for all.

In the quiet moments of solitude, Ranjit found solace in his memories of Rajiv, cherishing the bond they once shared. "I'll make it right, Rajiv," he whispered to the wind, his voice trembling with emotion.

This commitment had led him to volunteer for an undercover operation in the small city of Calicut, offered as an option to him. His mission: to uncover the intricate web of conspiracy woven by the drug ring. The rumor that he was on punishment transfer to Calicut was a ruse to throw the culprits off his back and mislead any informants or moles in his own department.

Ever since his first week in Calicut, he had been gathering intelligence on the drug racket and smuggling operations in Kerala. Some leads led him to the KK brothers and their business, but he lacked concrete evidence against them. Then, unexpectedly, Nandini approached him about her brother Arjun's death. Investigating Arjun's death brought Inspector Ranjit to the KK brothers' doorstep, revealing how closely it was tied to their business. Now, ACP Ranjit had solid evidence to proceed with his investigation.

Ranjit met the DIG & Commissioner of Police in Calicut in his elegant office to detail him on the findings. "Sir, I need to reveal my true credentials. I am appointed and authorized by the Intelligence Bureau in New Delhi. I was transferred to Calicut from Delhi for a covert operation. My mission is to unearth reports of ganja and drug smuggling from North India to Kerala, funding terrorist cells in the process. I have been operating from the Town Police Station, along with two of my colleagues, Sooraj and Kartik assisting me in the operations."

"Well, that is a surprise!" exclaimed the Commissioner. "I too have been kept in the dark. I was given to believe that your posting in Calicut was part of a mild punishment transfer for you."

"Yes Sir," Ranjit smilingly replied, "That was a deliberate white lie circulated to divert attention from my true mission and keep tongues from wagging. I'm sorry, Sir, but I had to keep it from you as well."

The Commissioner laughed aloud. "And you have been successful in pulling the wool over all our eyes."

Ranjit chuckled.

"I need your help and support to nab this gang, Sir. I have gathered sufficient evidence as to the working of this gang. What is needed is to round up the key players and put an end to it once for all." Ranjit's demeanor became serious. He carefully outlined his plan of action.

The Commissioner listened attentively and replied, "Go ahead, my boy. You have full authority to lead the operation. Let me know if you need any resources and reinforcements."

"Sure Sir and thank you." Ranjit saluted him and took leave.

In the labyrinth of intrigue and deception, Ranjit's mission gained momentum. The Commissioner, recognizing the need for specialized assistance, officially reached out to the recently established Narcotics Control Bureau (NCB), securing their involvement in the impending operation. The Narcotics Control Bureau, known for its proficiency in tackling drug-related crimes, pledged their full cooperation. The NCB in its own right was already investigating the death of the three schoolboys which had stirred a public outcry. The collaboration with NCB promised to bring together a formidable force against the cunning gang, setting the stage for a high-stakes operation. Forces were rallied against the common enemy.

Armed with a carte blanche from the Commissioner, Ranjit set his plan in motion. His quest for justice led him to a major decision as he reached out to the Commissioner of Police Coimbatore, seeking assistance in apprehending the elusive individual who had met Mohandas in Coimbatore and received the duffel bag of cash from him. The events in Coimbatore were about to take an unexpected turn.

Ranjit dialed the Commissioner of Police in Coimbatore and informed him of his credentials and the clearance he had from the Central Government for the operation. "Good morning Commissioner. This is ACP Ranjit from Calicut. I need your help to apprehend a key player in an important operation." He detailed the circumstances and how Mohandas was followed to Coimbatore on two occasions and was found handing over an alleged payoff to a suspect. "The suspect could have terrorist links, I suspect though I do not have any proof. I request you to arrange to pick him up and question him. I am sending you a few photographs of the suspect receiving a duffel bag from Mohandas who is one of the suspects here in Calicut, and details of his vehicle registration."

The Commissioner, intrigued by Ranjit's urgency and the seriousness of the situation, agreed to help. He proposed that they could apprehend the culprit while he accepted a payment from Mohandas. They would catch him in the act with the evidence.

"Yes Sir, perfect." Ranjit responded, "However, I don't want Mohandas to be apprehended yet along with him because I still need to find some of his connections in Calicut. So, it would be best if you arrest the culprit after he leaves the meeting with Mohandas."

Ranjit continued, "From what we gathered from the records, his name is Basha and most probably he is one of the gang of persons who are functioning as terrorist sleeper cells in this country. The Intelligence Bureau and the Narcotics Bureau are also onto him. We need to unravel the layers of this conspiracy. I am in touch with both the organizations for co ordinating the operations. I will keep you updated. My guys here are shadowing Mohandas day and night. I will inform you as soon as I find that he has left for Coimbatore."

"I will put a couple of shadows here on Basha discretely and apprehend him after the handover is made," promised the Commissioner.

"Thank you, Sir," Ranjit felt that matters were proceeding according to plan.

With the Commissioner's approval, Ranjit convened a combined meeting at Calicut along with the other Police Chiefs in the district.

The higher-ups listened attentively as Ranjit divulged his undercover mission, highlighting the crucial role played by his team members, constables Sooraj and Kartik. Their true identities concealed, they had worked undercover at the Town police station in Calicut, gathering intelligence that had now led to the threshold of a more significant threat. He showed them the photographs they had taken from the godown at Mahe.

The Commissioner, Kannur city remarked, "This is grave, Ranjit. We had no idea about the drug smuggling or the terrorism funding. What's the next step that you propose?"

Ranjit meticulously outlined the plan, explaining the need for a joint operation involving the Kannur and Thalasseri divisions to bring the entire gang to justice. The Commissioner, recognizing the gravity of the situation, pledged full support. Ranjit also informed them that officials of the NCB would also be with them during the operation.

Their support was unanimous. "We will coordinate with the respective police stations. You have our full backing, Ranjit. Launch your operation. You will be in charge of the nitty-gritties of the operation. Leave no loop holes, leave no stone unturned to bring these criminals to book. Good luck."

"We need to stay vigilant," Ranjit told them. "Once the next batch of illegal goods enters Kerala from the north, we need to act quickly putting our plan into motion." The days leading up to the operation were filled with meticulous planning and strategic coordination.

The wheels of justice began turning as Basha was apprehended along with the duffel bag full of cash, by the Coimbatore police as he left Mohandas with the payment. He was quickly whisked away to an unknown destination for questioning. The operation had been smooth and flawless. Mohandas, however, was not aware of Basha's capture, as he had returned to Calicut immediately on effecting the handover.

As the interrogation of Basha in Coimbatore unfolded, shocking revelations emerged, adding new facts to the already complex narrative. Basha revealed, on interrogation, that he was part of a sleeper cell operating from Tamil Nadu. They were being controlled by their handlers located in a neighboring country. The news sent shockwaves through the law enforcement agencies, realizing that the treacherous dealings extended far beyond their initial suspicions. They were financed by the sale of cannabis and Ecstasy, which was smuggled into the country across the border from the same country that was promoting and controlling the terrorist sleeper cells. These drugs were then transported and distributed by Mohandas and his associates in Kerala and the nearby Tamil Nadu. The sales proceeds of the drugs were being passed on to Basha and his associates by Mohandas. Mohandas in turn received a substantial commission for his part in this illicit venture. It was all a well-planned operation on the part of the cabal. The money was used to fund the terrorists and the sleeper cells.

Ranjit meanwhile received information that two trucks belonging to the KK brothers returning with fertilizer from North India had crossed the check post at the Kerala border at Thalappady which is the northernmost village in Kerala. Ranjit alerted his special action team immediately and set in motion the plan of action.

As plans were set in motion, Ranjit found himself at the helm of a joint task force, orchestrating the convergence of intelligence, law enforcement, and specialized agencies. The team members' conversation was filled with excitement and anticipation, as they discussed the upcoming confrontation, recognizing the importance of every word spoken in relation to the mission.

Sooraj, the constable, met Ranjit in his office, "Sir, this is bigger than we thought. Are we ready for what's coming?"

Ranjit's eyes reflected a steely determination. "We have no choice but to be. There is no going back now. The truth must be exposed, and justice served. We have come searching for the truth, let us now get into action."

The joint task force, fueled by a collective sense of duty, prepared to descend upon the treacherous gang like a storm. Ranjit, at the epicenter of this covert operation, knew that the unraveling of the conspiracy would reshape the landscape of justice in the region.

Chapter 34

Inspector Ranjit, having decided to question Divya and her mother further, had brought them to the police station. The station buzzed with activity as he meticulously planned his interrogation of Divya and her mother. He had sent a female constable Merin to their house to bring Divya and her mother to the police station. The constable Merin, with a grim-faced expression escorted the duo into Ranjit's office.

He asked the constable to seat Divya's mother in the waiting room outside and bring Divya alone into his office.

Inspector Ranjit, a picture of authority behind his desk, gestured for Divya to take a seat. Her posture mirrored her tension. Constable Merin stationed nearby, provided silent vigilance, ready to intervene if needed.

As Ranjit's gaze fixed on Divya, she felt the weight of his scrutiny, a silent accusation hanging in the air. The room seemed to shrink around her, suffocating her with its starkness.

"Divya," Ranjit's voice cut through the silence like a knife, "I need to ask you some questions. And I expect frank answers. Mind you, no hide-n-seek games with me this time. I know quite well that you have not been honest with me."

Divya swallowed hard, her resolve wavering under the intensity of Ranjit's stare. She glanced at constable Merin, seeking solace in her presence, but the constable's expression remained impassive, betraying nothing.

"Tell me about your relationship with Arjun," Ranjit pressed, his tone unyielding.

Divya hesitated, torn between truthfulness and self-preservation. Every word she uttered felt like a step closer to the edge of a precipice.

"We were close friends," she admitted, her voice barely above a whisper.

Ranjit leaned forward, his eyes boring into hers. "Just friends?"

Divya shifted uncomfortably in her seat, her mind racing to concoct a plausible story. She kept silent.

Ranjit's lips curled into a knowing smile, his skepticism evident. "And yet, there's more to this story about your *friendship*, isn't there? Come on, we know all about your relationship with him."

Divya's heart pounded in her chest as she struggled to maintain her composure. She knew she was walking a tightrope between truth and deception, and one wrong move could spell disaster.

"I..." she faltered, her words caught in her throat.

Ranjit raised an eyebrow, his patience wearing thin. "Don't make this any harder than it needs to be, Divya. Tell me everything. Be frank."

Divya glanced at Merin once more, silently pleading for guidance. But the constable remained silent, her gaze unwavering.

Realizing that she was trapped, with a resigned sigh, Divya began to recount her interactions with Arjun, each word laden with guilt and regret. She spoke of their meetings, their conversations, their mutual affection and the growing tension that developed between them when Arjun turned an addict.

"We loved each other and wanted to chart out a life together," she concluded. "But Arjun's addiction changed all that."

Ranjit listened intently, his mind working overtime to piece together the puzzle of Arjun's demise. He assumed that Divya might hold the key to unlocking the truth, and he was determined to pry it from her, no matter the cost.

As the interrogation dragged on, the atmosphere in the room grew increasingly tense, each question digging deeper into Divya's psyche. She felt like a mouse trapped in a maze, with no way out and danger lurking around every corner.

But amidst the fear and uncertainty, Divya clung to one glimmer of hope – the truth. She knew that no matter how slippery the path ahead, she had to stay true to herself and face the consequences head-on.

And as Ranjit continued to probe, his relentless pursuit of justice fueled by a thirst for the truth, Divya knew that she had a choice to make – to stay silent and betray herself, or to speak up and confront the demons that haunted her every waking moment.

"When did you see Arjun last?" Ranjit's voice sliced through the dense silence, the weight of his suspicion palpable in the air. "You better come out with the truth, unless you want to be arrested for his death." His voice had turned menacing.

Divya, feeling the intensity of his scrutiny, involuntarily shifted in her seat, her gaze avoiding the penetrating eyes of the inspector. "A few days before he died," she admitted, her words hanging in the air like a delicate confession, each syllable a whisper of unspoken secrets that threatened to unravel.

Ranjit, undeterred by her admission, confronted Divya with the letter, passed to Nandini, Arjun's sister by her, which now lay exposed on the table between them.

"I gave that letter to Nandini, Arjun's sister," Divya agreed, her voice carrying a hint of trepidation, a subtle tremor betraying the unease beneath her composed exterior. "That was the last letter Arjun had written to me. I had left it unopened."

The inspector's attention turned to the sensitive issue of her engagement, as his inquiries had revealed the complexities of her relationships. He had been apprised of this by Nandini and Elias.

"Who are you engaged to be married to?" Ranjit inquired, his words laced with the weight of suspicion.

Divya, with a composed demeanor, responded, "Mohandas... cousin to Sukumaran and Divakaran; the formal engagement ceremony was only about three months ago even though the decision was taken more than six months ago," her words echoing the testimony provided by both Nandini and Elias.

Ranjit, with a cunning glint in his eyes, continued his relentless pursuit, probing into Divya's interactions with Arjun. "Did you tell Arjun about your engagement to Mohandas?"

The room seemed to tighten its grip on Divya, the air heavy with unspoken revelations. She hesitated, her eyes darting around the room as if seeking an escape from the impending truth.

"No, I never told him about Mohandas. I told him that I was getting engaged to someone and he should not disturb me hereafter," she confessed, her voice carrying the weight of a guilty secret.

"When was the decision about the engagement and marriage to Mohandas finalized and from where?"

"Just three days before Arjun's death. It was decided in the presence of my mother and brothers at my home when Mohandas and his mother came for a formal visit to meet me and my family." Divya looked sullenly at the floor. Suddenly she looked up in panic as she realized her faux pas.

The intensity of the interrogation escalated each question chipping away at Divya's defenses.

The inspector smiled. "You said that you had not seen Arjun for a long time before he died. If so, *when* did you tell him about the decision regarding your engagement which happened only *three* days before his death?" Ranjit persisted, his eyes probing for the slightest crack in her composed façade, like a lawyer cross examining a witness on the stand.

Divya, feeling the walls closing in around her, began fumbling for words, her mind racing to navigate the treacherous terrain of deceit. She knew she was cornered.

"Well...er...I...I..." she stammered, her voice faltering. She suddenly understood that she was caught in a lie. The room felt quiet and tense, making the situation even more stressful.

"Come on, out with it; don't play games with me." Ranjit leaned back in his chair, a sly smile playing on his lips. As Divya's lies came out, the situation became more difficult and dangerous. She realized that now. She buried her face in her hands and wept.

"You met him on the evening he died, didn't you?" Undeterred, Ranjit's raised voice sliced through the air, the accusation hanging between them like an invisible thread.

Divya, under the weight of Ranjit's forceful glare, wilted with despair. A sense of dismay settled in, amplifying the tension in the room. With tears brimming in her eyes, she could no longer deny the truth. Slowly, she nodded, the admission a bitter pill to swallow. Tears welled up in her eyes.

As the revelation unfolded, Ranjit leaned forward, a threatening gleam in his eyes. "Well, what happened on that day? When did you meet him? From where?" The inspector's questions were rapid-fire, each word laced with a sense of urgency and determination. His voice was threatening. "You had better come out with the truth... or else..."

Under the pressure of interrogation Divya succumbed, silently sobbing as emotions overwhelmed her. The burden of guilt and impending consequences weighed heavily upon her. With a trembling voice, she began recounting the events of that ominous day, her words painting a vivid picture of her last bitter encounter with Arjun.

"Arjun came to my home around four-thirty in the evening," she confessed, as she gazed out the window, as if revisiting the haunting memories of that fateful evening.

The room, silent witness to the unraveling drama, seemed to absorb the gravity of her words. Ranjit, with a calculated patience, urged her to describe the sequence of events that transpired on that fateful evening.

"He walked in just as my phone was ringing," she continued, her voice a fragile thread in the heavy air. Divya shuddered as she described the moment when Arjun abruptly snatched the ringing phone from her and dropped it on the table savagely with a bang.

"Was he drunk or seem dazed on drugs?" Ranjit's inquiry cut through the narrative.

Divya, still immersed in the recollection, shook her head. "No, he seemed perfectly sober when he came to my house. My mother and I were alone at that time. Mother was in the kitchen making tea for us. Arjun seemed a bit agitated, that's all."

Ranjit probed further, his eyes like a pair of piercing daggers. "Then what happened?"

"Arjun accused me of spurning him," she admitted, her voice trembling with the weight of confession. "He said he still loved me, more than before, really; but I had betrayed him. He claimed to have given up alcohol and ganja after his mother's death, having not smoked or drunk for the past several days."

The room was now a silent witness to Divya's revelation as the narrative unfolded. Inspector Ranjit, absorbing the gravity of her words, leaned forward, his gaze unwavering. The atmosphere was tense, charged with unspoken secrets.

Ranjit, curious and sharp, took advantage of the chance to probe further into the events of that crucial evening. He repeated his question, "Are you absolutely sure that he was not drunk or under the influence of drugs?"

Divya, grappling with the memories, shook her head. "Yes I am sure... he was perfectly sober when he came to my house." she repeated.

The inspector, his mind working like a well-oiled machine, pressed for more details. "Then what happened?"

"It was then that I told him that, on my brothers' insistence, I was getting engaged to be married to another person," Divya's voice wavered as she recounted the crucial moment in her encounter with Arjun. The room seemed to hold its breath, the weight of her confession lingering in the air. "I begged him to avoid seeing me in future. At this, he became furious, and a fit of rage overcame him."

The memory of Arjun's fury haunted her like a relentless specter. She closed her eyes in silent contemplation of the moment.

"He became furious, claiming I belonged to him and no one else. *I will not allow you to marry anyone, whoever he is. You are mine, and*

257

mine only. *I will not spare anyone who comes in our way*, he shouted," she recounted, the chilling words reverberating in the room, leaving a lingering sense of treachery.

"Did you tell him whom you were engaged to?"

"No, I didn't... I did not tell him that I was being engaged to Mohandas. I was scared to tell him that."

Ranjit, with an inscrutable expression, leaned forward, his eyes searching for the nuances in Divya's narrative. "Tell me what happened next," he probed, his voice a low, measured undertone that underscored the gravity of the situation.

A shiver ran down Divya's spine as she recollected the memory. "He pulled me by my arms, his grip like a vise shaking me and gazing into my eyes, he shouted that he would not tolerate anyone coming between us."

Ranjit's keen observation did not waver. "Where was your mother when all this was going on?" he inquired.

Divya, now submerged in the complex detailing of her recollections, responded, "She was in the kitchen making tea." The image of her mother, unsuspecting of the impending storm, added further complexity to the scene. "On hearing Arjun shout and threaten, she came out of the kitchen with tea and *Neyyappams* for us. She handed Arjun his cup of tea, and I picked up a cup for myself. Mother then sat on the sofa, sipping her tea, unaware of the tension in the room."

"And then...?" Ranjit prompted.

"He ate a couple of *Neyyappams* and drank his tea."

Ranjit, eyebrows raised in anticipation, "Then...?" he prompted, inviting her to continue.

"When he saw my mother, Arjun calmed down a bit and sipped his tea silently, as he tasted the *Neyyappams*." Divya narrated, her words carrying the weight of the unspoken truth. "Then, abruptly, he got up to leave. Before he left, he turned to me and yelled, *Don't think that you have seen the last of me. I will be back.*"

The lingering threat in Arjun's parting words added a chilling undertone to the narrative, leaving a sense of foreboding in the room.

Ranjit, deeply involved in the unfolding story, sat back in his chair, thinking about what he had just learned. The room felt tense, hinting that there might be more surprising truths to come.

Inspector Ranjit's stern gaze bored into Divya's eyes, searching for any hint of deception. The room seemed to resonate with the heavy silence around them. He had stumbled upon a puzzle, and the pieces were perhaps falling into place to unravel his understanding of the case.

"Is that all?" Ranjit's voice echoed in the room, sharp and probing. He leaned forward, his eyes narrowing with suspicion.

"When did Arjun leave?"

Divya hesitated, her gaze flickering towards the window as if seeking escape from the inspector's intense scrutiny. "It must have been five o'clock or a little after that," she finally admitted, her words measured and cautious. "He left in a huff angry at me."

The inspector frowned, a deep furrow forming on his forehead. "What was his condition when he left? Was he sober?" Ranjit's tone was insistent, betraying an undercurrent of concern that danced with suspicion. Something about this scenario gnawed at his heart, and he couldn't dismiss the feeling that there was more to the story.

"Yes, of course, he was sober, but in a rage," Divya replied, her eyes avoiding direct contact with the inspector.

"Did you give him anything else to eat or drink while he was with you in your home?" Ranjit's question cut through the room like a knife, the weight of its implication hanging in the air.

"Why, no… Why do you ask?" her innocence seemed to be real. The tension in the room escalated, and Ranjit sensed that the key to the mystery might lay in the unspoken words and concealed motives.

Inspector Ranjit's shock at these new revelations lingered as he processed the unsettling disclosures surrounding Divya and her mother. He rose from his seat and approached Divya, seating himself on the table his presence looming like an unspoken threat above her.

"After Arjun left your house, he went straight to the house of the brothers, Sukumaran and Divakaran. He seemed to be a bit drowsy when he was there," Ranjit revealed, his tone steady but laced with an underlying tension.

Divya, on the defensive, responded with a curt, "I don't know anything about that." Her eyes darted away, avoiding the intensity of Ranjit's probing gaze.

Ranjit, sensing the need for clarity, raised his voice, a sharp contrast to the calculated calmness he had maintained hitherto. His eyes bored into Divya's, his voice threatening, "Did you add anything to his tea?" The point blank question hung in the air, a grave accusation that sought to expose any deception in her statements.

Divya, seemingly caught off guard, raised her eyebrows in surprise. "Well... no... what do you mean? What are you implying?" Her perplexity seemed genuine.

"Don't hide anything from me!" Ranjit's voice thundered through the room, as he thumped the table exploding in anger. The atmosphere crackled with tension as the inspector confronted Divya with the damning evidence.

"A significant amount of a sedative substance was discovered in his blood at autopsy. It could not have come from anywhere else but your home." Ranjit made a blind accusation, gauging her reaction with a steely resolve. The room was quiet, waiting for the truth hidden in the tangled lies to come out. "Did you put anything in his tea to kill him?" Ranjit's question was harsh, loud and blunt.

Divya looked up at him shocked.

Divya's mother, seated in the adjacent room, had been listening with a keen ear to the unfolding dialogue. A painful awareness crept over her as she saw the inspector in his relentless pursuit of truth bawling at her daughter. She sensed the danger closing in on her daughter.

Unable to withstand the intimidation of her daughter any longer, she abruptly rose from her chair with determination, a silent storm brewing within her. Crossing the threshold into the room where Divya faced the inspector's scrutiny, she faced the inspector.

"Inspector," she began, her voice carrying an apologetic tone tinged with tears that glistened in her eyes, "I have something to say."

The room seemed to hold its breath, awaiting yet another revelation that lingered on the edge of her trembling words.

Ranjit, his gaze flickering between Divya and her mother, commanded the lady constable, "Merin, pull up a chair for mother." The tension escalated as Divya's mother took her seat, a palpable unease settling over the room.

Seated, Divya's mother continued in a firm tone, her words hanging in the air like a delicate confession. "Don't harass my daughter, Inspector. It was I...I... who added the sleeping pills to Arjun's tea."

The room fell silent, her confession making everyone feel cold and uneasy.

Ranjit's shock was obvious in his facial expression as he absorbed the gravity of the situation. "You!" he exclaimed, his voice a mixture of shock and accusation. "What did you add... and why? Why would you do such a thing?" he shouted turning to her, his voice a mixture of disbelief and curiosity. Divya, hearing this new revelation, stared in disbelief at her mother.

Inspector Ranjit's calm demeanor shattered like glass as the shocking revelation unfolded before him, adding a startling twist to the narrative. The room reverberated with the heaviness of his disbelief.

Divya's mother, eyes red from crying, was caught in the middle of the turmoil. The room was tense as she tried to explain what had happened. Her words, filled with both sadness and explanation, aimed to clarify the situation.

"Seeing Arjun intimidate and threaten Divya, I was totally angry and upset," she confessed, her voice trembling with a mixture of regret and defiance. "On the spur of the moment, I went to my bedroom and picked up a few tablets of the sleeping pills from my bedside, which the doctor had prescribed for my sleeplessness. I came back to the kitchen and added it to Arjun's tea. I *personally* handed that cup of tea to him."

"What was the name of the tablet?" Ranjit queried.

"I don't remember the name... it started with an 'X'."

"Xanax?" Ranjit asked.

"'Ah, yes, that's the name."

"How many tablets did you add to his tea?"

"May be four or five, I did not exactly see how many."

Divya watched her mother with a mixture of surprise and agony. This was an unexpected turn of events.

The room seemed to reverberate with her words. Ranjit, his shock transforming into a calculating focus, probed further. "Why did you do it?" His question hung in the air, a demand for a deeper understanding of the mother's cunning actions.

"At that moment, as a mother, I did not know what to do," she explained, a delicate balance between remorse and justification. "I did it to get rid of Arjun from my daughter's life. She was engaged to be married to Mohandas, and I didn't want him to disrupt that. I am sorry if I was the cause of his death. I... I... never intended to kill him." Her words quivered with genuine guilt, and she succumbed to sobs that echoed through the room.

The room became a battlefield of conflicting feelings, where a mother's protective instincts clashed with the harsh reality of the unintended consequences for Arjun. The unexpected truth made them feel unsure about what to do, and now the inspector had to figure out what to do next.

Inspector Ranjit, still reeling from the shocking confession, turned his attention to Divya, as he sought more pieces to this enigmatic puzzle.

"Divya," Ranjit's voice sliced through the charged atmosphere, "You said that the phone was ringing when Arjun walked in, and he snatched the phone from you and put it on the table. Who was on the phone?"

"After Arjun left, I picked up the receiver and tried to listen, but it had been disconnected," Divya replied. "I did not know who called. The call was not repeated."

Ranjit, his senses sharp, pressed further. "So, you don't know who tried to contact you?" His question was met with a simple shake of her head. "Okay, it is not difficult to trace who called you around that time. I will find out."

Divya's mother, wiping tears from her eyes, interjected with an impassioned plea, "Don't blame or take action on my dear daughter sir.

She is innocent. I am the one who put the tablets in the tea. Punish me if you have to..." Her words hung in the air like a desperate plea of maternal sacrifice echoing through the room.

Ranjit, rising from his seat, contemplated the unfolding drama before him silently. "Let us see. You may go home now but be ready to come in for further questioning if needed." His words were a measured directive, and he motioned for Constable Merin to escort them back home in the police vehicle. "You have to give your signed statements to the constable outside. Merin here will guide you. You may go."

ACP Ranjit now sat down to jot down the rough timeline of Arjun's movements on that fateful evening.

4.00 pm	Arjun leaves the house of Satya - Janaki.
4.30 pm	Arjun arrives at Divya's house.
5.15 pm	Arjun leaves Divya's house.
5.30 pm	Arjun arrives at the KK brothers' outhouse.
6.45 pm	Arjun leaves the outhouse.

What happened after that ....?

A perplexed Ranjit sat at his desk deep in thought, grappling with the puzzling developments that had unfolded. The unexpected nature of the situation lingered, and he was left uncertain about what astonishing revelations were yet to come.

Chapter 35

Nandini was surprised to receive a long-distance call in the morning before heading to the hospital. It was her friend Dr. Soumya from Trivandrum. "Hey, Nandu, my husband Shekhar wants to talk to you."

Dr. Shekhar got on the line and explained Arjun's autopsy report in detail. "Hi, Nandini, from the report, I could see that Arjun had alcohol and traces of ganja in his system. But neither were near lethal levels. Also, the Alprazolam found in his system was higher than the usual therapeutic level but hardly enough to cause death. I can assure you that Alprazolam didn't cause his death. Even the mix of these three substances wasn't enough to kill him. As the autopsy report says, his death was due to drowning in seawater. What caused the drowning is something the police need to find out."

"Thank you doctor," Nandini told him.

Dr. Shekhar's words partly comforted Nandini, but she still had many questions about why Arjun took his own life if suicide was the cause. She decided to phone Ranjit about this later in the day.

Inspector Ranjit meticulously laid the groundwork for his sting operation against the smugglers. The final plans for the mission were drawn up in the conference room of the Commissioner of Police, Calicut. With the unwavering support of the Commissioner, Ranjit's plan took shape scrupulously like a spider spinning its web, each thread carefully woven to ensnare the unsuspecting targets. Hours of strategizing and coordination had led to this moment, as Ranjit stood, his resolve as unyielding as steel. He glanced at the figures surrounding him, his team poised for action, their eyes gleaming with anticipation as he imparted the final instructions to the group. Ranjit had also reached out to the NCB, their expertise and resources a valuable asset in his mission.

"Tonight, we strike," Ranjit murmured, his voice barely a whisper in the stillness of the night. "Their two trucks are due tonight. We should get those crooks at any cost. There can be no room for error."

The Commissioner's nod was all the confirmation he needed, a silent acknowledgment of their shared mission. With a sense of purpose burning in his chest, Ranjit turned his attention to the head of the Thalasseri police team, his allies in the darkness, their presence a silent reassurance in the face of danger.

"We'll need all the backup we can get from your side," Ranjit said, his voice tight with determination. "This won't be easy. It is a tough uphill task. We may encounter casualties. There can be no room for error."

As the hours ticked by, Ranjit's anticipation grew like a storm on the horizon, each passing moment bringing them closer to their moment of reckoning and a sense of urgency driving him forward.

"The pieces are falling into place," Ranjit thought, his mind a whirlwind of plans and contingencies. "It's now or never."

With the stage set and the players in position, Ranjit knew that the time for action had come. With a silent prayer on his lips, he gave the signal, setting the wheels of their operation in motion. They proceeded towards their destination in a silent convoy of vehicles aided by the darkness that was setting in.

As they moved through the shadows, Ranjit felt a surge of adrenaline coursing through his veins, each step bringing them closer to their elusive prey. But amidst the chaos and uncertainty, Ranjit remained steadfast, his determination unwavering in the face of danger.

But even as they closed in on their targets, Ranjit knew that their greatest challenge still lay ahead. With the fate of their mission hanging in the balance, Ranjit steeled himself for the final showdown, his heart pounding in his chest as he prepared to confront the enemy head-on.

For Inspector Ranjit, this was more than just a mission. He was dedicated to remembering his beloved brother, Rajiv, who was fatally hurt by the criminal deeds of these deceitful people. Inspector Ranjit hoped that no more young people would suffer from the drug problem caused by these criminals. It was a battle for justice, a fight against the forces of darkness that threatened to engulf the world. It was his life's commitment. And as he stood on the brink of victory, Ranjit knew that he would stop at nothing to see their mission through to the end.

The night draped over the godown like a heavy blanket, its darkness a fitting cloak for the treachery that lurked within. Inspector Ranjit, his nerves taut with anticipation, stood guard, his eyes scanning the shadows for any sign of movement. Beside him, Kartik and Sooraj, his trusted lieutenants, crouched in the small wooden shed adjacent to the godown, their cameras poised, ready to capture every damning detail of the impending confrontation.

"Stay sharp, boys," Ranjit murmured, his voice barely a whisper in the stillness of the night. "We can't afford any mistakes. The evidence needs to be ironclad. See that you get the maximum number of snaps. Focus on the faces of all the culprits and the registration number of the vehicles even though they may turn out to be fake."

Kartik nodded, his fingers deftly adjusting the focus on the camera, while Sooraj, with his video recorder leaned in closer, his ears straining to catch the faintest sound. The air crackled with tension, each heartbeat a drumbeat of anticipation as they waited for their targets to make their appearance.

In the dark shadows of the godown, Mohandas paced like a caged predator, his mind a whirlwind of schemes and calculations. Every step, every glance, was calculated with precision, his movements enveloped in the darkness as he awaited the arrival of his illicit cargo. The motorcycle he had arrived in was carefully concealed in the shadows, to evade detection.

With each passing moment, the tension in the air increased. Mohandas checked his watch impatiently, the minutes stretching into eternity as he waited for the telltale rumble of approaching trucks.

And then, the sound of the truck engines filled the air, the metallic groan of vehicles heralding the arrival of the trucks. Two trucks, bearing the unmistakable insignia of the KK Transport, rolled into the godown, their cargo concealed beneath a facade of innocent fertilizer.

With practiced efficiency, the drivers and helpers set to work, unloading bags of fertilizer to reveal the bags of contraband hidden amidst their cargo. As the trucks were unloaded, two motorcycles roared into the godown, followed closely by a sleek black Ambassador car. Their arrival was swift and purposeful, their occupants moving with the fluid grace of seasoned professionals. Their timing was perfect.

Ranjit's soft voice cut through the silence, sharp and commanding. "Let's do this," he whispered his words a rallying cry to his team. Kartik and Sooraj had already leaped into action, their movements swift and purposeful as they set about their task of recording every move.

In the shadows, Ranjit's minions, Kartik and Sooraj, watched with bated breath, their cameras poised to capture every damning detail of the illicit exchange that was taking place. Sooraj's video camera whirred noiselessly, the lens capturing the scene in vivid detail, while Kartik's camera with a telephoto lens clicked softly, freezing each moment in time with ruthless precision, zooming wherever necessary.

The transfer of contraband was swift, the packets of contraband disappearing into hidden compartments in the two motorbikes and the car with the deftness of practiced hands. Mohandas, the puppet master orchestrating it all, presided over the exchange with a sense of cold detachment, his eyes glittering with greed as he accepted the duffel bag of cash from the passenger in the car.

With a sense of triumph, Mohandas unzipped the bag, his fingers caressing the stacks of bills nestled within. A nod of approval was all it took to seal the deal — the unspoken agreement between buyer and seller.

As the minutes stretched into eternity, Ranjit watched with bated breath, his heart pounding in his chest like a drumbeat of anticipation. Every snap, every frame, brought them one step closer to their goal, one step closer to justice.

The motorbikes and the car left the godown as the rest of the bags of fertilizer were being reloaded into the trucks. Mohandas remained back to supervise this. It would take another half an hour to forty-five minutes.

In the shadowy recesses of the shed, Inspector Ranjit huddled with his constables, his voice a mere whisper in the stillness of the night. "I hope you got those snaps and videos perfect," he urged, his eyes glinting with steely resolve. "We needed clear shots of the faces of those criminals."

"All okay, Sir," the constables whispered in unison. "We have the evidence on camera."

The tension in the air was palpable. This was the moment they had been preparing for, the culmination of endless hours of meticulous planning and surveillance. Every detail had been carefully accounted for, every contingency planned for with ruthless precision.

As soon as the motorbikes and car slipped away from the godown, Inspector Ranjit silently moved into the shadows, his walkie-talkie crackling with urgency as he relayed orders to his team lying in wait along the road. With a quick response, the team, moving like ghosts in the darkness, planted spike strips on the road, their movements swift and silent in the darkness.

The criminals, oblivious to the danger that lay ahead, barreled down the road, their headlights dimmed to avoid detection. But as they approached the concealed traps, disaster struck. The sharp spikes shredded their tires, sending the bikes careening out of control and the car lurching to a halt.

Before they could react, chaos erupted in a cacophony of sound and fury. The night was rent with the screech of tires and the sharp crack of gunfire as the waiting police and NCB team unleashed a barrage of fire to apprehend the fleeing criminals.

"You're surrounded! Hands in the air!" shouted the leader of the team, his voice cutting through the chaos like a blade. "Don't make us use force. Surrender now!"

But defiance flared in the eyes of the gang members, one of them drawing a revolver and opening fire on the approaching officers. In an instant, the quiet night exploded into open warfare as more gang members emerged, their weapons gleaming in the dim light.

Meanwhile, Ranjit and his team of constables arrived on the scene, their presence a welcome reinforcement in the midst of chaos. With grim determination, they joined the fray, their guns blazing as they sought to quell the uprising from behind the gang. "Get down!" Ranjit shouted to his constables, diving for cover as bullets whizzed past them, the air thick with the acrid smell of gunpowder.

In the heat of battle, tragedy struck, as a bullet injured Ranjit's left arm, the searing pain a grim reminder of the dangers they faced. But even as he faltered, his resolve remained unyielding, his focus unwavering as he fought alongside his comrades.

The gang assaulted from the front and back could not hold for long. Amidst the chaos, two of the gang members fell to the ground, injured and defeated, while the remaining four surrendered, their weapons clattering to the ground as they raised their hands in surrender. With the battle won, Ranjit and his team moved swiftly to secure the scene, their victory tinged with the bitter taste of sacrifice. One of the police officers was injured in the leg. Another took a bullet in his arm. But luckily, none of the injuries were serious.

As they stood amidst the wreckage of the night, they knew that their triumph was just the beginning. For the fight against crime would never truly be over, and they would continue to stand vigilant against the forces of darkness that threatened to engulf their city. This was only a partial closure.

Luckily, the chaotic burst of gunfire had clashed with the rhythmic bursts of fireworks in a nearby temple which was celebrating its annual festival, creating a cacophony of sound that masked the violence unfolding in the shadows. Inspector Ranjit, despite his injury, with his team, moved with swift efficiency, his movements precise and calculated in the chaos of the night.

While the gunfight was raging on, Ranjit's gaze flickered to the nearby temple, where colorful explosions lit up the sky in a dazzling display of light. It was a God-given stroke of luck, he realized, that the celebratory noise drowned out the sound of gunfire, concealing their covert operation from prying eyes. The aerial pyrotechnics also gave them enough brightness to carry out their operation to an effective conclusion.

Even before the last echoes of the fireworks faded into the night, Ranjit and his team had bounced into action, their focus unwavering as they secured the scene. The car and motorcycles were swiftly taken into custody by the Thalasseri police, their presence erased from the scene like ghosts in the night.

Meanwhile, the gang members, their weapons confiscated and their bravado shattered, were herded into a waiting police van, their faces grim with defeat as they were whisked away in handcuffs to an unknown destination for interrogation by the police and the NCB.

Mohandas remained oblivious to the chaos unfolding in his absence far away from the warehouse, unaware of his empire crumbling around him. He had no inkling of the swift surgical strike that had apprehended red-handed the gang of drug peddlers along with their booty and vehicles.

In a matter of minutes, the scene was cleared and sanitized, every trace of the encounter meticulously erased to leave no evidence of the encounter that had taken place. Ranjit and his team worked with practiced efficiency, their movements swift and sure as they ensured that no stone was left unturned in their quest for justice. The whole operation lasted hardly fifteen minutes.

The team melted back into the darkness, like silent specters leaving behind nothing but a faint whiff or cordite in the air. Ranjit knew that their work was far from over. For the fight against crime was an ongoing battle, a relentless pursuit of truth and justice in a world shrouded in darkness. And as long as there were criminals to apprehend and justice to be served, Inspector Ranjit and his team would be there, ever vigilant in their quest to uphold the law.

In the heart of the turmoil, Mohandas remained blissfully unaware of the unfolding drama that had transpired just moments ago. He stood amidst the quiet calm of the godown, his mind consumed with thoughts of profit.

He never realized that a fierce battle had erupted on the road, a mere stone's throw away from where he stood. But as the sound of gunfire mingled with that of the fireworks from the temple fair faded into the night and the echoes of the confrontation dissipated, Mohandas remained none the wiser, his attention fixed solely on the task at hand. With practiced efficiency, he supervised the reloading of the trucks, his movements deliberate as he ensured that every last bag of fertilizer was securely stowed away. And as the final preparations were made, he mounted his motorcycle, the engine roaring to life beneath him as he prepared to return to Calicut.

As the trucks rumbled out of the godown and onto the open road, Mohandas followed close behind, his thoughts consumed with visions of the riches that awaited him in Calicut. Little did he know, however, that his carefully laid plans were about to come crashing down around him like a pile of dominoes.

Inspector Ranjit watched from the shadows, a cunning smile playing at the corners of his lips as he observed the two trucks rumble past them. The team had hidden in the bushes on the sides of the road hearing the sound of the trucks approaching. Mohandas followed close behind in his motorcycle. The inspector had allowed the smuggler — for that was what Mohandas was, to believe that he had was in the clear, knowing fully well that the truth would soon come to light.

As Mohandas disappeared into the night, Ranjit's mind raced with possibilities. With his co-conspirators already in custody, it was only a matter of time before Mohandas and his friends, the KK brothers, met the same fate. The giant sharks were still swimming free. But for now, Ranjit would bide his time, allowing the trap to close in around his unsuspecting prey.

For Inspector Ranjit, the game was far from over. With every passing moment, he edged closer to victory, his determination unyielding in the face of adversity. And as he watched Mohandas disappear into the darkness behind the trucks, he knew that their next encounter would be one for the history books.

Chapter 36

The night hung heavy with anticipation as Inspector Ranjit meticulously crafted his next plan to bring to book the perpetrators at the heart of the smuggling ring. With each passing moment, the net closed around the KK brothers and Mohandas, their grip on power slipping away with every move Ranjit made.

Ranjit had endured a harrowing ordeal amidst the chaos of gunfire, an unexpected casualty of the tumultuous clash. The searing pain had torn through his left arm as a stray bullet found its mark, threatening to shatter his world in an instant. Yet, by a twist of fate or perhaps a sliver of luck, the bullet narrowly skirted past his brachial artery, sparing him from a fate far graver than the agony he presently endured.

The surgeon's deft hands had skillfully extracted the offending bullet and meticulously sewn the torn tissues back together. The wound, though tender and throbbing, now bore the mark of healing, a testament to both the resilience of the human body and the marvels of modern medicine. Ranjit's left arm lay ensconced in an arm sling.

In a covert meeting shrouded in secrecy, Ranjit coordinated with the Punjab police and the NCB, laying the groundwork for a comprehensive operation that would shake the very foundation of the criminal underworld. With every detail meticulously planned, he awaited the perfect moment to strike. The police in Punjab intercepted the KK Transport trucks as they were being loaded with illegal goods concealed within empty fertilizer bags. The individuals responsible for this crime were caught red-handed in the act during a shootout and taken into custody. The operation occurred during the night when smugglers from across the border transported the contraband and loaded them onto trucks. The police and the Narcotics Control Bureau (NCB) lay in wait, concealed in the shadows. In a gunfire exchange, they apprehended the culprits along with the contraband.

The news of the operation in Punjab reached the KK brothers as panic swept through their ranks like wildfire. The tension in the air was palpable as they received word of their trucks laden with packets of illicit contraband being seized in Punjab, thus directly implicating them in the illicit smuggling. The weight of betrayal lingered in the atmosphere as their suppliers from across the border were apprehended in a swift and decisive mission by the Punjab police, an anti-terrorism squad of the central government and the NCB in a coordinated swoop.

The covert mission at Thalasseri, however, was not known to the KK brothers or Mohandas, as the six apprehended gang members were promptly removed from the scene to unknown destinations to be interrogated regarding the details of the drug distribution network in the state. The police Commissioner had asked the press to keep this sensitive news quiet, ensuring it didn't appear in newspapers or media.

With each passing moment, the walls closed in around them, leaving the KK brothers reeling in disbelief. Their once unassailable empire was crumbling before their eyes, their carefully constructed façade of power disintegrating to dust in the face of Ranjit's relentless pursuit of justice.

The source of the illicit cargo was identified as belonging to a neighboring country. More suppliers and terrorists were apprehended in a swift raid from an old building in Amritsar in Punjab and faced interrogation at the hands of the authorities. The harsh glare of the spotlight bore down on them, their lies being exposed with every question asked. But even as the truth threatened to consume them, they remained defiant, their resolve unbroken in the face of adversity. The whole gang was subsequently rounded up.

Detailed interrogation of the rounded up gang had revealed their agenda behind the smuggling of drugs and cannabis into the country. The future of India depended on its youth. By harming the youth of India, you harm the country itself. This was the ulterior motive of our neighboring country, which supports and nurtures these militants. They had been sending them across our borders and supporting terrorist sleeper cells within our country, aiming to weaken and destabilize India by targeting its young population. This was their treacherous plan to destabilize the country. The drugs and cannabis were intended to weaken the youth force of this country by getting them addicted.

The method of terrorism employed was unconventional yet devastating, sparing bloodshed but corroding the very fabric of the nation's progress. By insidiously fostering drug addiction among the youth, even within the confines of schools, the terrorists executed a calculated assault on the economic and fiscal stability of the country. This grand scheme was their weapon of choice, opting for the slow erosion of societal integrity over brute military force. Their scheme extended to fomenting religious intolerance among minority communities by targeting the youth, intending to sow discord and hinder the nation's advancement. They selected the state of Kerala to develop their traitorous operations because they saw the young population there as a fertile ground to implement their new terrorist tactics.

Ranjit was promptly kept updated of the developments in Punjab and Delhi. With each victory, he grew ever closer to his ultimate goal – the dismantling of the criminal empire that had plagued their city for far too long. But even as he reveled in his triumph, he knew that the battle was far from over. For in the world of treachery and deceit, the line between friend and foe was often blurred, and danger lurked around every corner.

He believed that the major part of his task, which brought him from New Delhi to Calicut, was complete. The mission to stop the flow of illegal drugs and catch the main people involved in transporting and distributing marijuana and drugs in the Malabar area of Kerala was successful. He had exposed the kingpins behind the conspiracy. It was up to the higher agencies like the NCB and the anti-terrorism squads of the Central Government to pursue the leads and bring the culprits to book. His secret assignment in Calicut had achieved its goal. He experienced a sense of satisfaction and contentment regarding it. He felt he had paid the debt to his brother, Rajiv and fulfilled the promise made to his mother and his deceased brother.

Ranjit had remained steadfast, his resolve unfaltering despite the daunting circumstances. Ready to confront the trials ahead, he was confident that nothing could hinder his pursuit of redemption. It was not over. The arrest of the trio – Sukumaran, Divakaran and Mohandas would be the ultimate goal which would complete his mission in Calicut. That he would leave to the Central government agencies. He had handed over the evidence and the data he had gathered to the agencies. They would haul them in for questioning.

What remained now for Ranjit was to unearth the intrigue surrounding Arjun's death. He felt he needed to do that for his friend Nandini.

Amidst the chaos of their crumbling empire, the KK brothers found themselves plunged into a state of panic once more as yet another wave of disaster struck. With each blow, the walls closed in around them, leaving them teetering on the brink of ruin. As news of the latest raid in Punjab reached their ears, a chill swept through their veins.

Three more trucks, laden with their illicit cargo, had been intercepted after they crossed the border into Kerala, their journey cut short by the swift hands of justice. The trucks were intercepted at Muzhappilangad, 17 kilometers from Kannur and the contraband seized by the Narcotics Control Bureau assisted by the Kannur police.

In a matter of moments, their world came crashing down around them, leaving them reeling in disbelief. The trucks, once source of their ill-gotten gains, now lay impounded, their contents seized by the authorities as damning evidence of their wrongdoing. With each passing moment, the noose tightened around their necks, leaving them gasping for air in a sea of uncertainty.

Meanwhile, Inspector Ranjit basked in the glow of victory preening himself in satisfaction. With the evidence against the KK brothers now nearly watertight, he wasted no time in facilitating a simultaneous raid on all offices of the KK Transport in Kerala. The full force of the law bore down heavily upon them, leaving them scrambling to salvage what little remained of their shattered empire. Their assets and bank accounts were frozen by the central government authorities. Notices were issued for them to be available for questioning.

As the NCB and the Enforcement Directorate descended upon them like avenging angels, the brothers found themselves powerless to resist. Their once formidable veneer crumbled in the face of overwhelming force, leaving them broken and defeated.

For Inspector Ranjit, the battle was far from over. With each victory, he drew closer to his ultimate goal, the complete and utter dismantling of the criminal empire that had plagued their city for far too long. And as he watched the KK brothers squirm beneath the weight of their own corruption, he knew that their reign of terror was nearing its end. For in the end, justice would always prevail, no matter how cunning or treacherous the enemy.

Mohandas had stayed updated about the misfortunes of the KK brothers and their business, yet he held onto the hope of escaping trouble using his political connections in Delhi. Although ACP Ranjit had meticulously gathered compelling evidence against him, the cautious inspector aimed for an airtight case before arresting Mohandas. Knowing his crafty, slimy nature and political connections, Inspector Ranjit sought to cover all bases. Unmindful of the chaos in Thalasseri that night, Mohandas naively believed he was beyond suspicion and could control situations from the safety of his political affiliations like a puppet master.

With a false sense of security, Mohandas reassured Sukumaran and Divakaran, his voice dripping with misplaced confidence. "Fear not, my friends," he declared, "Through my political connections, I shall get us out from this predicament. My contacts in Delhi will ensure our safety, mark my words."

But even as he spoke, doubt gnawed at the edges of his mind, a nagging voice whispering tales of impending doom. His dreams were depending on his friends in politics. They were his only hope for eluding the law.

Yet, despite the mounting pressure, Mohandas exuded an air of unwavering confidence, apparently a mask to hide the fear that churned within. With each passing moment, the noose tightened around them.

Meanwhile, Inspector Ranjit watched from the sidelines, a silent observer in the twisted game of cat and mouse. He allowed the tension to build, skillfully letting the trap close in on Mohandas and the KK brothers as the central agencies strove to gather more solid evidence against them.

Right now, he waited patiently, choosing not to take action as part of a careful plan in a dangerous game of trickery. He coordinated his efforts with the NCB, the Income Tax department and the Enforcement Directorate to gather additional evidence to prosecute them. As time went on, the evidence against them became stronger, bringing their eventual downfall closer with each passing moment.

Mohandas, however, remained steadfast in his resolve, his faith in his political connections unwavering. Little did he know, however, that the storm of justice loomed on the horizon and was moving towards him to engulf him in its fury.

In Coimbatore, the police officers worked tirelessly, fueled by a sense of duty and determination. "We must ensure that no stone is left unturned," declared the police chief, his voice resolute. "Every lead, every piece of information could be crucial in bringing these criminals to justice."

Following Basha's capture, the Coimbatore police, alongside the central government's anti-terrorism unit, launched extensive search operations. These efforts resulted in the identification and arrest of all sleeper cell members throughout Tamil Nadu and Kerala. Similar units in the North India were also targeted, with actions already underway. The operations were meticulously planned, synchronized, and executed, leaving no room for terrorists or their allies to slip through the cracks. Ranjit's tip-off regarding the Coimbatore operations played a pivotal role in this successful nationwide crackdown on terrorist groups. Raids were conducted in multiple locations across India, swiftly rounding up culprits planning terrorist activities in well-coordinated covert operations. Terrorist sleeper cells were identified and dismantled.

Meanwhile, in the central government's anti-terrorism cell, the atmosphere was one of focused intensity. "This is our chance to make a real difference," remarked one agent, her gaze fixed on the task at hand. "We owe it to the public to ensure their safety and security," added another, his expression reflecting a steely resolve.

The media had a field day in Tamil Nadu. As news of Basha's arrest spread, a sense of relief washed over the community. "Finally, some peace of mind," remarked one resident, his voice tinged with gratitude. "We can sleep easier knowing these threats are being dealt with," echoed another, her eyes reflecting a mixture of apprehension and hope.

Across Tamil Nadu and Kerala, families breathed a collective sigh of relief as the arrests were made. "I can't believe this was happening right under our noses," mused one resident, her voice filled with disbelief. "But I'm grateful to the authorities for taking swift action," she added, her tone tinged with admiration. "I feel that our children are now safe."

In the north, similar sentiments echoed as the crackdown on sleeper cells continued. "We must remain vigilant," cautioned one official, his words a stark reminder of the ongoing threat. "But with each arrest, we inch closer to a safer, more secure nation," he concluded, his voice infused with a sense of quiet determination.

Through the coordinated efforts of law enforcement agencies and the bravery of individuals like ACP Ranjit, the nation stood united in its resolve to combat terrorism. And as the dust settled on the successful operation, there remained a sense of hope — that perhaps, in the face of adversity, unity and perseverance would always prevail.

As Nandini entered Inspector Ranjit's office, the air felt tense with unsaid things. She hoped for answers in a time of confusion. The flickering light of the overhead lamp cast long shadows across the room, lending an air of solemnity to their meeting.

"Good afternoon, Inspector," Nandini greeted him, her voice tinged with a hint of concern. "I hope I'm not interrupting anything important. What happened to your arm?" She asked seeing his left arm in a sling.

Ranjit looked up from his desk as he motioned for her to take a seat. "Oh, that... it is the result of an injury during an operation. I am okay now. Please, have a seat. What brings you here today?"

Taking a deep breath, Nandini settled into the chair opposite him, her hands folded neatly in her lap. She had already informed Ranjit over the phone about the details from Dr. Shekhar regarding the autopsy report.

"I came to inquire about any progress in Arjun's case," she began, her voice barely above a whisper. "It's been days since you questioned Divya and her mother, and yet we still have no answers."

"Sorry, Nandini, I was totally engrossed during the past few days in a very crucial investigation, so that I could not concentrate on Arjun's case fully." He explained to Nandini the specifics of his interrogation with Divya and her mother. Nandini listened calmly, surprised by the secrets that Divya and her mother had been hiding from them.

Ranjit's gaze softened, a flicker of sympathy crossing his features as he listened to her plea. "I understand your concern, Nandini," he replied, his tone gentle yet firm. "Rest assured, Arjun's case still remains a top priority for me. However, as I said, recent developments have necessitated my attention elsewhere."

Nandini's brow furrowed in confusion, her eyes searching his face for any hint of explanation. "What kind of developments?" she pressed, her curiosity piqued.

Ranjit hesitated for a moment, not sure whether he should share the information with her. Weighing his words carefully before speaking, he said, "I'm afraid I can't divulge all the details at this time," he admitted, his voice tinged with regret. "Suffice it to say, a recent operation of national importance has taken precedence, but rest assured, I haven't forgotten about Arjun's case."

Nandini nodded, though a flicker of disappointment danced in her eyes. "I understand, Inspector," she murmured, her voice tinged with resignation. "I just want justice for Arjun and to know if there had been any foul play, that's all. I wanted to know the truth."

Ranjit offered her a reassuring smile, his eyes meeting hers with unwavering determination. "And justice you shall have, Nandini," he vowed, his voice carrying the weight of his conviction. "I won't rest until we uncover the truth behind Arjun's death, no matter where the path may lead."

With a grateful nod, Nandini rose from her seat, a sense of resolve settling over her like a comforting blanket. "Thank you, Inspector," she said, her voice filled with gratitude. "I appreciate all that you're doing for Arjun's case."

As she turned to leave, Ranjit watched her go, a sense of determination burning bright within him. He could now concentrate on Arjun's case. And as he prepared to face the challenges that lay ahead, he knew that no obstacle could stand in the way of his pursuit of justice for Arjun.

After Nandini left, his office the inspector Ranjit, determined to find answers, asked his dependable head constable, Raghavan, to join him. Raghavan's years of experience added seriousness to their mission.

"Raghavan Sir, please come in," Ranjit called out as the head constable entered the room, his posture rigid with respect.

"Sir, did you call for me?" Raghavan inquired, his voice tinged with anticipation.

"Yes, Raghavan Sir," Ranjit replied, his tone serious yet resolute. "I need your assistance in pursuing Arjun's case more aggressively. We cannot afford to let this investigation languish any longer."

Raghavan nodded, his expression mirroring Ranjit's determination. "What do you need me to do, sir?"

"I want you to go to the fishermen's colony on the beach and locate Ramu," Ranjit instructed, his voice steady. "He was the one who discovered Arjun's body, and I believe he may have valuable information that could aid our investigation. Bring him to the station to meet with me as soon as possible. Let us start with him."

"Consider it done, sir," Raghavan affirmed, offering a crisp salute before turning to leave.

As Raghavan departed, Ranjit couldn't shake the feeling of unease that lingered in the air. Arjun's death weighed heavily on his mind, a constant reminder of the unfinished business that loomed before him. He was determined to honor Arjun's memory by seeking justice for his untimely demise. Many new facts had now emerged regarding his last days. But he had no concrete answer as to the reason that led to his death.

Doubtless, it was the inquiry into Arjun's death that had led him to the KK brothers and thereby uncover the smuggling schemes masterminded by Mohandas and the KK brothers. He credited Nandini and her deceased brother, Arjun for his success in capturing those responsible for the extensive smuggling operation. Perhaps Nandini's doggedness and Arjun's sacrifice had led to the capture of the whole gang of smugglers and terrorists. They were intricately linked.

Hours later, Raghavan returned to the station with Ramu in tow, the fisherman's weathered face a testament to the hardships he had endured at sea. Ranjit greeted them both with a solemn nod, his eyes reflecting the gravity of the situation.

"Thank you for coming, Ramu," Ranjit began, his voice gentle yet firm. Ramu preferred to stand despite being offered a seat.

"I understand you were the first to discover Arjun's body on the beach. Can you tell me everything you remember about that day?"

Ranjit listened intently as Ramu recounted the happenings on that fateful morning, his mind racing with possibilities. "Did you see anyone else in the area at the time?" he pressed.

Ramu shook his head, his expression troubled. "No, sir," he replied.

Inspector Ranjit leaned forward, his gaze fixed on Ramu with unwavering intensity as he outlined his plan. "Ramu, I need your help," he began, his voice grave with purpose. "I want you to spread the word in your fisherman community. Ask if anyone saw or heard anything unusual on the beach on the evening prior to the day you found the body.

Ramu nodded solemnly, his weathered features reflecting the seriousness of the task at hand. "I understand, sir," he replied, his voice tinged with determination. "I will talk to the others and see what they remember. There are always a few boys playing on the beach in the evenings. They might have seen something."

Ranjit offered him a grateful nod, his appreciation evident in the depths of his eyes. "Thank you, Ramu. Your cooperation is invaluable to our investigation," he said, his voice tinged with gratitude. "Anyone who provides genuine and useful information about Arjun's death will be rewarded five hundred rupees. Make sure everyone gets this message too." The inspector was well aware that money talks.

With a sense of purpose, Ramu nodded, his resolve unwavering as he prepared to carry out Ranjit's instructions. "I'll get started right away, sir," he affirmed, his voice filled with determination. "I won't rest until I've spoken to everyone in our colony."

As Ramu made his way out of the station, Ranjit watched him go with a sense of anticipation, his mind already racing with the possibilities that lay ahead. He knew that the key to unlocking the truth behind Arjun's death may be hidden amidst the shadows of the past. The truth lies out there, he thought remembering Nandini's words.

Alone in his office, Ranjit allowed himself a moment of quiet reflection, his thoughts consumed by the weight of the task before him. With each passing moment, the mystery surrounding Arjun's death seemed to deepen, casting a shadow over the lives of all who were touched by it. He seemed to be nowhere near the truth despite his intense investigations. For in the depths of his soul, he knew that the truth would prevail, no matter how long the road or how steep the climb to reach it.

Ranjit felt a profound sense of responsibility towards Arjun and his determined sister, Nandini, who tirelessly sought closure regarding Arjun's death. It was Ranjit's solemn duty to unravel the mystery surrounding Arjun's demise, whether it was an accident, suicide, or something more sinister. He had compiled a lengthy roster of potential suspects who might be connected to the incident. Among them were Divya, along with her protective brothers, Sadanandan and Prabhakaran, who couldn't be ruled out from his list of suspects. The trio consisting of Sukumaran, Divakaran, and Mohandas also found themselves under suspicion. As Ranjit pondered over the possibilities, he couldn't dismiss Arjun's own brother, Satya, and his wife, Janaki, who had been implicated in the disappearance of the necklace. Yet could the culprit be someone entirely unexpected, lurking outside of his immediate suspicions? Ranjit was left grappling with these questions, his mind racing with scenarios and potential motives.

The weight of the investigation bore heavily on Ranjit, his determination matched only by the complexity of the task ahead. The quest for justice for Arjun had become a deeply personal mission, driving Ranjit to seek answers and closure no matter the cost.

With a fresh determination, he started his job, his strong determination unwavering as he got ready to explore further into the complicated mess of hidden truths and deceit that encircled Arjun's unexpected death. He understood that with every move he made, he came nearer to revealing the truth that had been hidden from everyone for a long time.

Chapter 37

Two days later, Ramu appeared at the police station, accompanied by a young adolescent lad. Inspector Ranjit, sitting behind his desk cluttered with files, glanced up, his expression curious, silently prompting Ramu to explain the presence of the boy. Upon seeing the inspector, Ramu respectfully lowered his partially folded *lungi*, unwrapped the towel from his head and stood in front of the inspector.

"This boy here has something to say about what he saw on that evening you were asking about, Sir," Ramu offered, his voice tinged with urgency.

Ranjit's gaze shifted to the teenager. "What is your name?" he inquired, his tone firm yet not intimidating.

"Hassan, Sir," the lad responded promptly, meeting the Inspector's gaze with a mixture of apprehension and anxiety.

Ranjit leaned back in his chair, folding his hands across his chest. "What did you see on the day prior to the death of the youngster on the beach? Give me the details," he prompted, his interest piqued.

As Ranjit listened attentively, Hassan began to recount his tale, the words tumbling out in a rush. "My friends and I were playing volleyball on the south beach that evening when I saw a car drive up to the beach. Two persons got out of the car and walked towards the pier in the sea."

"What time was it?" Ranjit interjected, his brow furrowing slightly as he sought to piece together the sequence of events.

"About six forty-five or seven, I think," Hassan replied, his voice steady despite the weight of his revelation. "The sun had just set, and it was not yet dark. It was twilight."

Ranjit nodded, absorbing the details. "Could you see clearly in that light?" he inquired, his tone gentle yet probing.

"Of course, Inspector," Hassan affirmed, his conviction unwavering.

"How far were you from those two persons?" Ranjit pressed on, his mind already constructing a mental map of the scene.

"Maybe around forty or fifty feet," Hassan estimated, his memory sharp and precise.

"Did you see their faces clearly?" Ranjit continued, his curiosity unabated.

"As dusk was falling, I could not make out their faces clearly as they were walking away from me," Hassan admitted, his brow furrowing in concentration. "But one of them was a tall, young man, a youth. The other was older, middle-aged probably."

"Can you describe what they were wearing?" Ranjit's voice carried a sense of anticipation, as if each word held the key to unraveling a tangled web of the mystery.

Hassan, recounted the attire of the mysterious duo with a clarity that surprised the inspector. "The youngster was wearing a red-colored T-shirt and jeans. The elder one was in dhoti, sporting a light-colored shirt."

Ranjit's eyes narrowed, his mind racing to piece together the puzzle. "How can you remember the color of the T-shirt so clearly after all this time?" he prodded smiling, his tone laced with suspicion.

A shy smile danced across Hassan's lips as he met the inspector's gaze head-on. "Sir, I have a similar-colored T-shirt which I had bought for Ramadan, that's why I remembered the color," he explained, his response calculated to disarm any doubts.

Ranjit nodded, though his mind buzzed with skepticism. "Can you remember anything more? Anything about the car? What make was it?" he pressed on, his curiosity insatiable, his senses attuned to every nuance of the boy's testimony.

The boy furrowed his brow in concentration, casting his mind back to that fateful evening. "It was a red Maruti car," he recalled, his voice tinged with uncertainty. "On the back glass, there was a color picture of Gandhiji, and below that was written '*Satyameva Jayate*'."

A flicker of admiration crossed Ranjit's features, though he remained guarded. "In Hindi?" he inquired, his tone neutral, masking the tumult of thoughts raging within.

"No, Sir, in Malayalam," Hassan confirmed, his words dripping with innocence. This was a hot piece of information that excited Ranjit. The car could be traced easily. There would not be many red Maruti cars with the picture of Mahatma Gandhi on the rear windshield.

"Did you see the number of the car?" Ranjit's enquired, sharp with anticipation, as he sought to extract every possible detail from the young witness.

"Oh, no sir, it was quite distant for me to see the number and it was too small to be seen from far away. I didn't pay any attention to the number." Hassan replied earnestly, his eyes wide with innocence. "I only noticed the picture and the writing on the glass."

Ranjit nodded, his mind already racing ahead, mapping out the next moves in his intricate game of cat and mouse. "Okay, Hassan, good work," he praised, rising from his chair to approach the boy. With a conspiratorial wink, he added, "Fine, now don't go around telling this to every one of your friends. I want you to keep this information to yourself. I will see that the reward is given to you after a few days. I will contact you. Leave your address with the constable."

"Thank you, Sir," Hassan responded, grinning eagerly, his gratitude shining in his eyes as he followed Ramu out of the police station.

287

Inspector Ranjit wasted no time in setting his plans into motion. Calling for the Chief Constable Raghavan, he wasted no time in getting to the heart of the matter.

"Raghavan Sir, can you find out who drives a red Maruti car with the picture of Gandhiji on the rear windshield with the..."

Before Ranjit could even finish his sentence, Raghavan's voice interrupted him, cutting him off mid-sentence. "That's Mohandas's car, Sir. I am sure. I have seen it many times."

Ranjit was astonished, his mind reeling with the implications of this damning revelation. "My God!" he exclaimed, his voice barely above a whisper. "That throws a whole different light on the case."

An early morning meeting had been convened in the Government Rest House in Westhill, Calicut, signaling the appointment of a candidate for the state elections to be held shortly. Mohandas, summoned urgently by the party's state secretary Krishna Raj, felt a surge of anticipation coursing through his veins as he prepared to step into the realm of electoral politics.

Krishna Raj, the party's formidable state secretary, greeted Mohandas with an air of intimacy, his smile masking the complex intrigues unfolding behind the scenes. "Congratulations, young man," he hailed, his words dripping with honeyed promises. "You have been selected as the candidate to contest in the elections from your constituency for the seat as an MLA. The party is extremely happy with your work and your generous contribution to the party's coffers."

Mohandas, overwhelmed by the magnitude of the moment, felt a lump form in his throat as he struggled to find the words to express his gratitude. "Thank you, Sir," he managed to stammer, his voice choked with emotion. "This is an unexpected windfall for me. I am overwhelmed. I do not know how to express my gratitude."

"Yes," continued the party secretary, "The high command in Delhi has approved your candidature in the coming elections. And the state committee has endorsed it."

The party secretary, sensing the swell of emotions in Mohandas, offered a reassuring nod. "You can help the party by keeping the flow of funds into the party's exchequer steady and generous," he suggested, his tone filled with expectation, hinting at the symbiotic relationship between power and patronage.

As they settled in for a cup of tea, Mohandas found himself immersed in a whirlwind of discussions, the contours of power and influence shifting with each passing moment. Yet, amidst the euphoria of his newfound political ascent, a nagging realization gnawed at the edges of his consciousness. The responsibility given to him was enormous.

He knew all too well that a portion of the profits from his illicit dealings with the notorious KK brothers had found their way into the party's treasury, greasing the wheels of influence and securing his place in the echelons of power. It was a treacherous game of give and take, where morality blurred into shades of gray, and ambition trumped principle. However, Mohandas found the attraction of power and status more important than the ethical dilemmas lurking in the background.

The news of Mohandas's nomination as the candidate for the upcoming state elections had spread like wildfire, igniting a fervor of excitement among his devoted supporters who had amassed in large numbers outside the Government Rest House in Calicut. Their fervent chants and slogans reverberated through the air, punctuating the atmosphere with an electric energy as they eagerly awaited the arrival of their beloved, charismatic leader.

As Mohandas descended the steps of the Rest House, his heart swelled with pride at the sight of his enthusiastic supporters, their faces alight with admiration and respect. With a wide grin plastered across his face, he greeted them with feigned humility, his hands folded in gratitude as they garlanded and showered him with fragrant flower petals.

For Mohandas, this moment marked the pinnacle of his political career, a validation of years of tireless dedication and unwavering commitment to his party's cause. He basked in the adulation of his followers, reveling in the euphoria of their collective triumph. As a leader of the youth wing of the party he had made significant contribution to the party's progress in the state of Kerala.

Yet, amidst the jubilant celebrations, a sense of anxiety nibbled at his mind. He knew that with his newfound stature came a weighty responsibility, one that would require him to navigate the murky waters of political intrigue with finesse and cunning. He would require additional funds to allocate to his election campaign. His thoughts raced as he pondered how to obtain these funds through his dealings with the KK brothers.

With a sense of determination burning in his heart, Mohandas resolved to seize the opportunity afforded by his nomination, to leverage his newfound influence to further his own ambitions and secure his place at the forefront of the political landscape.

As he made his way through the throngs of jubilant supporters, his mind raced with future plans and strategies, his thoughts consumed by the promise of power and the allure of victory in the coming elections.

Little did he realize, however, that amidst the revelry and applause, a shadow loomed on the horizon, casting doubt upon the bright future that lay before him. Unknown to Mohandas, unseen forces were at play, ready to challenge his ascent and test his resolve in ways he could never have imagined.

As he descended the steps of the Rest House, he found a smirking ACP Ranjit waiting near his car. The inspector was in civil clothes instead of his official uniform. He seemed to be enjoying the fun that was being enacted before him. As he approached the waiting ACP, a sense of foreboding washed over Mohandas, his instincts tingling with unease.

Concealing his apprehension beneath a false smile, Mohandas beamed as he approached Inspector Ranjit. The inspector, in turn, reciprocated the gesture with a perfunctory handshake congratulating him, his expression masking a deeper undercurrent of suspicion.

As they exchanged pleasantries, Ranjit seized the opportunity to draw Mohandas aside, away from the prying eyes of the crowd, his voice lowered to a hushed whisper as he delivered the ominous news.

"Mohandas," Ranjit began, his tone measured and somber, "I would like to ask you some questions regarding a case that I am investigating. I want you to come to the station with me right now. It will be best if you quietly get into my car without much fuss. I came in my private car and not in a police vehicle in order not to embarrass you."

Mohandas's initial shock gave way to a torrent of protestations. "Sir, what have I done? I do not know anything. Why do you want to question me?" His incredulity was palpable, etched upon his features for all to see.

The inspector's silence spoke volumes, his gaze unwavering as it bored into Mohandas with a steely intensity.

"Inspector," Mohandas pleaded, desperation creeping into his voice, "I will come to the station in my car after a while. I have to speak to the party workers who have gathered here. Please do not make me lose face in front of them."

Ranjit's smile was tight-lipped, his nod curt and decisive. "Okay, speak to your party colleagues," he acquiesced, though his expression remained stern. "I will wait here till you finish, and then you will come with me in *my* car, not in yours." The inspector was not willing to take any chances with the likes of Mohandas.

Mohandas realized the precariousness of his situation, the specter of humiliation looming large should he defy the inspector's authority. With a resigned sigh, he turned to address his supporters, his words hurried and terse as he sought to mollify their curiosity.

As the minutes ticked by, tension hung thick in the air, the anticipation of what was to come casting a pall over the celebration. Finally, after what felt like an eternity, Mohandas approached Ranjit, his resolve steeled for the ordeal that awaited him.

"I am ready to come with you to answer your questions, Sir," he announced, his voice tinged with resignation.

Ranjit, with an unreadable expression on his face, signaled towards his parked car silently and they headed towards the Town Police Station.

Chapter 38

As Mohandas found himself sitting in front of ACP Ranjit, the air thick with tension and suspicion, Ranjit wasted no time in laying bare the pieces of damning evidence before him. With a calculated precision, he scrutinized the phone records spread out on the desk before him, his gaze flickering up to meet Mohandas's with a steely resolve.

"Mohandas," Ranjit began, his voice low and measured, "I have a phone record here which shows that you had phoned Divya on the evening before Arjun's body was discovered. Is it true? Your phone records are in front of me."

Mohandas felt the weight of the inspector's gaze bearing down upon him, a sinking realization settling in the pit of his stomach. He knew he stood on the verge of being discovered, his carefully constructed facade crumbling under the weight of incriminating evidence.

"Yes," Mohandas admitted, his voice barely above a whisper, the admission hanging heavy in the air.

Ranjit's lips curled into a knowing smirk, like a predator toying with his prey. "What did you speak about?" he pressed, his tone deceptively casual, though his eyes bored into Mohandas with a penetrating intensity.

Caught off guard, Mohandas's mind raced to concoct a plausible explanation, his thoughts dancing on what to reply. He knew all too well that he had not spoken to Divya on that fateful evening.

"Well..." Mohandas hesitated, his words faltering as he struggled to maintain his composure, "She did not speak to me. She lifted the phone, but there was no conversation between us as she did not respond or speak to me." He decided to come out with the truth.

Ranjit's smile widened, though there was no warmth in it, only the cold satisfaction of cornering him. He had expected as much his net closing tighter around Mohandas with each faltering word.

"Is that so?" Ranjit mused, his voice laced with thinly veiled skepticism. "It seems rather convenient, don't you think? You never had any conversation?"

Mohandas's heart sank as he realized the seriousness of his predicament.

"Are you sure? Was there no conversation at all?" Ranjit persisted, his voice probing and insistent, like a hunter tracking his prey. "The records here show that your call lasted about fifteen minutes."

Mohandas's eyes darted nervously, a flicker of uncertainty dancing within their depths. He swallowed hard, the lump in his throat betraying his growing unease. "I... I heard some conversation in the background," he confessed, his voice faltering slightly under the weight of Ranjit's scrutiny.

"And...?" Ranjit prompted, his tone laced with anticipation.

"Divya was upset, probably," Mohandas continued, his words tumbling out in a rush as he recounted the fragments of conversation he had unwittingly overheard. "Arjun was shouting and accusing her of being engaged to someone else and seemed to be in a rage."

Ranjit leaned forward, his gaze unwavering as he pressed for more details. "What did you do?" he persisted, his tone soft but insistent, like a chess player maneuvering his pieces into position for the final checkmate.

"I listened for a while and then disconnected the phone," Mohandas replied, his voice steady despite the turmoil raging within him, "Deciding to talk to her later." He paused, a furrow creasing his brow as he recalled the events of that fateful evening. "I did not call her on that day again as I was busy otherwise."

Ranjit nodded remembering Divya's narrative previously, "I see," he murmured, his mind already racing ahead, piecing together the fragments of Mohandas's story in search of the elusive truth.

Mohandas watched anxiously as Ranjit scribbled notes on a pad, each stroke of the pen echoing like the ticking of a clock counting down to his inevitable reckoning. He knew that the inspector's relentless questioning was only the beginning, a prelude to the storm that loomed on the horizon.

As the interrogation stretched on, Mohandas couldn't shake the feeling of being ensnared in a web of deception, each carefully crafted lie pulling him deeper into the abyss.

"Did you see the KK brothers that evening?" Ranjit's voice cut through the tension in the interrogation room, his eyes, unblinking, fixed intently on Mohandas, searching for any hint of deception.

Mohandas shifted uncomfortably in his seat, the weight of Ranjit's scrutiny bearing down on him like a leaden cloak. "Yes, after calling Divya, I went to their outhouse to meet them," he confessed, his voice tinged with a note of resignation. It were best if he spoke the truth, he thought.

"Did you meet them?" Ranjit persisted, his tone unyielding.

"Yes, I did," Mohandas replied, his words hanging in the air like a fragile thread.

"Both of them?" Ranjit pressed further, his gaze piercing through Mohandas's defenses.

"Well... no, I met only Divakaran," Mohandas admitted, his voice faltering slightly as he recalled the events of that evening. "Sukumaran was not there. He had gone to Mannarkad as he had some work in his branch office there. Divakaran said that he would return only by night."

Ranjit nodded thoughtfully, his mind working overtime to piece together the puzzle laid out before him. So far, Mohandas's account seemed to align with the information gathered from other sources like the statements of Elias and Divya. But Ranjit knew better than to take anything at face value — especially Mohandas's. In the murky world of interrogation, truth was often a fleeting shadow, elusive and ephemeral.

As he pondered his next move, Ranjit's gaze softened, a subtle shift in his demeanor signaling a change in tack. "Tell me, Mohandas," he began, his voice taking on a gentler tone, "Who else was present there?"

After a moment of hesitation, Mohandas finally spoke up, his words measured and cautious. "Arjun came there after some time," he began, his voice tinged with uncertainty. "He was in an angry mood and accused Divakaran and me that we were not honest with him about our business."

Ranjit's eyes narrowed, his curiosity piqued by Mohandas's revelation. "Honest? What did he mean by that?" he probed, his tone sharp with intent.

Mohandas shifted uneasily in his seat, acutely aware of the weight of Ranjit's scrutiny bearing down upon him. "Well... he thought that we were not giving him his share of his profits adequately," he confessed, his words faltering slightly under the weight of Ranjit's piercing gaze. "He wanted more money as his share of his profits."

Ranjit's brow furrowed, his mind racing to connect the dots as Mohandas's narrative unfolded before him. "What did you tell him?" he pressed, his tone laced with a sense of urgency.

"We told him that as the business was new profits were low; we expected more profits as the business improved," Mohandas explained, his voice tinged with a hint of defensiveness. "Right then, the profits were limited and we were giving Arjun the share proportional to his investment."

As Mohandas spoke, Ranjit's mind flashed back to the statements of Elias, the pieces of the puzzle beginning to fall into place. He knew that Arjun's accusations against Mohandas and Divakaran ran deeper than mere financial disputes. No mention was made by Mohandas about the smuggling operations. But Ranjit remained silent, choosing to bide his time and let Mohandas continue to weave his web of deception.

Ranjit was fully aware that soon after his interrogation the Narcotics Control Bureau (NCB) would take in Mohandas for questioning, examining the dark depths of the illegal drug trade that lurked beneath the surface. Ranjit decided to leave that part of the questioning to them. The truth, he knew, would soon come to light, and when it did, the consequences would be swift and unforgiving. But for now, Ranjit remained patient, watching and waiting as the pieces of the puzzle slowly fell into place. He purposefully avoided referring to the smuggling operations or their business and confined his questions to Arjun's case.

Ranjit's interrogation continued. With a sense of purpose, he leaned forward, his gaze fixed intently on Mohandas, as he probed deeper into the interrogation.

"When did you leave Divakaran's house?" Ranjit's voice sliced through the silence of the interrogation room, sharp and incisive.

Mohandas paused, his mind racing to recall the events of that fateful evening. "Around six-thirty or shortly thereafter," he replied, his voice steady despite the tumult of emotions seething within him.

"Was Arjun still there when you left?" Ranjit's question hung in the air.

"No, Arjun had left about five to ten minutes before I did," Mohandas answered, his words tinged with a note of finality. "I returned after Arjun left the outhouse."

"Did you both leave together, by any chance?" Ranjit's eyes probed into Mohandas's.

"No, not at all... as I said, Arjun left before I did."

Ranjit's brow furrowed, his mind already racing ahead to the next line of inquiry. "Where did you go from there?" he pressed, his tone insistent.

"I went home to rest," Mohandas replied, his voice tinged with weariness. "I had had a hectic day and went to bed early after dinner."

Inspector Ranjit's demeanor shifted, his posture straightening as he rose from his seat and approached Mohandas with a sense of purpose. Sitting on the edge of the table, he fixed Mohandas with a stern gaze, his eyes boring into his very soul.

"Are you sure that you did not go anywhere else?" Ranjit's voice held a note of warning, a subtle reminder of the gravity of the situation.

Mohandas met Ranjit's gaze head-on, his resolve unwavering despite the weight of suspicion bearing down upon him. "No, I went home from there," he replied firmly, his voice unwavering. "I was at home after that. I did not go anywhere else. You can verify with my mother."

As Mohandas spoke, a palpable tension hung in the air, thick and suffocating. Mohandas knew that his alibi would be checked, as Ranjit's relentless pursuit of the truth threatened to expose the dark secrets hidden beneath the surface.

"By the way, Mohandas, do you wear dhoti and a white shirt most of the time?"

Mohandas was surprised when he noticed that the line of questioning was changing.

"Of course, I wear them most of the time I am in Kerala. Being in politics, I wear light colored *Khadi* shirts and dhoti. Most of the politicians wear that. What has my dress have to do with this investigation?"

"Nothing, I was just verifying some random facts."

Ranjit maintained a stoic silence, his gaze locked with Mohandas's in a silent battle of wits. Mohandas returned the stare defiantly, his expression a mask of unwavering resolve, as if daring Ranjit to challenge his statement. But beneath the facade of defiance, a flicker of uncertainty danced in Mohandas's eyes, betraying the inner conflict raging within him. After a prolonged moment of tension, Mohandas finally averted his gaze, his eyes dropping to his hands folded in his lap, a silent admission of defeat.

Ranjit decided to play his trump card. "Look here, Mohandas," he began, his voice edged with a hint of steel, "Don't lie to me. There is incontrovertible evidence that your car was spotted at the south beach near the pier at around quarter to seven that evening. Why are you lying to me? There is a dependable witness who saw it. It is better if you come clean."

Mohandas's face registered genuine shock and disbelief at Ranjit's accusation. "Me?... My car?... By the beach?..." he sputtered, his voice tinged with incredulity. "Oh no, it cannot be. I was nowhere near the beach on that evening. You must be mistaken. You may be..." His voice trailed off, uncertainty creeping into his tone as he struggled to make sense of Ranjit's accusations.

Ranjit, his expression inscrutable, waited for Mohandas to continue.

"Oh, no... yes... I did not have my car with me," Mohandas interjected hastily, a note of desperation creeping into his voice. "I had lent my car to Sukumaran that day. His car was at the workshop, and he had borrowed mine to go to Mannarkad. It is impossible that my car was seen at the beach. Suku had gone to Mannarkad in my car and was not in Calicut. Someone has made a mistake in identifying the car or given you false information. I had been using my motorcycle the entire day."

298

Chapter 39

As Mohandas left ACP Ranjit's office, officials from the NCB were waiting outside to whisk him away for questioning in connection with the drug smuggling.

Immediately thereafter, Ranjit decided it was the right moment to interrogate Sukumaran about Arjun's death. He instructed the head constable to bring in Sukumaran for questioning. Raghavan left with two other constables to Sukumaran's residence. Sukumaran arrived, appearing confident and unaware of the purpose behind his summons.

As Sukumaran entered the station, he could not understand the intention brewing within the inspector's mind. He stood confidently before ACP Ranjit's scrutinizing gaze with a certain amount of defiance.

"Sit down, Sukumaran," Ranjit gestured towards a chair, his voice measured and authoritative. "We have matters to discuss."

Sukumaran obliged, his hands clasped tightly in his lap as he awaited Ranjit's inquiry. He sat rigidly in the uncomfortable chair, facing ACP Ranjit across the desk in the cramped office. Though the summons to the police station had caught him off guard, leaving him puzzled and apprehensive, he put on an apparent brave front.

Dressed in his customary attire of a white *dhoti* and a sky blue short-sleeved shirt, Sukumaran appeared almost nonchalant, his attire belying the gravity of the situation. With one leg casually crossed over the other, he met Ranjit's probing gaze with an unwavering stare, as if daring the ACP to uncover any secrets he might hold. His mind churned with calculations and strategies. He had been briefed previously by his cousin, Mohandas, who had assured him of his political connections in Delhi and their ability to sweep aside any legal obstacles regarding the smuggling. This assurance had bolstered Sukumaran's confidence, convincing him that he was untouchable and beyond the reach of the law.

Sukumaran had entered the station, his heart pounding with nervous anticipation, though he managed to put on an apparent attitude of confidence. He believed he was there to answer questions about his trucks being seized, unaware of the barrage of questions that awaited him. As Ranjit's gaze bore into him, Sukumaran's palms grew sweaty, his confidence wavering under the pressure. He knew he had to stick to his fabricated story, no matter what. But deep down, a seed of doubt gnawed at him. What if Ranjit saw through his lies? What if he couldn't keep up the facade?

As Ranjit began to question him, Sukumaran's mind raced with the instructions Mohandas had drilled into him. He recalled how he was supposed to deflect any inquiries about the packets of illegal cargo found in the KK brothers' trucks. He was to pretend he knew nothing and shift the blame onto the drivers and helpers in the trucks. With this deceptive plan in mind, Sukumaran felt somewhat prepared to face the interrogation.

Despite his attempts to remain composed, Sukumaran's nerves betrayed him. His voice wavered as he spoke, his eyes darting nervously around the room. He felt a knot form in the pit of his stomach.

"So, how have you been, Sukumaran?" ACP Ranjit initiated the interrogation with an air of casualness, attempting to lull Sukumaran into a false sense of security. "It's been a while. I trust everything's been going smoothly with your business?"

Sukumaran's smile lingered, a mask of congeniality concealing the anxiety simmering beneath the surface. "Yes, indeed," he replied, his tone carefully measured. "No complaints on that front." He knew that the inspector was toying with him.

Ranjit leaned back in his chair, his demeanor deceptively relaxed as he continued his line of inquiry. "And how is your father faring after his stroke? I heard he's been on the mend."

Sukumaran's expression softened, a flicker of genuine concern momentarily breaking through his facade of composure. "Thank you for asking," he replied, his voice tinged with gratitude. "He's improving steadily, able to manage with a walking stick now. We're hopeful for his full recovery with active physiotherapy."

The conversation veered towards mundane topics, a superficial exchange of pleasantries masking the underlying tension between interrogator and suspect. Ranjit's probing questions disguised as casual banter, each word carefully chosen to elicit a response from Sukumaran.

Noting the light blue color of Sukumaran's shirt, Ranjit's gaze lingered for a moment before commenting, "That's quite a striking shirt you have on. Do you have a penchant for lighter colors?"

Sukumaran chuckled softly, his smile never faltering as he played along with Ranjit's charade. "Indeed," he replied, his tone light. "I find pastel shades more soothing, you could say. They suit my temperament."

Ranjit's next question was more pointed, a subtle shift in tone that did not escape Sukumaran's notice. "I couldn't help but notice your attire," he remarked, his voice casual yet probing. "Do you always stick to traditional attire like the *dhoti*?"

Sukumaran's demeanor remained unruffled, his response swift and practiced. "Ah, yes," he replied, a hint of amusement coloring his tone. "When in Kerala, the dhoti is my preferred choice. But when venturing beyond state borders, I do opt for pants. Jeans, however," he added with a smirk, "Are not quite my style. They tend to... lack sophistication, don't you think?"

As the interrogation unfolded, the atmosphere in the room grew increasingly charged, each exchange laden with unspoken tension. Ranjit's questions probed deeper, his scrutiny unrelenting as he sought to unravel the truth hidden beneath Sukumaran's carefully constructed facade. And amidst the facade of cordiality and camaraderie, a silent battle of wits raged on, each man striving to outmaneuver the other in a deadly game of cat and mouse.

Ranjit's laughter filled the room, a brief moment of camaraderie amidst the tension. "Indeed," he agreed, a hint of amusement in his tone. "The dhoti has been our traditional attire for generations. A symbol of our heritage."

Sukumaran nodded in agreement, though his mind raced with apprehension. He realized that the inspector was monkeying around with him. 'Something was not right,' his inner voice told him. He did not ask anything about the trucks or the fertilizer business. Despite the levity of the moment, he knew that the conversation was merely a prelude to some crucial interrogation. He looked at the inspector warily and remarked, "But I am sure that you did not summon me here to discuss about my sartorial tastes."

The joviality swiftly disappeared as Ranjit's expression grew solemn, and he became serious. "Indeed, Sukumaran," he replied, his tone sobering. "Our discussion today pertains to a far more important matter."

Sukumaran's heart skipped a beat, his pulse quickening with a sudden surge of apprehension. "Of course," he replied, his voice carefully neutral. "I'm at your disposal, inspector."

Ranjit wasted no time in broaching the subject at hand, his words measured and direct. "I have reason to believe that you were acquainted with Arjun, the young man whose untimely demise we are investigating," he began, his gaze unwavering.

Sukumaran's brow furrowed in confusion, a flicker of unease dancing behind his eyes. "Arjun?" he echoed, as if his mind were scrambling to recall details about the deceased. "Yes, definitely, he was a partner with us in our business. I knew him quite well. Poor chap, I don't know why he committed suicide."

But Ranjit pressed on, undeterred by Sukumaran's feigned naivete. "It has come to my attention that Arjun visited your residence on the evening of his death," he continued, his tone probing. "Is that correct?"

Sukumaran's heart sank as he realized where the interrogation was leading. "That evening? Yes, my brother mentioned it to me." he repeated, his voice tinged with disbelief. "But I assure you, inspector, I was not even in Calicut at that time. I was nowhere near my house that evening. I was away in Mannarkad."

Ranjit's demeanor appeared to shift abruptly, as if a sudden revelation had dawned upon him. "Ah, I see," he exclaimed, his tone now tinged with a hint of realization. "My apologies for the confusion. It seems there has been a misunderstanding."

Sukumaran's heart skipped a beat, a glimmer of hope flickering in the darkness of his despair.

Ranjit leaned forward, his expression inscrutable as he continued, "I stand corrected. It appears that Arjun did indeed visit your residence that evening, but not to see you. Rather, it seems he met with your brother, Divakaran and your cousin Mohandas."

Sukumaran was silent.

Ranjit's lips curled into a faint smile, a silent acknowledgment of the unfolding revelation. "According to our sources," he explained, his tone measured, "Arjun arrived at your residence with some troubling accusations against your brother. It seems there was an altercation, after which Arjun departed in an agitated state."

"My brother told me the next day when they discovered his body. He had come there in the evening with some accusations. Only Divakaran and Mohandas were at home... I mean in our outhouse. Arjun met them and had an argument with them, I was told. And then he left in a huff."

"Oh! so, you're certain you never saw Arjun that evening?" Ranjit's tone was firm, each word a carefully aimed dart.

Sukumaran's throat felt dry as he struggled to maintain his composure under Ranjit's relentless scrutiny. "No, I didn't," he asserted, his voice edged with alarm. "As I mentioned earlier, I had business in Mannarkad that morning. I didn't return until late in the evening."

Ranjit stared intensely into Sukumaran's eyes, a silent challenge lurking behind the piercing gaze. "And what time exactly did you arrive home?" he pressed, his voice betraying none of the impatience that churned within.

Sukumaran's mind raced as if racking his memory for the precise details of that fateful evening. "It must have been around seven-thirty or eight," he replied, his tone uncertain. "Though, I can't be certain of the exact time."

"What kept you so long?"

Sukumaran's mind raced, scrambling to concoct a plausible explanation that would satisfy Ranjit's probing inquiry. "I had paperwork to attend to at Mannarkad," he replied hastily, his words ringing hollow even to his own ears. "Accounts to balance, invoices to review. The usual business affairs."

"Nevertheless," Ranjit continued, his tone serious, "Let's focus on the matter at hand. Now, about your trip to Mannarkad..."

"Did you have a driver with you when you went to Mannarkad?"

Sukumaran braced himself for the next line of questioning, his mind racing to anticipate Ranjit's intentions. "I drove myself," he reiterated, his voice steady despite the unease churning within. "I prefer to undertake short journeys within Kerala on my own without a driver."

A flicker of interest lit up Ranjit's eyes at Sukumaran's response, a glimmer of shared camaraderie evident in his smile. "Ah, I can relate to that," he remarked, a note of apparent warmth creeping into his voice. "There's something inherently therapeutic about a long drive, don't you think? I love long drives."

Sukumaran's shoulders relaxed slightly at the unexpected camaraderie, a fleeting moment of connection amidst the tension of interrogation. "Indeed," he agreed, a hint of relief coloring his tone and a smile curling on his lips. "It offers a sense of freedom, a chance to clear one's mind of life's burdens, if only for a moment."

But Ranjit's expression grew serious once more as he steered the conversation back towards its intended course. "Now, let's return to the timeline of your journey," he prompted, his gaze unwavering. "What time did you leave from Calicut that morning?"

Sukumaran's brow furrowed in concentration as he mentally retraced the steps of his journey. "I left around seven-thirty," he replied, his voice measured. "And I arrived in Mannarkad by half past ten, give or take a few minutes."

Ranjit nodded in acknowledgment, a faint smile playing at the corners of his lips. "A three-hour drive, then," he mused, his voice contemplative. "Quite efficient, if I may say so."

Sukumaran nodded in agreement, his mind still unable to discern the direction of Ranjit's inquiry. "Yes, it's a familiar route," he conceded, unaware of the hidden currents beneath the surface of their conversation. I have driven there many times."

As Ranjit's questions continued to probe deeper, Sukumaran remained oblivious to the web of suspicion closing in around him, his confidence unwavering in the face of uncertainty. Little did he know that every word spoken brought him to the inevitable reckoning that awaited him.

Ranjit's inquiry shifted gears, his tone casual yet laden with significance, "And what vehicle do you drive, Sukumaran?" he asked, his eyes fixed on Sukumaran with a subtle intensity.

Sukumaran's confidence wavered as he sensed the conversation veering into perilous territory. "I have a Premier Padmini," he replied cautiously, his voice measured.

"It's a reliable car, quite comfortable for long drives, isn't it so?" Ranjit's hand moved to his pocket, retrieving a handkerchief with practiced ease. As he dabbed at his face, his gaze remained fixed on Sukumaran, observing his reaction with keen interest.

A sudden shift in Sukumaran's facial expression caught Ranjit's attention. A flicker of apprehension seemed to cross his features. His once relaxed and confident visage now suddenly became wary as if he sensed a trap ahead.

Ranjit noted the change with a raised eyebrow, a silent acknowledgment of the shift in dynamics. "So, you used your Premier Padmini for the journey?" he probed, his tone deceptively casual.

Sukumaran hesitated, his gaze flickering as he struggled to maintain his composure under Ranjit's relentless scrutiny.

"Actually," he began, his voice faltering, "My car was undergoing repairs at the workshop. I... I had to borrow a vehicle from a *friend.*"

The room felt tense as Sukumaran's confession lingered, making him uneasy with uncertainty. Ranjit's gaze bored into Sukumaran, searching for any sign of deception or evasion.

A trace of fear crept into Sukumaran's features, betraying the cracks in his carefully constructed facade. His confidence and arrogant attitude seemed to have crumbled before the inspector's gaze. His mind raced, searching for a plausible explanation to account for the sudden change in his story.

Ranjit's probing continued, his tone laced with subtle suspicion. "So, you couldn't use your own car and had to rely on a *friend*," he remarked, his emphasis on the word *'friend'* hanging heavily in the air. "I'm curious, Sukumaran. Who was this *friend* of yours?"

Sukumaran's palms grew clammy as he felt the weight of Ranjit's scrutiny bearing down on him. He licked his lips which had become dry. With a gentle gesture, Ranjit placed a glass of water before him, urging him to take a sip in an attempt to ease his obvious discomfort.

"Relax," Ranjit reassured him, his voice surprisingly gentle despite the underlying tension. "But I do need to know, Sukumaran. Who lent you his car?"

Sukumaran's throat felt dry as he hesitated, the name caught in his throat like a bitter pill. "It was... Mohandas," he finally stammered, his voice barely above a whisper.

A flicker of seeming surprise crossed Ranjit's features at Sukumaran's response, quickly masked by a facade of neutrality. "Ah, your cousin and your partner in business," he remarked, his tone carefully measured. "It seems odd that you didn't mention him earlier, considering your close relationship."

Sukumaran shifted uncomfortably in his seat, a heavy silence descending upon the room as he wrestled with his thoughts. Ranjit's scrutiny was relentless, leaving him feeling exposed and vulnerable.

"Well, let's move on," Ranjit continued, his voice brisk as he redirected the conversation. "What time did you leave your office in Mannarkad?"

Sukumaran's mind raced as he seemed to struggle to recall the details of that fateful day. "I... I'm not exactly sure," he admitted, his voice tinged with uncertainty. "It must have been sometime in the late afternoon, after I finished my work. May be four or four-thirty."

Ranjit's eyebrows arched inquisitively, a silent prompt for Sukumaran to provide a more precise answer. "Can you give me a more specific time?" he pressed, his tone insistent.

Sukumaran's gaze faltered under Ranjit's intense scrutiny, his mind scrambling to piece together the fragmented memories of that day.

Sukumaran's words hung in the air, the weight of his admission casting a pall over the interrogation room. "Four-thirty. Yes...I left at four-thirty."

Ranjit roared, his voice booming with an undercurrent of disbelief. "Are you trying to deceive me?"

Sukumaran's anxiety was palpable as he reached for the glass of water, his hand trembling slightly as he lifted it to his lips. Beads of sweat glistened on his forehead, betraying the turmoil churning within.

Ranjit's demeanor remained stern as he riffled through the pages of a file before him, his expression unreadable. With a sudden movement, he looked up, fixing Sukumaran with a penetrating stare. "According to our records," he began, his voice measured, "You left your office much earlier, at three o'clock in the afternoon. Your Mannarkad office has confirmed this."

Sukumaran's heart sank at the revelation, his mind racing to reconcile the conflicting accounts. "I... I must have made a mistake," he faltered, his voice strained. "Perhaps I left earlier than I thought, I did."

But Ranjit's scrutiny was relentless, his gaze unwavering as he pressed for clarification. "A mistake?" he echoed, his tone laced with skepticism. "Or a deliberate attempt to conceal the truth?"

Sukumaran's throat felt dry as he struggled to find an explanation that would appease Ranjit's suspicions. "I assure you, Inspector," he began, his voice quavering, "It was an honest oversight. I may have miscalculated the time in the midst of my busy schedule. It was months ago."

Ranjit's expression seemed to soften slightly at Sukumaran's plea, though the skepticism lingered in his eyes. "I see," he murmured, his tone thoughtful. "Well, let's move on."

Ranjit's interrogation pressed on, each question a calculated strike against Sukumaran's defenses. "And what time did you finally arrive in Calicut?" he inquired, his tone sharp with expectation.

Sukumaran shifted uncomfortably in his seat, his mind racing as he struggled to recall the details of his journey home. "I reached home around seven thirty," he replied hesitantly, a note of uncertainty creeping into his voice. "My brother can verify that. He was at home when I arrived."

But Ranjit's patience wore thin, his frustration bubbling to the surface. "I asked when you reached *Calicut*, not your *home!*" he snapped thumping on the table, his voice a sharp rebuke.

Sukumaran's heart sank at Ranjit's stern admonishment, a sinking feeling settling in the pit of his stomach. He knew he was caught in a web of his own making, his lies unraveling before Ranjit's relentless scrutiny.

A heavy silence descended upon the room as Ranjit stared down Sukumaran, his gaze unwavering. He knew he had Sukumaran backed into a corner, his lies exposed.

"Look here, Sukumaran," Ranjit began, his voice tinged with anger. "You've been spinning one lie after another, and it's clear you're in deep trouble. You can't evade the truth forever. It's time to come clean about what really happened."

Sukumaran's throat felt dry as he stared back at Ranjit, the weight of his guilt pressing down upon him like a suffocating blanket. He knew he had no choice but to face the consequences of his actions, no matter how dire they may be. As the interrogation wore on, Sukumaran's resolve began to falter. The pressure mounted with each passing moment, and he struggled to maintain his façade. Behind his mask of confidence, fear lurked, threatening to expose the truth he so desperately sought to conceal.

Ranjit's words hung in the air like a silent challenge for Sukumaran to finally come clean and confront the truth. The tension in the room was palpable, the atmosphere charged with anticipation.

Sukumaran's world seemed to collapse around him, the weight of Inspector Ranjit's scrutiny bearing down on him like a crushing burden. Beads of sweat gathered on his brow, his nerves frayed with the knowledge that he stood on the brink of total disaster. Ranjit's relentless pursuit of the truth left Sukumaran feeling exposed and vulnerable, his every word being dissected under the harsh glare of interrogation.

The air in the cramped interrogation room grew thick with tension. The steady whirring of the fan overhead provided a discordant backdrop to the high-stakes drama unfolding within its walls, its erratic rotations mirroring the turmoil of Sukumaran's troubled mind.

In the end, as Ranjit continued to press him for answers, Sukumaran found himself teetering on the edge of confession. The weight of his guilt bore down upon him, threatening to consume him whole. Yet, even in the face of imminent exposure, he managed to cling to his lies, knowing that to admit the truth would be to seal his own fate. He understood he had no escape and had to confess to the truth that had haunted him since that fateful evening.

With a heavy heart, Sukumaran lowered his gaze, his eyes fixed on the worn floor tiles beneath his feet. With a deep breath, he began to recount the events of that fateful evening, each word weighed down by the gravity of truth.

Inspector Ranjit listened intently as Sukumaran's narrative unfolded, his eyes widening in wonder at the revelations being disclosed. He leaned forward, perched on the edge of the table, his attention fully captured by the unfolding tale.

"I killed him... I killed Arjun," said Sukumaran with downcast eyes.

Chapter 40

Sukumaran cleared his throat, steeling himself and beginning his narration of the events on that catastrophic day.

"It was on that eventful evening," Sukumaran began, his voice faltering slightly as he glanced at Ranjit, "When everything changed."

He could feel the tension in the room palpable, almost suffocating. Each word he uttered felt like a confession, a release of the burden he had been carrying for too long in his mind.

"I left Mannarkad earlier than usual in Mohandas's Maruti car," Sukumaran continued, his eyes fixed on a distant point as if reliving the moment, "Anticipating the crucial meeting with Mohandas and Divakaran."

Ranjit's gaze remained unwavering, urging him to continue the narrative.

"The meeting was about supply of fertilizer from another state in the Northeast. We were planning to expand our business," Sukumaran explained, his voice tinged with bitterness. "Mohandas had assured us that his political connections in Delhi would help us establish some contacts in those areas."

He paused, memories flooding back with a surge of emotion.

"I left Mannarkad around three o'clock," Sukumaran resumed, his tone growing more solemn with each word. "I wanted to ensure I reached home in time for the meeting, without any delay."

Ranjit listened intently, a silent observer to Sukumaran's unraveling tale.

"I didn't stop anywhere along the way," Sukumaran emphasized, a note of resignation creeping into his voice. "Not even for a cup of tea."

The silence that followed was heavy, pregnant with unspoken questions and lingering doubts. Ranjit nodded, a silent signal for Sukumaran to continue, his expression unreadable as he awaited the recital of this intricate tale of deception and betrayal.

Sukumaran's voice trembled slightly as he recounted the events of that fateful evening, his words laced with an air of uncertainty.

"I remember it vividly," he began, his gaze fixed outside the window on a distant point as if searching his memory. "It was around six-thirty when I reached Calicut."

The weight of the moment hung heavy in the air, each word he uttered echoing with the gravity of his testimony.

"As I approached our home," Sukumaran continued, his voice faltering slightly, "I spotted Arjun, emerging from our gate."

The memory seemed to play out before his eyes, like a scene from a long-forgotten dream.

"He seemed... disturbed," Sukumaran recalled, his brow furrowing with concern. "His face was flushed with anger, and he was in a rage."

"I slowed down my car," Sukumaran recounted, his hands gripping the imaginary steering wheel, "Hoping to catch his attention."

"Arjun recognized me," Sukumaran recalled, his voice tinged with regret, "And before I could even utter a word, he lashed out."

"He pounded on the bonnet of my car," Sukumaran continued, his voice trembling with the weight of his confession, "His anger unleashed in a torrent of accusations."

The confrontation threatened to spiral out of control, a tempest seemed to be raging within Arjun's mind.

"I knew I had to defuse the situation quickly," Sukumaran admitted, his words a whisper. "So I coaxed him to get into the car with me, hoping to go to some place to talk things over."

"But even as we drove, the tension between us remained palpable. 'We need to talk, to find some solution to the problem that was vexing you,' I said to him."

And so, we drove on. We drove towards Calicut beach.

Sukumaran's narrative unfolded like the ebb and flow of the tide, each word carrying the weight of the memories he struggled to reconcile.

"We made our way towards the south beach pier," Sukumaran recounted, his voice tinged with nostalgia.

"As we parked the car and moved towards the beach, I couldn't shake the feeling of unease that gnawed at the edges of my heart. The sun was setting," Sukumaran continued.

"Arjun was bent upon walking on to the pier and sitting there. He wanted to discuss matters with me, he said. He seemed to be preparing for a showdown."

"I cautioned Arjun and told him that it was a bit risky to move on to the old pier as some of the wooden planks on the pier were loose and rickety. It might not be safe. But Arjun insisted on walking on to the pier and I had to give in. He was in a dazed state as his breath reeked with alcohol... and perhaps had also smoked ganja."

"I felt that Arjun's determination was a reckless abandon that bordered on madness."

"He brushed aside my concerns," Sukumaran recalled, a note of frustration creeping into his voice. "His eyes were ablaze with a devilish fervor I could not comprehend. It was a type of frenzy that I had not seen in his eyes ever before. It was like the eyes of a madman."

"As we ventured onto the pier, my heart hammered in my chest, a relentless drumbeat of fear and uncertainty. The sea roared around us, its fury unleashed upon the wooden beams of the dilapidated pier that stretched out below us like the skeletal remains of some ancient leviathan. The planks beneath our feet groaned with each step. I was really scared out of my wits."

"I hesitated," Sukumaran confessed, his voice barely above a whisper. "But Arjun showed no fear, his frenzied, demoniac laughter ringing out against the backdrop of the crashing waves. His eyes glimmered with rage, as if he were possessed by some inhuman spirit."

"In that moment, I couldn't help but wonder at Arjun's recklessness, a defiance that bordered on madness. It unnerved me."

"And then..." Sukumaran trailed off, his voice faltering as he struggled to find the words to continue.

Ranjit's gaze bored into him, a silent urging for him to unravel the mysteries that lay hidden within the depths of his memory.

"Arjun's accusations cut through the air like a knife," Sukumaran began, his voice heavy with sorrow. "He spoke of betrayal and deception, his words a bitter reminder of the deception which he thought we were carrying out. He did not trust us. He felt that we were cheating him in the business."

"As Arjun poured forth his grievances, I could feel the weight of guilt settle upon my shoulders. I tried to reason with him, and assure him that his suspicions were unfounded, and we had never intended to deceive him."

But Arjun's anger burned like a wildfire, consuming everything in its path.

"He accused Divakaran, Mohandas and me of smuggling ganja and drugs," Sukumaran continued, his voice trembling with emotion.

"And then he turned on us," Sukumaran recalled, his voice barely above a whisper. "His words dripping with venom as he hurled accusations at me, my brother and Mohandas, accusing us of ruining his life. He accused us of turning him into a drug and alcohol addict and of ruining his life. He blamed us for Divya getting separated from him. He went on to accuse us of conspiring to arrange her marriage with Mohandas."

"I tried to reason with him," Sukumaran repeated, his voice a plea for understanding. "But his rage knew no bounds, he suddenly began slapping and punching my face with a fury born of betrayal and resentment. He was mad with rage. He appeared to possess a diabolical strength."

"In that moment of chaos and confusion, my mind was consumed by a single, desperate thought that I would topple into the sea." And so, out of sheer desperation, I... pushed him...," Sukumaran confessed, his voice barely above a whisper. "I pushed that unfortunate youngster from the pier into the churning depths of the raging sea below."

The memory of Arjun's fall lingered like a scar upon Sukumaran's soul, a painful reminder of the choices he had made in the heat of the moment.

"I heard a loud thud as he fell, possibly striking one of the pier's beams with his head. And then in a moment, he was gone," Sukumaran whispered, his voice choked with emotion. "Lost to the raging sea, swallowed whole by the darkness that awaited him below."

Tears welled in Sukumaran's eyes as he relived the moment of Arjun's fall, his heart heavy with the weight of his guilt and remorse. Burying his face in his hands, he sobbed silently.

Inspector Ranjit remained silent, his expression sphinxlike as Sukumaran laid bare the events of that ominous evening. The weight of Sukumaran's words hung heavy in the air, a silent condemnation of the choices that had led him down this path.

As Sukumaran's tears flowed freely, Inspector Ranjit watched on in silence, offering neither consolation nor interruption. He understood the importance of allowing Sukumaran to unburden himself, to confront the truth that lay hidden within the depths of his conscience.

After what felt like an eternity, Sukumaran's sobs began to subside, his trembling hands reaching up to wipe away the tears that stained his cheeks.

"It happened so quickly," Sukumaran murmured, his voice barely above a whisper. "One moment he was there, and the next... he was gone."

The memory of Arjun's disappearance lingered like a specter in the recesses of Sukumaran's mind, a reminder of the irreversible consequences of his actions.

"I wanted to save him," Sukumaran confessed, his voice heavy with regret. "But the sea... it was merciless in its fury, its waves crashing against the pier with a ferocity that left me paralyzed with fear."

"In that moment of chaos and confusion, I was left with no choice but to bear witness to Arjun's demise, and silently observe the tragedy that unfolded before my very eyes."

"I returned home with a heavy heart," Sukumaran continued, his voice hollow with grief. "Haunted by the memories of that fateful evening, burdened by the weight of the truth that I alone carried ever since that fateful evening. I never told this to anyone."

The silence that ensued was oppressive. He could feel the weight of Ranjit's stare, a silent judgment pressing down on him heavily.

"What next?" Sukumaran's voice was barely a whisper, his eyes pleading for absolution, for guidance in the midst of the storm that threatened to consume him whole.

Inspector Ranjit rose to his feet, his expression grave as he summoned his head constable Raghavan. Having heard the details regarding Arjun's last moments, he turned to face Sukumaran, his words a solemn decree that sealed Sukumaran's fate.

"Sukumaran," Inspector Ranjit intoned, his voice grave with authority. "I hereby place you under arrest for the murder of Arjun."

The words hung heavy in the air, a stark reminder of the consequences of Sukumaran's actions.

Dispassionately, Inspector Ranjit directed the constable to prepare the FIR.

Outside Inspector Ranjit's office, the atmosphere was filled with tension as officers from the Narcotics Bureau awaited the completion of Sukumaran's interrogation by ACP Ranjit. The looming specter of the ganja and drugs smuggling case cast a shadow over the proceedings, each passing moment bringing them closer to the inevitable interrogation that awaited him.

Divakaran and Mohandas had already been taken into custody by the Narcotics Bureau, their fate hanging in the balance as they faced the relentless scrutiny of the law.

As Inspector Ranjit sipped his tea, a small reprieve amidst the chaos that surrounded him, he couldn't help but feel a sense of satisfaction at the progress he had made in unraveling the mystery of Arjun's death. Hours of tireless interrogation had led him to this moment, the pieces of the puzzle finally had fallen into place as he prepared to bring Sukumaran to justice. The truth had been revealed in the end, after all,

With a sigh, Ranjit closed the file that lay before him. He was glad having closed Arjun's file.

Now all that remained was to face Nandini with the distressing truth. He would meet her tomorrow with the news, he thought.

Chapter 41

It was almost six months since Nandini had come to India. Her husband, Rajaram, from Australia, was constantly calling her to come back. Aathira, her daughter was now feeling her mother's absence. Nandini's leave for five years had luckily been sanctioned by the Kerala Government and she had been relieved of her duties from the Medical college at Calicut a couple of days ago.

The only thing that was holding her back was the non-closure of Arjun's case. The truth about his death, which had been eluding her was still not known. She realized that Inspector Ranjit, despite his busy schedule and heavy commitments to other cases, was taking a keen interest in this case. Knowing how busy he was, she felt guilty pestering him very often about the case and its outcome. She had not met him for the past one month and had avoided going to his office so as not to annoy him. She did not want to be a thorn in his flesh. Having already booked her tickets to Australia via Singapore emplaning from Madras, her last minute preparations were on.

Before leaving for Australia, she wanted to meet Ranjit and thank him for the active interest that he had taken in Arjun's case. All her possessions were packed to be shipped to Australia. This was her farewell to India. She did not plan to return to India in the near future were she to get her Fellowship in Australia.

As Nandini stood before the imposing facade of the *Nalukettu*, a sense of melancholy washed over her. With each step she took, memories of days gone by flooded her mind, a bittersweet reminder of the joys and sorrows that had unfolded within these walls.

Nandini stood at the threshold of her ancestral home, her heart heavy with the weight of memories that lingered within its walls. The air was thick with the scent of old wood, a familiar fragrance that tugged at her heartstrings and transported her back to a time long since passed.

With trembling hands, she unlocked the door and stepped inside, the musty scent of old wood and faded memories enveloping her like a familiar embrace. Tears blurred her vision as she wandered through the corridors of her childhood, each room a treasure trove of nostalgia and longing.

As she wandered through the rooms, every corner held a memory from her past, a small piece of a life that now felt far away. The creak of the wooden stairs beneath her feet sounded like a melody of memories.

She traced her fingers along the worn edges of family photographs that adorned the walls, each image a snapshot of a moment frozen in time. Faces smiled back at her, their eyes twinkling with the memory of days gone by, a reminder of the love and laughter that had once filled these hallowed halls.

The large ancestral house, the *Nalukettu*, stood stoic and silent, a sentinel bearing witness to the passage of time. Within its walls lay the echoes of countless memories, each corner steeped in the rich medley of a family's history. But now, it stood forlorn and desolate, its future uncertain. The *Thulasi Thara*, positioned in the center of the *Nadumuttam*, now contained the remains of a dried-up *Thulasi* plant.

In the hall where laughter once echoed, now only the ghostly whispers of the past remained, a haunting reminder of the joy that had once filled these halls. In the bedroom once belonging to her mother, sorrow and loss lingered like unwelcome guests. Memories of *Amma's* struggles weighed heavily on her heart, evoking a profound sadness. Despite the challenges, her mother's unwavering devotion to her children never faltered, always graced with a warm smile and a willingness to fulfill their every desire.

As she gazed upon her father's empty easy chair, memories of his affection flooded her mind. The echoes of his hearty laughter reverberated within her, bringing both comfort and longing. His words of guidance and admonition resonated deeply, underscoring the pivotal role of a father in shaping a child's character and growth.

But it was Arjun's room that held the deepest wounds, his absence a gaping hole in the fabric of their family's history. As Nandini stood before his photographs mounted on the wall, a silent sob escaped her lips, the weight of guilt pressing down upon her like a leaden weight.

"Why did you let me down?" Arjun's smiling face seemed to ask, his eyes accusing and pleading all at once. Nandini bowed her head in shame and sorrow, the truth of the words piercing her heart like a dagger.

She had promised herself that she would uncover the truth about Arjun's death before leaving Calicut, but time had slipped through her fingers like grains of sand. The truth remained elusive, a shadow lurking just beyond her reach.

But as she stood there amidst the echoes of the past, Nandini vowed to carry Arjun's memory with her wherever she went. His spirit would guide her on her journey, a beacon of light in the darkness that threatened to consume her.

With one last lingering look around the ancestral home she was about to leave behind, Nandini whispered a silent farewell, her heart heavy with the weight of unfinished business and unspoken truths. Instinctively, she understood that she would never return to this house again.

Satya, Nandini's brother, had taken on the solemn responsibility of overseeing the sale of their ancestral home. With Anandu residing in Pune and Sreeni and Mamta settled in the United States, Nandini felt the weight of their absence like a heavy burden upon her shoulders. The ties that once bound them to this place had begun to dissipate their paths diverging as they embarked on their own separate journeys.

After casting a final glance at the ancestral Nalukettu, she went back to her home — the outhouse.

As Nandini sat in the rocking chair in the outhouse, ruminating on the memories of the past and pondering reaching out to Ranjit, the phone in her home rang, breaking the silence like a bell tolling in the distance. With a sense of anticipation, she picked up the receiver, her heart quickening at the familiar voice on the other end.

"Hi, Nandini, how are you?" Ranjit's voice was a welcome respite from the solitude that enveloped her. "It's almost a month since you came to see me."

A pang of guilt gnawed at Nandini's conscience as she listened to Ranjit's words. "I'm sorry, Ranjit," she began, her voice tinged with regret. "I've been caught up in a whirlwind of bureaucracy, trying to get my leave sanctioned from the Government of Kerala."

She could almost see Ranjit's understanding nod through the phone line as she continued, "I've had to make multiple trips to Trivandrum, pushing papers and navigating the labyrinth of bureaucracy. It's a far cry from the efficiency of abroad, I can tell you that much."

Ranjit's response was sympathetic, his own experiences with the bureaucracy of Kerala's government mirroring her own frustrations. "I understand completely," he reassured her. "It's no small feat, getting leave sanctioned from the government."

Nandini let out a sigh of relief, grateful for Ranjit's understanding. "Thank you, Ranjit," she said softly. "I've only been relieved of my duties at the hospital a couple of days ago. I've been contemplating seeing you before I leave for Australia."

Ranjit's voice carried a note of excitement as he spoke, his words tinged with anticipation. "Oh! you are leaving? I have some important news to share with you," he revealed. "That's why I called. Since today is Sunday, are you free to meet us in the evening? My wife and son will be with me."

Nandini's heart skipped a beat at the prospect of meeting Ranjit and his family, the promise of important news adding a sense of anticipation to their meeting. "Of course, Ranjit," she replied eagerly. "I'll be there. Where should we meet?"

Ranjit suggested the Sea Queen Hotel in Calicut beach, its cozy atmosphere the perfect setting for their meeting. He was excited, "I want you to meet my wife Revathi and my little son Aarav. Why don't you join us in the Calicut beach today?"

"Oh, sure, I'd love to," Nandini was enthusiastic, "I have not met your family till now."

"We will be in the lobby of the hotel. Will five-thirty be okay for you?"

"Sure, I'll be there." With a sense of anticipation, Nandini agreed, her mind buzzing with excitement at the prospect of meeting Ranjit and his family before leaving for Australia.

Sharply at five-thirty, Nandini made her entrance into the lobby of the Hotel Sea Queen, her pista-colored chiffon saree billowing gracefully around her, the fabric whispering against her skin with each step. The subtle scent of Nina Ricci perfume trailed behind her, leaving a lingering trail of elegance in her wake. Ranjit's eyes lit up as he caught sight of her, rising promptly from his seat to greet her.

Revathi, Ranjit's wife, a petite woman with a warm smile, approached Nandini with genuine delight. "It's so lovely to finally meet you, Nandini," she exclaimed, her voice tinged with warmth. "Ranjit has spoken so highly of you."

Nandini returned Revathi's smile with a playful glint in her eye. "Oh, has he now?" she teased lightly, a hint of mischief dancing in her tone. "Spoken only good things about me, I hope," she replied laughing.

Laughter bubbled between them that echoed the camaraderie shared between old friends. Aarav, their son, a bright-eyed ten-year-old with an endearing charm, joined in the exchange, offering Nandini a polite greeting. "Good evening, Nandini aunty," he chimed in, his voice filled with youthful exuberance.

Despite the lighthearted banter, an underlying tension lingered in the air, casting a shadow over the jovial atmosphere. As the conversation faltered, an awkward silence descended upon them, each grappling with unspoken words and unresolved emotions.

Sensing the need for privacy, Ranjit interjected, coming to Nandini's rescue with a proposal. "Why don't you two head to the restaurant and treat yourselves to some refreshments?" he suggested turning to his wife and son, his tone gentle yet firm. "Nandini and I have something important to discuss. We'll join you shortly. Keep Aarav entertained," Ranjit instructed his wife, "We won't be long, just fifteen or twenty minutes."

With a nod of understanding, Revathi ushered Aarav towards the restaurant, leaving Nandini and Ranjit alone in the lobby. Once they were alone, Ranjit motioned towards the exit, his expression grave yet determined. "Let's take a walk," he suggested, his voice low and solemn. "There's something I need to tell you, Nandini."

"Sure," Nandini rose from her seat, a sense of anticipation mingled with anxiety tugging at her heartstrings.

Nandini and Ranjit stepped out onto the bustling south beach road the world around them a blur of motion and noise.

Together, they traversed the familiar path towards the beach, the salty breeze caressing their faces with a gentle embrace. The sand beneath their feet felt warm and inviting, a stark contrast to the cool indifference of the sea beyond. Ranjit scanned the shoreline, his eyes searching for a secluded spot away from the prying eyes of onlookers.

"Let's find a quiet place to sit," Ranjit suggested, his voice a soft murmur against the backdrop of crashing waves. With a nod of agreement, they veered off the beaten path, seeking refuge amidst the solitude of the shore.

As they settled onto the soft, golden sands, Ranjit's gaze softened, a hint of nostalgia flickering in his eyes. "Nandini," he began, his voice laced with a bittersweet warmth, "Do you see that pier over there?"

Following his gaze, Nandini turned towards the weathered structure jutting out into the horizon, its skeletal frame a haunting reminder of days long past. A frown creased her brow as she turned back to face Ranjit, curiosity mingling with apprehension in her gaze. 'What about it?" she queried, her tone tinged with uncertainty.

Ranjit took a deep breath, steeling himself for the words he was about to speak. "It's about Arjun," he began, his voice barely a whisper.

"That was where Arjun met his end... I am sorry," Ranjit's voice carried the weight of sadness as he narrated the events responsible for the haunting truth to Nandini, his words hanging heavy in the air.

Nandini sat quietly, shocked, as Ranjit told her about what had happened and the details of his investigations into Arjun's death. As he spoke, Nandini's eyes widened with a mix of horror and sadness. Tears welled up, blurring the setting sun on the horizon as she struggled to control her emotions.

"Nandini, I have finally unraveled the mystery surrounding your brother's demise," Ranjit began, his voice carrying a weight of solemnity. "He did not commit suicide but was murdered."

For a moment, silence enveloped them, the weight of her grief rendering words unnecessary. In the stillness, memories of Arjun danced at the periphery of Nandini's consciousness, a bittersweet memories of her beloved younger brother.

Ranjit proceeded to succinctly detail his investigation, shedding light on the circumstances leading to Arjun's tragic death and the involvement of Mohandas and the KK brothers. Ranjit also touched upon the nefarious conspiracy concocted by the trio ensnaring Arjun in their web of deceit taking advantage of his innocence and naivete. Furthermore, Ranjit elaborated on their illicit activities, particularly their engagement in smuggling ganja and drugs from North India. The inquiry into Arjun's passing had inadvertently unearthed a Pandora's box, exposing the culprits behind an international drug smuggling ring. Additionally, it had revealed their participation in anti-national activities, thus bringing their nefarious deeds to light. He painted a vivid picture of Arjun's unwitting entanglement in their web of deceit, his innocence leveraged by forces beyond his control.

He also shared with her the story of his brother Rajiv, who had tragically fallen victim to drug abuse, and his determination to uncover the truth behind his death. Rajiv had meant to him what Arjun meant to Nandini. This was the driving force behind his request for a transfer from Delhi to the city of Calicut.

As the tale unfolded, Nandini listened in stunned silence, her heart heavy with the weight of sorrow and indignation. Every revelation stabbed her soul like a dagger, reopening wounds she had believed were long healed.

When Ranjit finally concluded his narrative, Nandini found herself engulfed in a maelstrom of emotions, tears cascading down her cheeks in silent anguish. Beside her, Ranjit too was moved, his empathy a silent testament to their shared loss. A wave of grief washed over Nandini, memories of Arjun flooding her mind like a torrential downpour. She remembered his infectious laughter, his unwavering optimism, and the countless adventures they had shared together. And now he was gone, leaving behind nothing but a void in their hearts. Tears rolled down her cheeks as Nandini struggled to come to terms with the truth.

In the hushed aftermath of their revelation, they sat silently in somber reflection, their hearts heavy with the weight of truths long buried. In the quietude of the beach, the echoes of her grief mingled with the gentle lull of the waves, a haunting melody of remembrance and lamentation.

Finally, as the sun dipped low on the horizon, casting a warm glow across the golden sands, Nandini stood up, a sense of closure settling over her like a comforting embrace. "Well, Ranjit," she began, her voice soft yet resolute, "Thank you for unraveling the puzzle that had haunted me for so long."

Ranjit nodded solemnly, his gaze lingering on the fading light of the day. "What's done is done," he murmured, his words tinged with a hint of melancholy. "But the truth was always out there, waiting to be uncovered. Through his demise, Arjun has contributed to uncovering the mystery and complexity surrounding drug smuggling and distribution, as well as exposing a massive international terrorist plot."

With a grateful smile, Nandini expressed her heartfelt appreciation. "You have given me closure, Ranjit," she said, her voice tinged with emotion. "For that, I am truly grateful."

As they made their way back towards the hotel, Nandini found herself opening up to Ranjit, sharing her plans for the future. "I've decided to move to Australia," she revealed, her tone tinged with excitement and anticipation. "There's a Fellowship opportunity waiting for me there. I leave on Wednesday."

Ranjit listened attentively, his silence a comforting presence amidst the tumult of emotions swirling within her. "Thank you for being here for me," Nandini added, her voice tinged with gratitude. "It means more than you realize."

As they walked, the distant chatter of children playing on the beach and the faint clanging of the ice cream vendor's bells gradually faded into the background, replaced by the serene melody of the sea lapping against the shore. The setting sun had painted the sky in shades of orange and pink, a distressing reminder of the passage of time and the inevitability of change.

In the distance, the haunting cries of seagulls echoed across the vast expanse of the Arabian Sea, their mournful call a moving reminder of the fleeting nature of life and the eternal rhythm of the ocean. Together, Nandini and Ranjit made their way towards the hotel, each step a testament to the enduring bond forged through shared sorrow and newfound closure.

"Goodbye, Nandini," Ranjit bid farewell to her. "Keep in touch even though you will be far away from us."

"I sure will," Nandini replied, looking into those bright eyes that had brought her comfort and peace.

Epilogue

2024

Nandini sat on her balcony, perched on the twentieth floor of a tall apartment building overlooking the Calicut Beach. Dressed in a light blue kimono, she ran her fingers over its soft folds, recalling fond memories of her trip to Japan seven years prior. With her husband, Rajaram, and their daughter, Aathira, she had explored enchanting cities like Kyoto, Osaka, and Tokyo. As she swayed gently in her rocking chair, echoes of their adventures filled her mind, each memory a vivid picture.

Holding a delicate porcelain cup, Nandini savored the aroma of freshly brewed coffee, watching the steam blend with the salty sea breeze. Her silver-grey hair danced in the wind, a testament to the passage of time and the memories she held dear.

As she settled into the familiar rhythm of the rocking chair, Nandini couldn't help but be transported back to a bygone era, a time when her father, Anantharama Iyer, would occupy the very same chair, lost in contemplation as he rocked back and forth with solemn grace. The memory of his dignified presence hung in the air, vividly etched into her mind as if he were still sitting beside her with his palm leaf fan swaying to and fro.

Lost in memories, Nandini gazed at the distant horizon as the sun dipped below the Arabian Sea, painting the sky with hues of gold and pink. In the twilight, she found comfort in thoughts of loved ones gone but not forgotten. With each sway of her chair, she intertwined past and present, finding solace in life's journey.

Recently turning seventy-five, Nandini felt the weight of memories, especially that of her brother Arjun, whose absence left a profound void. With each passing year, the pain seemed to deepen, his memory etched into her very soul.

However, Arjun wasn't the sole loved one Nandini had lost in life's journey. Her elder brother Anandu had passed away three years ago, succumbing to a sudden heart attack that took away yet another pillar of support. Left behind was his wife, Uma, a resilient woman facing her own battles in Poona. Afflicted by osteoarthritis and asthma, Uma stood strong despite her frailty, spending her days in an old age home.

As Nandini reminisced, her thoughts turned to Anandu's two sons — Akhil and Aadi. Despite the distance, she found comfort in knowing they had found their paths in distant lands. Settled abroad with families of their own, they had moved beyond the challenges of their homeland.

Coming from a forward community, they harbored uncertainties about the opportunities available to them and their descendants for education and employment in their homeland, where caste and politics often dictated outcomes. Throughout their schooling, their parents had encountered obstacles in gaining admission to prestigious educational institutions based solely on merit. They faced setbacks in comparison to their peers from less privileged backgrounds. These experiences drove Anandu's sons to consider pursuing their futures in foreign countries, where such discrimination was absent, and success was determined solely by merit and performance. Their decision to seek their fortunes abroad was not taken lightly. It was a choice born out of necessity, a quest for a brighter future unburdened by the shackles of discrimination. As they set their sights on distant horizons, they carried with them the hope of a better tomorrow, where merit alone would pave the way to success. Their success abroad served as a reminder of time's passage and the inevitability of change.

In their retirement, Sreeni and Mamta sought comfort in the peaceful surroundings of Florida, where sunny beaches and swaying palms welcomed them. Moving to the Sunshine State was a thoughtful decision, offering relief from the harsh winters up north that worsened Mamta's arthritis. Here, the gentle warmth of Florida's climate eased her joint pain, allowing her to bask in the soothing rays of the sun.

However tranquil their new home was, challenges emerged. Sreeni, recuperating from a recent cardiac bypass surgery, attributed to the fast-paced life in the US, grappled with the daily physical toll of his health condition. Despite their trials, the couple found strength in the steadfast support of their only daughter, Pooja, who had married an American and built a life in bustling California.

In the peaceful twilight of retirement, Satya settled in Trivandrum after bidding farewell to the bank where he had worked for most of his life. Now residing in Janaki's ancestral home, a cherished legacy from her father, Sadasiva Iyer, Satya sought comfort in the echoes of generations past.

The old house, weathered and creaking, held memories in every corner, whispers of days gone by. For Satya, it was a sanctuary—a place of peace away from the noise of the world. Sadasiva Iyer had been Satya's mentor and guide throughout his life, even until his last moments.

However, amidst the quiet of their ancestral home, Janaki battled illness, her vibrant spirit dimmed by medical afflictions. Day by day, she fought against the burden of sickness, her strength fading. Despite her struggles, Janaki found solace in the lives her two daughters had built in North India. Married and settled, they had ventured beyond tradition, finding happiness on their own paths.

Together, Satya and Janaki faced life's challenges, supported by their ancestors' legacy and the love of their family. In the gentle streets of Trivandrum, they moved forward, guided by the wisdom of the past and the hope of tomorrow.

Nandini felt a wave of relief wash over her, grateful that the turbulent storms of her past had finally calmed, leaving behind a sense of peace. The journey had been difficult, testing her resilience and inner strength.

The memory of her late husband, Rajaram, remained strong in her heart — a reminder of the battles they had fought against his blood cancer. For nearly five years, they had fought together, clinging to hope even in the darkest times. However, fate dealt a cruel blow when Rajaram passed away suddenly from a cerebral hemorrhage two years ago, leaving Nandini to navigate grief on her own.

Despite the shadows of loss, Nandini found comfort in her daughter Aathira's successes. With determination, Aathira pursued her dreams and earned a Master's degree in Environmental engineering from the esteemed University of Wisconsin in the United States. Because of discrimination against the 'privileged class,' opportunities for her too in India were restricted. As she belonged to the forward community which encountered considerable hurdles in India, Aathira found herself caught in the grip of this discrimination. She realized that politics and caste based discrimination in the academic and employment sectors would prove to be the bane of the country.

This year — in 2024, the country once again headed to the polls to elect a new government. However, Nandini couldn't help but sigh, realizing that regardless of who held power at the center, the longstanding policies of discrimination and favoritism towards 'real' minorities (whom they called the forward communities) would persist for decades to come. This was because politics, power, and bureaucracy were tightly intertwined.

While in the US, Aathira met her fiancé, a young man who shared her ambition. They embarked on a journey of success and prosperity, both in their careers and personal lives. Their love flourished in the lively streets of Boston, where they found jobs and created a life full of hope and opportunity.

Truth often proves stranger than fiction, for Aarav, Aathira's fiancé's father turned out to be none other than Inspector Ranjit, a man whose life had crossed paths with theirs before. In the intricate tapestry of fate, their coming together seemed predestined, a testament to the enigmatic ways of destiny.

The birth of their son, named Arjun in memory of Nandini's lost brother, filled Aarav and Aathira with immense joy. His arrival brought hope and a sense of new beginnings. Fate had intertwined their lives in unexpected ways, creating a complex web of connections that surpassed their wildest imaginations.

Having retired from a distinguished position within the Research and Analysis Wing (RAW) in New Delhi, Ranjit now found himself retired alongside his devoted wife, Revathi, in the bustling city of Gurgaon. Despite the comfort of their settled life, a longing tugged at their hearts, a yearning to reunite with their only son who resided across the vast expanse of the United States. Plans were underway for a permanent relocation, a journey that would see them traversing continents in pursuit of familial bonds and new horizons in the US.

As Nandini pondered the mysteries of fate, she marveled at its puzzling ways of connecting and separating souls. Life, she reflected, resembled the ocean's ebb and flow, guiding individuals like the flotsam on its surface. Sometimes, it brought them together in unexpected harmony, only to drift them apart again like scattered driftwood. Sadly, some met their end prematurely on fate's unforgiving reefs, their lives extinguished by its whims.

With a nostalgic sigh, Nandini watched the sun sink below the horizon, painting the sky in golden hues. She knew that tomorrow would bring a new day, full of possibilities and opportunities. For her, each sunrise symbolized a fresh start, a chance to embrace the unknown with optimism and determination. As the sun disappeared, Nandini found solace in the belief that every day offered the chance for new beginnings and connections, like weaving a tapestry of life with threads of hope and strength.

Yet amidst the shadows of sorrow, there flickered a glimmer of hope, a silent promise that even in the darkest of nights, the light of love would continue to guide her onward, illuminating the path ahead with its gentle glow.

GLOSSARY

Aattukattil	A swinging bed found in traditional homes in Kerala and Tamil Nadu
Adisayama Irukku!	Means, *"It is surprising"* [Tamil]
Agrahaaram	Rows of houses on either side of the road with a temple at the end of the road. Seen in villages.
Akka	Elder sister [Tamil]
Amma.	Mother [Tamil, Malayalam]
Ammamma	Grandmother : Mother's mother.
Angavastram	A rectangular piece of unstitched fabric worn on the shoulder and torso by adult males usually with borders decorated with golden braids. [Tamil]
Anna	Elder brother [Tamil]
Appa	Father [Tamil]
Beedi	A thin cigarette or mini cigar filled with tobacco wrapped in a tendu leaf tied with a string. It is smoked by the village folk in India.
Bhagawan	God [Hindi, Tamil, Malayalam, Sanskrit]
Bhagavad Gita	Means, "Song of the Lord" It is a dialogue between Bhagavan Krishna and Arjuna, It is part of the epic 'Mahabharata'.
Bhatura	A thick leavened and fluffy flat bread made from all-purpose flour. Common in the Indian Subcontinent. It is rolled and flattened into discs that are deep fried in oil.

Chai	Tea [Malayalam, Hindi]
Chittappa	Father's younger brother [Tamil]
Chitti	Chittappa's wife : Mother's younger sister. [Tamil]
Deerga Ayushman Bhava	Means, *"May you live long"* [Sanskrit]
Deerga Sumangali Bhava	Means, "May you remain married to your husband for long". [Sanskrit]
Devi	Goddess. [Hindi, Tamil, Malayalam, Sanskrit]
Dhaba	A casual roadside eatery in India.
Dharma Sastha	Lord Ayyappa in Sabarimala in Kerala.
Dhoti	A loincloth or lower garment worn around the waist by men in parts of India.
Elelo Eilasa	A Theme song of fishermen [Malayalam]
Ellaam Pocchu	"All is gone" : "I have lost everything" [Tamil]
Enna	Means 'What' [Tamil]
Ennada, nalla than irukken	Means, 'Hey, I am keeping fine" [Tamil]
Enna Aachu?	Means, *"What happened?"* [Tamil]
Etta	Elder brother [Malayalam]
Excess baggage	'In laws' are often euphemistically called 'excess baggage' derogatorily.
Ezhunthirungo	Means, "Wake up". [Tamil]
Ganesha	A Hindu God with the head of an elephant and body of a human. Also called "Elephant God."

Grihasthasrama	Means 'Householder's Life' : In Hinduism, there are four stages of life called Brahmacharya, Grihasthasrama, Vanaprastha and Sannyasa. [Sanskrit]
Guruvayurappan	Another name for Lord Vishnu, one of the Trinity in Hindu pantheon.
Hum Honge Kamyab	Means, 'We shall overcome' [Hindi]
Iddli	Steamed rice cakes, the most common breakfast item in South Indian Households. [Tamil, Malayalam]
Jayate	Win : Victory.
Jeera	Cumin seed
Kanna	Means 'Dear' – an endearing way of addressing one's child. [Tamil]
Keerai Molakoottal	A classic stew made from Spinach, dal and coconut gravy. Special in South India. [Tamil]
Kettela	Meaning, "*Did you hear?*" [Tamil]
Ketu Dasa	A bad period of seven years in a person's life as per his horoscope (astrologically) when the planet Ketu influences the person's life.
Khadar	Hand-spun, hand-woven fabric for making clothes. Promoted by Gandhiji in India and usually worn by most politicians. Also called *Khadi* [see below]
Khadi.	Hand-spun, hand-woven fabric for making clothes. Promoted by Gandhiji in India and usually worn by most politicians. Also called *Khadar*
Kolam	A traditional decorative art where designs are drawn on the floor with

	rice flour. Seen in the front courtyard of Tamil Brahmin homes. Called Rangoli in North India. [Tamil]
Kurukankaattil	Family name of the KK brothers. The literary meaning of the term is "In the Jungle of Jackals" [Malayalam]
Kutty	Meaning, 'child' [Malayalam, Tamil]
Lacha	A traditional ankle length Indian skirt worn by women, mostly in North India.
Lakh	One hundred thousand.
Lungi	Lungi is a type of sarong – usually a colored cloth that is worn by men around the waist in the Indian subcontinent. Unlike the dhoti which is usually white, the lungi is often colored and with designs.
Mahabharata	One of the great epics or Puranas in Hindu scriptures.
Mahalakshmi	Goddess of Wealth.
Makara Sankranti	A Hindu festival celebrating the transition of sun from the southern to the northern hemisphere. Usually falls on January 14th or 15th.
Mama	Uncle : Mother's brother. [Tamil, Hindi]
Mami	Aunty : Mama's wife. The way elderly women are addressed. [Tamil]
Manni	Elder brother's wife : Sister in law [Tamil]
Moksha	Salvation : Freedom from the eternal cycle of birth-death and re-birth. [Sanskrit]

Mundu	Dhoti : Garment worn around the waist- a long white cloth worn around the waist Worn by South Indians. [Malayalam]
Nadumuttam	Central courtyard in a Nalukettu house in Kerala.
Nair	A sub caste of Hindus in Kerala – they are Malayalees.
Nalukettu	Traditional Architectural style in Kerala. The house has four blocks with a central courtyard.
Naam Peruvomei Vettri	Means, 'We shall overcome'. [Tamil]
Naan	A light, fluffy textured flatbread, a staple cuisine in India. It is baked in a clay or metal oven called a Tandoor.
Nanna Irukku	Meaning, "*Very nice*" [Tamil]
Neyyappam	A sweet rice based fritter fried in ghee. Jaggery is added for sweetening.
Nivedyam	Offering to a deity in the form of fruit or cooked items.
Paal	Milk - Paal Paayasam stands for 'Milk Pudding' [Tamil]
Paavadai	Long frock usually worn by girls in south India extending from the hip to the ankles. [Tamil]
Padippura	A traditional arched gateway that leads to the main building of the house.
Padmanabha Swami	The deity in the temple in Trivandrum, Kerala. It is the idol of Lord Vishnu in the lying down pose.
Palada Pradaman	Thick, creamy pudding made with milk, rice flakes called 'Ada', cardamom, sugar.

335

Panchagaccham	A five-yard-long piece of fabric worn around the waist and drawn up between the legs. Worn by brahmins. [Tamil]
Panchayat	Village council in India.
Pappadam	Thin crispy Indian flatbread made from lentil flour. [Tamil, Malayalam]
Paayasam	Sweet rice pudding. Called 'Kheer' in Hindi. [Tamil, Malayalam]
Phoren	A slang way of saying 'Foreign'
Podimass	Spicy South Indian mashed potatoes.
Pongal	Harvest festival celebrated by Tamils – usually coincides with the Makara Sankranti : The dish made on this day is also called '*Pongal*'.
Rasam	A traditional, spicy, and tangy South Indian soup-like dish made with tamarind juice, spices, and herbs. [Tamil, Malayalam]
Sambar	A popular lentil-based vegetable stew common in South Indian Cuisine. [Tamil, Malayalam]
Sapthaham	A recital and explanation of the contents of the Srimad Bhagavatham, a Hindu Holy scripture by a scholar over a period of seven days.
Saraswathy	Goddess of Knowledge.
Satsang	A spiritual discourse in Hinduism. [Sanskrit]
Satyam	Truth [Tamil, Sanskrit, Malayalam]
Satyameva Jayate	Meaning, "Truth Alone Triumphs". It is India's National Motto. It is a

	mantra from an Upanishad. [Sanskrit]
Subramanya	A God who is the son of Lord Siva, younger brother of Ganesha.
Suprabhatham	Means "Auspicious Dawn" [Sanskrit]
Tamizh-le paadu-da	Means, 'Sing in Tamil' [Tamil]
Taqiyah	A white skull cap worn by Muslim men. [Arabic]
Thani kudithanam	Means, 'Separate Family Set-up' : The couple live separately after marriage away from the joint family.
Thara	A traditional raised platform built of stone in front of Hindu households where the Thulasi plant is grown for worship.
Tharavadu	Means, '*Family Home*' or '*Ancestral Home*' [Malayalam]
Thatha	Grandfather [Tamil]
Thulasi	It is a shrub known as 'Holy Basil' or *Ocimum tenuiflorum* seen in Indian subcontinent and Southeast Asia.
Uttarayanam	The Hindu festival marking the transition of the sun from the Zodiac sign of Sagittarius (Dhanu) to Capricorn (Makara). It begins with the Makara Sankranti – Jan 14th or 15th
Va	Come : A way of inviting someone into the house. [Tamil]
Vaidyar	A practitioner of traditional medicine like Ayurveda.
Vanaprastha	Means 'Retiring to the forest'. [Sanskrit]. In Hinduism, after the grandchildren are born, the aged

337

couple withdraw into solitude, detach themselves from material things and practice ascetic living.

Vastu Shastra	Traditional Hindu system of architecture based on ancient Hindu texts.
Vendakkai Pacchadi	A dish made with Ladies' Finger (Okra) and curd. [Tamil]
Venkatesa Suprabhatham	Hymns traditionally sung or chanted in the morning to awaken Lord Venkateswara from his celestial sleep. The term Suprabhatham is a Sanskrit word that means "auspicious dawn".
Venkitachalapathy	Lord Vishnu in the Tirupathi Hills Temple.
Veshti	Dhoti : Traditional dress of males in Tamil Nadu and Kerala. A long cloth worn around the waist.
Vibhuti	Sacred Ash worn on the forehead by Hindus. Also called 'Bhasma'
Vilakku	Lamp usually lit with oil or ghee and used in traditional festivals at home and in temples by Hindus. [Tamil, Malayalam]
Vishnu	Lord Vishnu is one of the Trinity in Hinduism. He is the "Preserver"
Vishnu Sahasranama Stotram	The hymn extolling the thousand names of Lord Vishnu.
Yama	The Hindu God of 'Death' and judges of the souls of the dead.

MORE BOOKS BY THE AUTHOR

How to Face the Challenges while Growing Old - Problems of Elderly Book 1

https://amzn.to/3NmPmkm

Old Age Health Challenges and Solutions - Problems of Elderly Book 2

https://rxe.me/B86F7R

Tell Me a Story, Grandpa -Short Stories for Children Book 1

https://amzn.to/3LsTeOp

Grandpa, Tell me More Stories -Short Stories for Children Book 2

https://amzn.to/3qOoFea

Understanding the Electrocardiogram - Medical Book on ECG

https://relinks.me/B0BZLSN59M

Demystifying Hinduism - Understanding Hinduism Book 1

https://relinks.me/B0C7J5GPMQ

The Avadhoota - Whispers of Wisdom Understanding Hinduism Book 2

https://rxe.me/MPWP4Q

Daily Musings - Understanding Hinduism Book 3

https://relinks.me/B0CJL9SY1G

In Search of a Bridegroom - An Autobiographical Fiction

http://relinks.me/B0B6YS16XF

How to Master Essential Life Skills - Skill sets for Success Book 1

https://mybook.to/tcklL

How to Achieve Professional Excellence. - Skill sets for Success Book 2

https://relinks.me/B0CT5F6XH3

Milton Keynes UK
Ingram Content Group UK Ltd.
UKHW020640140524
442690UK00001B/85